PRAISE

I didn't know what to expect when I started reading The Six. I had seen it compared to Narnia and Harry Potter, and this was where my apprehension set in. I'd read Narnia when I was about ten, and I'd never read Harry Potter, so I was afraid that some of the magic would be lost on me. I also wasn't sure how invested I would become in a group of thirteen year olds and their adventures, but I was pleasantly surprised. The Six caught my attention right away with Darcy and her young teen angst and later by Hoyle's excellent depiction of an alternate world called Alitheia.

The Six was full of magic and action, which bridged the gap between young adult and adult readers. Once Darcy and her friends step into Alitheia, it was nonstop action and adventure. I have to admit that this novel is my first encounter with many of the magical creatures Hoyle talks about. Once I stepped into Alitheia, it took me a few pages to switch gears and catch up on the lingo, but I got there eventually. It was a bit of an abrupt transition, and I would have liked to see a little more world building and introduction to these new types of creatures so that I didn't spend any time feeling lost. But like I said, it didn't take long to acclimate to Alitheia, and once I did, the magic began—literally and figuratively!

Not only was this an exciting fantasy-adventure novel, but it was full of strong characters and relationships. I really enjoyed the characters Hoyle crafted from Darcy and her initial sullen and woe-is-me me attitude, to Sam and her over exuberance, to Perry and his tough guy persona. These kids felt authentic with their demeanors, their dialogue, and their attitudes towards each other. They were believable, and this was a big part of what drew me into this novel. It didn't matter that this was a younger crowd than I usually read about; a well-depicted character was a well-depicted character! I also loved the growth in Darcy's character. Hoyle incorporated themes like friendship, loyalty, and forgiveness that appeal to any audience, especially the younger adult crowd. These relationships added another layer to the story, making it more than just a fantasy novel.

The Six is an exciting, action filled and magical novel that will appeal to both young and not so young readers! The story has enough meat to appeal to adults who are fans of YA, but it is also a clean enough story to be appropriate and relatable to younger teens, so it really is the best of both worlds. I recommend this book to anyone who loves the magic and adventure of the Chronicles of Narnia and is looking to get lost in another world for a few hours!

~ Bonnie Speers-Bauman: Words at Home blog

The Gateway Chronicles

Book 1

The Six

By

K. B. Hoyle

First published by The Writer's Coffee Shop, 2012

The Writer's Coffee Shop
(Australia) PO Box 447 Cherrybrook NSW 2126
(USA) PO Box 2116 Waxahachie TX 75168

Paperback ISBN- 978-1-61213-300-3
E-book ISBN- 978-1-61213-053-8

A CIP catalogue record for this book is available from the US Congress Library.

Cover image by: © Eric Gevaert © rossco
Cover design by: Megan Dooley

www.thewriterscoffeeshop.com/khoyle

About the Author

The Gateway Chronicles Book 1: The Six is K. B. Hoyle's first published novel. Ms. Hoyle lives outside of Birmingham, Alabama, with her husband and two sons. She is a teacher at a local classical school. Her hobbies include travel, reading, and of course, writing.

Dedication

To Adam

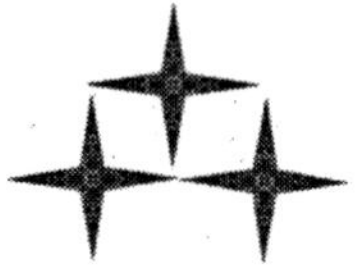

Special Thanks

Beth Mitchell, Julie and Brad McGuffey, Ross Boone, Jenny Combs, Sharen Watson, Melissa Bell, Hayley German Fisher, the lovely ladies in my writing group, and all my students who read my manuscript and gave insightful feedback. You know who you are.

"If I find in myself a desire which no experience in this world can satisfy, the most probable explanation is that I was made for another world."

C. S. Lewis

CHAPTER 1
FAMILY VACATION

The pouring rain outside did nothing to improve Darcy's mood. The steady thrum mixed with the squeak of the windshield wipers and the swish of passing cars made up a chorus of gloom, of which Darcy was the conductor. She didn't dislike rain itself, but if she had to listen to percussive sound, she preferred the beat of horses' hooves on solid turf to liquid hitting wet pavement. In fact, the rain only served as a reminder to her that she would not be attending Gregorio's Equestrian Camp this summer, nor would she be riding Timmory, her favorite horse, for at least another year. Instead, she was expected to spend the week in Michigan at some lame camp building "family unity" and making friends with people she didn't care about and would probably never see again.

Her dad's job change had messed everything up. Usually when summer break rolled around, Darcy went off to Gregorio's for two weeks of learning about horses and horseback riding, her ten-year-old brother Roger went to science camp in Florida, and their mom and dad took a Caribbean cruise together. That was the way things had been for four years, ever since Roger was old enough to go to camp, and Darcy didn't understand why it had to change now.

When her dad left his job and opened Pennington Furniture Surplus, Darcy thought he'd gone mad. Her mother assured her, however, that he had always wanted to run his own business, and when the opportunity had come along to buy the furniture store, it was too good to pass up. But, as Darcy's mother also explained, the family was going to have to make a few changes, because owning the store did not pay as much as they were used to. That meant no more Gregorio's, no more science camp, and no more cruises.

Darcy snapped her gum angrily just thinking about it and huffed on the car window, adding her own fog to the condensation from the rain. With her forehead against the glass, she watched a car with one headlight out drift past on the water-logged highway. She heard movement on the seat next to her before she felt the punch to her arm. "Ouch!" She turned to glare at her brother.

"P'diddle!" Roger grinned impishly and bounced up and down. He didn't seem too glum about missing science camp.

"Mom!" Darcy whined, rubbing her arm.

Sue Pennington's keen eye appeared over the passenger headrest, her perfectly sculpted eyebrow arched indignantly over her heavily made-up lid. "Roger, don't antagonize your sister." She looked back down at the magazine she was reading.

Roger's grin only widened and he stuck out his tongue at his sister. Darcy rolled her eyes and landed a retaliatory punch on his arm. "Leave me alone!" she hissed. She fished her iPod out of her pocket and began to shuffle through her music. She needed to find an appropriate tune to fit her mood; anything to drown out the rain and her brother.

Poke poke. *Just ignore him.* Poke, poke, poke . . . poke, poke. "What?" *I swear I'm going to kill him. My brother will never see the sixth grade.*

"Do you want to play the alphabet game?"

"No."

"The license plate game?"

"No."

"Twenty questions?"

"No!"

"How about . . ."

Darcy looked up from her iPod and glared. "Roger, I'm just going to make this simple for you, whatever the game is, the answer will always be no. Got it? No! Now leave me alone."

Roger sat back and pouted. "Why are you so grouchy? We're on vacation!"

"I wouldn't exactly call this a vacation," Darcy grumbled under her breath.

"What was that?" Darcy's mom's eye reappeared over the headrest.

Shoot. "Nothing." Darcy ducked her head and tried to look busy. Roger chortled and bounced on his seat.

"Darcy Marie, we've been over this. I don't understand why you can't get on board with the rest of us. Mrs. Palm said that Cedar Cove is a very lovely camp, and there will be plenty of kids your own age there for you to play with."

"Mom, I'm thirteen, not five; I don't play anymore."

"*And* she said that Samantha loves it there." Her mom went on, pretending she hadn't heard Darcy's comment. "They've been attending for thirteen years, ever since Samantha was born, imagine that. I think it would be nice for us to be able to build that sort of tradition as a family together." She smiled and reached over to rub her husband's shoulders.

That's not the reason we're going, though. We're going because we don't have enough money to do anything else, Darcy thought, but wisely kept her mouth shut.

"Samantha Palm is such a sweet girl, Darce, I think this summer is going to be really good for you two. I don't understand why you haven't made friends before."

Samantha Palm. Blond, blue-eyed . . . and overweight. She'd lived at the end of their street since before Darcy could remember, and every summer she tried to make friends with Darcy, to no avail. Darcy liked to think that her avoidance of Sam had nothing to do with the girl's weight, but if she was truly honest with herself, she knew that deep down she did not want to be friends with the fat girl at school. *I have a hard enough time making friends at school without hanging out with someone like Samantha Palm,* she'd argued to herself more than once. And that was beside the fact that along with Samantha came Lewis Acres. Darcy rarely saw one without the other. Lewis was a quiet, nerdy boy who was never seen without his backpack on and a notebook in his hands. When she'd found out that the Acreses also attended Cedar Cove every summer, Darcy had just about died of mortification. She had a dreadful, sinking feeling that she wouldn't be able to disassociate herself from Samantha Palm or Lewis Acres ever again.

Once Sam had found out that the Penningtons were going to be joining them at Cedar Cove that summer, she'd been impossible to shake. It seemed that every time Darcy stepped out her door, Sam was there, bubbling over with some obscure fact she just *had* to tell Darcy about this or that at Cedar Cove. And oh, wasn't Darcy just going to *love* it there. And wait until Darcy met so and so, and apparently there was a really cute boy named Perry—Darcy remembered *his* name—that Darcy was just going to die over, and on and on . . . Darcy had started taking to staying indoors a lot.

Her one consolation was that Lewis Acres apparently could not care less that she was going to Cedar Cove with them that summer. While he followed along in Samantha's wake like a piece of toilet paper attached to her shoe, he never looked overly excited to see Darcy and had never offered any encouragement aside from the occasional "Yeah, it's great" at Sam's insistence. Their mutual dislike was somehow satisfying to Darcy, and she hoped that Lewis Acres rubbed off on Samantha before the week was up.

"Darcy. Darcy!"

She suddenly realized that her mom had been talking to her while she was lost in her musings. "What?" she mumbled.

"I said, Mrs. Palm told me that there are plenty of trails to hike, and a large beach and boats and a recreation hall and everything. I don't think you'll be bored."

"Sounds great."

Her dryness was not lost on her mother. "Oh, come on, Darcy."

"Darcy doesn't like any of those things unless they involve horses," Roger taunted.

"Maybe there will be horses there, Darcy. You never know," Allan Pennington spoke for the first time from the driver's seat.

"There's not," Darcy said, her irritation with her entire family mounting to new heights, "I already asked Sam." That was the one tidbit of information that she had sought from her enthusiastic neighbor—whether or not perfect Cedar Cove had stables—because according to Sam the camp had everything else. Sam's bright face had fallen for a fraction of a second before she had launched into a description of all the *other* great things there were to do.

Finally she found a song she wanted to listen to. Darcy jammed her earphones in her ears as her mother took a breath to harangue her some more. "I'm tired, Mom, I want to take a nap." She feigned a yawn and rested her head back against the plush leather seat of the family van, the strains of her music carrying her into gloomy restfulness.

"Who wants lunch?" Darcy jolted awake at her father's voice and realized that not only had she actually fallen asleep, but she had to have slept for at least an hour. When she'd closed her eyes, they were roughly two hours north of the Illinois-Wisconsin border, and two and a half hours north of their home in the northwest suburbs of Chicago. Peering out the window she saw terrain that she didn't recognize and a weak sun poking through a shifting cloud cover.

"Darcy?"

"What? Lunch? Um, yeah." She rubbed her eyes sleepily and stretched, her fingers pushing into the cushiony ceiling of the van. She yawned deeply as she pulled her earphones out and looked around. "Where are we?" She slipped her flip flops on and leaned forward to look out the front windshield. She saw a pretty town and a quaint park bordering a river with a brown visitor center and an interesting collage of cars and people.

"Marinette," her dad answered, maneuvering the minivan into a spot angled between a rusty Volkswagen and a pickup truck towing a beat-up camper. The sounds of dogs barking, birds chirruping, and children squealing sounded crisp and refreshing to Darcy's sleepy ears after the long hours on the highway. It took her a moment to remember that she was not happy to be there.

Roger slammed his side door open and hopped to the gravel with a whoop.

"Roger!" His mom called after him as he made a dash for the park. "Come back and help with the cooler! You can run around when you are finished eating." He waved distractedly at her, pretending not to be able to hear what she had said, and joined in with a group of boys who were tossing a Frisbee around. That was Roger—able to make friends with anybody.

Darcy was slower getting out of the car, her brain still a little fuzzy from her nap, and she blinked as the sun suddenly broke through the clouds in full force. It must be around noon. "Where's Marionette?" she asked her dad. "Are we in Michigan yet?"

"Marinette," he said, correcting her. "We're still in Wisconsin."

Darcy groaned. "And we still have to go *all* the way to the Upper Peninsula?"

"Don't get grumpy, Darcy, just be thankful that you don't have to drive."

"Dad," Darcy said, rolling her eyes, "thirteen, remember?"

He chuckled and pointed past the visitor's center in the park. "See that river, and all these people?" She nodded, shielding her eyes. "That's the Menominee River. Once we cross that we will be in Michigan. This is a popular tourist stop because it's right on the border and it's close to Green Bay. Marinette is also known for its waterfalls and hiking trails."

"Fascinating," she said dryly.

"Darcy, carry this," her mother interrupted and handed her a pack of water bottles. "Allan, will you take the cooler? I don't know where Roger ran off to."

Roger, like a true ten-year-old boy, reappeared the moment the food was spread out on a picnic table. In five minutes flat he inhaled a ham sandwich, a bag of chips, and a bottle of water, and disappeared before his mother could make him eat a banana. Darcy watched him with ill-concealed disgust and picked at her sandwich. She didn't like ham. She didn't know why her mom couldn't remember that.

"What's the matter? Aren't you going to eat?" her mother finally asked. "Roger's already done and we're not going to sit here all afternoon. We still have a long way to go."

Darcy peeled open her sandwich and showed it to her mom. "It's ham."

"What's wrong with ham? You like ham, don't you?"

"No, Mom, I don't."

"Since when?"

"Since never."

"You're too thin, Darcy—"

"Sue," her dad interjected quietly. Her mom tutted loudly and looked away, drumming her manicured nails on her crossed arms.

Darcy rolled her eyes and snagged a banana. After making sure there were no bruises on it, she tucked in, turning to watch her brother play with the other boys. Why couldn't she make friends like that? She wasn't fat, she wasn't ugly, and she thought that she was a tolerably nice person, but . . . she sighed through her bite of banana. She just couldn't talk to people, not like Roger could. The moment she met someone new, her mind went blank and she was suddenly aware of how big her hands were, how uncoordinated her feet were, and how stringy and high-pitched her voice came out when she was nervous. She felt comfortable around animals—kind, quiet, unjudging animals. Speaking of which . . . she discreetly tossed her uneaten sandwich to a gull that landed nearby while her mom wasn't looking. She grinned as a flock of gulls instantly descended on the first one, their raucous cries ringing in the air as they fought for the biggest piece of bread, cheese, and ham.

"You know, you shouldn't feed them," her dad said, looking over. "They're never going to leave you alone now."

"That's okay." She smiled. She liked to watch them.

She finished a bag of corn chips as her mom cleaned up the garbage and her dad carried everything back to the car. She let her gaze roam over the river into Michigan. She had never been to Michigan before. Maybe it wouldn't be that bad. *No*, she thought firmly, *I will* not *enjoy this trip*. She couldn't give her parents, or Samantha Palm, that satisfaction.

"Roger, Darcy, let's go," her dad called from the minivan. He tapped his watch to indicate that it was time.

"Later!" Roger shouted to his new friends, and jogged to the car. Darcy followed slowly behind, imagining as she went that she was going to her doom.

CHAPTER 2

CEDAR COVE

Four more hours in the car had reduced Darcy, out of sheer, desperate boredom, to play the alphabet game with Roger.

"But I swear, if you cheat, I'm not playing anything with you for the rest of the trip."

They were both stuck on "Q" at the moment, and Darcy was only half-heartedly scanning the road signs and town markers for the elusive letter. The time zone change meant that it was 5:30 p.m. and her stomach was starting to grumble about the small lunch she had eaten in Marinette. The scenery in the upper peninsula of Michigan was pretty, she had to admit. Early glimpses of Lake Michigan had quickly given way to dense forests of cedar, birch, and pine trees, and picturesque small towns popped up in the most unexpected places along the two-lane highway. Her dad said that they were heading for a town called Loggers Head and that the camp was just six miles past that.

"Q!" Roger suddenly shouted and pointed. "Quentin Road!"

"I give up, Roger, you win," Darcy said, bored. She didn't feel like playing anymore.

"Wha— No! Come on, Darce, you promised you would play with me."

"I'm too tired, Roger, I just want to sit." She yawned to punctuate her point. "Besides, you know as well as I do that whoever gets the Q first usually wins."

He pouted and looked out the window. "I'll let you have that Q," he said hopefully after a moment of silence.

"Those aren't the rules and you know it."

"Fine." He was quiet for a moment before a malicious grin spread over his face. Puckering his lips he made a distinctive popping noise. Darcy ignored him. He did it again. And again.

"Stop it," she finally said.

Pop. Pop.

"Roger," her voice threatened.

Pop.

"Roger, please, for all of us," Allan growled from the driver's seat.

Roger sighed deeply and started bouncing his foot.

"Why don't you play your Nintendo game . . . thingy?" Darcy asked.

"Don't wanna."

"Why not?"

"Mom says it rots my brain."

Darcy raised an eyebrow at him. "Right." She watched the trees skim by out her brother's window. Suddenly she caught a glimpse of deep grey and blue sky. "Ooh, look! You can see the lake again."

Despite her best intentions to hate Michigan, the sight of Lake Huron stretching to the horizon and white gulls gliding over smooth sandy beaches momentarily took her breath away. Living in the Chicago area she'd been to Lake Michigan plenty of times, but this felt different. There was an untamable quality about the landscape surrounding them and an aura of mystery and adventure. At the same time, it felt very, very peaceful. She found she desperately wanted to get out of the car and dig her feet into the white sand.

"Dad, can we stop and walk on one of these beaches?"

"Sorry, Darcy, we're too close to Loggers Head. We'll be at the camp in a half hour and you can walk on the beach there."

But at the camp there will be Samantha and Lewis, and other people I don't know that I will have to meet and talk to. Her chest felt constricted for a moment and she pushed the thoughts away. "Um . . . I have to go to the bathroom. Bad."

Her dad glanced in the rearview mirror. "Nice try."

"Seriously."

"You can hold it for half an hour."

"If I explode, it will be your fault," Darcy grumbled under her breath. Well, there was nothing for it. She was a half hour from Cedar Cove and a whole week of discomfort. She had better steel herself for the experience. The constriction in her chest came back with full force and she felt as though she would smother under her anxiety. Not even her dad knew how afraid of meeting new people she was, or how desperate she was *not* to be friends with Sam. *Just focus on the scenery. Look at how beautiful it is. Don't think about Cedar Cove.*

Their maroon minivan was cruising through the town of Loggers Head long before Darcy was ready for it to be. Her dad slowed to thirty miles an hour, the van swerving slightly as he turned his head from side to side to take in the town.

Quaint houses lined the highway and a single gas station with two pumps looked lonely on the corner of the only traffic light in town. On the left hand side of the road the largest building in Loggers Head boasted a sign that read “Loggers-Mart” in plain black letters. Just past the Loggers-Mart the highway climbed over a hill and Loggers Head disappeared behind them as the speed limit reverted to sixty-five.

Darcy’s dad whistled. “Phew! Blink and you’ll miss it. We certainly aren’t in Kansas anymore, Toto.” He grinned at his joke. His wife smiled wanly at him.

“Look at that, kids!” he said a moment later.

Darcy craned her neck to see that the trees broke to reveal mountainous piles of small white rocks. Metal chutes stood on framing over and around the pyramid-like piles and an ocean-liner rested a short distance off in the bay.

“Whoa,” Roger said, plastering his nose against the window.

“Must be some sort of mining operation up here,” her dad mused as her mom made a noise of agreement next to him.

Darcy didn’t respond. She was having difficulty breathing past the growing lump of anxiety in her throat.

The tree line to their right thinned out and the lake grew ever nearer to the highway as the bay they were passing bulged inwards. Then the highway angled inland again—or the bay receded out, Darcy didn’t know which—and the view was lost in the trees once more.

“Okay, kiddos, we’re looking for a sign that says ‘Cedar Cove, East Entrance, Glorietta Bay.’ It should be on the right side of the road.”

“Mrs. Palm said that it’s a light brown sign with black, carved letters,” Darcy’s mom said, looking out her window with interest.

“There it is!” Roger shouted, pointing.

Sure enough, a large sign reading “Cedar Cove” swung slightly in the breeze just a few hundred feet up the road. Darcy’s dad slowed the minivan and flipped on his right blinker but then said, “Whoops, that’s the West Entrance, to Mariner’s Point. We want Glorietta Bay.”

He accelerated and soon the trees broke again to reveal a picturesque bay. Tall reeds bent gently in the wind, their bottoms sunk deep in the water near the road, and cedar trees hugged the sides of the bay. Crisp white daisies were strewn among ferns wherever the sun’s rays could reach and the occasional bright orange lily poked out from behind mossy rocks. Darcy could see dark brown buildings and a few colorful sailboats a mile across the bay on what she could only assume was Mariner's Point, and beyond the point the lake opened up to deep blue water with a green island dotted on the horizon.

All of these things she took in quickly as the trees stretched in to hide the view, and her dad proudly announced the appearance of a second sign.

"*Here* we are," he said, slowing to take the turn. "Cedar Cove, Glorietta Bay."

Their tires crunched loudly on gravel as the van swung into dense, cave-like tree cover. Darcy felt like she was being swallowed whole as her dad inched their vehicle along the drive, the late afternoon sunlight slowly disappearing behind tall cedar limbs. Another gravel drive branched off to their left, but her dad stayed straight and a moment later they pulled into a small, rough parking lot. Trees all but enveloped the cramped lot, but Darcy could see that a gray-sided building with heavy-looking metal doors and a wood-planked walkway rose up in front of them. Sunlight peeked down over the building and in patches in the parking lot. With a final crunch, her dad turned the van into a spot next to another family van and turned off the ignition.

"Well, we're here!" He yawned and stretched.

Roger was tying his tennis shoes as fast as he could in his excitement to get out of the car, but Darcy just sat still in her seat, taking advantage of the tinted rear windows to observe the people milling around the parking lot. She saw families with very small children—harassed moms and dads holding tight to wiggling arms and trying to wrestle suitcases out of trunks. One boy about her own age was leaning casually against a tree trunk while his three older brothers unhooked fancy-looking mountain bikes from the roof rack of a medium-sized sedan. The boy was tall and thin with close-cropped dark brown hair, but he certainly wasn't good-looking enough to be Samantha's Perry.

Darcy jumped suddenly as her door rolled open without warning. Roger stood grinning impishly at her; she hadn't heard him get out of the car.

"Whatcha doin'?" he asked loudly. "You starin' at that boy?"

Her eyes flew wide, and she felt her ears redden as the casual boy looked up at her, pulled a questioning face, and turned his back, seemingly unconcerned with her personal drama. "I'm gonna *kill* you!" she hissed at Roger, who barked a laugh and dodged away. She fumbled with her seatbelt and hopped down from the van, feeling like she was jumping into a swimming pool without first testing the water. Roger had totally disappeared and she realized that she was standing outside the van all alone. She shivered slightly, although the air was warm, and wrapped her arms around her ribcage, feeling exposed.

"Darcy."

"Yes?" She answered her mother too quickly, eager for a distraction.

"Take your suitcase, and for goodness sake try not to look like you're going to your own funeral." Her mom shoved her plaid-patterned suitcase into her listless arms and stuck her head back into the trunk.

She felt an arm around her shoulder and turned into her dad's hug. "It's going to be a fun week, kiddo, I promise."

"Okay, Dad," she said, but quickly pulled away. She didn't want to appear *too* strange to the other kids.

"Go ahead and take your suitcase into the lobby of that building there—I assume it's the lodge—and then come on back to help clean up the car. I'll see if I can find your brother and put him to work, too."

She nodded wordlessly and turned toward the grey building. As she walked over the white, crunching gravel to the looming building, she caught a glimpse of a familiar face. Lewis Acres was helping his mother unload luggage from the back of their station wagon, for once without his notebook in hand—although he did have his backpack on—and their eyes locked for a brief moment. He paused, looked like he was going to say something, but then went back to work with a slight shake of his head, his eyes unreadable behind his wire-rimmed glasses. Darcy nodded, that was fine with her.

She lumbered over the wooden walkway to the door, her feet making hollow thumping noises on the graying wood, and reached with one hand to pull open one of the heavy metal doors. Before she was able to get a handle on it, however, it suddenly swung open with a bang and she heard a high-pitched squeal as she felt a large, soft, bushy-blond-haired missile hit her with the force of a small Mack truck. "Oof!" Samantha Palm had found her.

Chapter 3
Meetings and Greetings

"You're *here!*" Samantha shrieked, rocking Darcy vigorously back and forth.

"Samantha, I . . . can't . . . breathe." Darcy spit out strands of blond hair and wished with all her might that Sam would let her go.

"Oh," Sam said breathlessly, finally releasing her. "Sorry. Here, let me help you with that." She wrenched Darcy's suitcase from her hands and Darcy was left with nothing to do but hold the door for Sam as she entered the lodge with all the grace of a young elephant. Darcy rolled her eyes and discreetly looked around to see if anybody was watching them, and then slipped through the door behind Sam, who was talking as though Darcy had been by her side the entire time.

"So this is the lodge, as you probably guessed, and through that door is the boardwalk to the beach and the rec hall that I told you about. We don't have time to go out there right now, though, because the dinner bell is about to ring. Oh, Darcy." She dropped her suitcase and wheeled around to hug Darcy again, "I'm *so* glad you're here. We are going to have *such* a good time. You can't even imagine. Hey, do you know what room you are in? I could take your suitcase up for you, or—"

"Actually, Sam, my dad told me to leave my suitcase here and go back out to the car to help clean up."

Roger banged through the door behind them and dropped his suitcase in a heap. "Dad's looking for you!" he called, accentuating her point. He stomped back out the door.

Darcy moved her and Roger's suitcases against the wall and shrugged at

Sam. "See? Don't let me keep you from doing what you want to do, though. Um, I'm sure I'll see you after dinner." *Please,* please *don't follow me outside.*

"Don't be silly. What I want to do is help you, come on." Sam linked her arm through Darcy's and skipped them out the door.

Once they were back in the parking lot, Sam stopped so suddenly that Darcy stumbled against her and almost fell. She straightened up and glared at Sam, wondering what on earth had gotten into the girl.

Sam was standing ramrod straight, her eyes closed and her nose tilted in the air, breathing deep. "You smell that?" she whispered.

"What?" asked Darcy grouchily; she was losing patience.

"The *smell* here; the cedar trees, the flowers, the dirt, the ferns . . . it smells like Heaven to me." Her eyes flew open and she smiled dreamily. "Isn't it unlike anyplace you've ever smelled before?"

Darcy sniffed cautiously just for good measure and shrugged her shoulders. "Um, I guess so." *I knew it, she's crazy.*

Sam started forward again just as suddenly as she'd stopped, and Darcy let herself be dragged along in her wake. "Oh, now I see your van. I was watching for you to pull up for like an hour, but you managed to pull in just as I was in the bathroom. Isn't that funny? Hi, Mr. Pennington!" She finally dropped Darcy's arm to wave at her dad and Darcy quickly tucked both her arms close about herself, hoping to discourage any further touching.

"Hi, Samantha." Darcy's dad smiled at her and looked at Darcy. *Be nice*, his expression seemed to say.

"Darcy, have you seen the beach yet?" Roger hopped out of the van with his arms around his pillow. "It's *sweet*."

Sam beamed.

"How did you have time to see the beach already?" Darcy asked, accepting the cooler and a grocery bag full of goodies from her mom.

Roger grinned and shrugged. "I get around."

"Can I help with anything, Mrs. Pennington?" Samantha asked.

"Ahhh . . . here you go, sweetie, you can take Darcy's pillow and camera for her. Allan, why don't you go inside and find out what room we are in?"

"I'll show you where the registration desk is, Mr. Pennington," Sam offered.

"Um, okay. Thanks, Sam. Hey, are your parents around?"

"They're in our room unpacking. Number five. We've been in the same room for eight years!" Sam said proudly.

Are we supposed to congratulate you on that? Darcy snorted and quickly turned it into a fake cough. The cooler was heavy and she could hardly see around the bag of groceries on top of it. "Can we go in?" she pleaded.

"Lead the way, Sam," Mr. Pennington said, gesturing with his hand.

Sam grinned and led them back to the lodge, Darcy's pillow swinging from one hand and her camera looped around the other. Once inside, she waited with breathless anticipation as Mr. Pennington found out their room number and where to find bed linens and towels. "You're right across the hall from us!" She gushed when she heard that they were in Room Six.

Joy, Darcy thought.

Sam led them through a sitting room area packed with people chattering happily around wooden benches to a large staircase that formed a sideways V against the opposite wall. "The rooms are all upstairs, over the dining hall," Sam explained as they climbed to the landing and turned to climb the remaining set of stairs to the second floor.

They alighted and looked around. Directly before them a smaller stairway led up to what looked like a loft area, to the left a single hallway stretched, dead-ending in a closed door, and to the right the hallway quickly ended in a window overlooking the parking lot. Worn orange and brown patterned carpeting covered the floor and dark wainscoting came up to Darcy's waist on the walls.

"Bathrooms are to the right," Sam said, pointing down the shorter end of the hallway toward the window, "and the rooms are to the left." She turned triumphantly and marched down the hall, stopping before the dark, wooden door with a golden number six on it. "Here you are!"

Darcy's dad swung the door open to reveal a small room with two windows on the far wall. Swaying cedar trees were visible beyond the glass. One tall dresser, a single end table and two bunk beds with bare mattresses made up the rest of the furnishings in the room. "Cozy," her dad said, looking around.

Darcy grunted and dropped the cooler with a *thunk*. A slightly musty, yet earthy smell hung about the lodge and she wrinkled her nose a little. She stepped around the cooler to the window and looked out. A short stretch of pale green grass scattered with picnic tables was directly beneath them—a buffer between the lodge and the tree line. To the left the grassy area widened to become a small field, and beyond the field was another, smaller, gray building. A single wooden swing set hugged the trees on the side of the field, and a large bell on a wooden pole sat in a dip in the ground even with the far corner of the lodge. As she watched, a man in a white apron walked toward the bell and took hold of the handle. Within a second its clangs echoed clearly through the lodge.

She turned to Sam. "What's that?" She was surprised at how loud it was.

"That's the first dinner bell," Sam said, putting Darcy's pillow on one of the lower bunks and handing her the camera. "It means to gather in the seating area outside the dining hall. Then in a few minutes they'll ring the second dinner bell, in the hall, and we can go in and find our tables. I wish I could introduce you around before dinner, but we'll have plenty of time afterward."

Darcy saw Roger dash past their room over Sam's shoulder, followed shortly by her mom hauling her suitcase and travel bag. "Mom!" she called, "we're in here."

Mrs. Pennington reappeared a moment later and dropped her things by the dresser. "Allan, get Roger to help you with the two suitcases in the lobby, and then I think we need to go down to dinner." She looked at Sam. "I ran into your parents, Sam, on my way up. They asked me to send you along to dinner if I saw you."

Sam pouted slightly but quickly recovered and waved brightly at Darcy before heading out the door and down the stairs.

Darcy let out a breath that she felt she'd been holding since she first ran into Sam and sat down on the lower bunk next to her pillow. She suddenly felt like her appetite was gone.

"Get up, Darcy."

"Why?"

"Because your father and I get the bottom bunks. You and Roger can sleep on the top. Now move." She swatted playfully at her, and Darcy bounced up with a yelp. Grumbling slightly under her breath, she moved her pillow to the top bunk.

Roger careened into the room with a whoop, dumped his suitcase on the floor, and made a flying leap for the wooden ladder on the end of the closest bed. "I call top bunk!" He tossed Darcy's pillow on the floor and sat up on the bed like a triumphant house cat.

"We both get top bunk, you idiot, and I already called that one. Get down."

"Why don't you make me?" He stuck his tongue out at her.

Darcy groaned and snatched up her pillow. Walking to the opposite side of the room, she tossed it up on the other bunk bed. "Happy?"

"Too bad, so sad."

"Shut up, Roger."

"Come on." He shifted gears as fast as only a ten-year-old could. "Let's go get some grub."

"Wash your hands first!" their mom called to his retreating back. Darcy knew he wouldn't. "You too, Darcy. Let's go to the bathroom, and then we can go down together."

They edged past her father, who was talking loudly to Mr. Acres in the hallway, and went to the bathroom.

"We're supposed to share this one bathroom with all these people?" Darcy asked incredulously, looking around the pale blue bathroom that contained only three stalls, two sinks, and two showers. "You've *got* to be kidding me."

"We have a mirror in our room for makeup and whatnot," her mom said, smoothing her hair and checking her eye shadow. "I'm really not concerned, Darcy."

"Whatever." Darcy looked at her own pale reflection in the mirror and decided that her ponytail definitely needed a redo. She deftly let down her long brown hair and tried to add some life to it by shaking her head back and forth. She would never look as put-together as her mother, but this was the least she could do. She didn't like to wear makeup, like her mom, nor did she have the same auburn hair and perfect porcelain complexion as Sue Pennington. Sometimes, in the right light, Darcy could see that she had red highlights in her hair, but it was really just brown. Plain brown. Her skin, instead of being creamy, just looked pale, and her grey eyes looked washed out and tired. A smattering of freckles covered her pointed nose and cheekbones, and tolerably full lips rested above a softly rounded chin. She lifted her chin slightly and studied her face and neck. She hoped that when she grew up she would have more defined features, like a supermodel, or her mother. She scowled and washed her hands, wishing she could take a shower and go straight to bed.

"Hurry, Darcy, I hear the second dinner bell."

Her mom was right; Darcy faintly detected a much softer bell clanging beneath them. She squared her shoulders, tried not to think about throwing up, and followed her mom out of the bathroom.

Somehow she made it down the stairs, through the sitting room, into the dining hall, and to her seat without having to make eye contact with anybody she didn't know. Only when she was pulling out her wood and wicker chair did she allow herself to look up and carefully glance around. The dining hall was spacious, full of heavy round tables, and smelled of warm rolls and casserole. A salad bar stood off to the right of the kitchen, and cheery windows lined the wall behind her, offering a breathtaking view of the beach and lake. Darcy almost gasped, but caught herself in time. The view was stunning and serene. The green, tree-clad island she'd seen from the road when they'd driven past Mariner's Point looked closer from Glorietta Bay, which faced it head on.

She reluctantly turned back to the table and sat down in her chair. "Pennington-4" was penned neatly on a little standing note card on the table next to another that read "Marks-3." She looked up and dropped the basket of rolls her mother was handing her. Rolls bounced to the floor as she stared at the boy across the table from her. Golden blond, deeply tanned, and athletic-looking, there was only one person this could be: Perry.

"Darcy!" her mother said, exasperated.

"Sorry," she gasped, ducking under the table to retrieve the fallen rolls in mortification.

She emerged from under the table with flaming ears, wishing that her hair was down to hide her blush, and stood awkwardly, staring at her feet.

"This is our daughter, Darcy."

Her dad was introducing her, she should really look up.

"She's thirteen. Is that how old you are, Perry?"

"Yes, sir."

He has a nice voice.

"Darcy, this is Mr. and Mrs. Marks and their son Perry. They have a daughter who's away at college and won't be here this week."

"Hello," Darcy mumbled. She didn't look up; she couldn't.

"Um, let's see . . . where can we get some more rolls?" her dad asked.

"Darcy, dear, if you take that basket up to the counter by the kitchen and tell them what happened, they'll get us a new basket." *That must be his mom talking.*

"Thanks." Darcy practically ran from the table. She'd barely been here half an hour and she'd already been embarrassed in front of *two* boys, no thanks to Roger. But that first boy was nothing, *nothing*, compared to Perry Marks. She wove between the scattered tables to the metal counter. As she waited for more rolls, she discreetly glanced back at her family's table. Perry Marks was saying something to her father, nodding his head vigorously and gesturing with his fork. *Dad! Don't say anything stupid.* Darcy groaned and scanned the rest of the room. She saw Samantha waving at her and jabbing her finger toward the Pennington/Marks table.

"Isn't he *hot?*" Samantha mouthed at her.

Darcy only smiled weakly in return. For once, she couldn't disagree with her. *Maybe the week won't be a total loss after all.*

Darcy slid back into her seat and set the rolls down *very* carefully. She was painfully aware of how tired she looked and fervently wished that she had taken the time to change out of her van-crumpled clothes. As it was, she was wearing a plain blue T-shirt with "Gregorio's" and a horse outline emblazoned in the upper left corner, and plaid Bermuda shorts with flip flops. Her charm bracelet with horses and horseshoes on it tinkled softly as she gathered items to her plate: a roll, a pile of green beans, and a small portion of chicken casserole. She wasn't sure if she'd be able to eat, though.

"So, Darcy, your mom tells us that you like to ride horses?" Mrs. Marks's kind voice sounded from across the table, and Darcy was finally forced to look up.

"Yes, Ma'am, but I don't own my own horse."

"Do you ride at a camp, then?"

Darcy nodded, careful to look only at Mr. or Mrs. Marks, letting her eyes skim quickly over Perry where he sat between them.

"We signed Perry up for a few lessons years ago, but he never really took to it," Mrs. Marks continued. "Isn't that right, Perry?"

Perry shrugged and continued vigorously downing his plateful of casserole.

Mrs. Marks turned her attention to Roger, and Darcy allowed herself to study the family with a bit more liberty. She shoved a forkful of green beans into her mouth and surreptitiously glanced at Perry. He definitely took after his mother. His father was a good-looking man, but he had dark hair and a rounded nose. Perry's golden waves—which were long on his forehead, but short in the back—dark lashes, blue eyes, and straight nose all belonged to his mother, who was beautiful, of course, even with liberal amounts of grey streaked through her hair. Darcy noticed that Mr. Marks and her dad were talking to each other, and she tuned into the conversation.

"So, this is your first summer here?"

"Yes. We usually go our separate ways in the summer," Mr. Pennington squeezed Roger's shoulders playfully, "but we thought that we'd try something new this summer."

"How did you find out about Cedar Cove?"

"Well, two families in our neighborhood come here every year—the Palms and the Acreses. When Sue mentioned to Kathy Palm that we were looking for a family vacation spot, she couldn't speak more highly of Cedar Cove."

"That's great. We've known the Palms and the Acreses for years; they're both great families. Lewis is a little bit . . . different . . . but he and Perry have always gotten along fine. Samantha Palm and Perry have practically grown up together."

Darcy thought she saw a flicker of irritation cross Perry's face and she suddenly felt very sorry for Sam. Apparently her undying infatuation with Perry Marks was not in the least bit returned. *Of course, did she really expect it to be? I mean, look at him and look at her—* Darcy stopped her train of thought abruptly and studied her plate, ashamed. She shouldn't think things like that.

"If Darcy's already friends with Sam, she should fit right in with the rest of them." Mr. Marks continued. "I'm sure Perry will help her to feel welcome." He nudged his son.

"Huh?" Perry looked up at her. "Oh, yeah . . . sure." He gave her a cursory smile and looked at his dad. "I think the dessert trays are out, can I go get one?"

His dad gave his permission and laughed when he left the table. "You know teenage boys, only concerned with food. You don't have long to wait with that one." He nodded at Roger.

"Sure don't."

Darcy pushed her mostly uneaten plate of food to her mother, who was scraping all the food onto one plate and stacking the empty ones, and tried to look alert and charming for when Perry returned with the dessert tray. He didn't even look at her when he returned, though. He handed around the tray with small bowls of apple crisps and tucked into his dessert with almost indecent gusto. Darcy found that she was actually very much in the mood for apple crisp and finally managed to eat everything that was in front of her.

Perry disappeared as soon as his dessert was finished and Darcy looked around the crowded room for some sign of where he might have gone. People were standing up and milling around, taking piles of scraped dishes and platters of uneaten food up to the counter, and the noise level in the dining hall had increased to an excited buzz. Darcy saw lots of people giving hugs and exclaiming over how much children had grown and wondered if her family was the only one that hadn't been going to Cedar Cove for years upon years.

Suddenly Samantha appeared at her elbow. "You all finished?" she breathed excitedly. "Come on, I want to introduce you to everyone." She practically dragged Darcy out of her chair and into the crowd of people. "You are *so* lucky!" she hissed into Darcy's ear. "I would kill to sit with the Markses. Isn't Perry amazing?"

"Um, yeah. So will we be sitting with them all week?"

"No, probably only for a day or two." She pointed at a pillar near the front of the hall where a seating arrangement was posted. "They generally try to move families around throughout the week so that people get to know each other."

"So maybe you'll get to sit with them later in the week?"

"Hopefully." Sam grinned and stopped by a group of young teenagers standing near a rear exit. Darcy's mouth went dry. "Guys, this is Darcy. Darcy, this is everyone!"

Well, she'd found where Perry had disappeared to. He was leaning against the wall chewing on a straw next to the dark-haired boy Roger had embarrassed her in front of in the parking lot. His name was Dean, Sam said, and he smirked at her when she looked his direction. Darcy looked quickly away. Next she was introduced to Amelia, who smiled cautiously at her. Amelia was a naturally pretty girl, and Darcy felt a stab of jealousy. She was tall and willowy—the next tallest after Dean, and just an inch or so taller than Perry—with very straight sandy hair that fell to her shoulders, pretty hazel eyes, and even, white teeth. Her perfectly clear skin would be the envy of any thirteen-year-old girl.

"And, of course, you know Lewis."

Lewis squinted at her from behind his glasses, his pale blue eyes wary. His lips twitched in an attempt at a smile, and Darcy returned the attempt in her own fashion. Silence fell among the group, and she panicked slightly. *Am I supposed to say something?* She was saved by Samantha's mother.

"Well, look at all of you! Dean, you just get taller and taller. So, do you guys think you are going to have a good week?" Mrs. Palm smiled sweetly at all of them.

Amelia shrugged and nodded as Dean said, "Don't see why not."

"Sam." Mrs. Palm turned to her daughter. "I want you to come upstairs and unpack your suitcase, and then you can hang out with your friends."

"Okay, Mom. Hey, do you guys wanna go for a walk in, like, fifteen minutes? It won't take me very long to unpack."

Darcy was about to say that she really should go up to her room when Perry looked at Dean and said, "Sure, I'll just need to let my mom know."

"Me, too," said Amelia. Lewis nodded.

Sam beamed. "Darcy?"

Perry's going. "Okay."

CHAPTER 4

SKIPPING ROCKS

Darcy stepped out onto the boardwalk and shivered slightly, crossing her arms over her chest. The sun was going down and the air was taking on a definite chill. *Maybe I should go get my sweatshirt?* she thought, but just as she turned she saw the dining hall exit swing open and Perry Marks hop down to the cement patio. *Never mind.* She straightened her shoulders and tried to appear casual as she cautiously walked over to him, but he didn't even look at her. Instead he was surveying a post as though he was thinking of climbing it. *Say hey, just say hey*, she told herself.

"Hey." Her voice sounded squeaky and unnatural.

He looked at her, both hands and one foot on the post. "Oh, hey. It's Darcy, right?"

"Yes." *What do I say now?*

He shook his bangs out of his eyes and went back to his conquest of the pole. Awkward silence ensued as he grunted and shimmied up the rough-cut beam.

Darcy's mind buzzed furiously, screaming at her to say something, but instead she just stood there dumbly. Finally, she forced her mouth open—it felt like it had been cemented closed—and said, "So, um—"

Bang! The crash bar on the dining hall door sounded painfully loud in the stillness of Cedar Cove. Samantha charged out, practically dancing with glee, and Amelia followed serenely in her wake. Darcy heard tennis shoes scrape on sandy wood behind her and turned to see Dean standing with his arms crossed, his head concealed beneath the hood of an army sweatshirt.

"Let's go!" Sam squealed.

"What about Lewis?" Perry swung down from the overhang of the porch with ease and landed next to Sam.

"His parents said that they had to have a 'family meeting.' " Sam did air quotes on the last two words.

Perry shrugged. "All right, cool. Lead the way." He dropped back to walk with Dean.

Sam linked an arm each through Amelia's and Darcy's and tugged them down the boardwalk. *Why is she always touching me?* Darcy inwardly lamented. *Do I look like I want to be touched?* She kept her arm as limp as possible, hoping to discourage the unwanted contact, but Sam was totally oblivious.

Sam nodded down the gently sloping boardwalk to where it ended about a hundred yards away at the smaller grey building Darcy had seen from the window in her room.

"That's the Stevenson Recreation Center, but we usually just call it the Rec Hall. The Sticky Branch, which is the camp store, is right inside those doors. You can buy candy, ice cream, soda, T-shirts, books, mugs . . . whatever! It's not open right now, though. There's also a library on the second floor, and foosball, table tennis, and bumper pool on the first floor. Classrooms for the little kids are down the hall along that side." She removed her arm from Amelia's to point. "But we won't be there for class. They'll probably put us in the loft this year." Without warning she careened off the left side of the boardwalk into the sand and plopped down to pull off her shoes.

Her arm liberated, Darcy sat down carefully on the sandy grey planks of the boardwalk to slip out of her flip flops. She'd taken the time to change her shirt in the fifteen minutes after dinner, but had decided that her Bermuda shorts and flip flops were suitably cool to keep on. Perry also had on Bermuda shorts, after all.

She dug her toes into the cool sand and suddenly felt a soft, prickly sensation, like there was a very small electrical current running through the sand. She jerked her feet out and swiftly looked up to see if anybody else was acting like they'd felt anything. Dean and Perry were already down by the water, laughing and chucking handfuls of wet sand at each other, and Sam and Amelia were still taking off their shoes and socks. *Okay . . .* Darcy's heart rate scooted up a notch and she cautiously lowered her feet once more into the sand.

There it was again, a thrumming, like the beach was alive and powerful. *I'm losing my mind. There must be some sort of natural explanation.* She stood slowly, delicately.

Amelia stepped down off the boardwalk and smiled broadly. "Gosh, I love it here. This sand always feels so good after a year away from it."

"I know!" Sam gushed, rolling up her jeans and joining them.

The effervescent tingling was traveling up and down Darcy's legs now, and she frantically thought of a way to ask about it. *Don't sound like a crazy person.* "Um . . . are there, like, minerals, or something, in the sand here?"

Sam looked at Amelia, for once at a loss. "I don't know. I guess there could be."

"Why?" Amelia said, her eyebrow raised.

"The sand just feels . . . different. Different from any other beach I've ever been on, that is."

"Different how?" Amelia sounded suspicious now.

Darcy opted for honesty. "Don't you guys feel the tingling?" *It's not in my mind.*

Amelia looked at Sam; her face seemed to say, "Is she always this weird?"

Sam rocked a little and smiled. "I don't feel any tingling, but the sand does feel amazing." She shrugged slightly. "Maybe your feet are still a little sleepy from the drive."

No. "Yeah, maybe." She took a cautious step toward the water, her mind working furiously. Why was she feeling a tingle that apparently only she could feel? *Maybe I've got cancer, or something. A brain tumor would explain it*. But she didn't really think that was the case. Suddenly, without warning, the tingle stopped. She froze mid-step and turned her head to look at Amelia and Sam. Amelia was still watching her scrupulously, but Sam was staring wistfully at Perry.

Darcy's face must have warranted pity, because Amelia suddenly turned to Sam and snorted. She poked Sam hard on the shoulder. "Hey! Don't be so obvious."

Sam started and blushed. She looked down. "Yeah, I know."

"You don't *want* him to know, remember?" Amelia rolled her eyes and shook her head.

"Yeah, yeah."

"Come *on*, you guys!" Perry hollered from the water. "Girls are *so* slow."

"C'mon, let's go," Amelia said, and Sam followed her. Neither one seemed to notice that Darcy was still poised with one foot half in the air, inhaling and exhaling with deliberate slowness.

Darcy cautiously placed her left foot all the way down. Nothing. She bounced up and down a little. Still nothing. The tingling was gone without a trace. *Strange*. There was nothing left for her to do but follow after the others. As she hurried to catch up with Sam and Amelia, however, she noticed something else that was strange. She didn't feel tired anymore—not the least bit. In fact, she felt the opposite of tired; she felt that at that very moment she could run a mile or do a hundred jumping jacks without growing weary. Invigoration coursed through her, and her heart pumped a healthy rhythm. *There's no* way *I can be feeling this good after eight hours in the car.* She couldn't actually remember *ever* feeling that good before. *It's not adrenaline, it's . . . It's like magic!* She snorted and choked down a laugh. *Okay, I'm not going to go there.* Perhaps there really was something special to Cedar Cove, after all. When she looked around at the other teenagers, however, she distinctly knew that this experience was her own. She was the only one who'd felt the tingle, and she was clearly the only one who felt the unnatural health and vigor. Sam was already panting slightly from the walk across the sand, and Dean, Perry, and Amelia were laughing together about some story from a previous year.

Darcy trailed after them to the edge of the beach and tried to act normal as they picked their way in among the piled rocks, large and small, that littered the lake's edge where the water met the trees.

"We don't have much light left," Amelia commented. The sun was setting behind the trees to their right and long shadows stretched across the surface of the water, turning silvery blue to charcoal grey.

"We've still got time to get a few good skips in," Perry said. He selected a rock from the ground and expertly sent it skimming across the water.

"I can never find a good one," Sam muttered. She tucked her bottom lip between her teeth as she searched the ground.

Dean hauled up the largest flat rock he could find and held it above his head. "Look out!" He chucked it in the water and ducked away, laughing.

Darcy gasped as cold water doused her legs.

Amelia turned keen eyes on her. "What's the matter? More tingles?"

"No. It's just . . . really, really cold!" She shivered again.

Sam chuckled. "Yeah, the water's pretty cold this far north. My dad says that it sometimes dips below fifty degrees in the summer, but it feels really good on a hot afternoon." She turned back to hunting for rocks and finally found one that she thought would do. It gave two feeble skips before disappearing below the surface. "Darn! I can never get more than two or three." She shot a furtive glance at Perry, whose rocks were flying across the surface as though they had wings.

Amelia skipped a few, but didn't seem too into the activity, and Dean moved farther down the shoals to find more good rocks for splashing. Darcy observed them all with a small amount of interest. Finally Sam noticed that Darcy hadn't skipped any yet and asked, "What's the matter? Don't you know how?"

Darcy shook her head. "I've never skipped rocks before. But that's okay, I don't mind watching."

Perry looked up. "You don't know how? It's easy, here." He came over and put a small, flat stone in her hand. Her heart gave a flip that had nothing to do with her experience on the beach. She felt her ears start to redden as he took her hand and showed her how to hold it. *I'm glad it's almost dark.*

"You angle it like this, and then throw it, almost like a Frisbee, out over the lake. Now you try." He stepped back with the look of an encouraging coach.

Darcy held the rock still for a moment. With the strange strength flowing through her body, she certainly *felt* that she could do it. She took a deep breath, wound her arm back, and threw it with all her strength.

The rock sailed in a perfect, smooth, gradual arc out over the water, hit once, bounced back up, hit twice, bounced again, hit three, four, five, six, seven times, skipped in tiny, rapid hops five or six more times after that, and then disappeared smoothly under the water.

Darcy stared, wide-eyed, holding her breath. There was no way she had just done that! She turned to Perry and smiled sheepishly. "Beginner's luck?"

He whistled quietly under his breath. "Um, yeah, okay . . . you sure you've never done this before?"

Darcy nodded.

"Holy cow, Darcy! How did you do that?" Samantha looked around their feet and snagged another rock. "Here, try again." She pressed it into her hand.

"Okay." Darcy let it fly, with the same result. She laughed a little shakily. "Honestly, I don't know what I'm doing." *What's going on?*

"Uh huh." Amelia sounded unbelieving, but Sam and Perry were grinning.

"Hey, guys, I think we'd better go in. I see my mom on the boardwalk and she looks anxious," Dean interrupted, popping up next to them. He had missed the whole thing. He ducked around them and hopped from rock to rock until he reached the sand.

"Yeah, okay," Perry said. He was still looking at Darcy with a quizzical eye.

Sam and Amelia were quick to agree with Perry, and Sam reattached herself to Darcy's arm once they reached the beach. "You surprised Perry because you can skip rocks better than him," she whispered happily into Darcy's ear. "Nobody's *ever* been better than him before."

Chapter 5

Night

When they reached the patio, Darcy said goodnight to Dean and Amelia, whose families both stayed in some of the special cabins that cost a little more money than staying in the lodge. Perry muttered something about taking a shower and disappeared through the lobby entrance, and Sam and Darcy were left alone in the gathering dark.

"I love the night sky out here," Sam said, craning her neck up. "Just wait. When it's completely dark out, the stars are amazing. You can actually see the arm of the Milky Way."

Darcy looked skyward with interest, but it was still streaked with lavender and scarlet; no stars had yet emerged. "At the equestrian camp I go to, Gregorio's, it's really pretty at night, too, but I don't think you can see the arm of the Milky Way. How do you know that's what you're seeing up here?"

Sam shrugged. "My dad told me."

"So, does everybody usually go to bed this early here?" Darcy looked around. She could only see a few scattered adults sitting in patio chairs or walking from one place to another. It couldn't be much later than eight thirty.

Sam giggled. "No. But people usually crash early on the first night. Everybody's always real tired from traveling. My parents usually like me inside by the time it gets dark, but I don't have to be in the room until ten."

The lobby entrance swung open with a creak and Lewis poked his head out. "Sam, do you want to play cards? My parents finally finished talking to us."

Sam brightened. "Sure! Darcy, do you want to play?"

Lewis scowled at her.

"Ahhh . . . no. I think my parents are probably wondering where I am." Darcy looked at Lewis and saw a flash of relief cross his face. *The feeling's mutual*, she thought grimly.

"Oh, okay." Sam's face fell a little.

They brushed the rest of the sand off their feet and pattered barefoot into the lobby, clutching their footwear. Darcy turned for the stairs with a curt nod and stopped only when Sam called her name again.

"Darcy?"

"Yeah?" She turned. Sam's face looked anxious.

"Did you have fun tonight?" She breathed the question out in a rush, as though she was afraid of the answer.

"Sure, Sam." She suddenly found that it was the truth. She *had* had fun with them, but she knew that it had little to do with Samantha, and a lot to do with a certain cute boy. *What Sam doesn't know won't hurt her,* she thought, but she said out loud, "It's really . . . nice here." And it was. Even her strange experience on the beach did not diminish the beauty and serenity of the landscape or the unique sense of community that she felt between the campers. *But it's not like being at Gregorio's.* She felt a pang and swallowed hard. She needed to be alone.

Sam, oblivious as always to Darcy's inner battle, smiled in a relieved sort of way that made her dimples deepen in her cheeks. "Good. I'll see you in the morning. Oh, and by the way, you may want to shower tonight. Sometimes the showers get congested in the mornings."

"Thanks for the advice." Darcy waved and smiled weakly.

Lewis sat on a bench shuffling a deck of cards. He didn't look up.

Darcy opened the door to her room quietly and slipped in. Her mother was lying on the bunk beneath Darcy's reading a Nora Roberts novel, and her brother's freckled hand hung over the edge of the bunk next to her head; loud snores issued from the vicinity of his pillow. Her mom looked up when Darcy entered and put a finger to her mouth. *I didn't make any noise coming in*, Darcy thought grumpily.

"Roger's sleeping," her mom whispered.

Duh, Darcy refrained from rolling her eyes, barely.

"He was so worked up all day that he just came up here and crashed about a half hour ago. Did you have fun with your friends?"

Darcy shrugged. She didn't miss the emphasis that her mom put on the word "friends." Sue Pennington was always pushing her daughter to be more social. "Yeah, I guess so. I found out that I'm pretty good at skipping rocks."

"Uh huh." Her mom's eyes had returned to her book.

Darcy sighed and went to the dresser. She'd noticed as soon as she'd entered the room that her bed had been made, and when she opened the top drawer of the dresser, she found her clothes neatly laid out for her. *Probably Dad's doing*. She grabbed her nightclothes (a large T-shirt and boxer shorts) and her overnight case from the top of the dresser and looked around for towels. "Mom?" she whispered.

"What?"

"Towels?"

"Use your eyes, Darcy. They're right on the hooks behind you."

"Oh." She took a plain, white, camp-issued towel off its hook. "I'm going to take a shower."

"Okay, honey." Her mom didn't look up.

Roger snorted in his sleep and rolled over. Disheveled orange curls stuck up oddly from his pillow.

Five minutes later Darcy was in the shower. The hot streams of water pushed satisfyingly into her back and shoulders and she felt herself relax. *Okay, now I have to figure out what happened on the beach tonight.* But try as she might, she couldn't come up with a logical explanation. Was she positive she hadn't imagined it? *Yes*. Was she sure that nobody else had felt it? *Yep.* Did she still feel strangely off, like she was a world-class tri-athlete? *Uh huh, but it's fading*. It was true; the more time that elapsed since the walk on the beach, the less she felt the lingering effects of the invigorating tingle.

She sighed and rinsed the shampoo out of her hair. Maybe there were some things in life that were simply beyond explanation, and maybe that was okay. Or maybe she really was different from everybody else, like she'd always thought. She'd never felt like she fit in, not with the popular kids, not with the nerds. Not with the athletes, musicians, drama kids, band geeks, or math clubbers. The closest thing she had to a best friend was Timmory—a horse that didn't even belong to her—and the only time she was ever truly comfortable was when she was all alone. A boy like Perry Marks would never like her. Every moment with other people was work to her, a discipline of stringing words together to form coherent sentences so that people wouldn't know how awkward she felt. A lot of other kids thought she was stuck up, she knew that from school, but she didn't know how to make them understand her. The only person her own age who'd ever shown genuine interest in her was Samantha, but Samantha drove her nuts. *And I don't* want *to be friends with Samantha.*

She scrubbed her feet, working the gritty sand out from between her toes. By about this time at home her mother would be hollering at her to get out of the shower.

A toilet flushed in the bathroom and a few women pushed through the door, their happy voices drifting through the partition into the shower area. Darcy quickly finished up; she didn't know why they had to make the shower doors transparent, anyway, and she didn't want anybody to see her. Her mom told her that she needed to get over it—"It's not anything other women haven't seen before, Darcy!"—but Darcy felt that there wasn't anything wrong with a healthy dose of modesty. She dove for the wooden bench and her towel in record time, wrapped a hand towel around her dripping hair, and quickly started the process of getting dressed beneath her towel, a discipline she'd mastered at school during the swimming unit of PhysEd.

When she emerged from the shower area to brush her teeth, she found Mrs. Palm and Mrs. Acres chatting in front of the mirror.

"Well hi, Darcy!" Mrs. Palm gave her a one-armed hug and smiled deeply. "Did you have a good time tonight?"

"Yes, ma'am." Darcy couldn't help but feel comfortable around Sam's mom. The woman had a natural proclivity for making other people feel as though they were dear and special, and Darcy wished that Sam were more like her, in more ways than one. Mrs. Palm was very pretty, and without all the added stuff that her own mom used. She wore very little makeup, but her eyes always sparkled and her mouth was always tipped up at the corners, as though it could break into a smile at any moment. She had the same corn silk blond curls as her daughter, but unlike Sam, she was very trim and fit. Darcy didn't know if she jogged or biked or anything like that, but she definitely was in better shape than her daughter. In fact, Darcy couldn't quite figure out why Sam was overweight; both her parents were thin, and her older brother was thin, but she and her younger sister carried around a lot of extra weight in their stomachs and thighs. Maybe it was just baby fat and would disappear with time.

Speaking of Sam's younger sister, Abigail Palm bounced into the bathroom with a flourish and tugged on her mom's sleeve. Mrs. Palm leaned down so her youngest daughter could whisper in her ear, smiled sweetly and whispered something back, and then ruffled her hair affectionately. Abigail smiled, too, her dimples deeper than anybody else's in the family, and bounced back out of the bathroom. Abby Palm was like that—full of little girl energy, but very, very quiet. *Sam could take a page or two from her book.*

"I'm sorry, Darcy, I didn't mean to interrupt you. You were telling me about your night?" Mrs. Palm prompted her.

Mrs. Acres ignored her. *Like mother, like son, I guess.*

"Um, yeah . . . we took a walk on the beach and skipped some rocks."

"That's nice. Did you get to meet everybody?"

"Uh huh. Perry Marks taught me how to skip rocks. I'd never done it before."

Mrs. Palm's eyes narrowed in a playful, knowing sort of way, and Darcy quickly shoved her toothbrush into her mouth. *Stupid, big, fat mouth.*

"I bet that was fun," Mrs. Palm said in a very measured tone.

Darcy nodded.

"Well, dear, I hope that you have a good time the whole week and that you won't regret missing your horse camp too much. We sure are glad to have you here."

"T'ank oo," Darcy managed to say through her mouthful of toothpaste.

Mrs. Palm packed up her things and left with a smile. Darcy shot a furtive glance or two at Mrs. Acres, but the woman continued her nighttime bathroom routine without so much as a nod. Darcy felt her familiar anxiety start to eat at her stomach. *There's too much silence. One of us needs to say something.* But Mrs. Acres saved her the trouble a moment later by turning her back and leaving. The door swung and thudded softly closed.

As Darcy crept quietly back to her room a few minutes later, she reflected on Mrs. Acres's behavior. *I know that Lewis doesn't like me, but I don't see why* she *has to act that way! What did I ever do to her?* she thought, hurt. She ran smack into her father's chest as he exited the room, his towel in hand.

"Oof!" he said, taking her by the shoulders and holding her out from him. "Lost in our thoughts, are we?"

"Sorry, Dad."

He continued to hold her shoulders, studying her face with his father's eye. "So, are you going to survive?"

"Huh?"

"Have we scarred you for life by bringing you here?"

"Oh . . . no. It's not as bad as I thought it would be," she conceded.

"Good, I'll take that." He released her shoulders and sidled past her, whistling to himself.

Darcy paused with her hand on the doorknob and turned back to her dad. "Dad?" she hissed. She didn't want to be accused of waking up other campers.

"Yes?"

"If I promise to have a good time this week, will you promise to let me go back to Gregorio's next year?"

Mr. Pennington hesitated; his face fell. "Well . . . we'll see, Darce."

"Okay." *I'll take that.* She slipped through the door.

CHAPTER 6

TALES AND TRAILS

Darcy woke to the sound of gulls calling and the rhythmic swish and pull of the waves hitting the shore. The Penningtons were in a "wood side" room, as Sam had told her, but the lake was still clearly audible. Darcy realized that it was a rare thing to hear nature sounds so clearly without the backdrop of suburban noise pollution. She lay very still in bed for a few minutes, certain that the unfamiliar sounds had woken her, because she was not usually an early riser. She eventually sat up and slid down from the top bunk, noticing that her brother's bed was empty and her parents were starting to stir. As her feet hit the short, worn carpet, she realized that no vestige of the unnatural strength from the night before remained any longer. She was herself once again. She didn't know if she was happy or disappointed, but supposed that it was really neither here nor there.

She dressed very carefully for the day, painfully aware of how many eyes were going to be on her, the "new girl," on this first, full day of family camp. Grey Bermuda shorts with a pattern of large, tropical blue flowers seemed "campy" to her, and a blue tank top from Gregorio's with the camp's emblem of a horse on the back felt appropriate due to her acute desire to be there, rather than here. Flip flops were always safe, and Darcy decided to fasten her charm bracelet around her ankle this morning, rather than her wrist. *Perry had an anklet on yesterday, maybe he likes them?* Her long hair had dried very wavy after sleeping on it wet, and she reluctantly wrestled it into a ponytail. She liked her hair wavy, but it was just too crazy to leave down for the day.

The light breaking through the shades was cheerful and promising, and

Darcy remembered what Sam had told her the night before about temperature fluctuations in upper Michigan. *"It will be cool in the mornings and at night, but it's usually warm, or even hot, in the afternoons."* Darcy nabbed her sweatshirt on her way out the door.

The outside bell started ringing as she descended the stairs. The crowd of people outside the dining hall was smaller than it had been the night before; clearly many people liked to sleep in. Roger's vivid head was bobbing through the crowd, and Darcy made directly for him. She didn't have a desire to hang out with her little brother, but she craved his easy-going familiarity and, above all else, did not want to find herself standing alone in a room full of people she didn't know.

She reached Roger, who was chatting animatedly with Jonathan Acres, Lewis Acres's younger brother, who was a year younger than Roger, and didn't seem to notice her walk up. She pasted herself against the wainscoted wall, trying to blend into the wood and plaster. But—she should have known—Samantha Palm could not be avoided for long.

"Darcy!"

She jumped. Where had Sam *come* from?

"What?" she snapped, a little more harshly than she'd intended. She never felt completely awake until mid-morning.

"After breakfast do you wanna walk around the camp with me and Amelia? I could show you all the trails and buildings and stuff." Sam's excitement, if possible, seemed even greater this morning than the night before.

"Um, I don't know. I'll have to ask my parents."

"Okay." Sam didn't seem concerned. "Oh, there's Amelia. Amelia!" She waved furiously, her blond curls bouncing.

Amelia edged through the growing crowd, her sandy head even with most of the adults in the room, and nudged up next to Sam. She gave Darcy a tight smile. "Hi."

"Darcy said that she should be able to explore with us this morning, but she'll have to ask her parents first." Sam filled her in with lightning speed.

"Okay." Amelia seemed to brighten a little and looked at Darcy with new interest. "I think you'll really like it here. I know that most of us feel so strongly about this camp because we've been coming here our whole lives, but it really is a very special place." Sam nodded enthusiastically as Amelia continued. "Dean's family's only been coming for four years, but he's already told us that he'll never miss a summer if he can help it. Perry's always threatening not to come back," Amelia scowled, "but he just says that to provoke us. His family's been coming since before he was born. His sister, who's, like, six years older than him, grew up here, as well. And Lewis, well, he doesn't say much, but we know he loves it here. Sam's parents got him to come, like, eight years ago, or was it seven?" She looked at Sam.

"Eight," Sam said cheerfully.

"Right, so, like, eight years ago, and they only missed one summer when his baby sister was born."

Darcy already knew most of this from Sam's unending monologue during the month of June back home, but she took new interest in it now that she had faces to place with the names.

The bell in the dining hall clanged and the crowd surged forward with purpose. Darcy was swept away to her family's table and found that her absolute favorite breakfast dish was set out on the table: french toast. There was also a breakfast bar against the wall, where the salad bar had been the night before, that boasted troughs of scrambled eggs and various breakfast meats and potatoes. Darcy took note of the long line and decided to dig into her french toast first.

Roger appeared at the table a few minutes later, his plate brimming with food from the breakfast bar. "I hope they feed us this well the entire week!" Roger exclaimed, diving into his plate with gusto. " 'Ey, 'Arshy?" he managed a moment later.

Darcy gave him a withering look; hash browns were sticking out of the corners of his very full mouth. "You'd better not let Mom see you talking like that with food in your mouth." She went back to her toast.

He swallowed hard and flicked a forkful of eggs at her plate. "Hey!"

"Gross, Roger. What do you want?" She glared.

He suddenly looked very innocent. "I was just wondering if you wanted to take a look around the camp with me after breakfast. Jonathan Acres told me that he'd show me all the best places to hang out."

Darcy's scowl melted a little and she felt a brief moment of chagrin. Sometimes she forgot that her brother was still a very little boy in many ways, and even though he gave her a hard time, he still liked to hang out with her. "Thanks, Roger, but I think I'm going to get stuck hanging out with Sam again."

A chair scraped the floor across the table and she looked up, startled. Perry Marks was sliding into his seat with his parents. He looked decidedly disheveled, like he hadn't yet woken up completely. *Oh no.* Darcy wished she could take back her last words. *Did he hear what I just said about Sam?* But Perry gave no indication that he even knew she was at the table and started piling french toast on his plate.

"Good morning, Darcy. Good morning, Roger," Mrs. Marks said. "Are your parents still sleeping?"

"They were just getting up when I came down," Darcy said quickly. "Normally they're up early, but I think they were tired from the drive yesterday."

"The time change can be difficult to adjust to, as well," Mrs. Marks said. "We come from Iowa and we always have to remind ourselves to change our watches, even after all these years." She turned to her son. "Do you guys have any plans for this morning?"

"Dean and Lewis and I are going to the other side to shoot some hoops, I think," Perry responded, distracted by the food.

Two thoughts immediately intruded on Darcy's mind. *Lewis plays basketball?* Was quickly pushed aside by, *Then there's no hope of him coming with me and Sam and Amelia to explore the camp.* She stabbed her french toast with more aggression than she'd intended. *Maybe Mom or Dad will say I can't go.*

They ate in companionable silence and Darcy's parents finally joined them just as the breakfast hour was coming to a close. As they exchanged pleasantries with the Markses, Darcy tried to figure out how she could ask them if she could explore with Sam and Amelia in such a way as to make them say no, but she couldn't think of a thing. She didn't want to be forbidden to explore, she just wanted to do it alone.

Just as she opened her mouth to broach the topic, Sam slid into Roger's vacated chair with an excited rustle and looked at her expectantly. "Have you asked them yet?" she asked in a conspiratorial whisper that nonetheless carried to the whole table.

"Asked us what?" Darcy's dad asked, looking between her and Sam.

No getting out of it now. "Sam was wondering if I could hang out with her and Amelia this morning so she can show me around the camp."

"Please, Mr. Pennington! I promise that we'll stay on this side. The ferry isn't even running until after ten o'clock," Sam said in a rush.

"Well, I don't see why not. You certainly know more about the camp than we do. I'm sure that Darcy will be very thankful for your expert knowledge and insight." Allan Pennington's voice was slightly teasing.

Thanks a lot, Dad.

Sam stayed at the table until Darcy finished eating. Darcy was usually a slow eater, but the fact that she had a full morning of Sam to look forward to made her drag her usual eating time out as long as possible. Sam busily helped Mrs. Marks clean off the table, and Darcy noticed that her eyes constantly darted to Perry during this time, as if seeking approval. The clock struck nine o'clock before Darcy was finally ready to go. She returned to her room to change into tennis shoes and then met Sam and Amelia on the boardwalk outside the dining hall. The boys were nowhere to be seen.

"Okay," Sam said, clapping her hands together with the air of a chef about to start a cooking class. Darcy quickly darted to the far side of Amelia, avoiding having her arm captured again by Sam, but the girl didn't even seem to notice. She took off down the boardwalk at a clipped pace and Amelia and Darcy trailed along behind her.

Cedar Cove in the morning was just as stunning as Cedar Cove at night, and Darcy tuned out Sam's chattering to enjoy the view from the boardwalk. To her right was the field with the swing set on the far side, and to her left was the beach. *Ah, the beach,* Darcy thought, tempted to step off into the sand to see what would happen, but she resisted.

The water was a deep, crystalline blue this morning, with starbursts of sunlight sparkling over its smooth surface. The ebb and flow of the lake on the sand was very subdued, and there were already a few little children building sandcastles and splashing in the shallow water. Trees hugged the bay on either side of the beach and Darcy could see the rocky shoals where they had skipped rocks the night before.

A shed was set up on the far side of the beach, even with the rec hall, in which hung oars for kayaks and canoes. Near a small wooden dock there were a few boats scattered about: canoes, kayaks, rowboats, and small, two-person sailboats that Sam later told her were called sunfishes. At the time, however, Sam was busily talking about the rec hall and Darcy decided that it might be time to pay attention.

"Here you go!" Sam held the heavy door at the end of the boardwalk open for them and they stepped into a shadowy hallway.

Darcy's eyes quickly adjusted and she looked around at the various things that Sam pointed out.

"Bathrooms are right here." Sam pointed down a branching hallway to their right, "stairs to the library are to your left. Life jackets for boating are hanging in the stairwell. And, of course, this is the Sticky Branch." The Sticky Branch was little more than a counter with goodies of all sorts piled within view of the register, but there was also, as Darcy quickly noticed, a small alcove just across from the counter with books, T-shirts, and other assorted items arranged artfully on the walls.

Sam hurried them forward to the main area of the rec hall, which was a loud, echoing room containing two foosball tables, ping pong tables, and bumper pool tables. A fireplace stood on the far wall and the plunked-out strains of "Für Elise" warbled from a piano in the corner where a pigtailed girl sat playing.

Amelia grimaced and shook her head. Sam chuckled at her. "Amelia's a musician. She plays, like, eight different instruments!"

"Five," Amelia corrected softly, but there was a distinct air of pride about her, nonetheless.

Darcy couldn't help but be impressed. "You play *five* instruments?"

Amelia nodded and tried to look busy watching a game of foosball.

"What are they?"

"Piano, flute, oboe, clarinet, and violin," Amelia supplied. "I started with the piano when I was three and, I don't know, it was just my thing, I guess." She shrugged her slender shoulders.

"Amelia wants to go to Juilliard someday." Sam sounded awed. "I think she'll make it."

"We'll see." Amelia moved to study a fourteen-by-sixteen portrait hanging on the wall. "This is why it's called the Stevenson Recreation Center, look." She pointed at the portrait and a small placard beneath it.

The faded image was of a pretty young lady of college age with long blond hair and large hazel eyes. The placard read "In Memory of Eleanor Stevenson, 1940-1959."

"What happened to her?" Darcy asked, interested despite herself.

"She disappeared at Cedar Cove fifty years ago," Sam said quietly.

"She was a college camper who came here with a school group back when the camp was still pretty young and the trails and whatnot were not as clearly marked as they are now," Amelia interjected. "They say that one day she just went hiking and never came back. They searched the woods for her for a week before she was found, dead."

"She wasn't killed by a wild animal, or anything, though." Sam continued, "It looked like she just got lost." Her voice dropped to a whisper and her eyes took on a mysterious gleam. "You know what is the weirdest part about it though, Darcy? When they found her body they said that she was laying peacefully, like she had just gone to sleep and a smile was on her face."

"*And* they say that she hadn't even started to decay even though she must have been dead for at least three days," Amelia added, but then laughed shortly. "Of course, every camp has to have its scary story. I don't really know how much of the story to believe."

Darcy and Sam straightened up. They had become crouched around the picture without even realizing it, and suddenly the sounds of the rec hall brought them back to reality.

Sam pouted slightly and chewed her lip. "I don't know, Amelia, there is something special about this place; almost magical, you know?"

"Yeah, but like, magical as in 'special,' not magical as in *actually* magical."

Sam looked unconvinced and Amelia laughed out loud. "Come on, first Darcy last night with the 'tingles' and now you actually believe the Eleanor Stevenson urban legend. You guys have been watching too much Sci-Fi channel." She tossed her sandy hair and put her hands on her hips. "Come on; let's go show Darcy the ferry dock. There's plenty to do out that direction, and I want to stop and get a hair tie."

"Okay." Sam brightened. "Let's take the trail; we can take the road on the way back."

Darcy didn't have any idea what they were talking about, but she followed them out a sliding glass door in the side of the building onto a woodchip path that led off into the trees. They entered the forest canopy, working their way along the path farther and farther from the lodge.

"Out there is where we skipped rocks last night." Sam pointed to their left through the trees where Darcy could see the sun glinting off the lake. "Down this path there are a few special cabins for people who don't want to stay in the lodge and share a bathroom. Amelia's family has been staying out here for about three years. Oh, look at the red squirrel! I *love* the red squirrels out here; they're so cute."

Darcy had also noticed the small, red squirrel that seemed to be keeping pace with them, launching itself from one branch to the next with ease. Chittering madly, it dove to a tree in front of them and clung, upside down, to its trunk. Darcy expected it to run away when they drew closer to it, but instead it stayed frozen where it was, fixing Darcy with an intense, studying stare. As Darcy sidled past, following Sam who was saying something to Amelia, the squirrel gave a slow, purposeful nod and suddenly scampered away. *Did that squirrel just* nod *at me?* Darcy stopped walking for a moment, tracking the squirrel's progress through the trees. It sure seemed to be going someplace in a hurry, now.

She shook her head and hurried to catch up with Amelia and Sam. *All this talk about magic has got me messed up. Now I'm imagining things.*

They stopped at Amelia's "cabin," which wasn't really a cabin so much as a small lodge tucked away in the trees. Amelia dashed inside to retrieve her hair tie, and Sam and Darcy waited outside on the path, enjoying the warming day. Darcy tied her sweatshirt around her waist, and they continued down the path after Amelia rejoined them. Darcy spent the next ten minutes listening to each of them exclaim over this or that tree or rock or cluster of flowers that was particularly special to them.

A branching in the trail led to either a nature center, which Sam said was in an actual old restored trapper's cabin, or the ferry dock. They chose the trail to the ferry dock and shortly found themselves out on a gravel road for a brief distance before re-entering the trees. The trail dumped them out on a long wooden dock that stretched into the bay that lay between the two sides of the camp.

They walked to the end of the dock and sat down, keeping their knees pulled up to their chests so that they wouldn't get their shoes wet. "Across the bay is Mariner's Point," Sam said, pointing. "There are *lots* of trails on that side. Maybe we can go hike one later this afternoon?"

Darcy gave a noncommittal shrug and Sam continued. "This is all part of Cedar Point," she gestured to the right and the left, "and down that direction is the highway, obviously. There is a nice hiking trail along Cedar Point that takes you deeper into the bay. I'll show you the trailhead on our way back. You reach it from the road." She stopped talking and seemed to study Darcy's face for a moment. "It's nice out here, isn't it?"

"Sure," Darcy said. Then, because she felt a little sorry for being so taciturn, "The view's real nice from here. I bet that the Cedar Point trail is pretty."

"It's pretty," Amelia chimed in, "but it's got nothing on Whitetail Point or Gnome's Haven. Just wait until you see those."

After another five minutes or so sitting on the dock, Sam jumped up and declared that they'd better move. "The ferry's about to make its first run," she pointed across the water to the boats and buildings of Mariner's Point, "and I don't want them to think that we need to cross. I promised your dad that I would keep you on this side of camp. Let's go!"

They took the gravel road back, as Sam had said, and Darcy thought that the crunch of gravel under her feet was a pleasant sound. It reminded her of riding Timmory along the trails at Gregorio's. She smiled slightly and closed her eyes, pretending she was there, and when she opened them, she saw the only sight that could really make her feel grateful to be at Cedar Cove: Perry Marks walking toward them. *Who cares that Lewis is with him?*

Perry was whistling loudly and carried a basketball under one arm. He smiled and waved at the girls and then all of a sudden he froze, his eyes looking off into the trees. "Look out!" he shouted one second before a large, black animal shot onto the path before them and knocked Amelia to the ground.

CHAPTER 7

COLIN MACKABY

"Eeeeekkk!" Darcy shrieked unwittingly, jumping and throwing her hands up to cover her face. Sam squealed next to her and clutched at Darcy's arm.

"Yaaarrrg!" The black creature roared and leapt off of Amelia and turned to face the other two girls.

"Ha ha ha!" Perry drew even with them and bent over doubled with laughter. He slapped his knee and shook his head with glee. "You guys should have *seen* your faces!" He gasped and slapped Dean's hand. "Nice one, Dean."

"That was *not* funny," Amelia said, scrambling to her feet and brushing herself off with as much dignity as she could muster.

"Every year; he gets you guys *every* year." Perry continued. Lewis just grinned.

Amelia scowled at him and turned to Darcy. "You're new here, so I'll let you in on a little secret. Dean thinks he's a navy seal, or something, and likes to hide in the woods and jump out at poor, unsuspecting girls."

Her heart rate finally returning to normal, Darcy was able to find some humor in the situation. She grinned. "Does he really get you every year?"

"Not *every* year," Sam said grumpily. "Last year he didn't."

"That was only because Lewis kept tipping you off." Perry shoved Lewis with one hand. "Traitor."

Lewis looked a little uncomfortable as he straightened his glasses. "I didn't want to be mean," he muttered.

"No, you didn't want Sam to stop tutoring you in math when you got home."

Lewis shrugged but didn't deny it. "We have a different math class this year," he said with a small smile.

Sam made a loud tutting noise and crossed her arms over her chest.

"At least I can take off this sweatshirt now," Dean said, still grinning. "It's getting hot out here." He shrugged off his black army sweatshirt and draped it over one shoulder.

"We're going over to the other side to shoot some hoops," Perry explained unnecessarily, slapping the basketball for good measure. "Come on, guys, we don't want to miss the ferry. See you girls after lunch."

"See you."

"Bye."

Perry saluted cheerfully and continued off down the road with Lewis and Dean.

A loud sigh issued from Darcy's right and she turned to see Sam staring wistfully after Perry. "I wish I was good at basketball, or any sport, for that matter. Then maybe he'd notice me."

"He notices you, Sam," Amelia said, still a little ruffled from her tumble. "He just doesn't realize yet what a beautiful and amazing girl you are."

Sam made a face at her. "Yeah . . . right."

"It's true!"

"Uh-huh."

Darcy stayed out of the conversation. She was glad that they didn't ask her opinion. As far as she was concerned, it was just fine if Perry didn't notice Sam.

"So, is Dean always like that?" Darcy asked a few minutes later, after Sam and Amelia had pointed out a few more interesting sights, including the trailhead to Cedar Point.

"Like what?"

"Like, always trying to scare you and stuff? He seems really into the whole army thing." Darcy had already noticed that he tended to wear army boots and carry his army sweatshirt everywhere he went. Even his haircut was army short.

Sam giggled and Amelia smirked. "Yeah," Amelia said. "We used to think he was really weird when he first started coming, but we soon realized that it's just his thing."

"He used to hide in the bushes and just watch us, and then follow real quietly after us when we went into the lodge or the rec hall."

"He even used to sleep under the bunk bed in the cabin or on the ground outside the tent whenever we did our class campout night." Amelia smiled, remembering.

"He still does that," Sam reminded her.

"Oh yeah."

"Anyhow . . . he doesn't say much, and he's a little strange, but he's cool. Perry really needed another guy his age to hang out with. I mean, he and Lewis are pals, but I don't really think they have much in common." Sam cut off abruptly and squinted down the road. "Oh no, Amelia, it's Colin."

"Great." Amelia's tone turned dry.

They lapsed into uncomfortable silence and Darcy curiously looked up to see who "Colin" was. What met her eyes was a boy about their own age with dyed black hair, wearing a heavy black trench coat despite the heat and painted black fingernails. He walked toward them on the road, kicking a rock in front of him, and seemed engrossed in his own thoughts until he looked up and spotted them. A wicked grin spread across his face as he stared at the three of them. Darcy started and felt her ears turn red as she quickly looked away. His face was frightening, magnified by one pale blue contact that he wore in his left eye.

They passed each other in complete silence, the three girls staring at the ground and Colin staring at them. Once they were a few feet beyond him, Darcy furtively looked over her shoulder and found that he was walking backward, still staring at them. She started again and quickened her pace, for once very thankful that she was not alone.

They heard him give a short bark of laughter, and all three broke into a slow jog. The backside of the rec hall was coming into view, though, and the sounds of children's laughter wafted their direction, making their fear seem pointless.

"Who was that?" Darcy gasped as they dodged around the rec hall and came out in the field.

"Colin Mackaby," Sam said grimly. "I never told you about him because, well . . . I didn't want you to be scared of coming." She stopped and faced Darcy anxiously. "Most years we hardly ever see him, honestly. He skips all the class times and hangs out alone in the forest."

"We have no idea what he does." Amelia added.

"He *obviously* doesn't want to be here, so we don't know why his family keeps coming."

Just because he doesn't want to be here doesn't mean that his family won't make him come, Darcy thought dryly. "So what's the deal with him?"

"Well, he's always getting into trouble. He tried to burn down the rec hall."

"What?" Darcy looked at the Stevenson Recreation Center. No matter how much she disliked it here, she would *never* do anything like that.

"We don't really know that, Sam," Amelia corrected her impatiently.

"Yeah, but everybody knows it was him."

"Everybody *thinks* it was him. The fire chief declared it an accident, so," Amelia shrugged, "he never got in trouble for it."

"When did it happen?" Darcy asked.

"Two years ago. The camp administration wishes that his family would stop coming, but they don't really have any solid reason to forbid them, so . . ."

"So he's here every year to darken our week," Sam finished disgustedly.

"Where do you think he was going?" Darcy looked back toward the road.

She really wanted to explore on her own a little, but she didn't want to run into Colin Mackaby.

"Probably to the ferry. We think he likes to snoop around the other side a lot," Sam said. She shivered slightly. "Come on. Let's stop talking about Colin and go inside for a snack. We still have an hour and a half before lunch."

Darcy looked around a little longingly. She didn't feel hungry for a snack and really just wanted to be alone with her thoughts. She was feeling sort of "people exhausted"—*more like "Sam exhausted"*—and wished that they would go inside and leave her alone for a while. *Amelia's not too bad, but if I have to listen to Sam's chatter anymore, I'm going to go crazy! I just need a break.* "You guys go ahead," she said. "I'm going to swing for a little bit." She turned toward the swing set.

"We can swing," Sam said. "This is the *best* swing set ever. It's been here since before I can remember. Do you wanna, Amelia?"

"Sure."

Shoot. "Oh, gosh, you know what?" It suddenly came to Darcy. It was such an easy little lie. And it wouldn't hurt anybody. "I *just* remembered that my dad said we have to have 'family time' every morning before lunch. He's probably looking for me now, and I don't want to get in trouble. I'd better go up to my room." *Brilliant! Why didn't I think of this before?*

"Oh . . . okay. Well, I guess we'll catch up with you after lunch, then."

"Sure." Darcy waved at them and headed for the rear door that led to a side staircase up to the second floor of the lodge with a new skip to her step. All she had to do now was hide out in her room for a little while until Sam and Amelia finished swinging—she could see the swing set from her window, after all—and then she could dash down the back stairs, be out the door and into the woods as fast as could be for a little exploration time alone. If she was lucky, she might even get a whole hour to herself. *Brilliant*, she thought again.

I don't think anybody saw me. Darcy slowed from a jog to a walk, her heartbeat racing much faster than her clipped gait warranted. She'd only had to wait about five minutes for Amelia and Sam to get tired of swinging and go into the lodge, and then she'd been off like a jackrabbit, down the stairs, out the door, across the lawn, and onto the road before anybody could have a chance to see her.

She felt exhilarated. She'd escaped. For the first time in over twenty-four hours she was going to have some real time alone. Without Sam's commentary on everything, she found that she was able to really appreciate the back road through the woods. She liked the way small boulders were scattered here and there along the side of the road, some of them moss-covered and growing plants of their own, some of them stark and white. Daisies were everywhere, and Darcy even noticed tiny splashes of red that she found to be tiny strawberry plants. *Although I'd probably not eat any; I don't want to get sick.*

She easily found the trailhead to Cedar Point and ducked off the road into the trees. She figured that she could probably hike to the point and back with time to spare before lunch. Amelia had told her that it wasn't a very long hike. She suddenly remembered Eleanor Stevenson and paused. *Maybe it's stupid to hike alone. I mean, I don't really know where I'm going.* But the trail before her beckoned softly, the gentle breeze through the trees seemed to whisper encouragement to her. She started forward again, this time a little more slowly. *If I get lost*, she reasoned, *all I have to do is find the lake, and then it's just a matter of following the coast either back to the ferry dock or out to the highway.* She quickened her pace confidently. *No problem.*

It was dark under the trees, but not a murky dark, more like a mysterious dark. The shadows were not gloomy, they were secretive, and the shafts of sunlight that pierced down through the cedar limbs shimmered off of floating particles in the air. This trail was rough cut, not groomed and wood-chipped like the trails by the cabins, but that only added to its charm. It wound around moss-covered boulders and under old, twisted cedar trunks, and the grey glisten of the bay was always visible off to her left side.

She hiked for about ten minutes with no sound other than her feet crunching softly over the mossy, twiggy trail when she froze. *What was that?* She thought she'd heard a child's laughter, but . . . not like any child she'd ever heard before . . . more wanton and wild. A bird called just above her head and swooped out over the lake. Darcy jumped and smiled in relief. *Just a bird*, she thought.

She came upon a slight bend in the trail, where it climbed slightly and bent between two massive boulders. Small cedar trees grew from the tops of the boulders and bright sunlight issued from the sky above, cutting through in wide shafts to the forest floor. *Wow*. "Beautiful," she whispered. She felt that at any moment an elf or a fairy would come dancing through that break in the trees, beckoning for her to follow. She smiled wryly to herself. It was all well and good to talk about magic, but there was no point in imagining things that could never be true. Her mom told her that she spent too much time with her nose in fantasy novels, but Darcy didn't care. In the great fantasy tales, animals could talk and ordinary people like her rose to meet great challenges. What was so bad about that? She didn't think that fairy tales were "only for children" as her mom said. She liked to dream.

She started forward again and crested the rise in the trail to see what could only be Cedar Point. The trail looked like it dead-ended near the swaying reeds of the waterline, but it actually bent around back the way she had come, clinging much closer to the shore. Darcy knew that it would lead back around to the ferry dock.

She stood still and stretched for a few minutes, enjoying the fact that she'd reached the point, and wondered whether she should go back by way of the ferry dock, or if she should turn around and head back the way she'd come. She had just made up her mind to go along to the ferry dock when she heard a loud snapping of twigs and froze. *Okay, this time it's not in my mind.* Cutting along the trail from the ferry dock direction was a black trench-coated figure. *Oh, great,* Darcy thought. She crossed her arms over her chest and took on her most intimidating stance. There was no avoiding him; he'd already seen her.

"Your name is Darcy; Darcy Pennington," he said when he drew up to her. He shook his long black bangs out of his eyes and peered at her closely. Darcy could clearly see the line of the blue contact in his left eye.

"Yeah, so what? Your name is Colin Mackaby." She tried to keep her voice steady, confident.

"You're new here this year."

"So?"

"So, Samantha Palm thinks that you're, like, best friends or something. But you're not." He smirked. "I can tell you don't like her."

How does he know so much about me? I've never even met him before. Darcy stared hard at him. *He's just trying to freak me out.*

He sighed dramatically. "I can't say that I blame you, really. I mean, look at the size of her. I wouldn't want to be friends with her, either."

Darcy's heart swelled indignantly on Sam's behalf, mostly because she knew he wasn't saying anything she hadn't thought before. Instead she said, "Yeah, well, you're not her favorite person either, so I think you're probably even."

He threw back his head and laughed loudly. "I like you, Darcy Pennington. You and I could get along."

"Doubt it."

"What?" He spread his arms wide. "You don't think I'm as good-looking as Perry Marks?"

She snorted. "You wish."

He dropped his arms and took a step closer to her. *Say something to make him stop!* Darcy thought frantically. "Did you really try to burn down the Stevenson Center?" she blurted out.

He paused and smiled slowly, malevolently. "Maybe."

"Why would you do that?"

He shrugged and took a step closer to her. "I didn't say I did."

Darcy's discomfort was reaching new levels and she clenched her sweaty palms next to her chest. "Why don't you just leave me alone?"

Suddenly his face turned very serious. "You're trying to pretend that you don't feel it, too, but you do," he said, almost hissing.

"Feel what?" Darcy's heart raced.

"The magic." His voice was a very low whisper now.

Magic, again. He's teasing me. "Shut up," she retorted. "Go away."

"You *do* feel it. Ha! I knew it. None of the others ever have. They're all too stupid and slow. But you . . . I've been watching you since you got here, and I know you feel something."

If magic really does exist, and the only other person who can feel it is Colin Mackaby, then I'd rather not be included. Darcy squeezed her eyes shut. "Leave me alone!" she shouted.

Silence. She didn't hear him leave, but she felt that when she opened her eyes he would be gone. Her heart thudded loudly in her chest, blocking out all other sounds.

When she finally opened her eyes the trail before her was clear. She didn't know if he'd gone back the way he'd come or if he'd cut off through the trees, but she didn't care. At least he was gone.

She dropped down to sit on a rock and put her face in her hands. She felt drained, sucked dry, as if he'd taken all the energy from her. She breathed deeply and tried to focus on the calling of the gulls and the splash of the waves behind her, but nothing seemed to help. She felt on edge and prickly, as though something virulent was watching her from the trees. She looked up slowly and scanned the tree line. Was it just her imagination, or was it much too dark under the trees for the time of day? She gulped and stared, feeling the whole time like malicious eyes were looking back at her. She stood slowly to her feet, reluctant to leave the warm sunlight and reenter the forest canopy, but desiring to be back at the camp—anywhere that other people might be. *I'll just go back the way I came; it's probably faster*.

She took a reluctant step forward and shivered as her leg descended into shadow. *What's going on?* She squinted into the trees to her left. There *was* something there, an indistinct shape; she could almost see its eyes. She squeaked and started shaking madly. *Don't scream. What sort of animals live in these woods? Wolves? Mountain lions? Bears?*

As if in answer to her thought, an enormous, brown, shaggy bear suddenly lumbered into view from the opposite direction of the menacing shadow. Darcy froze. Where had it come from? It had to have been down by the water all this time. It lumbered onto the path, not ten feet from her, and rose up onto its hind legs, pawing the air with plate-sized paws. Its eyes were not fixed on her, but on the shadowy spot beyond her.

Darcy regained use of her body with a lurch. The deep shadowy gloom was gone; she could see the path stretching clearly before her. She screamed and ran. She didn't care that you weren't supposed to run from a bear, she didn't care that she was pummeling through the forest at breakneck speed, and she didn't care that every breath of air she gulped in reissued from her in pitiful, horrified gasps. All she knew was that she had to get out of those woods. The ground shook slightly behind her and she thought she could hear the padding of enormous feet giving chase, but she didn't stop to look.

Before long she noticed tiny starbursts of light dancing just on the edges of her vision, and she once again thought she heard the wild, manic laughter of a child. She gasped and ran on, putting one foot in front of the other, but she knew that her pace was slowing, and the bear had not yet caught up with her. *It must not be chasing me. I'm imagining things again.* She tried to force herself to be reasonable and calm down. She could see the road through the trees.

With a final effort, she burst out of the trees and right into her brother's chest.

Chapter 8

In Trouble

"Ouch! Watch where you're going, Darcy." Roger rubbed his chest and scowled at her. "I've been looking for you everywhere. What's the matter with you?"

Darcy slowed her breathing and looked back up the trail. *Nothing*.

"Man, you look totally spooked!" Roger seemed excited by the prospect. "What happened, did you run into a mountain lion or something?"

"No, I ran into a bear," Darcy snapped.

"What? No . . . seriously?" Roger clapped his hands and jumped up and down. "No *way*, you're so lucky."

"I wouldn't exactly call it lucky, Roger." Darcy shoved him with one hand and bent over double, still trying to catch her breath. "And be quiet, I don't want it to hear us. I think it was following me."

"Sweet!" Roger craned his neck and took one or two steps into the woods.

"Roger." Darcy grabbed his arm. "What do you think you are doing? Are you crazy?"

"I just want to see." He shook her off. "Anyhow, you're not one to talk. You're in trouble with Mom and Dad."

Great.

"Hey! I think I see it!"

"What?" Darcy's head shot up and she scanned the trees. "Where?"

Suddenly Roger punched her on the shoulder. "Darcy, you idiot, you totally freaked out over nothing."

"Ow! What do you mean?"

"That's not a bear, that's a deer. See? I can see the antlers and everything." He shook his head and backed off the trail.

Darcy squinted. Sure enough, a large male deer stood back about fifty feet on the trail watching them carefully. "That's *not* what I saw, Roger! I think I know the difference between a deer and a bear."

"Right, whatever. We should get back. The lunch bell rang like ten minutes ago."

"You so don't believe me."

Roger shrugged and rolled his eyes. "Well, I don't know . . . I never heard anybody say anything about bears in these woods."

"Oh, okay, but a *mountain lion* would have been more believable?" Darcy's tone dripped sarcasm. *I know what I saw, and it was no deer.*

"I don't know. Jonathan Acres told me they can get them out here." He started to walk back toward the rec hall and the rest of camp. "Come *on*, Darcy. You're going to get me in trouble, too."

Oh yeah, I'm in trouble. With one more sidelong glance into the trees at the deer that still stood staring at them, she hurried to catch up with Roger. "So, why am I in trouble?"

Roger smiled wickedly and crossed his arms over his chest.

"Oh, come on, Roger," she pleaded. "You can at least tell me what I did. You said Mom *and* Dad are mad. Dad doesn't usually get mad at me."

"Well . . . let's just say that it isn't nice to lie to people." Roger seemed to be enjoying dangling the information just out of her reach.

"Lie to people? When did I lie to . . . anybody . . ." Darcy closed her eyes. *Shoot*. It looked like "family time" had been busted.

Roger seemed to guess that she had figured it out and became a wellspring of information. "Jonathan and I were hanging out on the beach and Sam and Amelia came up to us and asked me why I wasn't at 'family time' and I, obviously, had no idea what she was talking about, and I said so. And then that Amelia girl nudged Sam real hard in the rib cage and said 'I told you so' and Sam looked a little sad, but she said that she wanted to check with our dad, just to give you the ben'fit of a doubt—"

"Ben-E-fit," Darcy muttered, interrupting him. She felt rotten.

"Yeah, right, so she went and found Dad and he looked real surprised when she was talking to him and I heard him say something like there must have been a misunderstanding, but, man, Darcy, he looked *mad.* And then he disappeared into the lodge, I guess to see if he could find you, and I didn't catch anything else until the lunch bell rang and he told me to see if I could find you."

"How did you know where I would be?"

"Are you kidding me? I saw you running across the field when you left the lodge. I at least knew what direction you had gone." He looked up at her, exasperated. "If you wanted to be alone, why didn't you just say so?"

Ah, the cognitive ability of a ten-year-old. Everything was so simple for Roger. "You wouldn't understand," Darcy sighed. They were drawing up to the lodge and she could see her dad waiting on the porch outside the dining hall, arms crossed across his chest and face stern.

"Darcy saw a *bear*!" Roger shouted as soon as they were close enough for their dad to hear.

Mr. Pennington's scowl deepened and he pointed to the door. "Go inside, Roger. Your mother put together a plate for you."

Roger made one last face at Darcy and dashed into the dining hall. For a brief moment the sound of happy chatter and the clanking of flatware against plates filled Darcy's ears, and then the noises abruptly cut off as the door slammed closed. She took a deep breath and looked up into her dad's face.

For a long moment he just stared at her, the muscles in his jaw working angrily. Finally he said, "Do you know why we're out here?"

Darcy glanced at the windows to the dining hall next to her, imagining the people inside watching her torment. "Yes, sir," she whispered.

Her dad sighed deeply and uncrossed his arms. "Darcy, I just don't know what to do with you. What possessed you to lie to your friends?"

"They're not my friends—"

He held up a hand to silence her. "And on top of that, you snuck off to hike in the woods, by yourself. Do you have any idea how dangerous that can be?"

Darcy stared at her feet, pushing down the rising knot in her throat. *I will not cry*, she thought furiously. Her mother yelled at her at least once a day, but the rare anger of her father always devastated her. "I'm sorry, Dad." She hiccupped, the tears coming despite her every attempt to stem them.

"*Why* did you feel you needed to lie to get away from Samantha Palm?"

"Because . . . she . . . doesn't . . . understand me," Darcy choked out, her shoulders shaking.

Her dad made a deep guttural sound in his throat and pulled Darcy into a hug. "Ah, Darcy, it's always the same story with you, isn't it? Somebody wants to be your friend, but you won't give them the chance because they don't 'understand' you. What's so complicated, Darcy? What is it about Darcy Pennington that only Darcy Pennington seems to get?"

Darcy shrugged heavily, her shoulders pinned against her father's broad chest. She sniffed and pulled away. "Everybody's watching, Dad," she choked.

"Don't worry about everybody," he said sternly, taking her shoulders. "I want you to *promise* me that you will give Samantha Palm a chance this week."

Darcy nodded, penitent.

"And I want you to swear that you will not go hiking again unless you have at least one other person with you."

"Okay," she whispered, watching her prospects of a not-so-bad week go swirling down the drain.

"One more thing." He fixed her with a beady gaze. "You have to apologize to Sam. I can't imagine how she must be feeling."

"Oh, Dad . . . okay." *Will the mortification never end?* Darcy straightened her shoulders and wiped her eyes. She was starting to get herself together now that the worst was over. Darcy could count on one hand the number of times she could remember her dad really getting mad at her, and it was never a pleasant experience.

He slung one arm over her shoulder and cracked a smile for the first time. "That's my girl. Now pull yourself together before we go inside. What's this about a bear?" His gaze turned curious.

"Oh . . . um, I thought I saw a bear in the woods, but Roger thinks it was just a deer." *No reason to tell him the whole story; he'll just freak out again.*

"A bear, really?" He whistled. "I guess they could have bear up here, but I haven't heard any stories. We could ask Mr. Marks when we get inside. Are you ready?"

Darcy shrugged but nodded. She guessed that she looked as good as she was going to with a red nose and eyes. She wiped her face one more time for good measure and offered her father a wet, fake smile. "Ready."

"Okay, then." He held the door for her and Darcy imagined that people at the tables nearest the windows looked a little *too* interested in their food, like they had been watching her and her dad a moment before.

She slid into her seat as quietly as she could and picked up her fork. She had no appetite, but she needed something to do so that she wouldn't have to look around the table. Her mom had piled macaroni and cheese and salad on her plate. She started on the salad, delicately nibbling on the lettuce.

"Say, Frank," her dad said loudly, drawing Perry's dad's attention. "You haven't heard anything about bears up this direction, have you?"

"Bears?" Darcy could hear a note of incredulity in the man's voice. "I know there are some in upper Michigan, but there hasn't been a sighting at Cedar Cove in fifty years. Why do you ask?"

"Darcy thinks that she saw one today."

"Really?"

Darcy looked up at Mr. Marks. His eyebrows were raised slightly with interest, but he didn't look like he really believed her. She shot a glance at Perry and caught him watching her with ill-concealed disgust. He snorted softly and shook his head, going back to his near-empty plate of food.

"So there have been sightings here before, though?" Darcy's dad persisted. "Fifty years ago, you said?"

"Yep. Eleanor Stevenson, who the rec hall is named after, wandered out of the woods fifty years ago claiming that she'd seen a real big one, a massive brown bear. But according to her description there's no way the bear was actually as big as she claimed it was. Everybody assumed that she'd just seen a regular brown bear. When she disappeared later that week, a few people were afraid that she'd been attacked, but when they found her body she definitely had not been mauled. Oh, but don't worry," he added.

Darcy's mom's face had gone white and she sat with her fork poised in midair. "What happened to Eleanor Stevenson was a horrible tragedy, but it was an isolated incident. Nobody has disappeared from Cedar Cove since. The trails are clearly marked, now. I have no problem letting Perry hike with his friends." He clapped a hand on Perry's shoulder.

Darcy chewed her food thoughtfully, slight chills running up and down her back. *So Eleanor Stevenson saw a huge brown bear here, too. And it sounds like it was just as big as the one I saw.* She knew that nobody would believe her if she accurately described the size and breadth of the bear—how it towered at least ten feet above her head when raised on its hind legs.

"Well, Darcy's promised to stick with a group from now on," Darcy's dad said, breaking into her reverie. "And I'm sure you guys will keep your eyes open."

Darcy nodded.

Perry got up from the table abruptly and carried his plate and cup over to the kitchen counter, his shoulders rigid. Darcy watched him go with a sinking feeling in her stomach. Her intuition told her that it was not just Sam she had to apologize to, and it was not going to be easy. *I'd take bears again any day over this*, she thought grimly.

CHAPTER 9

GNOMES?

Darcy chewed very slowly and stretched out her lunch time for as long as she could before it became unavoidable; she had to get up and go find Sam. Samantha had not bounced over to her table the moment she was finished eating, which was telling all on its own, and Darcy knew that she might have to search a little in order to find her.

She sighed as she carried her plate to the kitchen counter, handing it distractedly to the cheerful worker. She *hated* this. If her parents had sent her to Gregorio's again this summer, none of this would have happened. *Obviously*, she thought grimly. She looked around the almost empty dining hall; they definitely weren't anywhere in the room. Shuffling her feet, she meandered out into the seating area and looked around. *Nope, not here either*. She passed through into the lobby and was just about to go through the double doors out to the boardwalk when she heard Sam's distinct voice waft toward her from a side room off the lobby.

"But I'm sure she didn't *mean* to ditch us," Sam insisted. "I still think it was some sort of misunderstanding."

Darcy inched closer to the doorway and stood out of sight, inclining her head carefully to eavesdrop.

"You didn't hear her at breakfast this morning, though, Sam." That was Perry talking. "She told her brother that she was going to get *stuck* hanging out with you again."

Sam had no response for that and the room fell quiet.

"Look." Amelia's even tone took up the dialogue. "She clearly doesn't want to hang out with us, so I don't see why we have to keep trying to be her friend."

"Yeah," Perry chimed in.

"She's not one of us, Sam," Lewis said quietly.

"Come on, guys, give her a chance," Sam pleaded quietly.

"We did; she blew it." Perry's voice was clipped and final.

"We thought Dean was weird when he first started coming, too." Sam tried another tactic.

"Hey!" Dean sounded a little indignant.

"It's true, and you know it!"

"Yeah, all right," he capitulated.

"But this isn't about her being weird," Amelia said. "It's about her being mean."

"Well . . . I don't care what you guys say." Sam sounded a little emotional now. "I think she needs a friend and I'm going to keep hanging out with her. If you want to hang out with *me*, you're just going to have to deal with that."

Silence fell again in the room and Darcy's heart felt like it was going to explode out of her chest with a dozen different emotions. She wanted to cry and she wanted to cheer, she wanted to storm in there and tell them all off, and she wanted to crawl in on hands and knees and beg them to like her. Instead tears that were still close to the surface leaked out of the corners of her eyes and she turned around to flee to her room.

She didn't get more than a few feet, however, before Mrs. Palm intercepted her. "Why, Darcy, what's the matter?" she asked kindly, steering Darcy to a wooden bench.

Darcy sniffed. "Nothing. I just need to be alone."

Mrs. Palm searched her face quietly and then said in a firm voice, "Actually, I think that's exactly the opposite of what you need."

"Mrs. Palm, I'm really sorry that I ditched Sam this morning . . . I just . . . I wanted to be alone and I couldn't think of a way to get Sam to leave me alone, and . . ." The words piled out of her in a rush and Mrs. Palm put a hand up to stop her.

"Darcy, what goes on between you and Sam is your business. But just between you and *me*, I know that Sam can be a lot to deal with at times, but she means only the best."

"I know," Darcy whispered.

"Now, what I think you need is some good, quality time with those wonderful kids in the other room. Why don't you give them a chance?"

"But they don't like me."

"Nonsense." Mrs. Palm waved her hand in front of her face as if dispelling an annoying fly. "They're angry with you, but they'll get over it."

I doubt it, Darcy thought, but she only nodded her head.

"Come with me," Mrs. Palm ordered. She stood and ushered Darcy out into the lobby with her, calling Sam's name.

Sam bounced out of the room and her face fell slightly when she saw Darcy. "Yes, Mom?"

"I hope you guys are making plans for this afternoon, because it is a lovely day outside. This would be a good day to go to the other side and hike Whitetail Point."

Sam's face brightened. "That's a great idea. Darcy, you'll love that trail." Then she stepped close to Darcy and gave her a squashy hug.

"Sam, I-I'm sorry." Darcy wheezed from within the tight hug.

"That's okay," Sam whispered into her ear. "I know you didn't mean to hurt anybody." Sam released her as quickly as she had grabbed her and went back into the other room, followed closely by Mrs. Palm. "Let me check with the others!" she called back over her shoulder.

Darcy waited nervously in the lobby, her palms sweaty. She couldn't hear what was being said this time, but she expected that Mrs. Palm was directing a certain amount of interference on her behalf. After a few tense minutes, the whole group of them emerged, but none of them smiled at her except Sam.

"Okay," Sam said. "The ferry leaves in a half hour, so let's meet back here in fifteen minutes to hike out there and catch it."

Darcy nodded quickly, avoiding everybody's eyes. She mumbled something about needing to ask her parents and ducked quickly away.

Darcy had no problem attaining her parents' permission. She didn't think that her dad actually believed her story of seeing a bear, which was probably to her benefit, but her mom did tell her to be extra careful. Within half an hour she was on the ferry sitting next to Sam with the cool wind blowing in her face and the shores of Cedar Point falling away to her right. The ferry was not really a ferry in terms of what Darcy would have normally thought. It was not anywhere near large enough to carry cars; instead it was a pontoon boat with bench seats on each side facing inward. Darcy guessed that it could probably carry between twenty and thirty people at a time. The driver was a cheerful man who stood behind the wheel, directing the ferry expertly back to the dock on the other side.

Darcy hopped onto the dock after Sam, looking around with interest. Mariner's Point looked a lot older than Glorietta Bay in terms of camp amenities. The buildings were painted brown instead of grey, and the dock system out into the bay was much more extensive. Several large sailboats bobbed gently in the wake of the ferry, and small one-room cabins lined the shoreline of the inner bay.

Sam explained to her that Mariner's Point had all the same things as Glorietta Bay—a lodge, rec hall, store, and special cabins—and it was all part of Cedar Cove camp. "This side is more often used for college groups, though," she explained. She glowered slightly at Amelia's back as she and the boys tromped past them without a word. "Don't mind them," she said quietly to Darcy. "They'll come around."

Darcy just shrugged her shoulders. She was really trying to give Sam a chance after how the girl and her mother had stood up for her, and she was trying not to let the behavior of the others get her down, but it was difficult. It had been a long, silent hike out to the ferry dock.

Sam waved a thank you to the ferry driver and pulled Darcy along the dock after the rest of the group, who were heading toward a small, central building. "The rec hall on this side," Sam exclaimed, slightly out of breath.

They hurried across a brief grassy stretch of land next to the beach and burst through the swinging doors into dim light. Like the rec hall at Glorietta Bay, this one boasted several different table games, but it was only one level and much smaller. Merchandise was littered on racks across the floor and the store counter stood on the far wall. The three boys and Amelia were settling into a game of foosball, two on each side of the table, and only Lewis looked up when Sam and Darcy entered. He nudged Perry.

"We decided that we don't want to hike out to Whitetail Point," Perry announced rather loudly. "We'd rather stay here."

"But . . . oh, come on, guys. It's a beautiful day. You don't really want to stay indoors, do you?" Sam pleaded.

"My mom told me not to get burned," Amelia said in a stiff voice.

"You never burn, you only tan," Sam retorted, but Amelia was studying her fingernails. "Well, fine," Sam snapped after a whole minute went by without anybody saying anything. "Darcy and I are going to hike out to Whitetail Point, and we're going to have a *great time.*" She continued to look around at her friends, clear disappointment written all over her face. "If anybody wants to come and find us, that's where we'll be." She spun around and exited the building, forgetting to grab Darcy's arm in her rush.

Darcy backed quickly out after her and felt immediate relief the moment her face hit the sun. Sam was sitting on the bench outside with her arms crossed sullenly over her chest. "I'm sorry about your friends," Darcy said quietly. "You know, you don't really have to ignore them just for me—"

"I'm not ignoring them, they're just being stupid." Sam hefted herself off the bench and looked around. "Well, are you ready to see Whitetail Point?"

"Sure!" Darcy offered. *The least I can do for her is act excited.* "What's so great about it?"

"Lots of things." Sam's eyes lit up and she clearly forgot about her quarrel. She took Darcy's arm to walk as she talked. "There's an old Indian totem pole and the hike across the isthmus is just beautiful. And then there's Gnome's Haven with all sorts of little gnomes stuck all over it, and since there aren't any adults with us, there's nobody to tell us we can't climb it." Her eyes sparkled mischievously.

"Climb what, exactly?"

"The rock," Sam said. "Gnome's Haven."
Oh. Then Darcy raised an eyebrow at her. "Gnomes?" she questioned.
Sam giggled. "Gnomes."

Chapter 10

Gnomes

Sam was right; the hike out to Whitetail Point *was* beautiful, particularly the part that took them along the isthmus to the section that would be an island if the water rose high enough. Sam told her that some years the water did cover the neck of the isthmus, but that it never was more than a foot deep, so people still hiked out to the point.

"I used to mess with my sister and tell her that the water rose and fell because herds of heffalumps were entering and exiting the water." Sam laughed.

"Heffalumps? Isn't that a creature from the Winnie-the-Pooh stories?"

"Yep." Sam smirked. "She was too little to know that, though. I think she still partly believes it."

The neck of the isthmus was about 200 yards long and covered in sun-bleached rocks. A few brave, scraggly bushes grew here and there along it, but nothing else. The green forestry of the main body of the isthmus loomed up before them. Darcy stepped onto the isthmus proper with a small amount of trepidation. They were about a mile from the main body of camp and the path before them was deserted. *But I'm not alone*, she reminded herself, *so Dad can't be mad.* She tried not to think about the fact that he'd given her permission to hike with the group, not just with Sam. But what was the chance that she would see another bear on the same day in a totally different part of the camp? Especially if the last bear sighting at Cedar Cove had been fifty years ago.

Darcy shook off her apprehension and tried to keep up with Sam, who was walking ahead of her with barely concealed excitement. "We've had our class campout here a couple times, but Amelia doesn't really like sleeping out here. Too many spiders." She made a face. "They put in permanent tents a few years ago, and they do tend to get a little spider infested, but Perry and Dean will play 'spider busters' if we make a big enough stink about it. I think it makes them feel macho." She was leading Darcy through a campsite that was a short distance into the trees and boasted four large canvas tents set up on wooden platforms. A fire pit in the center of the campsite was surrounded with cut logs, and Darcy saw another small path leading off to the right of the campsite. "The totem pole is back there," Sam said, noticing the direction of her gaze. "We'll go look at it on the way back."

They dove back under tree cover and Darcy noticed that this trail was a lot cleaner than the Cedar Point trail. The tree roots they clambered over were less gnarled, and the path cut a more direct route through the cedar trees. The limbs were also farther above her head, making her feel as though she walked under a canopy of green light. She tried to relax and enjoy the hike, but her mind kept wandering back to the other four teenagers at the rec hall. Were they still talking about her behind her back? Would they hate her the whole week? What could she do to repair their trust?

The trail branched again and this time Sam led her off to the right, following a cute wooden sign on a pole that said "Gnome's Haven" with an embellishment of a gnome pointing down the trail. The path almost immediately took on a more wild air as the trees closed in around them, and Darcy was reminded of her experience at Cedar Point. She shivered slightly and hurried to keep close on Sam's heels.

"So, you never told me what the gnome thing is all about," she called up to Sam.

"You kind of have to see it," Sam threw back over her shoulder. "I don't know when the tradition started, but I think it began with the college groups. Ah! Here we are, see?" Sam stopped next to a massive boulder and stood aside proudly.

Darcy pulled up next to her. The boulder was huge—the size of a house, at least—and it was pocked all over with nooks and crannies, with moss and plants growing off of it. The top of the boulder itself was forested, with a dense growth of pine and cedar trees reaching up to the sky, their roots intertwined all over the surface of the rock. The rock was made even more interesting by the little stone creatures that were tucked in almost every nook and cranny. Darcy walked forward to look more closely and could see that rocks of all sizes—some as small as her thumb, others as large as her head—had been painted by campers to resemble gnomes. Pointed red and blue hats, smart little jackets, and bearded faces winked at her from every surface of the rock, and Darcy founded herself grinning from ear to ear.

"Gnome's Haven," she said. "I get it. What a funny tradition!"

"I know," Sam said, smiling too. "It's always interesting to come here and look at all the gnomes. I think some of them have been here for ages."

"Did you ever paint one?"

"No . . . I think it's an activity that only the college students do." She pointed at one rock that had a male and female gnome painted on it holding hands. "Some of them have names and dates on them. Look, this one is from 1985."

Darcy reached out to take it and look at it more closely, but Sam pushed her hand down quickly. "We're not supposed to take them off the rock." She pointed at a small sign on a post by the boulder. "See?"

"Please leave the gnomes in their homes," Darcy read out loud. *That's a little uptight.*

"There are more around here," Sam said, pulling her around to the lake side of the rock, where there was a natural seating area of sorts. It looked like part of Gnome's Haven had sheared off of the boulder in years past, forming a platform of smooth rock about six feet up from the shoals lining the water. On this vertical side of the rock many more gnomes were stuck in their "homes" and Darcy looked around at them with interest.

"I've seen all these about a million times," Sam said suddenly, "so I'm going to start climbing the rock. It's totally safe," she assured Darcy unnecessarily, "but it takes me a little while since I'm so out of shape." She looked a little embarrassed by this last comment, but Darcy pretended not to notice.

"Where do you climb from?"

"Over where the trail ends. It's a real gradual climb from there, with lots of hand and footholds."

"Okay, I'll be over in just a minute. I want to look at a few more of these."

"Sounds good. You can catch me if I fall." Sam grinned at her and disappeared around the edge of the rock.

Darcy spent a good couple of minutes looking at the gnomes. She liked their funny little hats and charming smiles. Each one seemed to have its own personality, given to it by whoever the artist was, of course, and she relished a few moments alone with her thoughts. She didn't want to be accused of ignoring Sam again, though, so she meandered around to the other side of the rock to check on Sam's progress after a few minutes.

Sam had almost reached the top. She was clutching at two small saplings and smiled down at Darcy when she saw her. "Hey!"

"You almost made it," Darcy shouted back, even though Sam was only about twenty feet away.

"I know! Follow me up as soon as I reach the top and I'll help you find good grips."

"Okay." Darcy smiled to herself. It felt dangerous and adventurous, what they were doing, and she liked that. Sam wasn't turning out to be nearly as bad a companion this afternoon as she'd anticipated.

She whistled a tune to herself and moved closer to the boulder to examine a particularly large painted gnome sitting in a deep fissure. Her tune turned into an impressed whistle as she studied the handiwork on the stone. The gnome was painted in a little blue jacket and brown trousers, with a bright red pointy hat atop its white, curly hair. Laugh lines radiated out from its beady eyes, and its mouth was upturned in a smirk. The gnome was so lifelike she felt that it could almost jump right off the rock and run away into the woods. She grimaced slightly. *No more magic*, she chided herself.

She looked up again. Sam's feet were just disappearing over the top of the rock. Any moment now she would call down to Darcy to begin her ascent.

Darcy looked back at the fissure and almost fell over. The rock with the lifelike gnome on it was gone. She looked around her feet for some sign of it. *I must have knocked it down,* she thought wildly. *I hope I didn't break it!* But it was nowhere to be found—not at the ground by her feet, not deeper in the fissure, not in the woodsy undergrowth.

She felt chill bumps on her arms and told herself repeatedly not to freak out. Too many weird things were happening to her this weekend for it to be coincidental. She took two steps back from the rock. Sam still had not called down to her. *Maybe I should just start climbing.* She placed one hand on the boulder and froze. This time she was *sure* it was not a bird; a distinct childlike giggle had sounded from over her left shoulder.

She turned like she was going to face a firing squad and squinted into the trees. Cedar and birch limbs swayed benignly back at her, contradicting her rush of adrenaline. Mundane forest sounds called out to her, but wait! There . . . in those ferns. Something had definitely run through the ferns just five feet from her. They swayed tellingly in the creature's wake and Darcy took off after it. Whatever was going on at this camp, she *had* to know what it was. Sam would be fine without her for a few minutes.

She ducked under a low hanging branch and stopped to listen. Over there, to her right, she could hear the patter of little feet and sharp, excited breathing. Whatever sort of animal it was, it wasn't trying too hard to get away from her. She dodged right and passed between two trees, feeling a slight peculiar sensation—like she was pushing through a wall of pudding, but her momentum carried her through before she had time to stop and think. She turned a circle, listening for her elusive friend, took two more steps, and tripped over a root, landing flat on her face.

"Oof," she breathed out hard and lay still for a moment, catching her breath. Suddenly she heard the patter of little feet again, and the breathing stopped, very close to her nose. She raised her head slowly, cautiously; she didn't want to scare it off, whatever it was, and it was clearly curious about her.

For a moment she thought that her eyes were playing tricks on her. Tiny bare feet below brown trousers, blue jacket, white, curly beard, mischievous smile, beady eyes, red hat . . . it was the gnome from the rock! Except that it wasn't a painting on a rock, it was real.

"Oh . . . my . . . gosh!" she whispered hoarsely, a myriad of thoughts bursting through her head, chief amongst them being, *magic is real!*

The little gnome tilted his head sideways, like a dog listening to something out of sight, and pointed a dirty little finger directly in her face. "Boop!" he said loudly, poking her on the nose.

I felt that! He's really real! Breathe, Darcy . . . just breathe.

He suddenly jumped up and sprinted madcap away from her, his laughter filling the air.

"Wait!" Darcy wheezed. She scrambled to her feet and stumbled after him. "Who are you? What are you doing here? Are there more of you?"

Her last question was cut short as she stumbled out into a small clearing and gasped. The gnome had stopped in the middle of the clearing and was bent over double, laughing hysterically, but he wasn't the only one. All around her was a company of gnomes, hundreds and hundreds of them. It was as if every gnome on the rock had come to life and now surrounded her, pointing dirty fingers and laughing, endlessly laughing. Some of them peeked out from under rocks, others swung from high branches, and all of them were focused on her.

Darcy forced herself to breathe slowly, but her heart was jumping out of her chest. How could this be real? Did Sam know about this? *Sam!* Darcy started. She'd left her alone on the rock for at least ten minutes now! What if the gnomes were dangerous? What if they pushed her friend off the rock? Darcy had to get back to her.

She started backing up, but found her way blocked. An entire contingent of gnomes stood in her path, shaking their heads at her. Their smiles were gone, but the air practically crackled with their glee. She tried a different direction, but found it blocked, as well. Her panic started to mount. "Sam!" she called loudly. *Come on, answer me.* "Sam," she tried again. "Samantha Palm!" *I can't be* that *far away from her! "Sam!"* No answer.

The gnomes twittered madly, and some of them made weak imitations of her voice. "Sam, Sam, Sam." She heard them all around her.

Darcy stomped her foot and crossed her arms. What was she going to do? "Can you stop that?" she finally snapped at the gnomes who were continuing to mock her. "I'm trying to think." *I shouldn't even be talking to gnomes. I must have hit my head when I fell. This* must *be a dream.*

Suddenly the twitter of the gnomes grew more agitated, and Darcy turned around quickly to see what was bothering them. She started and almost screamed. A leather-clad man stood across the clearing from her, wielding a bow in one hand that he tapped methodically on his thigh, and behind him stood a creature she'd never seen before in her life. He looked like a man, but he had long, straight, blond hair, and large pointed ears that stuck out at an odd angle from the sides of his head. He was about the same height as the man next to him and wore what looked to Darcy like a long green dress.

The man in leather took a step forward, mouth open slightly and eyes penetrating. His gaze swept her from head to toe, and when he spoke he sounded deeply suspicious. "Who are you and where did you come from?"

Chapter 11

Alitheian Meetings

"I-I don't know—" Darcy backed up quickly and tripped over a log, landing hard on her bottom.

The gnomes burst into new paroxysms of giggles and some imitated her clumsy action. The man looked irritated with them and waved his hand distractedly. "Shoo! Go on, get!" he ordered. To Darcy's amazement, they obeyed, dispersing into the trees without so much as a backward glance.

Darcy's breath was coming in terrified, sharp bursts now. She was all alone in the woods with a strangely dressed man and a creature that *couldn't* be real. All she could think of was what her mother had always told her to do if approached by a strange man: run. He took another step closer to her and her breath caught in her throat. *That's it. It's now or never.* She jumped to her feet, whirled around, and ran. She'd always been a fast sprinter and she felt that her fear would give her an adrenaline advantage over the man and his strange companion. If she could just get back to the rock, then at least she would have Sam by her side. *Two are better than one.*

But she had barely taken two steps before the elf-like creature at the man's side appeared in front of her, blocking her way. She squeaked fearfully. *How did he get here so fast?* She spun the opposite direction, but there he was again, a relaxed smile on his strange, angular face. She gasped and back-stepped quickly.

"Veli." She heard the man's voice. "Stop toying with her and bring her to me."

Two hands were on her arms before she had a chance to see him move, and she felt herself propelled forcefully toward the man waiting in the clearing. She finally caught her breath and found her voice. With all her might she opened her mouth and screamed. The sound echoed through the forest until the creature holding her stuck a hand tightly over her mouth. "Great Gloria that was loud!" he muttered, but he didn't appear upset. He actually sounded rather cheerful.

The man in leather stepped closer and took a good look at her. "Why, she's only a child!" He stuck a finger in her face. "I doubt you are a spy, especially making such a racket like that, but we'll see. The council will have to decide." He had hard blue eyes and his hair was brown and shaggy around the ears. He smelled of earth and body odor, and his leather jerkin was soiled and stained. The *thing* that held her, however, did not smell unpleasant at all. His hand was right beneath Darcy's nose and she inhaled deeply without even trying to. He smelled of buttermilk, and . . . cherries. *What a strange combination*.

"Bring her, Veli," the man said and disappeared into the trees, apparently following some path only visible to his eyes.

She whimpered behind Veli's hand and deliberately dragged her feet, trying to make it difficult for the creature to move her forward, but he didn't seem perturbed by her at all. Instead he whistled a quiet tune and slung her effortlessly over his shoulder. "Now, no more screaming," he said pleasantly in a musical, lilting voice. "You never know who might be listening!"

Darcy didn't know why, but she obeyed the command. There was an air of authority and importance about these two that she'd never felt before, not even in the presence of her father or the school principal.

"Oy! Torrin," Veli called up to his companion after a few moments of passing through the trees. "Did you see this emblem on her ankle?"

"She carries it on her back, as well," the man called Torrin responded without looking back.

What emblem? What are they talking about? Darcy's stomach was pressed painfully into Veli's shoulder and she dangled, totally useless. *Sam!* she thought frantically, *I'm not ditching you on purpose!*

A few tree branches scraped the side of her face from time to time, but Darcy got the impression that Veli was working to keep too many from hitting her. She couldn't see where they were going, but she could hear a low murmur of voices drawing nearer, and fear clenched even tighter in her belly. What sort of people were these? What did they want with her? Was she hallucinating?

The busy murmuring abruptly stopped as Torrin and Veli, with Darcy over his shoulder, marched into a broad clearing. The two men—Darcy knew that Veli was not a man, but she didn't know what else to call him—stood at attention and Torrin bowed deeply. *I wish I could see what's going on.* So far Darcy's only view was the back of Veli's green tunic, and if she turned her head slightly she could see Torrin's legs, but she could sense numerous people behind her and knew that every eye was on her upturned bottom. She squirmed slightly, caught between wanting to be put down and wanting to disappear.

"Prince Tellius, Prince Cadmus, greetings!" Torrin's voice sounded again.

Prince! There aren't any princes in Michigan. But Darcy was getting a nervous, and excited, feeling in her stomach that she was not in Michigan any longer. She tried to pay close attention to the exchange of words.

"Yahto Veli," a deep voice sounded. *The princes must be old.* "Why do you carry this human girl over your shoulder, and where are her clothes?"

Darcy felt total confusion and slight indignation. *What does he mean? I'm dressed!*

"We found her in the woods near the old gateway, my lord, and this is what she was wearing." Yahto Veli's voice sounded amused. "We do not know why she would choose to be in the forest in her under-things."

"Perhaps she was washing her clothes and wandered away from her village?" *That sounded like a boy's voice.*

"All the way to the Point?" Torrin asked dryly. "I think it unlikely, your majesty."

Majesty? Are the princes just boys?

"So you think she is a spy?" the deep voice sounded again. "But she's only a child."

"Tselloch has used children before."

Silence fell and Darcy could hear the sounds of restless movement around her. Something snarled nearby and she shivered.

"There is another option, my lords, which would also account for her strangeness of dress," Yahto Veli spoke suddenly, shooting a furtive glance at Torrin.

"Aye." Torrin sounded a little apprehensive. "We did notice that she carries one of the emblems."

A burst of excited murmuring exploded around her, and she wished more than ever that Veli would put her down. Nobody seemed to care that she was hanging over his shoulder.

"One of the emblems?"

"Which one?"

"Where does she carry it?"

"Are you certain?"

"Can we see it?"

"You said you found her by the old gateway?"

Questions fired like gunshots all around the clearing and Torrin had to wait a few minutes before he could answer any of them. "The emblem is on her ankle"—Darcy felt a finger brush her skin—"and her back. Veli, put her down."

Darcy felt her world tilt crazily for a moment, and then her feet were on solid grass. She blinked black dots out of her eyes as the blood started draining from her face, and she realized that she was still facing backward.

Someone flipped her disheveled ponytail over her shoulder so that the back of her tank top was bared, and sharp gasps sounded from all around the circle.

"The horse," somebody said loudly. "Of course."

"Gre-go-rio's," somebody else sounded out. "Does she belong to this *Gregorio*? Is she a slave, do you think? Why would Pateros choose to send a slave?"

"*Did* Pateros send her?"

"What I want to know," sounded a gravelly voice that Darcy had not heard before, "is whether or not this girl is mute. Has she nothing to say for herself?"

Everybody grew silent once again, and Darcy suddenly realized that her shoulders were free. She could turn and face the odd assembly, or she could run for the woods. *Run.* Every sensible particle in her body cried; but the other half of her, the half that read fantasy novels as if they were the sustenance of life, the half that still looked under her bed at night for monsters, the part that really, *desperately*, wanted to believe that magic was possible . . . that part of her was stronger.

Darcy turned around. The variety of voices made sense when she saw the gathered assembly. *This can't be real.* Several human men looked back at her, all dressed similarly to Torrin, but finer. Another creature like Yahto Veli stood staring at her with arms crossed, but this one was female. Directly across from her a fine rug was spread out on the grass, and seated in two wooden chairs on this rug were two boys about Roger's age who were so similar in appearance that they could be twins, but one sat a little straighter in his chair and had wavy hair and a sharp, angular nose, while the other had a rounded nose and curly hair. They wore very fine, medieval-looking clothes and each bore a gold circlet on their dark brown hair. She took them in with a glance and moved her gaze to the most impossible of all the creatures there: the nymphs. A dryad, a naiad, and an oread, to be exact. Darcy knew them immediately. How many times had she read descriptions of them in her fantasy novels? They were very small, about the size of the boys on the rug, and they were all female. One of them, the dryad, was dressed in leaves from her head to her toes, and she trailed leaves when she moved. The naiad was clothed in what Darcy could only assume was water, because it moved and undulated with her small body and refracted the light from the sun. The oread was a little more puzzling in that she seemed to camouflage into whatever she was sitting on, so that at the moment she resembled the mossy rock she had perched on, and her eyes and hair were stone grey.

Darcy tried to keep her breathing even and her hands from shaking, but she was fighting a losing battle. Never before had she been unable to trust her five senses, but her brain was having a hard time putting together the pieces laid out before her. She swayed slightly, unintentionally, and Yahto Veli put a hand on the small of her back.

"I think our guest is overwhelmed," he said in his clipped, musical voice. "Will someone fetch a chair?"

There was a great deal of bustle at this request, and in a matter of seconds a rough, wooden chair was nudged toward her by nothing other than a massive mountain lion. Darcy recoiled and almost climbed back onto Yahto Veli's shoulder, but he smiled encouragingly at her and helped her to sit.

"Thank you," she said weakly, and she could swear that the lion dipped its head at her. It was then that she noticed the other animals and creatures flitting around the circle in the trees. Not only was there a mountain lion, but there was also a fox, a hawk, and a red squirrel, and Darcy's eyesight adjusted so that beyond them she could see various, tiny, sparkling images dancing on the tops of ferns and bounding from flower to flower. A tender tinkling reached her ears, broken only by the occasional loud chuckle of a gnome. And the trees and rocks and plants themselves. What a change! She hadn't noticed until now, but everything around her looked sharp, as though she was seeing it as it was really meant to be seen. She blinked hard, but the world remained the same. The difference between this Cedar Cove and the one she'd apparently left was the difference between watching a movie in high definition and watching one on VHS. Greens were greener, browns more rich, the blues and reds in the carpet beneath the chairs were the truest colors she'd ever seen, and every blade of grass was crisp, defined. Even the air smelled sweeter.

"Am I awake?" she whispered.

"More so than you've ever been before," Yahto Veli whispered back with a smile and a wink.

Chapter 12
The Council at the Pole

"Did you, girl, come through the gateway?"

"The what? I-I don't know . . ."

"Do you profess to be one of the Six?" The gravelly voice belonged to an elderly man on the fringe of the circle. He stood to the left of and slightly behind the two boys seated on the rug.

"One of the what?" she replied. She didn't know what else to say.

"One of the *Six*, girl, the Six. Don't you know what the Six are?"

Darcy shook her head and noticed several people frown.

"Can she be one of the Six and not know it?" One of the other men asked.

"It's possible," Yahto Veli declared. "She certainly is no native of Alitheia."

Alitheia. Darcy caught the name. *Is that where I am?*

"But we weren't expecting someone so young. Tellius is still only a boy, as well!" This protest came from the naiad.

"Pateros never said that he would send grown men and women, nor did he specify when or where they would arrive. Just that they would come," the other creature like Veli spoke up from the far side of the circle. "And she certainly bears the mark."

"Legend says that one would bear an emblem, and that the emblem bearer would lead the rest, so where are the other five if she truly is this one?"

The other five? They can't be referring to Sam and the rest, can they? Darcy's eyes flew around the circle; taking in all of those assembled, she finally noticed the thick wooden pole stuck in the ground to her left and slightly behind her. *Sam's totem pole*, she thought in disbelief.

"What is your name, girl?" the gravelly voiced man spoke again, piercing her with keen eyes.

"Darcy," she whispered. So many eyes were on her and she felt her familiar anxiety gnawing at her stomach.

"Strange name," the dryad muttered.

"Well, Darcy, are there, or are there not, *six* of you?"

"I'm . . ." Darcy thought frantically. Could he really mean what she thought he meant? "I'm afraid I don't understand, sir."

He squinted slightly, as if trying to assess whether or not she was playing with him. "Where you come from," he said slowly, "are there six of you of the same age and type?"

"There *are* five others that I've been hanging out with at camp," Darcy said, and immediately stopped because the crowd had once again grown agitated at her words. "There's . . . there's me, Sam, Amelia, Perry, Dean, and Lewis." Darcy finished quickly, hoping that she was saying the right thing.

"These names are foreign to us," the man continued, his gaze keener than ever. "Of you six, are there three girls and three boys?"

"Yes," Darcy all but whispered.

The oread squealed loudly and jumped up from her rock, clapping her hands together in a fit of glee. "It's her, it's her, it's her!" she repeated over and over. Several other people were smiling and nodding, but the taller, wavy-haired prince looked as though he had a bad smell under his nose. His curly-haired brother, on the other hand, was grinning from ear to ear and leaning forward in his chair.

"But why," another man asked, raising his hands in the air to get everybody's attention, "are you then alone? Legend clearly states that the one bearing the emblem would *lead* the others. Where are they?"

With a sharp pang, Darcy was suddenly reminded of the anger and dislike of the four teenagers she and Sam had left in the rec hall. "They didn't come hiking with me . . . except for one, and she's probably wondering where I've gone."

"Why didn't the other four go hiking with you?" the man dug deeper. He seemed intent on humiliating her, and Darcy began to feel rotten again.

"Because, well . . . because I was mean to them, I guess." *Might as well just get it all out there.*

"*Mean*? What do you mean, *mean?*" This question came from the taller of the two princes, his tone disdainful.

"Look, I've barely known them for two days. I just wanted some time alone, so I lied about having to be someplace and snuck away on my own." Darcy didn't know how it had come around to this again and was starting to wish she had never followed the gnome in the woods. "I didn't know that it would cause so much trouble, but I actually think they are all really cool, even Samantha, and I wouldn't have lied to them if I'd known how much it would hurt them." She thought she sounded stupid and immature before all these listeners, and she put her head in her hands miserably.

She felt a warm squeeze on her shoulder and heard Yahto Veli's musical voice above her head. "Her actions are between her and Pateros, and it can only be assumed that what has transpired has done so because he allowed it to. What is important now, is determining whether or not she and her five companions are truly the ones we seek."

"It is why we are here, after all, to re-evaluate the prophecy. What better time for them to appear?" another man spoke.

"You must bring them back with you," the gravelly-voiced man said to Darcy. "It is the only way."

"Can you do that?" Yahto Veli got down on one knee and looked her in the eyes. His were very light blue and danced beneath his pale lashes.

Darcy thought very carefully for a moment before answering. They were asking her to return to her world and convince the other five teenagers not only to hike back to Gnome's Haven with her, but to follow her through a magical portal into an unknown realm. Getting them to go with her would be a challenge all on its own, but getting them to believe her . . . well, that was just out of the question. But as she looked into the clear and honest eyes of Yahto Veli, she couldn't help but feel a thrill of empowerment. She *wanted* to share this secret with them. For the first time in her life, she actually wanted to be surrounded by other people her own age.

"I don't know," she finally answered. "What should I tell them? They'll never believe me. You don't understand what my world is like. We don't have magic, or anything!"

"You mean you don't have gateways in your world?" the shorter prince spoke in disbelief. "You've never met someone from another world before?"

Darcy laughed nervously. "No. Are you kidding me? I didn't even know that other worlds *existed* until now!"

"What a strange place you live in," the prince replied haughtily.

"Don't be so proud of the gateways in Alitheia," Torrin spoke suddenly, abruptly. "They are the reason we are in such trouble now, but they are also the reason that we need this girl to retrieve her companions." He, too, got down on one knee before Darcy and looked her in the eyes. "Tell your friends that they are needed—that you all are needed. Tell them that we are waiting for them . . . Alitheia awaits." He gestured to the pole stuck in the ground and Darcy really looked at it for the first time, taking note of the carvings.

It didn't look Native American at all; in fact, it looked older, much older, like it had been carved by the Greeks or the Romans. At the very top was carved a horse, its body wound around the pole. Clutching the horse's heel was a badger, and beneath the badger a bird. Following the bird a roaring lion was carved, standing on the head of a very wise-looking owl. At the very bottom was the clear image of a fox.

"Go and get your friends, and we will bring the animals," Torrin spoke softly to her and then raised his voice so that all could hear. “The animals will know.”

Chapter 13
Going Back

Darcy hurried back through the undergrowth with Yahto Veli. Torrin shadowed them, glancing keenly from side to side. "What is he looking for?" Darcy whispered to Veli.

"Eyes and ears," Veli replied cryptically.

They brushed through a patch of ferns and came to two trees standing side by side like a doorway. A slight haze hung between them and Darcy felt a sudden reluctance to pass through. What if she couldn't find her way back? What if the gateway closed? What if all of this really was a dream and the moment she passed between the trees she would wake up? *I don't want to go back to my boring life!*

She bit her lip and turned to look at Yahto Veli. "What if I can't get back to Alitheia?" she asked, her heart thrumming in her ears.

He smiled. "If you are the one, you will. You will not be able to *help* but come back. Could you control it the first time?"

She shook her head, her ponytail swinging between her shoulder blades.

"Then do not worry; Pateros will see you back."

Pateros. They've mentioned that name a couple of times. She wanted to ask what he meant, but her palms were slick with sweat and she felt that she had enough other things to worry about. "What do I do when I bring them back to Gnome's Haven?" she whispered.

"Follow the gnomes; they will guide you. Do you remember the big one with the blue jacket and red hat? The one that led you on your merry chase?"

Darcy nodded. How could she forget?

"His name is Brachos, and he will lead you back. The gnomes are mischievous, but they are loyal to Pateros. We will be waiting for you."

"Do you . . . do you think you could give me something magical? Some sort of proof, I mean, so that they'll believe me?" Darcy asked in a rush.

"Proof?" Veli's eyebrows rose on his high forehead and his ears twitched forward. "If they are truly your friends, your word will be your proof. You need nothing else."

Great, Darcy thought. But instead she said okay and squared her shoulders. "I'm ready."

Yahto Veli stepped aside and extended his arm toward the trees. Darcy took one step, stopped, took a deep breath and two more steps. She paused again, her nose just before the shimmer between the trees, took one more look back at Veli, and then plunged forward, holding her breath.

She once again felt the sensation of passing through thick pudding or Jell-O, but it only lasted a moment, and the next step she took was normal. Her foot crunched on a stick and she swung around to look behind her. The shimmer was barely visible on this side and looked more like a spider web. Yahto Veli and Torrin were gone.

"I can't believe this is happening," she murmured aloud. "I've got to find Sam."

She didn't know what to expect as she headed back toward Gnome's Haven. She must have been gone at least half an hour and she didn't know if Sam would have waited for her at the rock or headed back to camp. She sincerely hoped that the girl had not raised the alarm that Darcy had disappeared; she didn't think she could take another talking-to from her father.

"Sam?" she called tentatively as she came out next to the boulder. Brachos the gnome was painted on his rock, sitting tightly in the fissure. She squinted at him but he betrayed no hint of movement. "Sam!" she called again, looking upwards. "Are you there?"

"Hey! Sorry." Sam's head poked over the edge, smiling at her. "I was just making sure that there was enough space for us both to come up this way before I called down to you."

"O…kay." Darcy wondered if she sounded as puzzled as she felt. "Did that really take you a half hour?"

"What?" Sam made a face at her. "What do you mean? I've only been up here for, like, two minutes."

Darcy frowned deeply, her mind racing. "Are you sure?"

"Yeeesss." Sam drew out her answer and rolled her eyes. "What's the matter?" she called teasingly. "Did you fall asleep or something?"

"No." But suddenly Darcy wasn't so sure. "Hey, can you come down here? I want to talk to you about something."

"But I just got up here. Are you sure you don't want to climb up?"

"Not right now."

"Okay. Hang on." Sam lay on her stomach and started inching her way down the face of the rock, scrambling for foot and handholds as she did so.

Darcy watched her progress and called out encouragement from time to time, but her mind was busy, computing the turn of events. *Okay, so I was gone for at least a half hour, no question about that, but Sam didn't even notice! She claims that she was only on top of the rock for two minutes. So . . . either she bumped her head and didn't realize it, or time doesn't work here the same way it does in Alitheia. Maybe when you're there, time stands still here? I wonder if it works the same way going back? Maybe Yahto Veli and Torrin will only have to wait a few seconds for me to return. Or maybe,* a small voice at the back of her mind reasoned, *you're going crazy.* She shook her head to clear that voice. She'd only gotten a taste of the magical world and she desperately wanted to go back. She refused to entertain the notion that none of it was real.

Sam finally plopped to the ground by her side and brushed the moss and twigs from the front of her T-shirt. "Ta da!" she proclaimed. "See? Easy."

"Um, yeah . . . listen . . ." Now that it came down to it, Darcy didn't know how to begin. "Have . . . have you ever really needed to tell somebody something and didn't know how to say it?"

Sam pulled a face and waved her hand dismissively. "If this is about this morning, forget about it. I already told you that it's okay, and the others will come around."

"No—I mean, yes, that's great, but that's not what I'm talking about." Darcy bit her lip and stared hard into Sam's eyes. She didn't usually look people in the eyes; it made her nervous.

"What's the matter, Darcy?" Sam suddenly turned serious. "You look like you're going to be sick, or something."

Darcy exhaled forcefully and started to pace. *This is so hard.* "Okay. You know how you were up on the rock for a few minutes and I wasn't with you?"

"Uh huh."

"Well, I *really* wasn't with you."

"What do you mean?" Sam frowned at her.

"I . . . I thought that you had been up there for, like, a half hour. Did you wonder why?"

"Well, I don't know. I guess I figured you just misspoke."

Darcy shook her head vigorously. "Uh-uh; I didn't. I thought you'd been up there for a half hour because I was someplace else for a half hour, but apparently you didn't realize I was gone, so maybe the time doesn't work the same from one place to the other."

"Darcy, you're not making any sense."

"Argh." Darcy put her face in her hands. "I know. It's just, this isn't easy to say."

"Just say it. Come on, what's the worst that I could do to you? Laugh?" Sam teased.

"No." Darcy stopped pacing and looked Sam in the eyes again. "I think you're the last person on earth that would laugh at me, and that's why you have to be the first one to know."

"Know *what*?"

"That . . ." *Okay, here goes*, "that I've been to another world . . . and it's called Alitheia." Darcy watched Sam's reaction carefully, ready to laugh and say that she was just kidding if Sam didn't believe her. *But I'm* not *kidding, and I have to get everybody to believe me somehow!*

Sam's smile slowly slid off her face and her eyes widened. "What do you mean, *another world?*" she whispered. "Like, an actual *other world*?"

Darcy nodded, her eyes suddenly shining. "It was *awesome*, Sam. You were right; Cedar Cove is magical, but not magical as in 'special' like Amelia said. Magical as in *magical!*"

Sam was shaking her head from side to side as though she was trying to clear it, and she leaned back against the rock that was Gnome's Haven.

Darcy took advantage of her silence to continue telling her story. "I was waiting for you to call down to me and I noticed that one of the gnomes on the rock was missing. I started looking for it, and I accidentally passed through what they call a gateway and stumbled into Alitheia."

"They?" Sam questioned weakly.

"The Alitheians. Sam, there are real live gnomes and dryads and naiads and oreads and fairies, I think, and plenty of humans too, and they want me to come back. Well, not just me—all of us. I guess they were expecting us because I wasn't supposed to go alone, but I'm back now and you can help me to convince the others to come out here, as well, because they're waiting for us." Darcy spoke in a rush and knew that her story was coming out in a jumble, but she didn't care. Either Sam would think she was crazy, or she would help.

"So . . . what do you think?" Darcy asked timidly after another full minute of silence. Sam looked deep in thought. "It's crazy, I know, and I guess I didn't really expect you to believe me, but—"

"I believe you," Sam said quietly. "How could I not?"

"You do?" Darcy's heart swelled.

Sam looked up, her blue eyes bright and shining. "How could I not?" she repeated again. "I've been coming here my whole life, Darcy, and I always knew there was something special about this place . . . something special beyond the people and the locations . . . something otherworldly. And you, let's face it, didn't even want to be here this summer, so why would you make something like this up? If it is a lie, Darcy, then it is a very cruel lie, and I don't think you are a cruel person."

For the first time in her life, Darcy spontaneously hugged somebody. What she'd done to deserve this girl's trust, she didn't know, but she intended to earn it from now on.

"So how do we convince the others?" Darcy asked when she released Sam, a little embarrassed by her outburst of affection. "They said they need to see all six of us. Six seemed to be an important number."

Sam squinted her eyes and squeezed Darcy's hand. "You leave them to me."

Chapter 14
Convincing the Others

"So they're, like, just waiting for you to come back?" Sam asked. It was one of many questions she'd been shooting at Darcy since they'd started heading back toward camp.

"Yeah, I guess so. Yahto Veli, that's the strange-looking one, told me they'd be waiting. I guess that means they'll be by the gateway, but I'm not sure."

"And they said the gnomes would lead you?" Sam clarified.

"Uh-huh." Darcy stifled a little laugh; her nerves were making her jittery. "I thought the gnomes were annoying at first, but they're actually pretty funny."

"I can't wait to see them . . . for real, I mean, not painted on rocks—" Sam cut off suddenly and froze. They'd just re-entered the campsite on the isthmus and nearly bumped headlong into Perry, Dean, Lewis, and Amelia. "Oh, hi," Sam said. She shot a furtive glance at Darcy.

Perry scowled and crossed his arms, and Amelia and Lewis looked at their feet. Dean pulled his hood up over his head and looked off into the trees.

"Hi," Amelia finally said, breaking the awkward silence. She looked up and her gaze seemed to plead with Sam.

"What are you guys doing here?" Sam asked, surprised. "We were just heading back to find you."

"Lewis said he felt '*bad*' and Amelia agreed with him," Perry said, a little scornfully. "So we decided to come find you."

"Well," Amelia said, "the ferry will be running again in about twenty minutes, and we wanted to make sure that you and Darcy got back okay."

Lewis nodded, still studying his toes.

Sam looked at Darcy again and her eyes conveyed what Darcy was also thinking. *Twenty minutes to convince them.*

"Thank you," Sam said to the others. "That was nice of you."

"But unnecessary," Perry said, punching Lewis on the shoulder. "I told you they'd come back on their own."

"Um . . . actually, we weren't coming back to ride the ferry. We were coming to find you guys," Sam said hurriedly.

"To do what?" Perry snapped.

"Apologize," Darcy said quickly. *They're never going to believe me if they're still mad at me*. "I . . . I know I acted really horrible this morning, and I didn't mean to. I'm sorry."

The other four exchanged looks of incredulity and Darcy quickly amended her statement.

"That is, I *did* mean to do it, but I didn't think that it would hurt anybody. I'm just a really solitary person, you know? I like to be alone. But I didn't want to hurt Sam and Amelia's feelings by telling them to go away, so—"

"So you thought you'd lie instead?" Amelia finished for her, one eyebrow slightly raised.

"Um, yeah."

"Well, you know what? We can make it real easy on you from now on and just leave you alone, if that's what you really want. Come on, Sam."

But Sam didn't move.

"Sam, come on. You heard what she said; she likes to be *alone*."

Sam glowered at Amelia. "I heard what she said, and I don't think there's anything wrong with wanting to be alone. She's apologized to me and to you, all of you, so you need to forgive her and move on." Darcy couldn't help being impressed by Sam's spunk and once again felt bolstered by her loyalty.

The other four were starting to look a little uneasy and Dean finally shrugged and shoved his hands in his pockets. "I didn't know what the big deal was in the first place," he muttered. "I'm cool with Darcy."

Sam beamed and turned to Amelia.

"Come on, Amelia. Remember that summer when you and Perry couldn't stop picking on each other? Remember how miserable that was for everybody?"

Amelia rolled her eyes and crossed her arms defensively. "Fine. I forgive her." But she didn't look at Darcy.

Lewis and Perry both capitulated quickly once they found themselves outnumbered, and suddenly everything appeared normal between the five friends and Darcy, but Darcy knew that she still had a lot to do to gain their trust. *And I doubt what I have to say next is going to help*.

"So, are you guys ready to head back to the ferry?" Perry asked, he turned and looked behind him. "I don't think we should wait a whole hour for the next one."

"Well . . . not *exactly*." Sam looked at Darcy for help.

"We kinda have something we need to tell you guys," Darcy put in.

"What? There's more?" Perry asked.

"A *lot* more." Sam seemed to gain strength and plunged ahead. "Darcy found a gateway to another world!"

Talk about just jumping in. Darcy thought frantically as she studied the reactions of the four teenagers. Amelia rolled her eyes dramatically and tisked under her breath. Perry and Dean started laughing, and Lewis just frowned.

Sam stamped her foot impatiently. "It's true!"

"Yeah, right, we're supposed to believe that?" Perry was practically rolling on the ground with laughter. "Of all the things you could have said, *that* is the craziest."

Dean chuckled and Amelia looked at her watch. "We have ten minutes, guys. We have to start moving if we want to catch the ferry."

"Amelia! Come on, you've felt it before, too, you've said so!"

"Felt *what*?"

"The magic of Cedar Cove. And *you,* Perry." Sam stabbed a finger toward his face. "I seem to remember you telling your sister that you saw a real, live gnome out here—"

"I was *six*," Perry protested, but Sam pushed on.

"Lewis, I know that you've written about it in your notebook."

"That's private, Sam," Lewis muttered, his face growing red.

"I'm not going to give specifics, but you've imagined another world connected with Cedar Cove almost since you started coming! Dean, wouldn't it be awesome if it was true?"

Dean shrugged. "But it's not. It's totally impossible."

"Sam, please, this is embarrassing," Amelia said. "You and I stopped playing these games when we were nine."

"Ten," Sam corrected her dryly. "And why did we play pretend in the first place?"

"Because we were kids. But we're grown up now. We know better."

Sam shook her head. "I don't think we do."

It was time for Darcy to step in. "Listen, you guys. I know this is my first year and I don't have all the history that you guys have together. And I know that you have no reason to believe me, but . . . I *did* pass through a gateway into another world while Sam was climbing Gnome's Haven."

"It's true," Sam put in. "She was all confused and thought I should have been up on the rock for a half hour, because that's how much time she was gone in Alitheia, but I'd only been up there for, like, two minutes!"

Confusion and exasperation met their eyes. "Okay, scratch that part. It's a little confusing, anyway." Darcy continued. "The important thing is that these people I met over there, in . . . in Alitheia . . ." She felt a little foolish saying the name aloud. "They're waiting for us. They knew all about us;

that there were six of us and that three of us were girls and three of us boys. They said they need us all to come to Alitheia together—that they need us for some prophecy."

Of the four of them, only Lewis was starting to look like he believed her. He had gone white around his glasses and wore an expression like he had just swallowed a bug. Dean whistled softly, however, twirling a finger near his temple and mouthing "coo-coo" to Perry, snorted and said, "Somebody's been playing too much Dungeons and Dragons."

"That's not nice," Sam snapped. "There's nothing wrong with her head. Why would she lie about something like this?"

"Gee, I don't know . . . maybe to get us to think she's cool?"

"Cool?" Darcy sputtered. "In case you haven't noticed, I feel pretty geeky right now."

"Why don't you just come back to Gnome's Haven with us, and we can check it out?" Sam intervened with a different tactic. "Darcy said that we would be led through the gateway, right Darcy?"

Darcy nodded, feeling a little sick to her stomach. What if it didn't work? She would permanently be labeled the "crazy girl" at Cedar Cove.

"All right, then, let's go." Sam still sounded cheerful, despite everything.

"I suppose we've missed the ferry, anyways," Amelia grumbled. "Let's get this over with so we can catch the next ferry back for dinner."

A few minutes later they were hurrying down the path, Sam in the lead and Darcy right behind her. "They're actually coming!" Darcy hissed in Sam's ear.

"I knew they would," Sam muttered back. "They're really not bad, once you get to know them. Even Perry." She grimaced a bit and looked forward again.

They took the right branch in the trail and came upon Gnome's Haven in no time. The light slanting through the trees was slightly lower, and Darcy hoped she hadn't taken too long to convince the others.

"Okay, so where is this gateway?" Amelia asked, her arms akimbo.

"Um, I don't know exactly. I was a little distracted when I passed through." Darcy looked around frantically. "But they said that the gnomes would lead us. Well, one gnome in particular, Brachos."

"Brachos?" Amelia repeated. "That's great." Her voice dripped with sarcasm. She marched over to the sloughed-off part of the boulder and sat down with a huff.

"Which one is Brachos?" Sam muttered in her ear. Darcy noticed that her hands were shaking slightly and sweat gleamed on her forehead. She was nervous, too.

Where is that fissure? There. Darcy found Brachos's stone and pointed. "There he is."

"He looks pretty painted-on to me," Perry mocked. "Although, gee, I don't know." He raised his hands to his face in mock fear and clutched at Dean's sweatshirt. "Dean! Save me! The little painted gnome is going to jump off his rock and get me!"

Dean tussled with Perry, shoving him closer to the fissure. "Oh yeah? Why don't you kiss it? Huh?" The boys laughed together, but Lewis stood off to the side, staring at the fissure.

"Sam?" Lewis said quietly, staring. He took his glasses off and cleaned them. "Darcy?"

"Yeah?" Sam went to his side.

"I think that gnome just winked at me." Lewis put his glasses back on and looked at Sam. "Is this for real?" he mouthed.

Sam nodded eagerly.

"YYYAAARRGGHHH!" Perry's bellow echoed through the trees and a few birds took flight in indignation. "Get it off! Get it *off*!" Perry howled, jumping around. Brachos the gnome was swinging gleefully from Perry's nostrils.

Darcy's heart gave a flip. *Yes!* She thought.

Dean had released Perry and was standing back in shock, and Amelia stood stock-still, mouth agape at the sight before her.

Sam squealed excitedly and clapped her hands. "It's happening, Darcy. It's happening!"

"It's hurting me!" Perry continued. "Okay, okay, I believe you guys, now just *get it off*!"

But his last plea was unnecessary. With a madcap chuckle and a loud "Boop!" Brachos released Perry's nose, fell to the ground, and dashed away into the trees.

"After him!" Darcy shouted. "He's leading us to the gateway!" Without another thought, Darcy dove into the trees and underbrush, following the loud giggles and the pattering feet. When Brachos dove through the two trees, Darcy didn't even blink. She was about to follow him but told herself to hold up. Breathing heavily, she turned to make sure that she was not alone.

Sure enough, just behind her were Sam, Lewis, Dean, Perry, and even Amelia, looking scared and uncertain. "Are you ready?" Darcy breathed.

Everyone nodded but Amelia, who asked in a tremulous voice, "Can we get back?"

"Of course!" Darcy smiled. "I did." And with that she took a step and plunged back into Alitheia.

Chapter 15
The Test of the Animals

One thick, slow-motion step later, Darcy tumbled into the pale arms of Yahto Veli. She took a deep breath and smiled up into his blue eyes. "It worked!"

He set her on her feet and tilted his head at her. "You didn't think it would?" He chuckled and reached out to grab the next arm coming through.

Sam emerged in Alitheia wide-eyed and silent. She mouthed wordlessly for a few moments, pointing at Yahto Veli and making a squeaking noise in her throat, and then promptly sat down on the forest floor and started crying.

"Sam," Darcy said, a little exasperated and embarrassed. "What's the matter?"

"It's just," Sam warbled, "you don't know how *long* I've wanted to believe that something like this was *true!*" She howled and buried her face in her hands.

For goodness sake. Darcy patted her awkwardly on the shoulder and shrugged at Yahto Veli, who looked like he was barely containing his mirth. Her heart quickened a beat as the next person came through: Lewis. He looked around with gaping mouth and quickly sat down next to Sam.

Dean, Perry, and Amelia came through in a bunch, Amelia clinging to the back of Perry's shirt with her eyes closed.

"Whoa," Dean murmured.

"This is impossible," Perry said, putting his hands on his head.

Amelia opened her eyes and exhaled loudly. "Oh my," she breathed. "Everything is so colorful! Are we really in another world?"

"I wish I had my camera," Perry muttered. "What's the matter with Sam?"

"Don't ask," Darcy muttered. She rolled her eyes. "Guys, this is Yahto Veli."

Yahto Veli had helped everyone through the gateway and now stood off to the side, watching them with an enormous grin on his face. He inclined his head when Darcy introduced him and said, "It is a most high honor to welcome you to Alitheia, my lords and ladies."

Sam's wet face popped up out of her hands and she scrambled to her feet and bowed awkwardly; Lewis followed suit. Dean, Perry, and Amelia just stared.

"Dude . . . your ears," Perry said, squinting. "Is that, like, a deformity, or something? I bet you can hear real well."

Amelia punched Perry on the arm at the same time that Sam and Darcy gasped at him. But Yahto Veli didn't seem to mind; he merely smiled more broadly. "I can hear very well, actually," he affirmed, "but it is no deformity; at least, not among my people. Although I have been told that mine are particularly large, even for a nark."

"A nark?" Dean said. "What's that?"

"It's what I am. At the moment I am a day nark, and in a few hours you will meet my night nark counterpart. We come from elfish stock," he explained, but to Darcy and the rest of them it just added to their confusion.

Torrin suddenly appeared out of the trees and sized them up with a single glance. Amelia jumped when he appeared and Dean grinned. He was obviously impressed by the man's stealth.

"Good," Torrin said shortly, "they're here. The animals are assembled. We are ready."

"Then please lead the way, my good companion," Veli said.

Torrin turned back into the trees and disappeared without another word. Dean said "Come on!" to Perry and plunged after him. Lewis and Sam followed the two of them, and Darcy hung back with Yahto Veli.

"Um, I have a question for you, if you don't mind," she said quickly.

"At your leisure, my lady. I will do my best to supply an answer."

"Okay. I was just wondering how long you were waiting for me to come back with my friends?"

"It was not long. The sun dropped from there," he pointed and moved his finger in a slight arc, "to there. Why do you ask?"

"Well, because it appears that where we come from, time stops while we are here. At least, it did when I was here. Do you think it will remain the same for however long we stay in Alitheia?"

Yahto Veli looked thoughtful for a moment and eventually said, "That I do not know. It is strange magic, but it is certainly not beyond Pateros's reach. It would be a good question to ask Rubidius."

"Rubidius?"

"Our chief master magician—the alchemist."

Oh. "Do you think we'll meet him? I mean, will we be here for that long?" Darcy's pulse quickened with anticipation.

"Oh, I think so. If you are indeed the Six we seek, then you will be here until your job is complete or Pateros sends you back. He has much work for you to do this year."

Sweet! Darcy practically jumped up and down with anticipation but held herself in check.

"Are you guys seeing this?" Lewis asked quietly, and Darcy looked up.

"Seeing what?"

"The fairies!" Sam hissed.

Darcy looked into the emerald leaves of the ferns and undergrowth. Keeping pace with them—flitting and cartwheeling and flipping through the air—were myriads of fairies, each about the size of Darcy's hand. They were shimmery and difficult to see clearly when they moved, but they looked exactly like Darcy would have imagined: little winged people clothed in floating garments. They glowed slightly and each looked like it belonged to a specific flower or plant, based on the colors they wore.

"Do they always act this way?" she whispered to Yahto Veli. She was afraid of scaring them off.

"Not all the time," he replied, a smile in his voice. "Only when they are very excited."

"Why are they excited?" Sam asked, her voice awed.

"Because they are happy to see you."

"To see *us?*"

"Of course. This is a very exciting time for all of us."

"Why exactly do you need six of us from another world?" Darcy asked. She was starting to get the impression that there was a lot more to this whole thing than she had anticipated.

"I think it would be best if we save the prophecy telling for the elders at the council," Yahto Veli replied. "But don't worry." His hand on her shoulder was warm, reassuring. "Everything is about to be made clear."

"Wow!" Perry shouted. "Are you kidding me?"

"Unbelievable," Dean added.

Darcy and Yahto Veli followed them into the clearing with the totem pole, only this time it was a little more crowded. Six animals were waiting in a row at the far end of the clearing, and a few more people had joined the assembly, most noticeably an elderly woman with kind eyes and a curly-haired man in long robes.

"It's the totem pole," Sam said, looking to the center of the clearing. "But it looks different."

"Sam, there's a lion over there." Amelia sounded frightened and she wrung her hands repeatedly. "And a fox. This can't be safe."

"I don't think they're going to hurt us," Lewis said in a measured tone. "They're just sitting there with all those other animals." He looked at Darcy for confirmation and she just shrugged.

Indeed there was a lion, but it was not a mountain lion this time. This was a shaggy African lion with a full mane. The mountain lion was still present, but it lay off to the side with its head on its crossed paws and its ears twitched forward. The fox that had been present before had joined the line of animals, as had an owl, a songbird, a badger, and a horse. Darcy's breath caught and she looked toward the center of the clearing. They were the six animals from the pole. Her interest returned to the horse, which she felt was watching her, and indeed it was. A beautiful bay stallion with black socks, mane, and tail, watched her with a wide-eyed, intelligent gaze, betraying no nervousness in the presence of the lion. Darcy stared back, but before she knew it the gravelly-voiced man was addressing them, and the awed exclamations of her companions fell silent.

"Welcome to Alitheia, six travelers from another world," he said, spreading his arms wide.

Darcy and the others didn't know what they should do or say. Darcy and Sam curtsied slightly, Amelia bobbed her head and choked on something that she was trying to say, and the boys awkwardly nodded their heads. Lewis said, "Thank you, sir," but quickly blushed and looked down.

The man looked flummoxed for a moment. He turned to the twin boys sitting on the rug, and they stood. Darcy saw now that they certainly weren't twins, even though they looked so similar in the face, for the taller one was noticeably older, in both bearing and stature. Even though they both bore thin crowns on their heads, the taller boy wore a rich, brown, leather jerkin over a crisp linen shirt. On the chest of the jerkin in golden stitching was the image of a golden eagle with wings spread. On the eagle's breast were three four-point stars. His clothing was both rich and simple. The younger boy wore a leather jerkin, as well, but his bore only three stars in the center. Darcy was somewhat startled to see that although they were both yet boys, they each wore a belted scabbard and sword.

The older boy spoke and Darcy was struck with how different he was from Roger, even though he must be about the same age. "I am Tellius the Seventh of the House of Ecclektos. You have traveled to the land over which I am rightful ruler. It is by my leave and Pateros's will that you are here. Do you agree to abide by the laws of my land and submit to my sovereignty for the length of your stay in Alitheia?"

He spoke to all of them but looked only at Darcy, and she realized she must have been figured default leader among her friends. She swallowed hard. There were so many eyes on her. But she didn't feel the same paralyzing fear that she normally felt when meeting new people, and so she stepped forward with only a small amount of trepidation. "Um, I don't see why not," she said and then blushed. *I should have sounded more formal,* she chided herself.

Tellius looked at a loss for a moment but then nodded his head. He moved to sit down, but the elderly woman who had joined the council cleared her throat loudly and nodded at his brother. Tellius jumped up like there was a tack on his seat and gestured wildly at his brother. "Oh, yeah . . . this is Cadmus." Cadmus snickered while he sat, his ears flaming.

He blushes just like me, Darcy thought with a small degree of satisfaction.

The gravelly-voiced man stepped forward again, looking a little exasperated, and spoke loudly so the Six could hear him. "And I am Tullin Ecclektos, cousin of the princes' father and governor of Kenidros. Welcome."

How many times can they welcome us? Darcy almost rolled her eyes, but refrained. The silence from her friends told her they were just as flummoxed as she was.

Tullin Ecclektos looked around to his left and gestured at the assembled animals. "For many years," he began, "we have waited, and none have come. Foolhardy we would be if we blindly accepted the first six visitors from another world without the test of the animals." Darcy got the impression that he spoke more to the assembled Alitheians than to her and the other five. The lined-up animals were alert and watchful; they looked like they were straining at invisible leashes.

"Those whom we've long expected," he continued, "include a companion, a musician, a warrior, a spy, a scribe, and the king's intended. The animals will align with them. If these six animals, chosen long ago by Pateros himself, should bond without question to those people to whom they belong, then we can be certain that the time at last has come, and the Shadow shall be overthrown." He seemed to get emotional and Darcy felt a pang of discomfort. The assembly was very hushed. "Rubidius, if you please." Tullin stepped aside to let the curly-haired man step forward.

Rubidius looked keenly at the six of them, and Darcy squirmed under his gaze. He touched each animal on the forehead and then stepped back. As if released from springs, the animals sped toward them, and Darcy's heart lifted as she saw the horse make straight for her. She reached out her hand and felt a thrill as the stallion nudged it, blowing softly in the way that Darcy particularly loved about horses. She let him smell her and then ran her palm up the side of his cheek as he bowed his head and bumped her gently on the chest.

She looked to her right and noticed that each of her companions had received animals in similar fashion. Perry was doing his best to look brave and manly as the great African lion rubbed its mane all over him, purring like a giant housecat. Dean was down on one knee, grinning like a little boy at Christmas as he ruffled the head of the fox, which was wagging its tail like a common dog with both front paws on Dean's thigh. Amelia looked pleased through her trepidation as the songbird perched on her shoulder and trilled loudly, and Lewis was rubbing his fingers in the soft feathers of the owl that had landed on his outstretched arm. Sam was bent at the waist greeting the badger, which stood on hind legs and rested its front paws on her knees. Darcy felt that if badgers could smile, this one certainly would. She almost expected the animals to speak, but they made no sounds beyond purrs, snuffles, trills, and whines.

With a whoop and a holler from the younger of the two royal boys, the assembly as one let out its breath, and celebratory sounds began. “It’s them!” Tullin’s voice resounded above the crowd. “We’re saved!” a female voice cried. And from that point on Darcy could make out little else in the hullabaloo. Before she knew it, fairies were dancing circles around her feet and the dryad had appeared at her elbow with a large bouquet of flowers for her. She heard Sam crying and Amelia exclaiming and the boys laughing, and all she could think was, *what next?*

CHAPTER 16

STUCK

"I'm sorry," Amelia protested through the noise after each of them had been wreathed in flowers and ferns. "But I don't really understand what all of this means."

Darcy joined the other five as they nodded in agreement.

"What's so special about *us*?" Sam added as the assembly gradually quieted.

"They don't already know?" The naiad seemed perplexed.

"Now, Umi, we cannot expect them to know our history. Ah, excellent!" Tullin Ecclektos clapped his hands together once and stepped aside for two small goats trotting into the clearing dragging behind them a sled carrying a very old and battered chest.

The alchemist Rubidius extracted a long chain from his shirt and began to pick through a number of keys, muttering to himself the entire time, finally settling on a very small golden one. Gathering his robes around himself, he knelt beside the chest and fitted the key in the lock. With a click the latch sprang open and Rubidius dropped the chain of keys back inside his shirt. Carefully picking up the first item in the chest, he drew himself back up to his normal height and held the item up for all to see. It was a cloth jerkin, not unlike the leather ones worn by the princes, but longer, and yellow. On the front, embroidered in red, was a prowling lion. Above the lion's head were embroidered three four-point stars.

Without preamble, Rubidius declared, "For the warrior." And then he ducked his head and muttered, "Oh, yes, there is also that." Bending down again, he retrieved a long broadsword and scabbard from the chest. He marched up to Perry, who looked positively flabbergasted, and threw the jerkin over his head without so much as a "by your leave." Perry stood frozen, his hands raised in the air as though he were being fitted for a suit, as the alchemist buckled the loose jerkin around his waist with the scabbard. The sword point hung almost to the ground.

When Rubidius turned back to the chest, Dean whispered to Perry out of the side of his mouth, "Dude, nice sword!"

"For the scribe," Rubidius declared next, holding aloft a brown jerkin with an embroidered white owl and three stars above its head. He delivered the jerkin and a fancy red-plumed quill to Lewis with all the solemnity of a graduation ceremony.

"For the musician!" Amelia's jerkin was soft lavender with a blue songbird and stars on the front. Her item was a small, harp-like instrument, and her eyes lit up when she accepted it, her shoulders relaxing for the first time. She immediately began to test each string carefully, caressing the instrument as though it was a newborn baby.

"For the spy!" Dean perked up and accepted his forest-green jerkin and handsome bow and arrow set with unconcealed excitement. The front of his jerkin boasted a fox and the ever-present four-point stars.

"For the companion!" Sam brightened and happily allowed Rubidius to sling the blue jerkin with badger and stars embroidery over her head. He handed her a small leather pouch and, when he turned his back, she discreetly peeked inside.

"It's empty," she whispered to Darcy. "I wonder what it's for."

Darcy shrugged. She wasn't interested in Sam's pouch at the moment, for she was the only one left to be fitted with a jerkin and given a gift. She shook slightly, and she wasn't even sure why. She still didn't know what the significance of all this was. She expected Rubidius to go back to the chest, but he did not. Instead he stood aside and held out a hand to the older of the two princes.

Tellius hedged for a moment, shooting Tullin and Rubidius sullen looks, but he eventually stood and walked to the chest with all the dignity a boy of that age, who obviously did not want to do what he was doing, could muster. He reached into the chest and pulled out a jerkin of rich red, embroidered in gold like his own. The horse on the front glittered, as did the three stars, and Darcy heard Sam gasp quietly beside her. Tellius also held something in his hand, but he did not show the object to the assembly.

"For the king's intended!" Rubidius declared, louder than before, and Tellius approached her slowly, a look of utter discomfort on his aristocratic face. He was shorter than she, but only by a few inches, and as he came to stand before her, Darcy noticed that his serious brown eyes contained flecks of green, and his nose was slightly smattered with freckles like her own. He would look almost impish if it were not for his intense and haughty disposition.

Darcy bent her knees slightly, so that he wouldn't have to reach so far to put the jerkin over her head. She felt the cool material, which smelled musty and old, slip over her head and settle on her shoulders. She straightened and looked down at herself, struck by how much at odds the jerkin was with her Bermuda shorts and tank top.

Tellius stood before her with the air of someone who was preparing to do something very unpleasant. A throat cleared behind him, sounding very loud in the hushed gathering, and the prince huffed and rolled his eyes. Suddenly, he snatched her hand and shoved the object he was carrying into it, dropping her hand quickly as though he was afraid of being burned.

Darcy looked down and opened her palm to find a heavy golden ring engraved with designs and symbols she didn't recognize. In the center was a grouping of the now familiar four-point stars cut out of some amber stone. The ring itself, even without the stones, must have been worth a fortune. Darcy quickly tried to give it back to Tellius. "I can't accept this; it's too much!" she whispered frantically.

He shook his head and backed up. "It's yours," he answered. "Put it on." He turned on his heel and marched back to his seat.

Darcy swallowed hard and looked around. Every eye was on her. *That seems to be happening a lot.* She swallowed again and fumbled with the ring. It was too large for any of her fingers except her thumb, so she slipped it on the thumb of her left hand and smiled weakly. That seemed to be enough to please the assembly because everybody smiled and some exchanged looks that seemed to house secret meanings. Darcy wondered, not for the first time, what it meant to be the "king's intended." Everybody else's positions seemed to be clear, but not hers.

Tullin cleared his voice awkwardly and said, "It was assumed that you Six would be older, my lords and ladies, so I fear we must apologize for the . . . the impractical nature of the garments. But I think you will find that someday they will fit."

Darcy had noticed the length and width of her own jerkin, and as she looked down the line she saw that only Amelia's was not skimming the grass, and only Sam's fit in the chest. She wondered how long they would be expected to wear them.

Suddenly, and without warning, the assembly bowed as one to the six friends from Cedar Cove. Those who had been sitting stood, and the animals made various postures of obeisance before them.

Amelia's fingers froze on her instrument, Perry and Dean stopped examining their weapons, and Lewis and Sam exchanged awed looks. Darcy felt her ears grow red for what seemed like the umpteenth time that day.

When the assembly straightened out of their bow, a few men who appeared to be servants, emerged from the forest and placed wooden chairs behind each of the six. The servants offered hands to Darcy, Amelia, and Sam to help them sit, and bowed deeply to Perry, Dean, and Lewis. The lion, fox, and badger settled themselves onto the grass beside each of their companions, and the owl relocated to Lewis's shoulder. Darcy's stallion trotted to stand behind her.

As soon as the six of them and the princes were seated, the rest of the assembly found positions either on the ground or on rocks or tree stumps, and all looked expectantly at Rubidius, who remained standing.

The formerly redheaded alchemist tugged on his very curly beard and then began in a rich tenor voice. "The prophecy is really very simple, but perhaps it would be best if told in its original, poetic form." He cleared his throat importantly.

"Magic and mystery, good days and bad,
Alitheians, your worst disobedience is at hand.
With arrogance and spite a magician awoke,
The Shadow of whom no man has yet spoke.
Magic and mystery without warning will fail,
And Pateros will leave Alitheia to peril.
Despair for a while, but not over-long,
For out of another world will help come.
Pateros will call them, three women, three men,
To right what went wrong and with courage defend.
Abilities they'll have, the Six are presented:
Companion, Scribe, Musician, Spy, Warrior, Intended.
Companion, you are loyal above everyone else,
Great friend of the Scribe, who will write words of wealth.
Musician, your music will find what is lost,
Making steps for the Spy, who will seek despite cost.
Warrior, your blade will always strike true,
Penetrating shadow, rending bone from sinew.
Intended, you are truly unique,
For your skills men have sought, and always will seek.
At the end of all things to the king you'll be wed,
Marked by a ring and the deepest color: red.
Now comings and goings will lead to the end,
To vanquish the Shadow, Alitheia to mend."

Rubidius nodded his head when he finished his recital, seemingly pleased with a job well done. "Yes," he said after a moment, "that should clear up everything."

Before Darcy could voice any questions about the wedding part, Perry sputtered to life.

"That doesn't explain anything," he protested. "I mean, don't get me wrong, this is awesome, but you all don't actually expect us to *stay* in Alitheia, do you?"

"Stay? Indefinitely? Goodness no." Rubidius shook his head as though he was discouraging a fly. "You will come and go. I may not be able to penetrate the deepest secrets of alchemy yet, but I think that Pateros has revealed to me *some* amount of wisdom in all my long years. Even if, that is, he has not been *seen*."

"What do you mean, 'he has not been seen'?" Darcy interrupted. "From everything I've heard so far about how we got here, it seemed to me like you all said this Pateros person brought us here. How could he do that if he's not around?"

"Just because he's not been *seen* doesn't mean that he's not *around*," Rubidius answered Darcy quickly. "He's not a person, or something that can be summoned at will." He seemed to think the very idea amusing and grinned in a serious sort of way.

"I don't care about any of that," Amelia said suddenly, standing so quickly that the songbird on her shoulder took flight for a moment. "This whole thing is preposterous. I listened to your poem, and it said that we're supposed to help you. We don't know how to help you. We're only kids! We have to get back to camp soon, or we're going to miss dinner and our parents will be worried."

"Amelia, I don't think that's a problem," Sam said quickly, trying to calm her friend. "Time doesn't work the same way when we are here. No matter how much time we spend in Alitheia, we *should* return to Cedar Cove at the exact time that we left it."

"*Still*," Amelia protested, "am I the only one who thinks this is totally crazy?" She looked from her right to her left.

"I think it's cool," Dean said, crossing his arms across his chest. "It's certainly better than going home for the rest of the summer."

"We'll still have to do that, Dean," Sam interjected, but he only shrugged.

"I agree," Lewis said quietly, breaking into a tentative smile. "I think this is a once-in-a-lifetime opportunity. I don't want to go back yet."

"I'm not ready to leave," Darcy said quickly.

"Me neither," Perry said.

Amelia whirled on him. "I thought you were on my side!"

"I never said I wanted to leave, I was just trying to figure out what they expected from us." Perry looked down the line to Darcy and smiled in a way that made her pulse quicken. "If Darcy says that time stands still while we are here, I think we should believe her. She was telling the truth about this place *existing*, after all."

Amelia's chin quavered slightly and Sam stood up to put an arm around her. "We don't mean to gang up on you," Sam said to her quietly. "But I think we ought to stay."

"What if I just decide to go back on my own? What would you do then?" Amelia demanded, shaking Sam off.

"I'm afraid that's out of the question," Yahto Veli spoke. He had been quiet up to now, and when he stepped forward, Darcy thought that his hair and skin looked a little darker than they had before. "The gateway closed after you came through. Torrin verified it just a few moments ago. You are all meant to be here, and here you will be until the gateway reopens."

"And when will that happen?" Amelia asked, her face white.

"When Pateros wills it."

"So, you're saying that we're stuck here?"

Veli hesitated. "In a manner of speaking . . . yes."

Chapter 17

Escape

Amelia opened her mouth to reply but was cut short by the loud cawing of a crow that flew into the circle and alighted on top of the pole. All eyes went to it, and tense silence fell on the assembly.

Tullin Ecclektos and the two princes stood and stared intensely at the bird as it continued to caw. "One of ours?" Tullin growled fiercely, his eyes going to Torrin.

Torrin stepped closer to the pole and drew an arrow from his quiver. "One of theirs," he replied grimly.

The assembly dissolved into chaos, and Darcy saw Torrin send an arrow flying at the crow, which took off to avoid being hit. Yahto Veli lifted her to the back of her stallion with a lurch.

"You can ride?" he shouted at her. His eyes were definitely darker.

She felt a swell of pride. "Yes," she answered.

"Follow me!" he cried, and he was off.

What about my friends? Sam! She looked around in panic and saw that each of her friends was being hurried away in a different direction. Tullin and the princes had disappeared without a trace.

"Lady Darcy!" Yahto Veli called to her from the trailhead out of the clearing. "To me! The others will find their way."

She dug her heels into the stallion's sides, feeling a thrill of exhilaration, and cantered toward Yahto Veli, already several yards up the path. She marveled at his speed, which she thought must have been a characteristic of his race, and followed as closely to him as she could.

He was leading her down a path, the very same path, it appeared, that existed at Cedar Cove. Except when he arrived at the fork, he took the left trail, leading her away from Gnome's Haven and toward, Darcy assumed, the point of the isthmus. Veli's hair floated ahead of her and the horse cantered comfortably as if it already knew this path. She kept her head tucked close to the horse's mane to avoid getting her hair entangled in branches.

Only once did Veli stop them, and when he did, he pressed a finger to his lips and stood as still as a statue. Darcy resisted the urge to hold her breath and instead breathed very carefully in and out, fearful of making any noise. She could hear more than one crow cawing somewhere close by, but the sound faded, and Veli relaxed.

He turned a grim smile on her and whispered, "They won't know whom to follow, and hopefully enough false trails will be laid to confuse them even further." He extended a hand to help her dismount and then spoke softly to her horse, his mouth just a few inches from its ear. "Lay a convincing trail, Hippondus, and don't get caught. Meet us at Sanditha."

Hippondus tossed his mane in response and bumped Darcy gently against her cheek before turning and cantering back the way they'd come. As Darcy watched, he gained speed and was quickly out of sight. She felt an enormous sense of loss, even greater than when she left Timmory every summer. She swallowed and looked at Veli. "He'll be okay?" she whispered.

"Don't worry; Hippondus can take care of himself. It is you that I am more concerned about." Veli took her hand. "Follow me; we are near the point."

Darcy let him tug her gently to the end of the path where it spilled out onto rocky shoals, and she only tripped on the front of her jerkin once. The low sun sent colorful swirls across the water that stretched on for miles. The island that was visible from Glorietta Bay was away off on her left side, and only open water spread out before her to the horizon. Veli seemed to be looking for something, and finally he said "Ah" very softly under his breath and drew Darcy out to the water's edge.

"Do you see that spot?" he asked her quietly, pointing to a very small black mark bobbing out on the water.

"Yes."

"That is where help awaits us. Can you swim?"

Darcy swallowed hard and looked up at him. *Can I swim?* "Some," she stammered. "But I . . . I'm not that good." *Please don't make me do this.* The serene and picturesque surface of the lake suddenly looked ominous and threatening. Darcy had harbored a fear of deep, dark water since she was a little girl and watched a special on the Discovery Channel about sharks. She doubted that she could swim all the way to the dot on the horizon, even without the encumbering jerkin.

"It's the only way," Veli said quietly. "And you will have help. See?" He pointed out at the lake again, and Darcy saw a ripple break to reveal a human head and shoulders. The woman in the water had gills on the sides of her neck, and she waved cheerfully at Darcy.

Darcy's heart stopped. "Is that . . . is that a mermaid?" she whispered hoarsely.

"In a manner of speaking. She won't let you drown."

Darcy turned enormous eyes on Yahto Veli. "Won't you need help?"

He winked at her. "No, narks are good swimmers."

Narks seem to be good at everything. Darcy sighed heavily and kicked her tennis shoes off in resignation. The idea of a half-fish, half-human creature helping her along was only a small comfort to her. Who knew what sorts of monsters lived in the lakes of Alitheia? But she didn't know what else to do. "Okay, I'm ready," she said.

Following right behind him, she scrambled over the scattered rocks, wincing whenever her bare feet struck sharp stone, and waded into the frigid water. She shivered convulsively. She had hoped that the water would be warmer in Alitheia than it was in her world, but she had hoped in vain. The rocks beneath her feet were slimy with algae, and before she knew it, she had completely lost her footing and splashed headlong into the shallows. She returned to the surface and spluttered, certain that her lips were already turning blue. With a great deal of surprise she tentatively licked the water clinging to her lips. Salt! In Alitheia, it appeared, Lake Huron was an ocean or a sea. She doggy paddled a few feet out until she could no longer touch the bottom and came face to face with the mermaid. The girl smiled in a friendly sort of way and Darcy started, for it was none other than the naiad from the council.

"Umi?" she queried through chattering teeth. "Was . . . that . . . y-your name?"

"Yes, lady," Umi replied. "I take this form when I need to. May I help you to the raft?"

"Y-yes," Darcy gasped. Her arms were already growing tired from treading water, and Yahto Veli was pulling away from them with long, confident strokes.

"Okay, then," Umi said. She stretched her bare left arm across Darcy's back and grasped her in her armpit. Her right hand took hold of Darcy's right forearm. "Just keep your head up, and I'll do the rest," she said cheerfully. With a flip of her fish tail, they were off.

Darcy kicked her feet slightly because it felt weird not to be doing anything, but in reality she was taking a free ride, and only the occasional swell of water hitting her in the face caused her any real discomfort. They moved at such a clipped rate that she forgot to be afraid, and she almost forgot to be cold. They kept pace with Yahto Veli, who was a very fast swimmer, and only pulled ahead of him when they drew near the raft.

Umi slowed them to a stop, and Darcy tried not to think about the fathoms of water beneath her. The naiad handed her up to the waiting nark on board, the operator of the raft, who was the female nark from the council. Umi waved and disappeared. Darcy couldn't tell if Umi swam away or if she simply dissolved into the water, but Darcy was left all alone with the female nark for the minute before Yahto Veli joined them.

The nark slung a heavy woolen blanket around Darcy's shoulders and pressed a steaming cup of some sort of broth into her hands as soon as she was seated on the cut logs. "Voitto Vesa, your ladyship," the nark said. "That's my name. It is an honor to serve you." Her voice was distinctly musical, like Veli's, but higher and more lilting. It reminded Darcy of Irish music.

Darcy tried to reply but was shaking too much to put together any sort of intelligent sentence, so she just tried to smile through the water streaming down her face. *I must look like a drowned rat,* she thought grimly. The female nark, Voitto Vesa, seemed to understand, though, and went to the side of the raft to help Yahto Veli aboard. The craft rocked for a moment and then settled back into a gentle swaying motion.

"Did you elude them?" Voitto Vesa asked quietly of Veli as she handed him another blanket.

"We did," he said cheerfully. "And I'm confident that the others did, as well. Did you have any trouble reaching the raft?"

Voitto Vesa shook her long blond tresses. "The escape plan seems to have confused them, as usual."

"Excellent." Yahto Veli went to the center of the broad raft where there was a small pot hanging over a smoking basin and poured himself a cup of the broth that Darcy had. "You should drink that, my lady," he said, turning to Darcy. "It will help you regain your strength and help you sleep. Are you hungry?"

Darcy nodded her head, still shivering. Yahto Veli, although wet, seemed much warmer than she was. Voitto Vesa handed her a loaf of some sort of flatbread and a hunk of cheese as Veli sat down next to her. Darcy took a tentative sip of the broth before eating the food. It tasted like chicken broth, but with a rich, buttery undercurrent; she liked it. Nibbling on a corner of the flatbread, she asked, "Will my friends be okay? I kind of feel responsible for them."

"I feel certain that they will be, my lady."

"When will I see them again?" She took another sip of broth and felt warmed to her very core.

"Later tonight. We are meeting everyone at the rendezvous at Sanditha, but we must wait until dark. It would draw suspicion to the community if too many people descended on it at one time. Darkness will be our ally." He patted her on the shoulder. "It is safe out here on the water; the Shadow cannot reach us here."

"The Shadow? What is that? Everybody keeps mentioning it."

Yahto Veli hesitated for a moment, shooting a look at Voitto Vesa, who stood holding the long oars near the center of the craft. "I think it would be best for Rubidius to tell you about it."

Darcy frowned and bit off some cheese. "Okay, well . . . what about this 'escape plan' you mentioned? What was that? How could you have an escape plan in place for us if you didn't even know we were coming?"

Yahto Veli laughed. "The escape plan wasn't for *you*, per se; we just worked the six of you into it. We never meet together without a plan of escape."

"Why? Isn't Tellius the prince?"

"Yes, of course, but he is prince in name only. Alitheia has not been under human control for many, many years."

"Why—" Darcy began, but Veli held up a hand to stop her.

"When it comes to the Shadow's dominion over this land, I defer to Rubidius. It is not my place to train any of the Six." He looked very serious, but he couldn't keep the twinkling out of his eye. "Do not fret, my lady, all of your questions will be answered in due time."

"So, why were you meeting together today? Do you always meet at the pole?"

"One question at a time." He laughed. "No, we do not always meet at the pole, but it was of special significance to our purpose this day. We met to discuss how long we were willing to wait for the Six to arrive." Here he frowned and looked down. "*Some* among us felt that we had waited long enough and wanted to move forward with the rebellion." He looked back up at her, shadow clouding his face and eyes. Or was he really turning darker? "Was it mere coincidence that Pateros called you to Alitheia this day? I think not." He smiled wanly at her. "It has been a long day. When you finish eating, I'll make up a mat for you, and you can sleep for a time."

"I'm not tired, honestly. I'd rather talk."

Veli smiled paternally and nudged her drink toward her mouth. "You will be tired. Just finish your broth."

No way am I going to fall asleep. This is all too exciting! Darcy thought, but she obediently went back to eating. By the time she drained the last drop of broth, her eyes were hanging low. She yawned and stretched. Her clothes were beginning to feel stiff.

"Let's hang your garment, my lady," Voitto Vesa interrupted her thoughts. "I have some more appropriate clothing for you. This red jerkin draws far too much attention."

There was a splash off the side of the raft and Darcy jumped. Vesa smiled. "Veli will swim a short distance away so that you can change."

"He didn't have to get wet again," Darcy protested, feeling bad.

"It's okay, narks dry quickly, and Veli enjoys swimming. Here." She helped Darcy pull off the long red jerkin and then instructed her to strip off everything else, underwear and all.

Darcy obeyed her directions as quickly as possible while Voitto Vesa made herself busy over the cook pot. The cold air nipped at her exposed skin, and she was only too happy to slip into the clothes provided for her. The undergarments were strangely shaped and felt like linen, and the long brown dress she pulled on over the slip was roughly woven and scratchy. It felt like wool. Darcy wrinkled her nose a little, but felt much warmer than she had all evening.

“May I keep my bracelet?” she asked, holding the charm bracelet out for Vesa to see.

“I think it would be best if we kept it with your clothes from your home world.” Vesa took it gently from her and added it to the bundle that contained her shorts, tank top, and under-things. “Don’t worry; you will get it back before you return.” Voitto Vesa smiled, dazzling Darcy with her perfect teeth, and then whistled softly. The sound of subdued splashing announced the return of Yahto Veli, and he climbed aboard the vessel with a hand-up from Vesa.

“You look like a true Alitheian.” He smiled at Darcy as she stifled a yawn behind her hand. “And it looks like that broth is working.”

Yahto Veli laid out a folded blanket for her and she lay back on it sleepily, one arm folded behind her head. She stared groggily up at the sunset-streaked sky, and the last thing she remembered before falling asleep was the hushed, musical murmurings of the two narks.

Chapter 18
Rendezvous

Darcy cracked her eyes open. It was very dark and something had shaken her shoulder. For a second she thought that she was in her bed back home, but that couldn't be because she didn't have a waterbed. She squeezed her eyes shut and yawned, her ears popping slightly as they always did whenever she yawned very wide.

"My lady," a soft female voice said in her ear. "It's time to go."

Suddenly it all came back to her: Cedar Cove, the journey into Alitheia, the council at the pole . . . a smile twitched at the corner of her mouth and she propped herself up on her elbows. The night sky above her was so full of stars that she felt that she could reach out and grab one. They filled the sky from horizon to horizon and Darcy could only tell where the shore was because there was a black, irregular smudge on the right horizon that contained no stars at all. The raft bobbed quiescently on the waves, and the partial moon was reflected in ripples on the surface of the lake—*or sea*, she corrected herself mentally. The black smudge that was the shore looked closer than it had before she had fallen asleep, and Darcy wondered where they would be coming ashore.

A quiet hiss and a pop preceded a sudden glare of light, and Darcy closed her eyes. When she opened them again, the light didn't look so bright, and she saw that Yahto Veli was waving a lantern toward shore. The light shone out across the water, but Veli's back was deeply cloaked in shadow. Another light flared up on the shore and blinked twice. "They are ready for us. About time," he muttered. He sounded ill-tempered and Darcy sat upright, a little taken aback. During the day Yahto Veli had never sounded anything less than chipper, even when addressing difficult matters.

"Excuse me, Veli?" Darcy said quietly. He didn't turn. "Veli?" She tried again. "Yahto Veli?"

The nark finally swung around, and when the light illuminated his features, Darcy shrieked.

A warm hand swiftly covered her mouth. "Sssshhhh," Voitto Vesa hushed her. "It's all right. We mustn't make too much noise. It's only Yahto."

Darcy took deep, gulping breaths through her nose and nodded beneath Voitto Vesa's hand. The female nark released her and moved into her line of sight so that Darcy could see her face. The same strange phenomenon had happened to Voitto Vesa, as well.

Instead of white-blond hair, alabaster skin, and piercing blue eyes, both narks now had black hair, tan skin, and their eyes had changed shades as well. She looked from one to the other and gulped twice. Yahto Veli was scowling at her. "Y-you-you're different?" she stammered.

"I'm sorry," Voitto Vesa said. "We should have explained to you what would happen when the sun went down. Sometimes we forget that not everybody knows what a nark is." Vesa dipped her head thoughtfully and then said, "All of our physical bodies contain two narks: a night nark, and a day nark, reflected by our physical change."

"Are you the same person?" Darcy breathed.

Voitto Vesa tipped her head to the side. "Yes and no. Technically, I have not met you before. I am Voitto, a night nark. During the day I go to sleep and Vesa wakes up, the day nark. We have the same likes, dislikes, and interests, but separate consciousnesses and slightly different personalities. At least," she paused and shot a disgruntled look at Yahto Veli, "that's how it works for most narks. Vesa can keep secrets from me if she chooses, just as I can keep secrets from her."

"This is like multiple personality disorder," Darcy muttered.

"I'm sorry?"

"Never mind. So . . . when the sun comes up, you will go away?"

"I'll go to sleep," she corrected her gently. "I close my eyes and quickly communicate to Vesa anything she needs to know, and then I sleep and she opens her eyes. I'm not aware of anything that goes on during the day unless she tells me about it. In fact," she laughed softly, "I have never even seen the sun, except in images that Vesa sends me. I've seen the early light that precedes the sun, but the moment it breaks the horizon, I can no longer stay awake."

Darcy felt a pang of sadness for her. Imagine never seeing the sun! "Do you ever wish that you could switch places with her?"

"And miss all this?" Voitto swept her hands at the expanse of stars. "Never."

"So . . . you're *Voitto*, and he's *Yahto*?"

"That's right. But it's common for narks to go by their double name, as well. It is sometimes difficult for humans to remember which of us is which." She winked at Darcy.

"If you're quite finished," Yahto interrupted them, "I *would* like to reach shore *sometime* this night. Of course, we'll probably all be caught and killed anyway." He harrumphed loudly and covered the lantern with a blanket so that only a narrow halo of light illuminated the planking of the raft.

Voitto chuckled quietly as she leapt to her feet and took up the oars, which were hinged to be rowed like a row boat, but from a standing position. Darcy scrambled to her feet, much less gracefully than Voitto did, and went to the female nark's side.

"Why's he so grumpy?" she whispered to Voitto. "Veli isn't like that at all!"

"Well, Yahto Veli is something of an enigma in our community. While most narks retain almost the same personality from night to day, Yahto switches on and off like a lantern. During the day you couldn't find a more optimistic nark than Veli. But at night," she grinned and shook her head, "well, as you can see, he's less than pleasant to be around. Unfailingly pessimistic, Yahto is, but he is still a good nark. At his heart he is every bit as good as Veli. He just, in his own words, looks at things from a more 'practical' angle. Stick around him long enough and you'll learn to love him. *Both* of him." The oars dipped and splashed in rhythm beneath her words and the shoreline rapidly drew closer.

Yahto ignored both of them on the way to shore and Darcy tried to relax, but she felt herself shivering again. The air had definitely cooled off even more with the onset of night. "What time is it?" she asked Voitto through quavering lips.

"Almost the breaking hour," Voitto replied, looking skyward.

The breaking hour? Does she mean midnight? Darcy looked up as well, but couldn't see anything to indicate a specific time. Roger was into astronomy, but Darcy had never cared much about it. Maybe if she had lived in a place like this—a place far away from light pollution where every star was visible to the naked eye—maybe then she would have taken an interest in it. But she didn't even know if it would have done her any good in Alitheia; maybe the stars were different here. She yawned again and wrapped her arms around her chest. Her woolen dress was warm, but it didn't act as a windbreaker, and it was jumper style so her arms were only covered in the linen sleeves of the slip. Goose bumps ran up and down her arms and legs, and she yawned again. Why was it that being cold always made her yawn? She shook her head and tried to focus on what was coming.

She could hear the lapping of water on a beach now, and she stumbled when all of a sudden the raft ran aground. The lantern on the shore hissed to life again and a man whispered urgently, "Yahto? Voitto? Are you there? Is the king's intended safe?"

There's that phrase again.

"We're here," Yahto replied to the man on the beach. "How many of the others have arrived?"

"Half. We're waiting on two more after you."

Darcy heard a splash and suddenly the man was at the side of the raft. He wore dark clothes, but he had a pleasant face. He held out his arms. "If it pleases your ladyship, there's no sense in your getting wet."

Darcy hesitated, but Voitto pushed her forward. "Go on. His name is Boden; he'll carry you ashore."

Great, Darcy thought, but she obediently stepped up to him and felt him sweep her into his arms. Her own arms instinctively went around his neck, and she tried not to cling too tightly as he splashed through the shallows to the beach. He smelled of earth and soot, and he placed her gently on the sand, as though she was a fragile vase.

"I'll be right back, my lady." He left her for a moment to help Voitto to shore, but Yahto splashed to the beach on his own. Once they were gathered on the sand, Yahto with a bundle of belongings from the raft over his shoulder, Boden told them that he would take care of the raft. "You know where to go," he said covertly to Yahto, who nodded in response.

Without another word, Yahto turned and started off through the sand. Darcy struggled to keep up, but Voitto walked behind her so she didn't feel too exposed. It was very dark, as they had left the lantern on the raft, and Darcy didn't know how Yahto could tell where he was going, but his confident pace never slackened.

They crossed a wide expanse of sand, wider than the beach at Glorietta Bay, so Darcy knew that they were someplace different. Pretty soon Darcy felt gravelly rocks underfoot. She winced, but tried to keep up, until she finally stubbed her big toe and let out a gasp of pain.

"Yahto, wait a moment," Voitto called softly. "Do you not have shoes, my lady? I'm afraid I neglected to bring any for you."

Darcy shook her head. "I left them on the shoals where we entered the water," she whispered back to Voitto. "They would have been really heavy when we swam."

She heard a sharp intake of breath. "You left them where?" Yahto hissed. "Veli didn't tell me anything about that!"

"I-I don't think he knew . . ." Darcy trailed off, concerned.

"It's okay, Yahto," Voitto soothed. "If they find them, it won't tell them anything other than that we took to the water."

"Yes, but that jeopardizes us using that technique in the future," he growled back.

"It's neither here nor there." Voitto sounded a little impatient now and reached down to un-strap her sandals. "Take my sandals, Lady Darcy. I can walk barefoot just fine."

"But—"

"Really. Narks are very tough."

Darcy could hear the smile in Voitto's voice and so she reluctantly accepted the sandals. They were a little large on her, but they stayed on once she'd tightened the straps, and she knew that her aching feet would thank her.

She stood and Yahto started moving again without so much as a backward glance. They left gravel after a few minutes and started picking their way through dense forest growth. Darcy was getting downright tired of being hit in the face with leaves and tree branches and having to untangle her hair every few feet by the time Yahto finally halted. Night noises closed in around them, and Darcy wondered silently what Yahto Veli was doing. When they had been still for a whole minute, Yahto suddenly whispered, "Pateros trisopo."

There was the sound of a great rustling in the underbrush and a slight creaking as a trap door of some sort was raised. A very dim light illuminated a tunnel opening up at their feet and an auburn-haired young man grinned at them from the hole. "Quickly!" He waved them in.

They descended into the tunnel, stepping down hard-pressed stairs cut into the earth, and the trapdoor snapped closed behind them. The redhead waved cheerfully at Darcy and gestured down the stairs. "They're waiting for you in the great room," he said quietly. "I have to wait here for the others. Just two more!" He looked very excited.

"Thank you, Bayard," Voitto said warmly.

The stairs descended for about fifty feet. Torches were hung in brackets on the close, earth-packed walls, and Darcy struggled against her claustrophobia. She didn't have to fight it for very long, however, because once they reached the bottom, the tunnel opened up considerably, and torches were placed much closer together than in the stairway.

Yahto led them wordlessly down the tunnel and Darcy peered curiously into dark doorways that they passed on the right and left, but her attention was mostly riveted on the glow at the end of the hall.

They stepped into the great room, as Bayard had called it, and Darcy felt warmth on her face for only a moment before she was engulfed in a bone crushing, blond-haired hug that was so reminiscent of her arrival at Cedar Cove that she almost forgot where she was for a moment.

"I'm so glad you're here!" Sam cried as Darcy pried herself loose and grinned wearily at her.

"Did you have a hard time of it? I wish I could have gone with you, but Fylla told me everybody had to go separate directions to confuse the bad guys."

"Fylla?" Darcy asked.

"The dryad." Sam waved off the question and dove into more explanation. "We were the first to arrive and I've been waiting for you for *hours.* Lewis and Dean went to bed about an hour ago, and they told me that I should, too, but I told them that I just *couldn't* until you arrived. We're still waiting for Perry and Amelia."

Darcy looked around the room. The cave was high-ceilinged and brown-walled, but comfortable enough. Lanterns hung instead of torches, and a roaring fire crackled behind a large grate. Roughly upholstered chairs were scattered throughout, and a massive table capable of seating at least twenty people took up the center of the room. Voitto and Yahto had settled at the table and seemed to be discussing something important as Voitto kept shaking her head and pointing at him. A few other people stood around the room in pairs of two and three. Darcy didn't recognize anybody else from the council.

"Who are these people?" she whispered out of the corner of her mouth.

"Members of the rebellion," Sam replied. "I met them all, but I can't remember any of their names. Fylla didn't stay; she said she had to get back to her tree. I think the rest of them are going to have another council yet tonight, but they told me we don't have to be there."

Darcy nodded distractedly and yawned for the umpteenth time that night. It was warm and comfortable in the cave, and she was feeling very sluggish after all the excitement. "Are you going to stay up and wait for Amelia and Perry?" she asked through another yawn.

"I think so. What about you?"

Darcy shook her head. "I'm too tired. I only got a couple hours of sleep on the raft."

"The *raft*?" Sam's eyes got big.

"I'll tell you about it some other time." Darcy headed off the questions she knew were coming. "Where do I go to sleep?"

"I'll show you; we're all sharing a room—the girls, that is. The boys are sleeping together, as well." Sam started to lead Darcy back down the tunnel and stopped at a doorway with a curtain in front of it. Soft light played out on the dirt floor as Sam swung the curtain aside so Darcy could pass through. "They made all sorts of fuss about how sorry they were that we would have to share a room . . . something about space being really limited here. I told them not to worry about it. I share a room with Abby back home."

Three lumpy mattresses lay at intervals along the curved wall of the circular room, and a round table in the center held three linen nightgowns, a hair brush, mirror, bowl of water, and . . . "Is that a chamber pot?" Darcy wrinkled her nose at Sam, who giggled.

"Yeah, I think it is. Well, we can't exactly expect them to have bathrooms in a place like this."

Darcy sighed and started to tug out of her brown jumper. With a little help from Sam, she got the ties in the back undone, and then Sam left her alone to change into her nightgown and get ready for bed.

Darcy collapsed on the nearest mattress and stared at the torch on the wall. Soft feathers cushioned her from the floor, and her pillow smelled like honey. With a feeling of deep contentment, she watched the flames dancing against the wall. Here in this cozy cave it was difficult to imagine anything sinister lurking in the woods outside. She closed her eyes to sleep and did not awake until morning.

Chapter 19

The Lost Cottage

"Should we wake her up? She's been sleeping for hours."

"I don't know. What time is it?"

"Do they use clocks in Alitheia?"

"I wonder what our parents are thinking right now."

"They don't know we're gone, remember? We don't have to worry about that."

"Oh yeah."

The harried whispers fell silent, and Darcy groaned and stretched her arms over her head. "What are you guys whispering about?" she rasped. Her voice sounded like it hadn't been used in days.

"She's awake!"

"I'll go get her some breakfast." Bare feet pattered on the floor and Darcy could hear the soft swoosh of someone pushing through the curtain.

Darcy opened her eyes, expecting to see the bright rays of morning, but the room looked almost no different than it had when she went to bed the night before. *I suppose that's a product of sleeping in a cave underground*, she told herself. Of course there wouldn't be windows. The torch on the wall looked fresh and burned a little higher than the one before it, and Darcy leaned forward to prop her arms on her raised knees, yawning furiously.

"How long did I sleep?"

"Ten hours at least," Sam responded. Darcy's mattress depressed heavily to the side as Sam plopped down next to her. "Vesa said that you were probably still feeling the effects of the broth they gave you. I wish I'd gotten some. I was so excited I could hardly close my eyes!"

"Will you hand me the brush?" Darcy extended her hand as Sam retrieved it for her. She began to work the brush through her long tangles, wincing slightly with each stroke. "So, Amelia and Perry made it here okay?"

"Amelia showed up not long after you went to bed, but Perry didn't arrive until this morning. He said that he and Ulfred—that's one of the men from the council—spent the night at a cottage in some village. He seems pretty happy about being here this morning, so I think he had a comfortable enough night.

"You didn't even blink when Amelia and I came in. She wanted to wake you up and talk to you about everything, but I wouldn't let her."

Darcy grimaced and lowered the brush. Her long brown hair hung in a curtain on one side of her face. "Is she still mad about all this?" She lowered her voice; she didn't know when Amelia would return.

"I don't think so." Sam hesitated. "It's just that . . . Amelia has so many plans for her future, that I think she's afraid of doing something to mess them up. And, well, she's really something of a homebody. She doesn't like to travel much unless she's with her family. I don't know what she's going to do when she goes off to college."

A rustle at the doorway drew their attention, Darcy aware that her ears were red. Amelia stood holding a tray of food. She wore a similar dress as Darcy's and her shoulder-length sandy hair was pulled back into double braids. Her face fell a little when she saw Darcy and Sam's guilty expressions. She moved into the room and placed the tray on the low round table in the middle of the cave.

"Were you talking about me?" she asked quietly. Her gaze flashed accusingly at Darcy.

"No," Darcy said at the same time Sam said, "Yes, but it wasn't anything bad!"

"Um . . . okay, yeah. What Sam said," Darcy amended quickly. Then she added, "I just don't want you to be mad at me for all of this." She swept her hands around the room and bit her lip.

Amelia took in and let out a deep breath very slowly and sat on a three-legged stool by the table. "At first I was mad—really mad. But then . . ." She trailed off and her eyes focused on a spot on the wall. "I realized that this is important, us being here. I mean, how many people get to have an experience like this? Who knew that magic was real, that other worlds existed?" She smiled, flashing her perfectly straight teeth. "I know I'll miss my family, but if what you say about the time thing is true, then they won't even know that we've been gone." She pushed the tray of food toward Darcy and stood. "Sometimes I just need to sleep on things. I'm going to go see what the boys are up to." She waved and passed back through the curtain.

Darcy consumed the breakfast with relish, even though she wasn't normally an oatmeal fan, and dressed for the day with Sam's help. She put the same brown dress back on, not sure if there were any other clothes available for them. She and Sam braided each other's hair, Darcy's into a single, long braid, and Sam's into twin french braids, and left their room to join the crowd of people in the great hall.

They entered the hall unnoticed by everyone except Lewis, who sidled over to stand beside them by the doorway. Amelia sat at the table by herself, watching a cluster of people moving awkwardly together in the corner.

"They're doing morning forms," Lewis whispered to the two of them. "I'm glad I'm not required to do this."

"They" were Perry and Dean, who, along with a handful of other young men, were stretching and balancing in strange and awkward contortions that changed every few seconds. Darcy watched as the two boys tried to imitate the young men they were with, occasionally earning a sharp rap on an offending body part from a man carrying a stick who called out instructions with every change. Perry seemed to handle the balancing techniques better than Dean, but Dean more easily swept into the fluid stretches.

"I guess it's some sort of warrior training," Lewis continued. "They said there was no time like the present to start training Dean and Perry, but that I wouldn't be doing a lot of fighting, so I was exempt." He grinned at Sam and adjusted his glasses. "They've been at it for over an hour. The instructor said they usually start at daybreak, but he allowed people to sleep in because of the late council last night."

Darcy watched them with humor for a few minutes and then looked around the room. Some people were sitting at the table talking or eating, and others were reading books or practicing swordplay with wooden swords. It was such a strange assortment in one room that she found she didn't know whom to watch first. She went back to observing the men doing their forms. Perry, Dean, and Lewis were clothed very similarly to the girls, except that instead of brown woolen jumpers, they wore vests and trousers of the same material over white linen shirts with sleeves that puffed slightly at the wrists. They wore leather belts and boots, and Perry's sword and scabbard leaned against the far wall. "What happened to our jerkins?" she said to Sam, who was watching Perry with rapt attention.

"Our whatsits?" Sam replied distractedly.

"You know, our jerkins. Those colorful garments they gave us yesterday. Voitto Vesa said she was going to hang mine, but she never gave it back to me."

"Oh! I don't know. Fylla took mine and did something with it. I think they were mostly ceremonial. I still have my bag, though." Sam tugged the small leather pouch out of a pocket and held it up for Darcy to see. "That reminds me." She turned her full attention on Darcy. "Can I see your ring? The one Tellius gave you?"

"Oh, sure." Darcy had almost forgotten about the heavy gold ring that graced her left thumb, and as she held it up, the amber stars sparkled even in the dim light.

"It's beautiful. Look at it, Lewis." She pulled him forward by his sleeve. He glanced at it and shrugged, uninterested. "What do you think it means?" Sam breathed.

"I don't know. Everybody else's stuff seems to have a purpose, but mine is just a piece of jewelry."

"I don't know what my bag is for," Sam reminded her, swinging the light leather pouch in front of her face.

"Yeah, but still . . . I'm sure it *has* a purpose."

"Probably," Sam said optimistically, tucking it into her pocket. "They talked about us for a long time last night," she said quietly after a moment. "I wasn't trying to listen, but sometimes it was hard not to hear."

"Who?" Darcy frowned at her.

"The people at the late council. Some of them said they wanted to storm the palace right away, while others argued that we need to be 'trained up' and that our abilities haven't even been revealed yet."

"Our *abilities?*"

"Yeah. I think it has something to do with how we each have a title. You know," she pointed at herself, "the companion," She pointed at Lewis, "the scribe, etc." She gazed around the crowded room as if looking for someone and then pointed. "There, that Rubidius guy. He was definitely there, and his side seemed to win out."

Darcy looked over to see the old alchemist snoozing in an armchair, his mass of curly hair, red near the bottom, rose and fell on his chest as he breathed.

"And what was *his side?*" Lewis asked Sam.

"For us to receive training before any action is taken. He said that Pateros is not 'in the habit of sending people to battle unprepared.' "

To battle? Darcy shivered.

"Good morning." A warm hand on her shoulder caused Darcy to jump and turn. Happy blue eyes stared down at her from a pleasant face.

"Good morning, Yahto—I mean, Veli."

He laughed good-naturedly. "I know what you mean, either way." His eyes took on a teasing gleam. "What did you think of my counterpart last night?"

"Um . . . he was all right."

He winked at her. "I'll tell him you said so. Come, there are many who would like to meet you, all of you." He swept out his arm to include Sam and Lewis.

As Yahto Veli steered them toward the front of the room, the forms instructor in the corner swept his staff up in front of his face and called out to the group, "Hup! Breathing exercises, two minutes."

Amelia joined them, sticking close to Sam's side, and Perry and Dean popped up a few minutes later, sweat pouring down their faces.

"That was *brutal,*" Perry said, scrabbling to reattach his sword belt around his waist. "I should tell my soccer coach about some of those exercises."

Dean merely nodded and mopped his forehead with a sleeve.

"Esteemed comrades and fellows in arms," Veli said loudly, sweeping his arms out. Conversation ceased around the room and Rubidius gave a sharp snort in his chair, blinking bleary eyes open. Those who had been at the council waved or smiled cheerfully, but the rest of the people looked at them curiously.

"Here I present to you the Six." A hushed murmur ran around the room. It appeared that some of the people didn't know about them yet. "The scribe." Veli squeezed Lewis's shoulder and he waved, growing red in the cheeks. "The companion." Sam curtsied. *Where'd she learn to do that?* "The musician, the spy, the warrior, and the king's intended." Darcy settled on a short wave like Lewis's and tried not to look anybody in the eyes. *Everybody's staring at me.*

"This is an important time for us, as I need not remind you," Yahto Veli continued. "All of you will play important roles in the protection and training of these six young people before you today."

"Training?" a woman at the back called out. "How much longer do we have to wait?"

"Long enough for the Six to be prepared. They are new to this world and unversed in our opposition and their abilities. We cannot expect this to be a short or easy process."

"But the Shadow already knows they're here!" another man declared. "His blasted crows told him everything he needed to know."

"All the more reason to wait," Veli continued in a measured tone. "He will be expecting an immediate attack, and we mustn't give it to him."

"Why'd Pateros send children?" A middle-aged man at the table scowled at them.

"Irrelevant!" Rubidius declared, rising imperiously from his chair. He came to stand before them, facing the crowd and staring around as though daring anybody else to challenge Yahto Veli again. "If you're finished asking foolish questions, we can move on!" he thundered, and then he softened. "This is a time for celebration. What is another year of preparation after a hundred years of waiting?"

Amelia turned to Sam and Darcy behind Rubidius's back. *A year?* she mouthed to them. Darcy shrugged.

"The council decided last night: the children will be trained before any direct action is taken against Tselloch. Now that you all know their faces, remember to keep them in your thoughts and prayers. This will not be an easy time for them, and above all else, we must keep them safe until the time is right. Their training will take place here at Sanditha until arrangements can be made to move them to the stronghold at Paradeisos."

Silence followed his statements, and Darcy noticed with pleasure that more people looked encouraging than sour. Bayard, the auburn-haired youth who had let them into the hideout the night before, smiled and waved at them from the back of the room. Several people stood and made their way forward to wring the hands of the Six and tell them how happy they were to meet them. A few came close just to stare at them. One very elderly woman took Darcy's hand gently and kissed it, weeping profusely.

When all who wished to had come forward, Rubidius turned to face the Six and clasped his hands in front of him. "Well, that's that," he declared. "Let's be off, shall we?" Without another word he turned on his heel and marched toward the tunnel opening.

"Go on," Yahto Veli encouraged them. "You are in good hands."

With Darcy in the lead, the six teenagers followed the alchemist into the tunnel and down past their sleeping quarters. Rubidius stopped at a doorway near the foot of the stairs and held aside a curtain. "After you," he said, ushering them inside.

Darcy stepped into the room beyond the curtain and gasped. Instead of a dreary dark cave, the doorway opened up to the inside of a quaint cottage with stone-cut walls and a thatched roof. A warm fire crackled behind a grate over which hung a large bubbling cauldron with strange metal contraptions sticking out of it. A round, wooden table graced the center of the living space, and a log bed stood on one wall, complete with a colorful quilt and throw pillows. There were too many interesting instruments and objects scattered throughout to take them all in at once, but most surprising of all were two curtained windows on the far wall of the room. Cheerful sunlight poured in through the glass panes, and a cricket beat against one of them.

"How—" Darcy spun around and blinked. Instead of a curtain in the doorway, Rubidius was closing a sturdy wooden door that was curved on the top like a door to an English cottage.

"Aren't we underground?" Perry asked, moving to look out the window.

"We *were* underground," Rubidius corrected him. "I never go anywhere without my front door."

"But . . . how . . ." Amelia sputtered.

"It was really very simple," Rubidius said, waving his hand as if shooing away a fly. "An easy matter of connecting the doorway of the room in the caves to the front door of my cottage."

"Is it safe?" Sam asked, looking nervously at the windows. "I thought we were supposed to be in hiding."

"Of course it's safe." Rubidius sounded a little affronted. "Do you think I would take you somewhere unsafe?"

"But where exactly *are* we?"

Rubidius fumbled with his beard and made a great deal of harrumphing sounds before he finally stammered, "Well, now, to be truthful, that is, I don't *exactly* know. I've been taking my front door with me for so many years that I rather *forgot* where I left my cottage."

Dean sniggered slightly, and Perry looked exasperated. "You forgot where you *left* your cottage? How can you *leave* a cottage anywhere? Don't you remember where it was built?"

"Now, there's no need to get lippy, young lord. It's rather more complicated than all that. You see, I used to take my entire cottage with me whenever I travelled, but as I grew older, it became rather cumbersome. Once I figured out the handy spell that would allow me to leave my cottage in one place and only take the door with me, why, you can't blame me for doing that instead, can you? It is a great deal lighter." He looked around as if expecting them to sympathize with him. "At any rate," he said when they only gave him confused looks, "I can't remember the last blasted location that I left my cottage. So there you have it; it's lost. But it's neither here nor there because I *haven't* lost my front door, so I can always get to it when I need to."

"Why don't you just go outside and look around a bit?" Lewis pointed to a door tucked in the back of the cottage by the foot of the bed.

"Oh, well now, that *would* be dangerous. To exit that way would destroy the particular cloaking spell that I put on my cottage."

"Cloaking spell?" Darcy asked weakly, trying to keep up with the magician's ramble.

Rubidius snorted. "Well, of course I put a cloaking spell on it. I couldn't just leave it in full view for anyone who might amble by. That would be truly idiotic."

"But losing your cottage isn't?" Perry muttered to Dean, who quickly turned his laugh into a coughing fit.

Darcy frowned at the boys and asked Rubidius, "How does the cloaking spell work?"

"Ah! An intelligent question, at last. It's very rudimentary, my dear. The cottage is invisible to all unfriendly eyes, so long as I only use the front door to come and go. And *that*, in turn, only works because I placed the door removal spell on that particular entrance. To exit out the back door or any of the windows would break the spell."

"Couldn't you just go outside, look around, and then redo the spell?" Lewis asked.

"It's not as simple as that. A properly placed cloaking spell takes a great deal of time and energy to complete. Not to mention that I haven't any idea what might have happened in the vicinity of my cottage since the time that I lost it. For all I know, it may now sit directly in enemy territory. We wouldn't want to go blundering out in the middle of that! No, no . . . we must not use the back door unless it is a case of extreme emergency. Now." He clapped his hands together as he often did and gestured for them to take seats around the table. "I am expecting someone to come and talk with you, but until she arrives, I think we should get down to the business of discerning your talents." He busily pulled out chairs for the girls.

"What are all those instruments?" Darcy asked him as he went to the fire and moved the smoking cauldron to a wooden hot pad.

"Another time, dear, another time," he said dismissively. "Now—" But he was distracted by a soft knock on the door.

"Ah." His eyebrows rose. "She's early."

The door creaked open and the elderly woman who had been at the council at the pole stepped through. She was tall and thin, with a long silver braid wrapped around the crown of her head. She closed the door behind her and looked at them, kind hazel eyes serenely taking them in.

Without warning, Amelia gasped and stood, her chair scraping noisily across the cobbled floor. She went pale and her finger shook as she pointed it across the room. "*You're* Eleanor Stevenson!"

CHAPTER 20

HISTORY

Darcy blinked and looked closer. She did indeed bear an uncanny resemblance to the woman in the picture at the rec hall. But didn't they find Eleanor Stevenson dead in the woods at Cedar Cove? If she was dead there, how could she be alive here? Her initial question was answered almost immediately as the old woman smiled and moved forward to take Amelia's outstretched hand.

"It's very nice to meet you," the old woman said pleasantly, folding Amelia's hand into a warm handshake. "I haven't heard a Midwest accent in years uncounted!" She smiled and prompted, "And you are?"

"Amelia Bennet," Amelia breathed. She sat down hard when Eleanor Stevenson released her hand and moved around the table, gathering introductions.

"Lewis Acres."

"Perry Marks."

"Samantha Palm."

"Dean Stewart."

"And you, dear?" Eleanor held out her hand to Darcy.

"Darcy Pennington, ma'am."

"Oh! A Southern girl?"

"No, ma'am. I'm from Chicago, but my parents grew up in Birmingham, Alabama. I was born there—in Birmingham, I mean."

"Is that right?" The woman's eyes alighted on Darcy's ring for the briefest of moments, and Darcy thought she saw a look of pity cross the woman's face. But when she looked up, she was smiling once more. "I bet that you all are wishing that somebody would explain all of this to you."

Darcy looked around the table at her friends. Would it be polite to agree with her? They opted for silence.

Eleanor pulled a chair up to the table and sat down across from Darcy, between Dean and Perry. "I, like all Alitheians, have been waiting for you for a long time," she began with the air of somebody starting a long discourse. "But I have more reason than most to want to see you before I die. As you have guessed, I am from your world, but I have lived in Alitheia these fifty years."

"But you're dead!" Sam sputtered. "In our world . . . they found your body in the woods."

A shadow crossed over the elderly woman's face, and she looked down, resting her chin on her intertwined fingers. "It is, then, as I knew it would be," she said very quietly, almost to herself. She looked back up, and her eyes glistened with tears. "I was young—only nineteen at the time. It was my second summer at Cedar Cove, and I was working staff because my family was very poor and couldn't afford to send me to camp. I was walking one day, not following any path, just wandering through the woods. I always kept the lake on my left so I wouldn't get lost. I had recently seen a great bear, and I wanted to find it again. This particular day, as I was walking alone, I met him."

"Who?" Sam whispered.

"Pateros. He said he was waiting for me."

"Pateros can travel between worlds? Did he find a gateway?"

"Pateros does not need gateways to travel between the worlds, dear girl, no . . . he was just . . . there. He spoke to me. He told me dreadful news. Terrible news."

"What did he tell you?" Amelia asked, engrossed.

"He told me that I was going to die." Eleanor Stevenson closed her eyes as she recalled her tale. "I'd had headaches for months, bad headaches that were getting worse and worse. He told me that there was a problem inside my skull . . . he called it a mass, and said that it was next to my brain. There was no hope for it; I would die within six months."

Sam gasped and put her hand over her mouth, but Eleanor smiled at her. "It's all right, my dear, this is ancient history, and Pateros provided me with a solution and a choice. He told me that I could either go home to die with my family, or I could go with him to a new world—a world called Alitheia, where my illness would be gone. I had special talents, he said, that belonged in that world."

"What sort of talents?" Perry asked.

Eleanor looked at him and her eyes sparkled. "Magic. But we'll talk more about that in a moment."

"So you decided to go to Alitheia?" Amelia's tone sounded slightly accusatory. "Didn't you think about how your family would feel? Didn't you *want* to see them again?"

Eleanor sobered again. "Yes. I did. I wept, and Pateros waited patiently. But you must understand that my family was *very* poor. My father fought in the Second World War, and he returned home a broken man. He had difficulty holding down a job, and at the time he had been out of work for several months. My mother did what she could to help, but I was the eldest of six children, and there simply wasn't enough money to provide for us all. They could not have afforded my medical care, and I knew that it would crush their spirits to watch me, their daughter, die slowly in their house. It was for them, for the family that was so dear to me, that I chose Alitheia. When I asked Pateros how I would get there, he replied that I would simply fall asleep. He said he would preserve my body until it was found."

"They named the rec hall after you," Perry said abruptly.

"Did they now? How nice."

"Are we dead, too? Back home, I mean," Lewis choked out.

Eleanor laughed. "Goodness, no. You certainly have many comings and goings yet to undergo before the end, and much to do." Her eyes flashed to Darcy.

Rubidius cleared his throat loudly from his armchair near the fire.

"Ah, yes, speaking of which, perhaps we should tell you what it is that you will be doing, at least what we know of it. The council decided that I, along with Rubidius, would instruct you. You see, I have something in common with both you and Rubidius. They thought our common heritage would unite us. Would you like to join us at the table, Rubidius?"

"Harrumph! Inviting me to my own table! I can contribute very well from over here, thank you."

Eleanor didn't seem perturbed by the alchemist's gruff manner. "As you wish," she said serenely. "Why don't we start with questions." She raised her eyebrows and looked around at them.

Just as Darcy opened her mouth to ask what the "king's intended" meant, Sam quickly said, "What is the Shadow?"

"An excellent place to start," Rubidius chimed in from the chair. "Eleanor?"

"Yes, I quite agree with Rubidius. Perhaps it is best to begin with whom you are to help deliver Alitheia from. Let's see, where to begin . . ." She tapped a long finger on her chin.

"Well, you *have* to go back to the beginning," Rubidius said.

"That's right. Alitheia. As you all know, this world is not your own. It contains parallels in certain places, such as Cedar Cove, but outside of Cedar Cove, the geography is quite different."

"Lake Huron's not a lake here," Darcy chimed in. "It's a sea. I could taste the salt water when I swam to the raft."

"Exactly! That's an excellent example. Alitheia used to be populated only by magical creatures—the narks, dryads, gnomes, fairies, the high animals, and the lot—but it was an unorganized place. No one race wanted to take responsibility for all the rest, and so they coexisted, but were not led."

Darcy's mind raced back to history class. "Was it like Greece with all the city-states before the Persian Wars?"

Eleanor thought for a moment, and then shook her head. "Not quite, but I can see why you would draw that analogy. None of the magical races have heads of government, and so there was very little law. Crimes went unpunished and populations dwindled . . . Pateros was not happy."

"He was alive back then?"

"He was and still is, darling; he has no age."

Oh.

"Therefore, Pateros set up the gateways," Eleanor continued. "He set up several to connect to your—that is, our—world, and drew hand-picked human beings to pass through them into Alitheia. Earth was not the only world he drew from. There were rumors of gateways to other places, but very few beings ever came through. Once Pateros was satisfied with the number of humans he'd drawn through, he closed the gateways."

"Were they upset at being stuck here?" Sam asked in a hushed voice.

"No. Pateros always gives people a choice. Most of them had stories like me; some were fleeing terrible devastation in Europe. From what I've gathered in my research, I believe that this exodus took place during a great plague."

"The Black Death?" Darcy asked.

"No, much earlier than that; there have been many plagues throughout history. At any rate, Pateros charged the humans with the care of Alitheia, and all the world of Orodreos. He gave them one gift when they arrived. He gave them magic, and he promised that their descendants would have magic, as well. They were to use and develop it like any other discipline—art, music, arithmetic, science—and those who practiced and applied themselves excelled, while those who did not could do only the most rudimentary spells. As with all disciplines, some were born stronger in the magic than others, and a select few became magicians, and even master magicians, like our friend over there." She gestured at Rubidius, who was nodding off in his chair. "You'll have to forgive him," she chuckled. "He's an old man, and it was a late night last night. Now then, where was I?"

"You were telling us about how Pateros gave them magic," Amelia reminded her.

"Ah, yes. Well, they spread throughout Orodreos and flourished, easily taking leadership of the lands of Orodreos, of which Alitheia is only one. But some of them, as is commonly the case in all histories, grew prideful as they grew in power. A wicked person is bad, but a wicked master magician is devastating!" She sighed and clasped her hands before her. "Pateros had placed but one limitation on their magic, on all of our magic: They must not construct gateways."

Lewis furrowed his brow. "Why did he give them the ability to build gateways if he didn't want them to do it?"

Eleanor spread her hands. "Choice," she said simply. "But it is no easy task to construct a portal to another world. Many tried and failed, until one master magician arose who succeeded. Over a thousand years ago, Baskania of Alitheia constructed the first gateway since Pateros had closed his gateways. At first, nothing came through it. After all, he only had the power to make it, not to draw anybody through it. It sat unused for many years, and Baskania stewed. He knew that it was a gateway because he had sent many low animals through it, and they never returned. But he never went through it himself; he was too scared. But as he neared the end of his life, he grew very rash, and finally one day he stepped through to the other side."

"Where did it lead?" Darcy asked.

"We do not know its name, but it was a very dark place, indeed. Baskania was gone for a week, and when he returned he was mad. He ranted and raved about darkness and fire and terrible creatures, and then one day, not even a week after his return, he died . . . without destroying his gateway." She sighed deeply. "The people in his village searched long and hard for another master magician to come and close the gateway, but none were found who could do it. It was then that Alitheians realized gateways, once opened, could not be closed but by means known only to Pateros himself."

"So why didn't Pateros tell the people how to do it?" Dean sputtered. "How to close it, I mean."

"Pateros told them that if they opened gateways, they must live with the consequences of their actions for a time—a time that we believe to be coming to a close." She nodded at the six of them.

"But why would he punish everybody for what one guy did?" Perry retorted.

"Because the failing of one, reflected the failings of all. Why did no one challenge Baskania? Everybody knew what he was up to. Why didn't the king of Alitheia put a stop to it? Some, we believe, were excited for him to succeed, and others turned blind eyes. Once Baskania died, people started to realize the gravity of what he had done. A guard was placed on his gateway, but the position was never held for long. Prolonged proximity to the gateway led to paranoia, irrational fear, and eventually, in some cases, madness. Attempts to guard the gateway were abandoned, and those who lived in the area gradually moved away, claiming to be plagued with nightmares and inexplicable nightly noises.

"And so the gateway sat, unguarded and open. It was through Baskania's gateway that he whom we call Tselloch, the Shadow, came through, bringing with him his minions. It was a slow migration, at first. A few were sighted at a time, the first over five hundred years ago, but in the last quarter millennium the migration increased." She hesitated. "We believe that the tsellochim, as we call them, opened further gateways to their world, increasing their numbers. The tsellochim are Tselloch's minions that came through the gateways with him. They are of the same essence as him, but he is their leader and infinitely more powerful. And now," she heaved a heavy sigh, "all of Alitheia is under their control. The Shadow sits on the throne that Pateros designed for a human king, and his yoke bears heavily on the people. It has been so for a hundred years. The gateways are lost or hidden; we believe this was the Shadow's doing. No record survives telling us where they are."

"Can't Pateros at least show you where they are?" Perry asked.

"Alas, when the humans that Pateros brought to Alitheia began to turn to dark magic, Pateros left this land. It is said that he walks to and fro on our borders, awaiting the proper time of return. But I think that, at least, is folklore. Pateros is not such that he can ever truly be gone; he's simply not shown himself to anybody in many years."

"He showed himself to you," Darcy reminded her.

"Yes, but it was in our world." Her eyes glazed a little, and a smile played on her lips. "I would dearly love to see him again." She was quiet for a moment, and then shook herself. "And, at last, that brings me to you six, for we believe that now that you are here, we will see him again. When Pateros first brought humanity to Alitheia and gave them the warning not to construct gateways, he also set up the pole in the forest glade."

"The totem pole?" Sam asked in disbelief.

"Yes." Eleanor smiled, and then murmured, "I'd forgotten that it exists at Cedar Cove, as well. Pateros had the six animals carved on the pole and warned the people that if they set up gateways, terrible distress would fall upon them. But at that time, he said, when things looked the bleakest, he would open a gateway again for six people from their world, three males and three females, who would deliver them. He gave them the details of the prophecy, which you heard rendered in poetic style, and gave them the pole to help them remember. And that, my dears, is where you come in."

Chapter 21

Explanation

"Lunch!" Rubidius said suddenly, sitting up straight in his chair and leaning forward.

The six teenagers jumped; they hadn't known that he was awake. Darcy's stomach gave a rumble, and she realized that it was already the noon hour.

"Can't learn anything on an empty stomach," Rubidius rumbled, going to his cupboards and rustling around inside them.

Eleanor Stevenson chuckled and leaned back in her chair. "You are right, as always, Rubidius."

A moment later he set down with a clatter eight wooden bowls and cups and gruffly instructed Perry and Dean to pass them out to everybody. Then he went back to his cupboards and returned with a very crusty and dry-looking loaf of bread, a pitcher of water, and a moldy lump of cheese. He placed them on the table and then dragged his armchair up beside Darcy. "There, now, budge up, would you?" he instructed her, and she hurried to comply.

When he was seated, he looked around at their apprehensive faces with a perplexed frown. "Eh? What's the matter? Not hungry, are you?"

"Um, Rubidius," Eleanor said gently, "are you quite finished with the meal preparation?"

"What?" He squinted at the table. "Oh dear, *that* simply won't do." With a wave of his hand, the food before their eyes transfigured. The crusty loaf of bread became golden and soft, and steamed as though it had just been pulled from the oven, the mold disappeared from the cheese, and the water in the pitcher grew clear. "There, now, mind the pitcher," Rubidius said.

"It's pulling double duty, you know."

What on earth is he talking about? Darcy wondered, but she took the pitcher as Rubidius handed it to her.

"First into your bowl," he instructed. "Then your cup."

She obediently tipped the pitcher toward her bowl, and when the water hit it, it became a hearty stew that smelled of chicken. She tipped it to fill her cup, wondering what would happen. A deep, purple, frothy liquid filled it to the brim. *Grape juice?*

She passed the innocuous-looking pitcher to Sam next and eagerly took up her glass. She took a deep gulp and almost choked. The drink was pungent and almost bitter, tasting only remotely of grapes.

Eleanor Stevenson laughed as Darcy gasped and shook her head. "What *is* this?"

"It's wine, of course." Rubidius frowned.

"We can't drink wine!" Sam gasped. She set the pitcher down with a thunk. Her glass was only half full. "We're only thirteen. My parents would *kill* me!"

"Of course you *can* drink wine. To suggest otherwise is absurd. Everybody drinks wine. What will you drink at meal time if you don't drink wine?" Rubidius seemed utterly flabbergasted.

"Rubidius, things are a bit different where these children come from," Eleanor told him, her eyes still twinkling with mirth. "People do not drink wine until they are of age."

"What an absurd custom. Why ever not?"

"Because people get drunk," Eleanor said.

Rubidius snorted to show his disdain. "What a foolish thing to do."

"Yes, but there are those who get drunk in Alitheia, as well. It's not that strange."

"Of course it happens, but they ought to be ashamed of themselves!"

He glowered around at them as though *they* were the offending drunks until Eleanor suggested softly, "Perhaps something a little less . . . *mature*. I'm afraid our guests would become drunk, whether they wanted to or not, if they partook of the excellent beverage you have provided for them."

Rubidius harrumphed, but his eyes became thoughtful. He waved his hand again and the liquid in Darcy and Sam's glasses turned from dark purple to light pink. "There," he said, somewhat sulkily. "And I even watered it down."

Eleanor nodded encouragingly at Darcy, who took a tentative sip. It still carried the same pungent flavor, but it was much milder, and even a little sweet. She smiled at Rubidius; she could tolerate it.

Once everybody had their food, Amelia turned to Eleanor and asked, "How long do you think we will be here?"

"No business at the table," Rubidius said.

"Come, now, Rubidius. You don't expect us to eat in silence, do you? Of course the children have questions."

"Yes, but that does not make the questions intelligent. What sort of a question is that? How long will they be here? Irrelevant! They cannot get back until Pateros decides to send them back, and nobody knows when that will be. You could say that you think they will be here a month, and somebody else could say ten years, but neither opinion would be valid because there is no standard to measure it against. I, for my part, think that their initial training will take the better part of a year, which is no time at all."

"A year is a very long time to children," Eleanor reminded him softly.

"Only because they haven't been properly *perspectified*."

"I don't think that's a word," Lewis said.

"Eh now, what? According to whom?"

Sam giggled and took up her spoon.

"If we must discuss business at the table," Rubidius continued, glaring around at them, "I would prefer to take intelligent questions."

Darcy swallowed a large spoonful of soup and opened her mouth. She was almost afraid to ask. "Um, Rubidius, sir . . . I was wondering what my job will be. I don't really understand what it means to be the 'king's intended.' "

His expression cleared and he chewed very thoughtfully for a long moment before he answered. "Well, do you not know the meaning of the word *intended?*"

"Well, I guess it means to have a specific purpose, right?"

"Yes, but there is another, connected, translation of the word. Does anybody know it?" Rubidius had taken up the demeanor of a classroom teacher; turning from grumpy to encouraging at the drop of a hat.

"It means 'engaged,' " Amelia said after only a moment. "It's kind of old-fashioned, where we come from."

"Excellent. Did you know that already, or did you pick it up from the poem?"

"I knew it already."

"Do you think that we could hear the poem again?" Sam asked eagerly. "It was difficult to pay attention before with all those people watching us."

Rubidius nodded quickly and repeated the poem.

"Magic and mystery, good days and bad,
Alitheians your worst disobedience is at hand.
With arrogance and spite a magician awoke,
The Shadow of whom no man has yet spoke.
Magic and mystery without warning will fail,
And Pateros will leave Alitheia to peril.
Despair for a while, but not over-long,
For out of another world will help come.
Pateros will call them, three women, three men,
To right what went wrong and with courage defend.

Abilities they'll have, the Six are presented:
Companion, Scribe, Musician, Spy, Warrior, Intended.
Companion, you are loyal above everyone else,
Great friend of the Scribe, who will write words of wealth.
Musician, your music will find what is lost,
Making steps for the Spy, who will seek despite cost.
Warrior, your blade will always strike true,
Penetrating shadow, rending bone from sinew.
Intended, you are truly unique,
For your abilities men have sought, and always will seek.
At the end of all things to the king you'll be wed,
Marked by a ring and the deepest color: red.
Now comings and goings will lead to the end,
To vanquish the Shadow, Alitheia to mend."

Darcy choked slightly at the last stanza and dropped her spoon with a clatter. *Intended, engaged, wed.* The fearsome words flew through her brain. "You mean that my purpose is to get *married?*"

Rubidius nodded.

"To the *king*?"

He nodded again.

"But . . . but I'm only thirteen!" she protested.

"It doesn't mean, dear, that you will get married right away," Eleanor Stevenson intruded on the conversation. "It simply means that you are the one he is intended to wed someday."

"But, I don't belong here! I live in Chicago; how can I marry anybody in another world, even if it is in the future?"

Eleanor hesitated, and a shadow crossed her face again. "We don't know, but surely Pateros will work it out." She looked down briefly, and when she looked up, her eyes were very intense. "Do not be so certain that you do not belong here," she spoke softly, and only to Darcy.

An immediate protest sprang to Darcy's lips, but she never got it out. Is this why she never made friends in her world? Is it why she only felt comfortable when she was by herself or with animals? Was it why she, of all the others who had gone to Cedar Cove for so many years, was the one chosen to lead them through to Alitheia? She swallowed hard. She still had too many questions.

"And technically, he still has to declare you," Rubidius interjected.

"Who?" she asked faintly.

"The king, of course. Remember, Pateros always gives people a choice."

Darcy thought of the two princes she had met at the council at the pole. They were only boys, but they couldn't be that much younger than she. If they were almost her age, then their father—the king—must be nearly her father's age. *And* he would have been married before! She wrinkled her nose. Did this *Pateros* really expect her to marry an old man?

She licked her dry lips. "How old are the princes?" she asked Rubidius.

"Cadmus is nine summers and Tellius is ten."

She nodded; that was about what she would have guessed. "So, the king must be pretty old, then," she continued.

"Hm? What is this foolish talk! I just told you how old the king is." Rubidius returned to his grumpy demeanor.

"But I thought you told me how old the princes are. If they are close to my age, then their father must be old enough to be my dad."

"Oh, I see," Eleanor Stevenson said quietly. "Nobody has told you. Cadmus and Tellius are orphans. Their father, Tullin Ecclektos's older cousin, was murdered by the tsellodrin, along with his wife. The tsellodrin are human men or other intelligent races that have allowed the Shadow to indwell them. The boys survived because a trusted servant secreted them away from their hidden home once she knew that it was betrayed to the enemy."

"Don't let her modesty fool you." Rubidius snorted. "It wasn't just any trusted servant; it was the very woman you see before you who saved them. She is their governess and tutor."

Eleanor blushed and dipped her head. "It was five years ago," she said, "and I am blessed that Pateros chose to place me in their household."

Darcy didn't mean to be selfish by returning to her part of the story, but she was desperate to find out exactly what she was supposed to do. "So, that boy I met, who gave me the ring . . . that was the king?"

Eleanor nodded. "The rightful king. The royal line of Ecclektos has remained hidden and preserved since the Shadow took over the throne, and it is those two boys that Tselloch hunts more than any other. And it's not polite to call him 'that boy,' my lady," she chastised Darcy gently. "He is sovereign of this land, and he is presumably your future husband. Tellius Ecclektos will be a fine man someday."

"But he's *younger* than me!"

"First too old, and now too young!" Rubidius guffawed. "Is there no pleasing you, child?" He twiddled with his beard and studied Darcy for a moment. "I have actually given some thought to that," he said unexpectedly. "You've told us that time stands still in your world while you are here, but it does not stand still here while you are away. I conjecture that before the time comes for your marriage, Tellius will have aged beyond you."

Darcy decided to take her emotions out on her stew and, stabbing her spoon into the bowl, she said, "So, is that all that I'm here for? To marry some guy I don't know . . . someday?"

Eleanor frowned at her use of "some guy" but Rubidius chuckled at her ire. "Well, you didn't listen very carefully to the poem, now did you?"

"Oh, yeah," Sam said eagerly. "He's right, Darcy."

Rubidius winked at Sam and nodded. "The prophecy clearly states that in addition to being the king's intended, which is, in itself, a noble role, you also have a unique talent. It is something that men have long sought to be able to do or possess. Whatever it is, it will be great indeed."

Darcy couldn't muster a smile at his words, but she felt a little warmed inside. "You don't know what my talent is?"

"No." Rubidius didn't seem daunted by the fact. "Technically, we don't know what any of your talents are." He looked around the table. "We only know what the prophecy tells us, which gives us a pretty good idea on most of you."

"My music will find what is lost?" Amelia put in tentatively.

"That's right." Rubidius smiled at her. "How it will do that, or what exactly you are intended to find, we don't know."

"I will write words of wealth?" Lewis questioned. "What does that mean?"

"Well, obviously your pen will produce words of great value. Beyond that, I've no idea, but I'm sure we'll find out." Rubidius seemed overly cheerful at the road before them. "Do you see now why you need training up?"

All of them, except for Perry, nodded. He shrugged and said, "Mine seems pretty straightforward. I'm to be a great warrior, right?"

"Ah, yes, our warrior. The physical end of things tends to be less complicated than the rest. But I think that even with you, my young knight, unexpected magic will arise." He stood suddenly and clapped his hands. "If you're finished"—with a swoosh the bowls and cups cleared themselves and soared over to his counter—"we'll begin your training."

Chapter 22
Training

What followed that afternoon was a series of tests in which Rubidius placed strange-looking metal and wooden instruments before each of them in turn and asked them to "move this" or "change that" without touching anything. Darcy was the only one with any measure of success, which Rubidius waved off as "expected."

She brooded a little at his nonchalant attitude until Sam leaned over and whispered. "How did you do that? Make the pendulum swing, I mean?"

"It barely moved, Sam; it wasn't a big deal."

"Yeah, but still! None of the rest of us could do it."

Darcy shrugged. "I don't know. I just willed it to move . . . and it did. But it made me really tired."

"Those are the sorts of exercises that our very youngest children are given to do in their magic schooling," Rubidius said as he rejoined them at the table. His instruments and such were tucked away in a cupboard. "We thought it important to verify whether or not any of you had any magic aside from the talents that we have yet to discover."

"And?" Perry prompted.

"You don't. Except for Lady Darcy, who, it seems, has some degree of natural magical ability."

Eleanor smiled in a knowing way from across the room. Ever since lunch, she'd taken up residency in Rubidius's chair.

"Our royal tutor," Rubidius gestured at Eleanor, "exhibited a greater degree of magic when she arrived. I tested her myself," he said importantly.

"So, will any of us get to have this magic?" Perry continued. He seemed eager not to be left out.

"No. Either you are born with it, or you are not, which validates my suspicion concerning the nature of your talents."

"What's that?"

"They are not natural abilities, but special gifts from Pateros himself. I suspect that they amplify natural abilities that you already possess; that would be consistent with Pateros's nature."

"Ooh, yeah!" Sam said excitedly. Darcy could almost see the light bulb go off over her head. "It's like how Perry is really athletic, and Dean likes army stuff, and Amelia's a really good musician back in our world."

Rubidius nodded thoughtfully. "And, I would expect that you are a very loyal friend, am I correct?"

Sam blushed and shrugged her shoulders, but Amelia piped up, "Yeah, she is."

Darcy wanted to ask, *"What about me?"* but she held her tongue. Besides having an affinity with animals, she didn't really have any natural abilities. She was a good student, but not the head of her class, she could draw, but not well enough to win any prizes, she could sing, but she wasn't section leader in choir, and she could play sports, but she never got picked first for any teams in gym. She restricted herself to a small sigh and tried to pay attention to what Rubidius was saying, but the afternoon was wearing away and she was itching to get out of the cottage and do something else.

"Darcy has hers, too." Sam's comment suddenly broke into her reverie.

She started. "My what?"

"He just asked us who had their gifts on them," Sam whispered to her out of the corner of her mouth.

"Oh, yeah, I do." Darcy waggled her left thumb in the air.

Amelia, Dean, and Lewis did not have their gifts, and Rubidius instructed them to go and fetch them. While he waited for them to return, he sat back in his chair and hummed thoughtfully to himself. Darcy and Sam exchanged amused looks and sat quietly.

When the other three teenagers returned, Rubidius sat up suddenly and said, "Ah, yes! Excellent. Now for some instruction on your gifts, which you'll find will work only for you."

"You mean, like, nobody else can use my sword?" Perry asked.

"No, no, what a foolish thought! No, dear boy, it means that the special trait contained in your sword will work only for you; specifically its unbeatable nature."

"Unbeatable?" Perry asked in disbelief. His eyebrows disappeared underneath his bangs. "How can a sword be unbeatable?"

"Because I made it as such!" Rubidius harrumphed. "I am an alchemist, after all."

"Excuse me, sir, but I'm not exactly clear on what alchemy is here in Alitheia. In our world it has something to do with turning lead to gold, which is impossible." Darcy didn't want to sound disrespectful, but she was curious.

"Ah, yes. The ever-present pursuit." Rubidius sounded a little wistful as he waved his hand toward the metal tubing and odds and ends around his fireplace. "The one goal I have not yet accomplished. That is, of course, the ultimate end of all alchemy, but in magical terms it really has more to do with what the act of turning lead to gold represents."

"What's that?" Sam asked, her eyes wide.

"In simple terms, making the ordinary," he waved his hand over the table, "extraordinary." Following the sweep of his hand the table turned to gilt gold and the chairs became mahogany with rich upholstery. "But that's unnecessary," he muttered, returning the table and chairs to their rough wood finish.

"If you can turn the table to gold with a wave of your hand, why don't you just turn lead to gold the same way? With magic?"

"Cheating, my dear," Rubidius answered Amelia. "Hardly worth the ridicule I would receive from my peers." He peered around at all of them. "At any rate, I used my magic long ago to create gifts for five of you, assuming I would ever get to meet you. I planned on passing them onto a trustworthy successor, and so forth, until your arrival if you did not come in my lifetime, but I have been fortunate. All of them are objects that I have altered, either with enhancement or the addition of a special purpose. For instance, as I have already mentioned, Perry's sword, so long as he wields it, is unbeatable. He could fight the most experienced swordsman in all of Orodreos today and not lose the battle."

Perry's eyebrows lifted and he looked at his sword with new appreciation.

"Lewis's quill," Rubidius took the object from Lewis's hand and held it reverently before him, "is made of phoenix feather. It will always write exactly what Pateros wants to be written—no more, and no less. As long as Lewis is the one using it," he added, handing it back to the boy.

"Sam, your bag," he barked, holding out his hand. Sam obediently handed it over and Rubidius upended it for all to see. "Empty," he said needlessly. "But in times of great need, it will always fill itself with items for those to whom she is a companion."

"Oh!" Sam clapped her hands. "That's cool!" She accepted it back with a much greater degree of appreciation.

"Amelia's lyre," he took the instrument, "should aid her magical talent of finding hidden things." He sounded a little apologetic as he handed it back to her. "Because I do not know what the nature of the hidden things will be, it was difficult for me to do much more with it. But I promise it will be an enhancement to you," he added.

"Dean's bow and arrow. Ah. Now this is one of my favorites. A very clever idea, if I say so myself." He rocked back and forth smugly as he held up the weapon. "This is not an ordinary weapon, and it should not be fired as such," he warned Dean. "It is designed for the sending and receiving of messages. If you attach a message to an arrow and tell the arrow where to go, when you shoot it up in the air, it will always fly to your intended receiver. And if that receiver needs to send a message back to you, he needs only attach it and shoot it back in the air, and it will return to you."

"Cool," Dean said, grinning.

So that leaves me the odd person out again, Darcy thought glumly as Rubidius turned his gaze upon her.

"And for you, child, I made no gift because there was already one prepared for you. It contains no magic properties, but by rights it belongs to you, unless Tellius decides otherwise. It is the ring of the queen. It has been in the Ecclektos family since before the time of the Shadow and it is priceless. Cherish it," he said solemnly.

Darcy nodded obediently, but inside she was wondering why she couldn't have received a cool magic gift like everybody else.

"You need no special training with your gifts, but you should use them whenever possible. They will work for you regardless of whether you have used them once or twenty times, but it is always good to be familiar with that which is your own." He sat back, seemingly satisfied. "I will work with you one-on-one for a time. Individualized attention should reveal your talents in due course. I shall start with . . . Sam. The rest of you may go. In the morning after breakfast, I would like to work with Darcy until lunch, and then the rest of you may join us."

Darcy stood along with the others, feeling her limbs protesting after sitting for so long. With a stretch, she followed Amelia, Dean, Lewis, and Perry out the door and once again found herself in the tunnel. The curtained opening to Rubidius's cottage fluttered unobtrusively behind them.

Chapter 23
Musician

Perry let out soft whoop the moment they were a few feet down the tunnel and turned to face them, walking backward with ease. "That was a bit to take in, huh?" He grinned. "Kind of makes my head spin."

Amelia frowned at him. "I don't know why you are so excited. It sounds like we're right in the middle of a war. I don't think this is exactly going to be fun for us."

Perry scowled and tripped over a protrusion in the floor. He stumbled before he righted himself and faced forward once more. "If you look at it that way, of course it sounds bad. But, come on, who really gets to do stuff like this? I think it's awesome."

"I think it's cool," Dean said, lending his support to Perry's point of view. "Man, did you see all that stuff the old guy could do? Talk about amazing!"

"I always knew magic was real," Lewis added softly.

Amelia tisked and folded her arms. "It's not real, Lewis."

"What? How can you say that after what we just saw?" Perry said.

"What I mean is, it's not real in our world. This is a different world; the rules are different here."

"Okay, but how do you explain the gateway, then?"

She frowned and didn't respond.

"It's pretty cool about Eleanor Stevenson, though," Lewis said after a moment.

"Yeah, but what about her poor family?" Amelia said. "They thought that she was dead all this time, but she was really fine and dandy."

"I understand why she chose to come here, though," Darcy put in. "I think she was sparing her family a lot of pain. Besides, who wouldn't want to choose life over death?"

"I'm just glad that we didn't have to die to be here," Dean said.

"I'm just glad we're *here*," Perry added. He cocked an eyebrow at Darcy and smiled.

Darcy felt her ears warm and she quickly ducked her head to study her ring. If what Rubidius said was correct, it was really, really old—definitely the oldest thing she'd ever touched, let alone possessed. But, then again, she wouldn't actually possess it until Tellius "claimed" her as his intended bride. What a ridiculous thing! Why couldn't she just have a normal adventure like the rest of them? Why did she have to worry about marrying some strange boy someday? She tucked her thumb inside her fist and looked up. She didn't really want to think about it.

They emerged into the dining hall, and Darcy looked around self-consciously. It was much less crowded than it had been that morning, but their appearance still caused the heads of those people who were there to go together as whispers and comments were exchanged. She spotted Yahto Veli and Voitto Vesa against the far wall deep in conversation, and a few animals lounged around the large open space.

"All right!" Perry exclaimed as a large African lion paced toward him purring like an inflated housecat. The animal bumped Perry's face affectionately, almost knocking him over.

As Perry greeted his lion, Dean's fox trotted forward with its bottle-brush tail held high and jumped up on Dean's legs with an excited yip, and Lewis's owl and Amelia's songbird flew to perch on their shoulders. Darcy looked around expectantly, but she didn't see her stallion Hippondus anywhere. She sighed. *Left out again*. Turning to the others, she said, "What are their names? My horse is called Hippondus."

"This is Liontari," Perry said, patting the lion between the eyes. "He's totally harmless." The lion growled suddenly and bared sharp teeth. "Okay." Perry laughed a little nervously. "So he's not harmless, but he won't harm any of us."

"This is Alepo," Dean said; he ruffled the fox's long ears.

"This is Koukoubagia," Lewis said, "but everybody calls him Kouk."

"And this is Ptino," Amelia said fondly as the bird cooed in response to her name. "I think she's beautiful."

"Yahto Veli told me that Hippondus would meet us at Sanditha," Darcy said, looking around. "I assumed that was where we are, but I don't see him."

"This is Sanditha," Lewis said, "at least, part of it. I think that's the name of a region in Alitheia that we are in."

"You could ask Yahto Veli where he is." Amelia pointed across the room.

"I don't want to bother him," Darcy muttered, but as she spoke, Veli's ears suddenly twitched and he looked up at her and smiled. He placed a hand on Vesa's arm and made his way toward her.

No way, he heard me from all the way over there, Darcy thought incredulously. Her face must have betrayed her thoughts because Veli tapped his ear lightly and said, "Narks have good hearing, remember?" He winked and smiled around at all of them. "I see your animals have found you; they've been anxiously awaiting your appearance. Did you have a pleasant day with Rubidius?"

"Yes, sir," Darcy responded for all of them. "Sam's still with him for a little while."

"Ah, yes, I assumed that he would want some individual tutelage with all of you."

"How long until dinner?" Perry suddenly asked. "I'm starving."

"It's being prepared as we speak," Veli said cheerfully, waving his hand toward the kitchen entrance. "Now is the time to freshen up if you need to."

The three boys headed off to their room, Koukoubagia swaying slightly on Lewis's shoulder and Liontari and Alepo following along behind them.

"I think I'd like to practice on my lyre," Amelia said softly. "I haven't really had a chance to play it yet." With that, she, too, headed back to the hall, and their room, leaving Darcy and Yahto Veli standing alone together in the great hall.

"And you, Lady Darcy, what would you like to do?" Veli asked her kindly.

"If it's not a pain, could you tell me where Hippondus is? I'd like to see him again, and I thought you'd said he would meet us here."

"Of course," Veli replied, placing a hand on her shoulder and steering her toward the kitchen. "The great hall is no place for a horse. He's in the stables."

Darcy let the nark lead her through the kitchen entrance and along a smaller, dimmer hallway that slanted upward as they went. A question was forming in Darcy's mind as they walked, and she finally voiced it.

"It seems like the animals can understand us. Can they?"

Yahto Veli chuckled and dipped his head toward her. "Can they understand humans? I should say so. They can *even* understand narks." He added teasingly. "Of course, it depends on the kind of animal."

"What do you mean?"

"In Alitheia, and in all of Orodreos, there are high animals, and there are low animals. High animals have human intelligence and are to be treated with the same respect due to all intelligent inhabitants of Alitheia. They understand common speech but, alas, cannot speak the words themselves."

"But can they communicate between each other?"

"Only within species. It would be a great aid to Alitheia if the high animals could speak the common tongue, or if we could understand their animal speech, but it is too great a barrier to overcome. A few intrepid humans have, at times, tried to learn to speak certain dialects, like wolf or horse, but they always come up short."

"So, what about the low animals?"

"The low animals are of low intelligence," Yahto Veli answered simply. "They have no souls and may be used for menial labor and food. Sometimes an entire race is low, such as the rabbits, and sometimes it depends. Some birds, for example, are high while others are low."

"What if you don't know if an animal is high or low? What do you do then?"

"It's rather simple to find out. The high animals are usually capable of giving some sign to indicate their intelligence. But it is a great crime to kill a high animal for food or to treat them as a low animal. It would be the same thing as doing that to a human, or a nark."

"Why do you think they can understand you, but you can't understand them?" Darcy asked.

Veli shrugged. "It's the way Pateros made them. Ah. Here we are." He stopped outside a wide door off the tunnel and stepped aside to let Darcy enter first.

Familiar smells of hay and horse met her nose and she breathed deeply, allowing the pleasurable sensation to wash over her. Numerous stalls were cut out of the earth on either side of her, and lanterns hung between each one, giving off weak, warm light. A loud nicker from a rear stall met her ears, and she hurried forward, dodging pails and rakes and ignoring the other horses that stuck inquisitive heads out of their stalls as she passed. A stall gate swung open before her, and Hippondus met her in the walkway, his ears pricked forward eagerly. Darcy giggled as he snuffled her ear and nickered again.

"He's happy to see you," Veli commented behind her. Darcy could hear the smile in his voice.

"I'm happy to see him, too," Darcy responded, rubbing the side of his neck.

She spent a good twenty minutes in the stables with Hippondus and Yahto Veli before the nark commented that they should really get back for supper. She watched with amusement as Hippondus backed up into his own stall and pulled the door closed after him. She waved and promised that she would be back the next day, and then she and Veli walked back to the great hall together.

On the way, Veli explained how there was a large hidden entrance to the stables that the horses and other larger animals could use. "But we discourage too much coming and going," he said as they took seats at the table together, "as the entrance is too exposed when it's used too much and could pose a threat to our hideout."

Sam and Rubidius joined them at the table for supper, but Eleanor Stevenson did not reappear. When Darcy asked Rubidius where she was, he explained, rather impatiently, that she, of course, had duties to the princes and could not be expected to stay with them all the time.

"But don't the princes stay here?" Darcy asked, puzzled. She had been worried about bumping into Tellius ever since they'd left Rubidius's cottage.

"No, no," Rubidius replied. "They are someplace much safer." But he wouldn't say any more than that.

Darcy then turned to Sam, who was picking at her mushroom stew with a sick look on her face, and asked her about her training session with Rubidius.

"Oh, he just ran a few more tests on me," she answered distractedly. "Something about trying to narrow the scope of my abilities." She sipped a bit of the broth and made a face. "Do you think it would be rude if I didn't eat this?" she said to Darcy under her breath. "I hate mushrooms."

Darcy shrugged at her, a little annoyed at her lack of specifics regarding her session. "Dump it into my bowl," she said, holding it close to Sam's. "I like mushrooms."

"Thank you!" Sam exclaimed breathlessly. When the transfer was complete, she snatched a roll from a basket and chomped into it with a blissful look on her face. "Since I don't have inherent magic, like you, I didn't really have much to do. I basically just answered a few questions for him and sat around as he made notations and took measurements and whatnot." She waved her hand and grabbed another roll. "He said it was just preliminary stuff; not a big deal. I bet your session with him in the morning will be a *lot* more interesting."

"I hope so," Darcy murmured, but she had an inkling that it probably wouldn't be much different from Sam's experience.

After supper, the six teenagers were encouraged to explore the various texts scattered on shelves throughout the room—musty scrolls; old, cracking tomes; tiny, leather-bound books; and sheaves of loose paper in stacks—but Dean and Perry didn't seem too enthused by the prospect. Darcy quickly found a small book of nursery rhymes and settled into a squashy armchair to read. She noticed Sam and Amelia bending over an enormous book laid open on a table and Lewis was squinting at a thin book on a shelf across the room, his quill tucked jauntily behind one ear. Every now and then he would reach up and adjust his glasses. Dean and Perry were rescued from the task of reading by the weapons instructor who cornered them for a tutorial on forms and body movement. Darcy found it rather distracting to have Perry practicing forms in her periphery, so she readjusted in her chair so she couldn't see anything but her book and the wall. Tucking her long woolen skirt around her legs, she opened the book to the cover page.

"Cerdwin's Collection of Rhymes for Children" read the title in flowery gold letters. Darcy turned to the next page and smiled at the small, colorful caricature of a gnome leaning on the letter A at the top of the page. "*A Gnome in His Home*," Darcy read softly aloud. "*There once was a gnome in his home. He sat all alone. When he called for some friends, no one made amends, and he grumped and he groaned, all alone. Then his fairy friend came, him to find. She was kind. She asked 'what's the matter?' and when*

he had no reply, she suggested he go for a ride, oh so kind. 'What's this?' the gnome cried. 'Leave my home? No sir-ee. From my home never must I flee. A gnome must never be forced from his home and so I must ask YOU to leave; yes sir-ee.' The fairy, she chuckled, and went on her way. She left the gnome all alone. She'd forgotten the cardinal rule, you see: You must leave a gnome in his home." Darcy chuckled quietly to herself.

She stifled a yawn behind her hand and shook her head. It couldn't be that late; Yahto Veli hadn't even changed color yet, although his hair and skin were starting to look a little brown. She flipped through the pages of the tiny book, enjoying the colorful illustrations and playful poems, and it wasn't long before soft string music met her ears. She looked up to see that Amelia had pulled out her lyre and was strumming absentmindedly, her eyes half closed, in a chair by the fireplace. Sam sat on the floor at Amelia's feet, her head back against the seat of the chair and her eyes closed. Her fingers caressed the ears of her badger, Pinello, he was called, who was curled up in her lap.

As Darcy studied them, a great grey wolf approached her with measured steps. She shifted back in her chair, uncertain what this animal could want with her. The wolf stopped before her and slowly lowered his haunches to the ground, studying her with a measured gaze as he did so. His eyes, yellow orbs surrounded by smoky fur, were so intense that Darcy knew intuitively that he was very intelligent, probably more intelligent than she was. She swallowed and tried to look away, but she was held captive by his penetrating gaze. He growled deep in his throat, but Darcy didn't know if he was angry or content. She saw Sam straighten across the room and frown over at her, her movements imitated by Pinello.

The moment was broken when the weapons instructor let out a shout. Amelia jerked upwards and stopped playing, but the instructor waved frantically at her and said, "Don't stop! Keep playing!"

Amelia looked confused and she fumbled with the instrument as her fingers found the strings, but in a few seconds her music once again sounded throughout the room. Darcy saw Rubidius hurry forward to join the weapons instructor, and the two men bent over a spot on the floor. Darcy couldn't see exactly what was happening, but she could hear a slight crumbling sound and saw dust rising into the air. A moment later a distinct crunch was heard and Rubidius let out a triumphant shout.

The wolf at Darcy's feet rose and paced away, and she stood, eager for a glimpse of whatever it was that had happened. Amelia stopped playing again, and this time no one asked her to continue.

"What is it? What did you find?" Voitto Vesa hurried to the table on which the two men were placing a very dirty wooden box.

With deft fingers, Rubidius undid the clasp on the box and opened the lid. More dirt fell away as he swung it open, but the contents were perfectly dust-free. It was a scroll, a very old one by the looks of it. The stained parchment was rolled very tightly and tied with a string. Rubidius cut the string and unrolled the scroll out on the table, his eyebrows furrowed. Vesa and Veli each held a corner of the scroll down and bent their heads too closely together for Darcy to see what was written on it.

Finally, after what seemed like an interminable amount of time, Rubidius looked up and declared with a smile on his face, "It's a map. A map of Ormiskos, probably lain down after the initial construction of the palace."

"What do we need a map of Ormiskos for?" a red-faced man asked. "We have plenty."

"Yes, but we did not, until now, have *this* one," Rubidius replied impatiently. "A very important map, indeed."

"But why is it important?" the man replied stubbornly.

"Because this map details the initial construction, all of the initial construction, including the secret passageways into and out of the palace."

"Ah!" Yahto Veli exclaimed quietly as the red-faced man stood silent. The nark turned first to Amelia and then to the weapons instructor. "Baran, tell us what happened. How did you find this?"

The weapons instructor shrugged his shoulders and pointed at Amelia. "I was showing these boys the forms, here in this very same spot that I always have, and the musician was playing her music. All of a sudden the dirt at my feet started to move, like it was dancing or something, and I stepped aside because I noticed a crack forming in the floor. That's when I shouted and she stopped playin'. But when she started up again, the crack widened and pretty soon this whole area caved in around this small box. Then Rubidius and I brought it over here and you've seen the rest."

Rubidius turned to look keenly at Amelia, his eyes alight with possibilities. "I think we shall soon understand the depths of your talent," he said to her, and then he turned to Darcy. "I will meet with Amelia in the morning, instead of you. You may join me with your peers in the afternoon."

Darcy swallowed and nodded, but inside her feelings pricked. Shunted aside . . . again.

Chapter 24

The Grumps

Darcy slept fitfully that night and her dreams were filled with shadowy creatures that stalked her through dark forests. When she shouted for help, nobody answered, even though she could see the other five teenagers laughing in a cluster nearby. She awoke grumpy and taciturn in the morning, barely even pleased to find her dress and undergarments washed and folded at the foot of her bed.

When she wandered out to the breakfast table, Veli greeted her with a cheerful wave and invited her to sit next to him. He failed to cheer her up, however, because she was still stinging from his caustic attitude as Yahto the night before. When the sun had set and Yahto had awoken, he had ignored her completely, even going so far as to move whenever she came near him. Darcy knew that Yahto was a different person than Veli, but she couldn't quite bring herself to forgive him yet.

Veli seemed to read her mind as usual, though, and he leaned close to her as she sat pouting into her porridge bowl. "You know, Yahto didn't really mean any harm last night. He merely takes a while to warm up to people."

Darcy dribbled porridge off her spoon into her bowl, watching the unappealing pile it made, and mumbled, "Can't you tell him to be nice to me?"

"Tell him?" Veli laughed. "Of course I can, and I have. But I can only suggest it, not make it happen." He sobered. "He wasn't really being mean to you; he was just . . . standoffish. You should be encouraged by the fact that he shared his behavior with me this morning. He didn't have to, you know. I think it's his way of trying to make amends."

Darcy grunted and ate a spoonful of porridge. It wasn't bad, but it could use sugar. She took a few more bites and gave up, pushing the bowl aside. She preferred warm breakfasts like eggs and bacon or french toast.

"What are you going to do this morning?" Veli asked her, changing the subject.

"I was supposed to be with Rubidius, but now I guess I'll just sit around."

"Ah, yes, he's working with Lady Amelia this morning, isn't he?"

Darcy shrugged.

"Quite an intriguing development with her music last night," Veli continued. "I don't think any of us expected any of your talents to manifest so quickly or easily."

"Rubidius said there is still probably a lot more to it," Darcy reminded him.

Yahto Veli dipped his head. "As you say."

The subject of their conversation entered the great hall at that moment, rubbing sleep out of her eyes and looking around for food.

"Sam's just getting up," Amelia said with a yawn as she plopped down beside Darcy, a small bowl of porridge in her hands. She wrinkled her nose at it, but ate nonetheless. Her sandy colored hair was hanging loose about her face this morning, and she looked very pretty even with sleep circles under her eyes.

Darcy noticed Bayard, the redheaded teenager who'd let her and the narks into the hideout the first night, watching Amelia surreptitiously from the group of men doing their forms. Darcy scowled. He had to be at least four years older than her! But she supposed Amelia looked older than she was because she was so tall. She wished that boys would look at *her* that way.

She watched the men, young and old, as they went through a complicated pattern of what looked like martial arts moves. Dean and Perry, looking dead on their feet and stumbling to keep up, were the youngest men of the bunch.

Actually, Darcy reminded herself abruptly, looking at Amelia again, there *were* boys who looked at her like Bayard looked at Amelia, but they were always the weird boys. The ones who came to school with their pants tucked into their socks or their favorite science fiction characters displayed on every T-shirt they owned. And then there were the silent ones who never said anything but watched her and followed her from class to class. Yes, she attracted a lot of *those* kinds of guys, but never anybody like Perry.

"Well," Amelia said, standing and stretching, "I guess I'd better go see Rubidius. That is," she hesitated, "if he's up already."

"He's up whenever you need him," Veli said with a smile.

Bayard's eyes followed Amelia out the door, and he earned a sharp reprimand from Baran, the weapons instructor, when he tripped over the man in front of him and sent them both sprawling.

Darcy remained at the table and tapped her fingers on the wood grain. What *was* she going to do this morning? Pretty soon she was going to be joined by Sam, and she didn't think that she could handle the girl's irrepressible energy at the moment. She looked around the room. She couldn't hide very well in the great hall. There were plenty of chairs and nooks to sit in, but her presence would still be visible to any curious eyes, and she knew from experience that busying herself with a book or other activity would not dissuade Sam from bothering her.

"You know," Veli suggested, "you could visit Hippondus this morning. You did promise him that you would be back to see him today."

Darcy brightened. That was a great idea! But she'd better go quickly before Sam came out for breakfast, or she would want to go with her.

"Thanks, Veli," she said, rocketing from her chair.

In a few minutes she was back in the stable and all alone except for one or two grooms and the animals. She watched a groom brushing down a dun mare and asked tentatively, "Does it bother them?"

"Does what bother them?" the groom grunted, not looking up from his chore.

"Being treated like animals when they're just as intelligent as us?"

"They *are* animals," he replied. He lifted the mare's hoof to check her shoe.

"Yeah, but, isn't it demeaning to groom them and keep them in stalls and whatnot? I wouldn't want somebody doing that to me."

"Yes, but you are not a horse." He finally paused in his task and looked at her. "This would be the equivalent of somebody giving you a massage, feeding you, making sure you are neat and clean, and tucking you into bed at night. Wouldn't you enjoy that?" He snorted. "This is a luxury for them! Besides," he gestured at the stall doors, "none of these doors latch. They are free to come and go as they choose."

The groom went back to his work and Darcy patted Hippondus on the flanks. "Would you like a brush?" she asked softly. In response, the stallion dipped his head and snorted. She smiled. "Okay."

Taking a stiff-bristled brush off a hook on the wall, she let herself get lost in the task. She had always enjoyed rubbing down Timmory at Gregorio's; it made her feel closer to him.

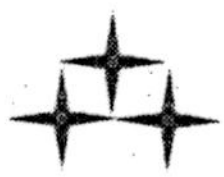

It wasn't until close to lunchtime that Sam came looking for her, Pinello trotting along at her heels. She seemed intimidated by the horses and told

Darcy that food was almost ready for them.

"Rubidius is finished with Amelia for the morning; it sounds like she had a much more interesting time than I did yesterday. Of course, she had a lot longer with him. He seems to think that the type of music she plays will influence what it will reveal, and he's trying to figure out what sort of things it will work on, like, does she need to write compositions? Play arpeggios like she did last night? Play whatever comes to mind? She said he had all those questions for her, and I think she's a little overwhelmed."

Fascinating, Darcy thought dryly; she wasn't all that interested. She said goodbye to Hippondus and washed her hands in a bucket of soapy water before following Sam back to the great hall. She couldn't smell anything when they passed the kitchen, but she found the long table laden with cuts of cold meat and cheese. Crusty rolls sat in baskets and pitchers of wine were interspersed throughout.

The woman who worked in the kitchen waved them forward and pointed to a pitcher. "Lady Eleanor spoke with me yesterday," she whispered to them. "This pitcher is already watered down for you young ones. I hope that it is satisfactory."

"Thank you," Sam said brightly.

Darcy sat down next to Amelia and watched the boys squabble over a basket of rolls. "What did they do all morning?" she asked.

"After Dean and Perry finished their forms," Sam replied, "Veli taught them a game with cards and dice."

"What do you think we'll do with Rubidius this afternoon?"

Amelia looked up. "He said something about lessons. I think it's going to be a lot like school."

Amelia was right. When the six of them joined Rubidius in his cottage that afternoon, they were met by a large pile of greenery on the table. A fire was crackling in the hearth and six pieces of blank parchment were laid out on the table before each of their chairs. The room was hot and stuffy with the fire going and the sun streaming through the window panes, and Darcy wished they could open a window for some fresh air, but she knew it was impossible.

"Part of your training," Rubidius started without preamble once they had each taken a seat around the table, "will consist of learning the ways, customs, and history of Alitheia, including how to survive. This resistance would not be alive today if we were not able to live off the land." He gestured to the pile of plants on the table. "I've gathered together a sample of common greenery that you would find in the woods of Alitheia. I'm going to spend time this afternoon explaining what each one is and its properties. I want you to take studious notes and ask questions if you don't understand everything," he admonished gruffly. "Don't use your quill!" he barked at Lewis, who lowered his phoenix-feather quill self-consciously. "I've provided ordinary quills for each of you."

At first Darcy thought the lesson was interesting, but after an hour or so, it became tedious. All the leaves began to look alike, and she really didn't care that such-and-such plant gave off green smoke when burned—hence the reason the fire was lit—and shouldn't be mistaken as such-and-such other plant that burned cleanly. Only Lewis and Amelia managed to still look interested by the end of the afternoon. Darcy had been staring at the same spot on the table for at least a half an hour, Sam was drawing tiny curlicues all along the edges of her parchment, and Dean was staring at Rubidius with a slack-jawed expression that bespoke someone who was trying to pay attention, but was completely checked out. Perry kept flicking ink onto Dean's parchment whenever Rubidius looked away, making it look like two armies of ink-footed ants had staged a battle on top of his notes.

Darcy suddenly realized that Rubidius wasn't talking anymore, and she refocused on the old man to find him scowling around at them.

"This may not be the most interesting information you've ever learned," he said, "but it could save your life someday." He raised his eyebrows at Dean's and Sam's parchments and shook his head. "Shameful."

Sam blushed deeply and put down her quill.

"We'll continue with plants for the rest of this week, and then next week we will move onto roots."

Darcy almost laughed at the expression on Perry's face, but she sobered immediately when she realized that once again she was being passed over for Amelia in the morning.

"I would like to continue working with our musician in the mornings," Rubidius continued, "for another week or more. I feel that I should take advantage of the early revealing of her talent."

"Please, sir," Sam began tentatively. "What was so important about that map she discovered last night?"

"It shows secret passageways, weren't you paying attention?" Perry said a little contemptuously.

"Yes," Rubidius interceded, "and it is very, very old, probably the first rendering of the castle and its environs. There are people already at work comparing it to existing maps and plotting out points of weakness. We think there may be passageways revealed on it that Tselloch himself does not even know about. But," he spread his hands, "we will see."

"But what was it doing here? Buried in the floor?"

Rubidius looked thoughtful for a moment, stroking his long, curly beard. "These warrens were constructed long before the Shadow arrived," he finally said. "Soon after the twin castles, Ormiskos and Kenidros, were completed, Alitheia faced a hostile invasion from a neighboring country. The fighting was fierce and lasted for thirty years. We believe that these tunnels were constructed during that time, and they remained a secret to all but a chosen few after the invaders were expelled from Alitheia. For some reason, I believe that one of the Alitheians buried that map in the floor of the great hall. Who knows why he did so? Perhaps they were afraid of discovery? Perhaps Pateros prompted him to do so? Regardless, the map is in our hands now, and it will surely prove to be a great aid." He snorted at all their upturned faces. "If you paid this close attention to the lesson today, you would all be a great deal wiser."

Rubidius stood and stretched, his fingers brushing herbs that were hanging in bunches from the rafters. "You should be getting to supper."

"Aren't you coming?" Dean asked as their chairs scraped away from the table.

"I have work to do this evening," the old alchemist replied. "I won't always join you for meals and almost never for the breakfast hour." He shuddered. "Breakfast should be a private time." And he dismissed them just like that.

They trouped back to the great hall, and Darcy ducked into their room to use the chamber pot before supper. When she was finished she delayed joining the others, straightening things about the room instead. She felt despondent and bored. Why didn't Rubidius want to work with her? Wasn't her talent supposed to be the most important one? Why teach them about boring plants and roots and stuff when they were stuck underground for goodness knew how long? The initial excitement of entering a new world had worn off, and Darcy started to wish that she'd brought her iPod with her, or at least that she had the freedom to travel back and forth between the worlds. Lewis had his backpack, but she hadn't seen him wear it since the first day, and she doubted that there was anything interesting in it. If she had to be here, she wanted to be trained to use magic, and she wanted to see more gnomes and fairies and nymphs, and she wanted to fight in a battle. She snorted. But they wouldn't even teach the girls forms; forms were only for the men.

She picked at a spot on her face and paced the room. She knew that she was entering into what her dad called the "grumps." But she didn't care. That, at least, was kinder than what her mother would say if she could see her now. "Self-absorbed" she would call Darcy, but *she* never understood why Darcy felt and acted the way she did. She didn't know what it was like to be invisible and second best; always second best.

She lay down on her bed. Her stomach rumbled in protest, but she didn't feel like being around anybody. The torch flickered on the wall, and Darcy felt an inexplicable lump grow in her throat. Couldn't they at least let them go outside? Didn't they know what lack of sunlight did to people? *You can see sunlight through the windows of Rubidius's cottage*, the little voice in her head reminded her. "That's not the same," she answered out loud.

She lay still for a long time before Sam's voice sounded from outside the curtain. "Darcy? Are you okay? Can I come in?"

"Fine," Darcy said, but she turned her back to the entrance.

"I noticed that you didn't come to dinner," Sam said, sounding much closer. "Are you feeling okay?"

Sam was the only one who came looking for me. "I wasn't hungry," Darcy lied. "I'm just resting. I'll come out in a little while."

There was a long pause before Sam said, "Okay." And the curtain fluttered as she left the room.

Darcy stayed where she was for as long as she could stand it, but eventually her stomach wouldn't let her lie still anymore. She wandered out into the great hall to find it still filled with people doing various activities. A basket of bread remained on the table, and she tried not to look too famished as she chose a piece. Sam, Amelia, and Lewis were sitting together in a corner with their heads together, and when Darcy drew close she heard Amelia say in a loud whisper, "She's just pouting because she's mad that Rubidius is paying more attention to me than to her."

"Well, she *is* supposed to be the queen someday," Sam responded in the same hushed tone. "I think I'd feel a little neglected if I were her, too."

Darcy quickly changed direction and went to a bookshelf before they could see her. Amelia's words stung because they hit so close to the mark. *But I wasn't pouting*. She found the book of children's rhymes that she'd read parts of the night before and took it to a chair. The cheerful tales failed to warm her spirits, however, and she found herself staring blankly into space again. Like the night before, the great grey wolf padded over to her feet and stared at her.

"Leave me alone," she muttered to the animal, but he only lay down and put his head on his paws.

When she rose to go to bed, she had to step over him, and she had the feeling that his eyes followed her all the way out of the hall.

Chapter 25

Dropping Eaves

If Darcy had known that that third day in Alitheia would set the pattern for the better part of the next several months, she may have marched straight up to Yahto Veli and begged him to take her back to the gateway. The only thing that kept her from doing so was the knowledge that the gateway was closed and she couldn't get home even if she tried. Every day was the same: breakfast in the great hall, mornings hiding from Sam in the stables, afternoons in Rubidius's cottage learning about obscure subjects, and evenings in the great hall staring blankly at a book while the grey wolf lay at her feet and watched her. Yahto Veli told her that the wolf was called Lykos and he was the wolf prince of Sanditha. Veli didn't know why he'd attached himself to her.

Darcy stopped looking in the mirror in the mornings. She didn't want to look at her pale complexion, her limp and stringy hair, or the deep circles beneath her eyes. She didn't want to see how her dress hung on her skinny frame, and she didn't want to be reminded of how she used to look before she came to Alitheia. Sam watched her with worried frowns throughout the day, but had given up trying to get her to talk about her feelings; Amelia mostly ignored her, lost in her own feelings of homesickness. She cried herself to sleep almost every night for a month.

Almost four months had gone by and Rubidius had not asked to work with her individually since that day that he had passed her up for Amelia. He worked with each of the others, but every time that Darcy thought he would ask to meet with her, he decided that he needed to test some new theory on Dean or Lewis. He'd made serious inroads in figuring out Dean's talent, and the others now knew that in Alitheia, Dean was really good at blending in. Darcy didn't exactly know what that meant, because she'd never seen him in action, but she assumed that it was important because Rubidius had spent the better part of the last month tucked away with the tall boy.

Eleanor Stevenson came and went during their training sessions. Her lessons usually consisted of history, customs, and language. She seemed to think it was important for them to learn what she called Old Alitheian, a language that sounded distinctly like Old or Middle English. Darcy tended to perk up during the history lessons, but her mind went blank when Eleanor turned to language. She'd almost failed Spanish in sixth grade and didn't expect to do much better at Old Alitheian.

She never saw Tellius, and she began to forget what he even looked like. The council at the pole seemed a distant memory, like the look and feel of green grass, sunlight, and fresh air. Nobody seemed to care that they were never allowed outside, and most of the adults excluded them from any real information about what was going on in the outside world. During the day, Yahto Veli offered her some respite from her gloom, but even he avoided digging much deeper than mere pleasantries.

The boys had their forms and other combat training to keep them busy. Lewis had decided to do the forms after all, probably out of boredom, and he showed a surprising propensity for them. She saw camaraderie emerge between Lewis and the other two boys that hadn't existed before. Early on, Voitto Vesa had mentioned training the girls in basic self defense and archery, but nothing had transpired on that front.

To make matters even worse, Darcy constantly felt like the others were talking about her behind her back. She felt their eyes follow her wherever she went, and more than once they stopped talking the moment she walked in. She started taking her breakfast back to her room in the mornings, agreeing with Rubidius that it should be a private affair.

She knew that four months had passed because Rubidius kept a small calendar of their training sessions in his cottage. Amelia had turned fourteen a month after their arrival, and Dean's birthday was fast approaching. Through the glass panes of Rubidius's windows, Darcy could see leaves falling and knew that the air outside must be considerably cooler than the last time she'd felt it.

Men argued every night at the table in the great hall, and most days Darcy ignored them, but one night their heated conversation caught her attention. She put her book down and listened in; she thought she'd heard Tellius's name. The wolf at her feet, Lykos, raised his head and looked toward the table as well.

A man had just joined the table, and he looked vaguely familiar to Darcy. Shaggy brown hair peeked out from the hood of his cloak, and he had a pleasant voice, even raised in agitation. Darcy remembered suddenly, closing her book and sitting up straighter. *The man who met us on the beach when Veli and Vesa brought me here.*

The two narks were also present, both as their night personas. As the days grew shorter, Darcy's interactions with Veli became shorter, too, and she was forced to spend more and more time in Yahto's company. Yahto was wearing his characteristic scowl at the moment, and Voitto had her hand on his arm as if trying to calm him. Besides the narks and the messenger, Torrin and two other men made up the huddle. One of the other men had a characteristic, gruff voice that Darcy thought sounded familiar.

Someone sat down on the arm of her chair and she jumped, looking up to find Perry's blond head bent over hers. "Your chair's closer," he whispered to her. "They're talking about moving us." He put a finger to his lips and studied the group of adults.

"What do you mean?" Darcy whispered back. She found that if she listened hard, she could barely make out the men's hushed voices.

"Listen," Perry admonished her, and she bent her ear toward the table.

"All I said is that it's time for us to do something with them." The gruff voice wafted over to her. "I'm not saying that I agree with the explosive factions."

"It is about time to relocate to Paradeisos," Voitto Vesa said thoughtfully. "Some of them are getting peaky, especially . . ." Voitto's voice dropped too low for Darcy to hear.

"Yes, but that's not what I hear Boden telling us to do." Yahto's voice rang out clearer. "He would have us send them into battle now!"

"Shh!" Torrin's eyes flicked their direction and Perry immediately looked down at Darcy as though talking to her. After a moment of tense silence, he spoke again. "Boden only brings us the news from Kenidros. It is understandable that Tullin is becoming impatient. He's certainly in the . . ." Darcy lost the rest of his sentence. It was difficult to hear, and the nearness of Perry's face distracted her. A few more lines were exchanged that she couldn't hear.

"Will he come here?" the old man with the gruff voice asked.

"Before too long," Boden, the man from the beach, answered. "Eleanor thinks it might help."

"I guess she would know," Voitto said in reply. "It would be good for him to come before the move."

"What move are they talking about?" Darcy hissed to Perry.

"I don't know, but I get the idea that we won't be staying here for much longer." He relaxed a little on the chair as the group at the table split into two factions, one of which made for the door. "Thank goodness," he added. "Although I think we would have been let outside soon, anyways. Rubidius keeps talking about getting us out in the 'field.' " He made air quotes.

"He does?" Darcy screwed up her face trying to remember. She couldn't remember much of anything from any of the recent classes.

"Only, like, every other day," Perry said. He looked at her a little strangely. "Geez, and I thought *I* didn't pay attention."

Darcy ignored the slight and gestured toward the remaining adults at the table. "Did you know who the old guys were? I knew who Boden was; I met him on the first night."

"The one who did some of the talking, with the really rough voice, his name is Ulfred. I stayed with him and his wife the first night before he brought me here in the morning," Perry said. "I think he's some sort of nobleman, but he lives with the peasants 'cause he represents them, or something like that. I didn't know the other guy."

"Did you hear who is supposed to be coming to see us? Was it Tullin?"

Perry shook his head. "No, I don't think so. I think they were talking about one of the princes, probably Tellius." He smirked slightly at her. "Your *fiancé*."

Darcy blushed deeply and stood. "He's not my fiancé." She spun around and marched out of the hall to her room, her blood pounding in her ears. Was Tellius really coming here after all this time? How could she possibly face him? She slammed her book down on the round table in the center of the room and crossed her arms over her chest. Why, oh why, did she have to be put in such an awkward and uncomfortable situation? At the very least, couldn't Pateros have arranged for him to be someone like Perry, rather than some gawky ten-year-old? Her energy suddenly left her with a whoosh and she felt very tired.

She left her clothes in a heap on the floor as usual and crawled into bed.

Her clothes were still in the pile where she'd left them the night before when she awoke in the morning, and she had a moment of confusion before she remembered that it was Resting Day. Every week on what was Saturday on planet Earth, the Alitheians carried out their version of a Sabbath day. They had a break from lessons and ate cold food that didn't require cooking preparation. It also meant that the cleaning girls who usually took care of the girls' clothes in the wee hours of the morning had the day off, as well.

Darcy felt self-conscious in her wrinkled dress as she gathered her breakfast food, and she was about to head back to her room when Yahto Veli's hand on her shoulder stopped her.

"Yahto tells me that you and Perry took an interest in our conversation last night," he said without preamble. "Is that true?"

Am I in trouble? Darcy panicked. "Um . . . yeah. Sorry. We just really wanted to know what was going on."

Veli's face relaxed into a smile, and he steered her toward the table with her food. She obediently sat, and he took the seat across from her. "It's okay to be curious," he said, "but I would prefer that you gather your information without eavesdropping."

"But how?" Darcy blurted out. "You never tell us anything!"

"Have you ever asked?" he countered.

"Well—I—" Darcy squinted hard, trying to remember. "I guess not. But I didn't think you would answer my questions."

Veli took a bite of breadstick and waved it in the air. "Why don't you run a few questions by me, and if I can't answer any of them, I'll let you know."

A hundred questions immediately popped into Darcy's mind, and she scrambled to think of the best one she could ask. "Why doesn't Rubidius want to find out what my talent is?" she finally said.

A puzzled look crossed Veli's face and he frowned. "What do you mean? Of course he wants to find out what it is."

"But he never works with me."

"Are you begrudging him the time he is spending with your friends? I'm sure that he will get to you when the time is right. But, come now, that is a question for Rubidius. Ask me one that I can answer."

Darcy thought for a moment. "What is the 'move' you guys were talking about last night? What does it have to do with us?"

"Ah! A good question." He shifted his weight forward. "Eat," he ordered her. "I'll talk. The members of the rebellion like to stay mobile. There are several hideout locations throughout Alitheia, but it is especially important now to stay close to the twin castles. The only other location that we could move to and still stay close enough is the ruins at Paradeisos. They are cloaked from the enemy, and we could allow you to be outdoors. We've been here for too long, and many of our number have already gone on to Paradeisos—"

"Is that why it's been so empty around here lately?" Darcy interrupted between bites.

"Yes; I'm glad you noticed." He looked at her keenly and nudged more food toward her. "Within another month, we hope to move the six of you, as well."

"Another month?" Darcy sprayed her food as her stomach dropped. *I can't survive another month underground!*

"I said *within* another month," he corrected her gently. "It could be sooner."

"Why can't we go now?"

"Well, we can't all go at once; too suspicious. And there are a lot of preparations that have to be made for you."

Darcy chewed quietly for a few more moments and then swallowed hard before her next question. "Is Tellius really coming here?"

Veli's eyebrows rose. "I shouldn't be surprised that you overheard that," he said wryly, "but yes, he is. Hopefully this week."

"Why?"

Yahto Veli hesitated, as though unsure whether to continue, but he did anyway. "Lady Eleanor seems to think that it will be good for the two of you to start getting to know each other."

Darcy's stomach dropped even further, and she pushed the rest of her food away.

"This is . . . displeasing to you?" Veli questioned softly.

Yes, Darcy thought, but she only shrugged her shoulders.

"Darcy!" Rubidius's brisk voice suddenly barked at her from across the room. The old alchemist swept toward her, his robes brushing the ground and his eyes keenly focused. "I expect to see you in my cottage tomorrow morning, just after breakfast. We have a lot to talk about."

Chapter 26

Not Ready

Darcy tried not to get too excited as she pattered down the hall toward Rubidius's cottage entrance. She was still spinning from the fact that he was actually going to work with her, and her hands shook as she knocked on the wall next to the curtain hanging in front of his doorway. From experience, she knew that the sound would resound as a knock on his door in the cottage, and she waited expectantly for his gruff "Come in!" but it didn't come.

Frowning, she knocked again, this time a little harder. Surely he hadn't forgotten about her. Her fears were baseless, though, as the curtain abruptly pulled open and Rubidius poked his face out. His curly hair and beard were frazzled, and he was red-faced and sweaty.

"Is it time already?" he barked. "Well, come in, come in. I just have a bit of a mess to clean up."

Darcy followed him into his cottage and surveyed the "mess." His cauldron, which was usually boiling by the fire, was overturned on the floor and scorch marks gave evidence to its landing next to its spilled contents. Rubidius was nursing a burn on his hand and mumbling angrily to himself. Darcy immediately knew that he wouldn't be in a pleasant mood this morning.

"Um . . . what happened?"

"What happened? This confounded experiment happened!" Rubidius shouted. "Why give us the drive to complete an impossible task?" He shook his good fist in the air, and Darcy got the impression that he was not talking to her. "First, it's too hot," he continued, mumbling quickly, "and then it's too cold. The next time it's too viscous, and when I try to correct that, it gets too opaque and gives off a foul odor. What is a self-respecting alchemist to do?" He waved his hand over the mess on the floor, and the spilled liquid started rapidly drying.

Darcy surveyed the scene. "Does this have anything to do with turning lead to gold?"

"Does it have anything to do with it? It has *everything* to do with it!" He gestured wildly and Darcy jumped.

"But why is it so important?"

The master magician mouthed at her like a fish out of water for a solid minute before turning away without giving her an answer. When his floor was clean, he dug a jar out of his cupboard and applied a thick salve to his burned hand.

As Darcy watched him do this, she had a revelation and giggled. "Did you *throw* your cauldron?"

He scowled at her. "Impudent," he said, but he didn't deny it.

Darcy sat in a chair at the table and smirked. At least *she* didn't get violent when she suffered from the grumps.

When he was finally finished cleaning up his mess and the cauldron was once again hanging on its hook by the fire, Rubidius sat down at the table across from her and surveyed her with very serious eyes.

"You're unhappy," he finally declared.

"I—"

"Don't deny it!" he barked. "I know why you're unhappy."

"You do?"

"You feel neglected, but you mustn't."

Darcy glowered at him, but she said nothing.

"I haven't neglected you, and neither has anybody else," Rubidius continued. "You've fallen prey to a false perception." He made a steeple with his fingers in front of him. "You are not ready to be trained in magic," he declared. "You possess magical abilities that none of your peers do, yet you are jealous of their revealed talents. You mope around the tunnels, avoiding people and responsibilities, and you do not pay attention in sessions."

"Yes, I do," Darcy protested weakly. This was not what she had expected.

His eyes narrowed. "What's the primary function of the humidorous fungi?" he asked her.

"To—to—to be . . ." Her voice trailed off. She had no idea.

"You can extract a liquid from them that will sustain you better than water," he said grimly. "We've discussed those particular fungi at least five times since I first mentioned it in the second week of sessions. You should have numerous notes on it, but," he pulled a stack of parchment from under the table and placed it in front of her, "you've written nothing of worth for weeks."

Darcy recognized the stack as being her notes and she blanched. If

Rubidius had thumbed through her notes, then she was truly in trouble. She knew the pages contained only doodles and half-hearted attempts at poetry. On a few pages she had written Perry's name and her own encased in a heart, and she sincerely doubted she'd had the presence of mind to scratch them out. She swallowed hard. She didn't know what to say.

Rubidius took her pieces of parchment to the fire and tossed them in. "Learn contentment," he said simply. "Confide in your friends and be happy for them. Encourage them, even. When you are ready, I will teach you." He went to the door and held it open for her: a clear dismissal.

"But don't you want to find out what my talent is?" she whispered. "I thought it was supposed to be the most important."

"Of course I do!" he snorted. "But if we discover it before you are ready, I am afraid of the repercussions that could follow. I will see you this afternoon."

Darcy slouched against the wall outside his cottage with her arms wrapped tightly around her middle. She'd never felt more rotten, and she squeezed her eyes shut against the deluge of tears that was rising. Self-pity and self-loathing battled for supremacy within her, and she shook her head back and forth, a fierce desire to prove Rubidius wrong aiding the self-pity side of the battle. It was unfair. Unfair of him to treat her like that, unfair of him to expect so much of her. How would *he* feel in her place? He couldn't even handle the failure of his alchemical experiments without flying off the handle!

Muffled voices and the tread of heavy boots announced the imminent approach of a group of men, and Darcy quickly ducked through a curtained entrance she'd never been through before. The room was dark, lit with only one sputtering torch, and full of supplies. She sat on a stack of potato sacks and waited for the group of men to pass by in the hallway. She heard their laughter and the lightness in their voices, and she finally lost the battle with her pain. Covering her face in her hands, she howled in misery.

A few minutes passed by until she felt a warm hand on her shoulder and smelled a waft of cinnamon. She was suddenly being hugged, and she squirmed, distinctly uncomfortable.

"Sam, get off," she muttered. The worst of her fit had passed, and she was reduced to puffy eyes and a runny nose. She sat up and pushed her away. Sam's anxious blue eyes peered at her, and Darcy felt a pang of remorse. "Sorry, I'm not mad at you."

"They said that somebody was crying in here," Sam said carefully.

Oh great. So now everybody knows. "Who did?"

"The men that just arrived . . . from the palace. They're preparing a visit for Tellius and Cadmus."

Even better. "I'm okay," Darcy lied. She took in and let out a shuddery breath. "I just had a . . . a bad morning, that's all."

"Are you homesick?" Sam asked.

"No."

"Did Rubidius get mad at you for something? He can be rather intimidating."

"Sam." Darcy felt a nudge of annoyance. "I don't want to talk about it."

"Okay." Sam looked over her shoulder at Amelia, who stood by the doorway holding something wrapped in thin cloth. "We brought you a cinnamon bun." Sam laughed a little nervously. "Food usually makes *me* feel better."

Darcy accepted the food offering but didn't eat it; instead she studied her feet and wished that they would leave her alone.

"Are you *sure* you don't want to talk about it?" Sam persisted after a very awkward moment of silence had passed.

"Yes," Darcy said. She shoved the cinnamon bun in her mouth to discourage more questions.

"Is Rubidius going to work with you now? I know that you've really been wanting that."

Darcy sighed through her nose and rolled her eyes. "No," she managed as soon as she swallowed.

"Why not?" Sam cried. "He's worked with all the rest of us, at least for one or two sessions."

Darcy glowered at her. "He said I'm not ready," she said shortly.

"Oh!" Sam's shock was almost worth the admission, Darcy thought glumly.

"But—"

"Drop it, Sam," Amelia finally spoke up. "She doesn't want to talk about it."

Darcy felt an unexpected rush of gratitude toward Amelia, but Amelia wouldn't look at her.

"Let's go." Amelia continued, "I don't think we're supposed to be in here."

Sam offered Darcy a hand up and helped her straighten her skirts, which had become badly twisted as she lay on the potato sacks.

"So, did they say when the princes are supposed to arrive?" Darcy asked in a vain attempt at sounding normal as the three girls exited the storeroom.

"I think sometime tonight or tomorrow morning," Sam said. She looked askance at Darcy as if afraid of her reaction. Suddenly she frowned and stopped walking.

"What is it now?" Amelia said impatiently.

"My pouch, there's something in it!" Sam said excitedly, fishing around in her pocket with eager fingers.

She managed to extract the small leather purse and pulled the strings apart with shaking fingers. Frowning, she pulled out a small, antique-looking metal square that was decorated with ornamental swirls.

"What's this all about?" Sam said, puzzled, but Darcy recognized the piece immediately.

"It's for me," she said dully, holding out her hand. Sam placed it in her palm and she turned the object over, marveling against her will that it could have magically made it all the way to Alitheia. Pressing a catch on one side, the object sprang open to reveal a brightly polished interior: a mirror. “It was my grandmother’s,” Darcy explained quietly. “But it’s just an old compact.”

“Why would that appear in my pouch?” Sam asked. “You don’t *need* a compact right now, do you?”

Darcy shrugged as she snapped it closed. *EMS*, her grandmother’s initials, were engraved on the bottom. “I don’t know. Maybe I need to look in a mirror.” But she had a sneaking suspicion that it meant more than that.

Chapter 27
Unexpected Talent

Darcy made an extra effort to pay attention in session that afternoon, and she successfully took three pages of notes on the new parchment that Rubidius provided for her, but she did it all out of spite. Rubidius thought she wasn't ready to be trained in magic? That it wasn't time to discover her talent? That she never paid attention in sessions? Well, she'd prove him wrong, and he'd be sorry.

She viciously dotted an 'i' and put her quill down. The communal pot of ink that they shared at the table was almost empty and the other teenagers were stretching and shuffling their parchment, ready to be done for the afternoon.

"Just one more thing." Rubidius held up a hand to get their attention. "The princes will be arriving soon, probably tonight, but tomorrow morning at the latest. I am not sure what this visit will mean to each of you, but I can guarantee that it will be important to at least *some* of you." His eyes flickered to Darcy. "Lady Eleanor has told me that you are not accustomed to royalty in your world and that you may not know how to act when they are here. I want to make it clear that although Tellius is but a boy, he is the rightful sovereign of this land and a person to be respected. By his allowance are you living and studying here, and you owe him your allegiance. But I also hope," his face relaxed a little and he smiled, "that you can come to be friends with him. You and he will have much interaction before your time is completed in Alitheia."

He spoke to the six of them as a group, but Darcy felt that he was targeting her with his words, and she groused inwardly as she packed up to leave. As if reminding her of her supposed future relationship with the coming prince, the royal ring on her left thumb caught a ray of sunlight from the window and reflected it into her eyes. She moved her hand quickly and did not look at Rubidius as she followed Lewis and Dean out of the cottage.

"Are you nervous?" Sam asked at her elbow. Darcy knew that she had wanted to talk about Tellius's impending arrival from the moment she'd found out about it.

Nervous, terrified, angry, uncomfortable . . . Darcy smiled grimly, only lifting the corners of her mouth. "I don't see why I should be. I mean, nothing's decided yet, is it?"

"Of course she's nervous!" Amelia snorted, trailing a short distance behind them. "Wouldn't you be? I can't imagine being in your situation, Darcy."

That doesn't help. "I guess I am a little nervous," she admitted. "But I'm trying not to be. I mean, come on. He's just a little boy!" She made a face.

They stopped at the entrance to the great hall. In the center of the room, surrounded by a group of people, was a little person trailing leaves behind her. She was so obviously otherworldly that Darcy's breath caught in her throat. They'd grown used to Rubidius's casual magic and the narks' unusual traits, but they hadn't seen any other magical creature since their first day in Alitheia, and Darcy felt suddenly revived at the sight.

"It's the dryad from the council!" Sam hissed excitedly. "Fylla! She took me to her tree when the council broke up. I wonder if she'll come say hi to me."

"Shhh!" Darcy shushed her.

"They've made it successfully out of the city and are travelling by horseback," the dryad Fylla was saying. "Lord Tullin is going to make it look as though they are on a foraging trip; he's hoping to avoid the checkpoints on the roads by cutting through the woods."

"But when will they be here?" a woman asked anxiously. Darcy recognized her as the cook.

"Not for another hour, at least. They will be coming in a very roundabout way," the dryad answered. "I said I would bring word, but I must return to my post!" With a flutter of leaves, she disappeared up the back tunnel toward the stables.

"Well, that's nice," the cook muttered, smacking a large wooden spoon on her palm in agitation. "I suppose they'll need feeding, then. I didn't expect them so early . . ." her mumblings faded away as she bustled back to the kitchen.

"Maybe we can help her," Sam said anxiously, peering over the gathered heads.

"Don't count on it," Veli said from behind them. His hair was already a golden brown, and his eyes had darkened to a deep-water blue. In less than an hour he would go to sleep. "Asa Rhea doesn't like interference in her kitchen, and she certainly would not consider it proper for one of the Six to help her." He yawned apologetically. "So sorry. Bedtime, you know. Shall we sit?" He guided Darcy and Sam to the table and held out a hand to include Amelia, as well.

Sam giggled and looked at Darcy.

"Um," Darcy began, "I don't know if you should sit with us, Veli. Yahto, you know, doesn't really like to sit with me, and last night you changed right in the middle of dinner." In mid-bite, Veli had suddenly stopped chewing and closed his eyes. His hair had quickly finished the transformation to midnight black, and his skin deepened its tan. When he opened his eyes after a few seconds, they were steely, charcoal grey, and contained no humor. As he'd started chewing again, he'd looked to his right to find Darcy next to him and had rolled his eyes with such exaggeration that Darcy had almost choked on her salad. He hadn't said a word for the rest of the meal.

Veli looked a little exasperated, but dipped his head in acquiescence. "I can only apologize for his behavior. I don't want to make either of you uncomfortable, so perhaps you are right. I'll sit with the young lords." And with that he joined Perry, Dean, and Lewis on the other side of the table.

They ate dinner with Darcy continuously looking over her shoulder, expecting fanfare or whatever it was that would happen when Tellius and his brother arrived. They did not come during supper, however, and Darcy breathed a sigh of relief. Perhaps she could escape to her room for the rest of the night and not have to bother with awkward re-introductions. When she stacked her plate and stood to leave, however, Yahto looked up and stopped her.

"You can't leave," he said dryly. "You have to be here for the prince's arrival."

"I know that," Darcy lied peevishly. "I'm just going to . . . to get a book." She felt his gaze follow her as she marched to a bookshelf and blindly stared at book spines. *No escape, no escape*, pounded over and over in her head.

Lykos rose from near the fire and prowled to her side, his deep growl sounding in his throat. He bumped her thigh with his nose and she reached down to push his snout away. "Cut it out," she muttered. She'd grown increasingly bold with the animal over the past couple months, and he no longer intimidated her. Sam didn't like him, though, which Darcy thought was odd. She'd never known Sam to feel unkind toward anyone, human or otherwise.

Lykos bumped her leg again, this time hard enough to make her stumble backward. "Lykos, what are you doing?" she hissed. She looked him in the eye, her thought exploding from her nonverbally, *Leave me alone!*

In that second she knew that something had happened. Lykos immediately ceased his rumbling and both of his ears shot up in the air. With two keen, intelligent eyes trained on her, a deep, inhuman voice entered her brain. It asked her a question. *Can you hear me?*

Darcy's heart thumped loud, and she dropped to one knee in front of the great beast. *Yes!* She answered him in her mind. *Yes, I can!*

What a great talent you have, Darcy Pennington.

Darcy gasped aloud, but nobody turned to see what she had exclaimed over because the people in the room had suddenly stood as one. When Darcy looked up, her eyes alighted on the figures of the young princes and their escort standing at attention in the rear entrance of the hall.

Lykos's voice entered her mind one last time before she stood, and he sounded approving, but stern. *We must keep this between us for now. It will be best that way. Do you agree?*

"Okay," she whispered aloud to him, but she knew that he understood. Too much was happening at once, and her mind whirled. As she stood and faced the princes, she felt that whatever connection she'd just had with Lykos was broken. *Lykos,* She reached out with her mind.

Yes?

Relief flooded her. *Never mind. Did you hear all my thoughts?*

I only heard my name, he replied. *I'm going now, but I'll return tomorrow*.

She felt the connection sever again as the great grey wolf loped to the main entrance and disappeared. She felt abandoned, alone, and horribly exposed. Why was she all the way over here by herself? Most everybody else was still at the table. They were announcing the princes now, but the words sounded fuzzy in her ears. She twisted her fingers over and over, uselessly wringing her hands.

They didn't look like princes this time. They were dressed commonly, even lowly, in rough, hand-spun fabrics that were worn and stained. Thick cloaks were draped over their shoulders, and Darcy noticed a dusting of snowflakes standing out against the dark brown. Four narks had slipped in with the boys and their cousin, Tullin Ecclektos, and they moved discreetly to various corners of the room. A couple servants stepped forward to take their cloaks, and Tellius's eyes flashed briefly to Darcy as he shrugged loose of the material and stepped forward to take a seat at the table. Asa Rhea, obviously eager to please, hurried forward with three steaming plates balanced on her capable arms and placed them before the weary travelers.

"Here ya are," she said, "this should warm your bones."

The boys and Tullin nodded their thanks, and Darcy noticed that Tellius was rather stiffer than his brother. They bent to eat, and low conversation began again in the room. Yahto leaned forward to engage Tullin in conversation, and Darcy let out a heavy breath. What should she do? Get a book and read? Go forward and greet them? Her stomach lurched at the very thought. Should she stand there like a marionette with no puppeteer? *She* didn't know what protocol demanded of her. Why didn't Rubidius or Eleanor better prepare them for this?

She licked her lips; they had gotten very dry in her tension and nervousness. She noticed Sam shooting her inquisitive glances, and she decided to settle on a compromise. Snatching a book off the shelf without even glancing at its title, she meandered back to the table and sat down next to Sam, every nerve in her body on edge. She wasn't so close to Tellius that she would have to say anything right away, and Sam seemed to understand what she was doing, because she didn't press the matter.

Darcy cracked the book open, intending to bury herself in it, and winced. *Celmian Importations and Their Economic Impact on Alitheia.* Not exactly what Darcy would consider a page-turner, but she was committed to her choice now; she would have to act interested. She turned the title page and read the first paragraph. Her eyes practically crossed. It was worse than her science textbook. There was no way she could lose herself in this, but she made a good show of it, staring hard at the words and even turning a page from time to time.

"Are you interested in economics?" a young voice invaded her consciousness, and she peeked above the book to find Tellius looking at her. He'd finished his meal and was leaning forward in his chair to look around the few people that separated them.

Darcy blushed against her will and closed the book carefully. "Not really," she admitted. "I just picked it up." She noticed that the conversations around them had ceased and people covertly, and some not-so-covertly, watched the two of them as if analyzing their interaction. Darcy felt a flush of anger. Why couldn't everybody just mind their own business? Her anger gave her a rush of boldness and she decided to counter Tellius's question with one of her own. "Do *you* like economics?"

He shrugged slightly. "I don't mind it, but it's not my favorite subject."

Darcy raised an eyebrow skeptically. "You've already studied economics?" She did not succeed in keeping the disbelief out of her voice.

It was Tellius's turn to flush angrily, and his ears flamed red. "I've studied it some," he said, and then he turned away from her and flashed his cousin an obstinate look. Some sort of silent struggle ensued between the two of them before Tellius abruptly stood. "I would like to be shown to my room," he demanded to the hall at large.

A servant hurried forward. "Right this way, your majesty."

He was led from the room, and Darcy felt a niggle in the back of her mind that told her she should have shown more tact. When she glanced at Tullin Ecclektos, however, she found him shaking his head and commenting to Yahto Veli about Tellius's behavior. Darcy felt a little better. She, apparently, was not the only one who had not behaved as expected.

She didn't feel like going to bed yet, even though she was much more relaxed now that Tellius was no longer in the room. But at least she was free to return the dreadful book on Alitheian economics to the bookshelf, which she did. Deciding that she couldn't focus on reading any book because of all that was running through her mind, she settled on observing the card and dice game that the boys settled in to play. She had never bothered learning how to play—a side effect of the grumps—and she watched with interest as they placed bets, rolled the die, and collected piles of chips.

Cadmus joined his older brother wherever their quarters were, and the remaining two night narks followed him out of the great hall, the first two having followed Tellius on his exit. Tullin announced that he was not staying and that he would be back in a few days to escort the princes home—wherever that was—and he left toward the stables.

The great hall once again contained only people who were regularly there, and Darcy breathed easier, finally allowing her brain to explore the unsettling revelation that she'd had with Lykos just a short time earlier. So *this* was her talent! She could mindspeak with animals! Or . . . she frowned thoughtfully . . . maybe she could only mindspeak with Lykos?

She was one step away from attempting to engage Pinello, who was curled in Sam's lap as usual, when she stopped herself. Lykos had told her that it would be best to keep it between the two of them for the time being, and she'd agreed. She knew that she hadn't made a binding promise, but she still felt that she'd given her word. What was one more day? She'd see the wolf again tomorrow and they could talk it over. Besides, she felt a slight thrill, it was kind of exciting to know what her talent was when even Rubidius did not; it made her feel important . . . empowered. Was it merely coincidence that on the very day he'd declared her unready for training she'd stumbled upon her talent on her own? Didn't that very fact prove the alchemist wrong?

She smirked and sat back in her chair, continuing to watch the boys play the game as though she were interested in what they were doing. What if Lykos could help her develop her talent to the point that she wouldn't even *need* Rubidius to teach her? Wouldn't he be surprised!

Sam poked her on the leg. "Are you coming to bed? Amelia and I are going."

"Not just yet; I'm interested in the game," Darcy said.

"Okay, 'night." Sam and Amelia stood and left.

"Do you want to learn how to play?" Perry asked her once the other two girls were gone. "I don't mind teaching you. You can share my hand."

Darcy's stomach twisted with pleasure, and she moved to sit on the floor next to Perry. She had a feeling that the grumps were on their way out.

CHAPTER 28

TELLIUS

"His majesty would like to speak with you."

Darcy looked up, her spoon halfway to her mouth, at the unfamiliar day nark speaking to her. "He does? Tellius wants to?"

"Yes, my lady. He's requested that you appear in his quarters."

"All right." Darcy put her spoon down and stood, accidently stepping on her skirt and falling against the nark's chest as she did so. "Sorry," she mumbled as he reached out a hand to steady her.

She followed the nark out of the great hall and into the tunnel. He didn't say anything else to her once his summons was delivered, and every question that popped in her mind died on her lips. Why couldn't Tellius just come and talk to her in the great hall? Why did he have to see her alone? He and his brother had completed their morning forms with the rest of the men in the great hall that morning, and she knew that he'd seen her at the table. Why didn't he just ask to talk to her then?

She sighed as the nark stopped beside a curtained doorway on the left side of the tunnel and held the fabric aside for her to pass through. Steeling herself, she entered the room and was immediately thrown off by its dimensions. She'd been expecting a small, cozy room like the one she shared with Amelia and Sam, not the cavernous space that she now stood in. Four large beds stood around the walls and a roaring fireplace was set in the back wall. A full-scale dining room table with high-backed chairs stood in the middle of the room, and bookshelves lined the walls. By the fire was a cluster of armchairs and small end tables, each containing a different game or set of instruments.

Tellius sat in one of the armchairs opposite his brother, playing a game on one of the small tables, and he only glanced up when Darcy entered. Two more narks stood on either side of the door inside the room. Nobody said anything for a long moment and Darcy was beginning to wonder if there had been a misunderstanding, when a figure suddenly rose from one of the high-backed chairs facing the fire and turned.

"Darcy!" Eleanor Stevenson said, surprised. "I didn't hear you enter. Come in, dear, come in." The elderly woman sent a reprimanding glance toward the two princes and gestured for Darcy to join them around the fire. "It's getting downright cold outside," Eleanor said as she pulled out a chair for Darcy. "I arrived by foot this morning and have been sitting by the fire almost since the moment I walked in the door. I just can't seem to warm up." She shivered and squeezed Darcy's hand. "Boys," she said seriously, turning her gaze upon the brothers, "your guest is here."

Darcy couldn't see Tellius's face because his back was to her, but Cadmus smirked and swept the pieces of their game to the side. "Not *my* guest," he said teasingly. Jumping up, he raced to the door. "Come on, Tova, let's go see the lion!"

One of the narks unfolded himself from the shadows and patiently followed the young prince out of the room.

Tellius took his time straightening the game pieces and then stiffly moved his chair to face Eleanor Stevenson, putting Darcy between them. He looked more his station today. His ratty clothes were gone and he was dressed in a simple tunic of burgundy and tan over brown britches. His dark wavy hair was combed neat and it gleamed in the firelight. He was only ten, but he sat very still. Darcy had never seen her brother sit still for so long without being asleep. She studied him discreetly, wondering what he had called her here for.

"Tellius wanted to ask you a few questions," Eleanor prompted, fixing the boy with a piercing gaze. "Isn't that right, highness?"

Tellius finally squirmed a little, the action showing his age, and opened his mouth. He looked as though he was going to be sick, but words came out instead. "What's your favorite color?" he asked unexpectedly. He didn't look at her.

"Me?" Darcy said, pointing at her chest. "What's my favorite color?"

"That's what I said."

"Tellius!" Eleanor said sharply.

"I mean," he finally raised his eyes to hers as he sighed, "Yes, my lady."

That's a strange question. "Um . . . I don't know. It changes all the time. I really like blue right now."

"How can your favorite color change?" he retorted. "If it changes all the time, then it's not really your favorite."

Darcy raised an eyebrow at him. Roger would have earned a punch on the arm for talking to her like that, but she could hardly punch the crown prince of Alitheia.

He watched her reaction seriously for a moment, and when she didn't rise to his retort, he asked another question. "What is your favorite season of the year?"

What is this? An interrogation? Darcy looked at Eleanor Stevenson for help, but the matronly woman merely nodded and smiled encouragingly. "Fall. I like the colorful leaves. What's yours?"

Tellius countenance immediately changed. "I like spring. I hate fall."

"What he means is that he prefers spring to fall," Eleanor interjected sternly. "Hate is a very strong word, Tellius."

"Well, I do!" His face took on a tortured look, and Darcy sank back in her chair, a little frightened by what she saw. What on earth was going on with this boy? It looked like fifty conflicting emotions were battling in his head.

It took Tellius a moment to compose himself, but he eventually did and rebounded with yet another trivial question. "What is your favorite activity?"

"Horseback riding. You?"

"I like archery, but horseback riding is okay, too."

"I would like to learn archery," Darcy said honestly.

Tellius didn't reply to her comment, but looked like he was searching for something else to say. After a very awkward moment, Eleanor interjected for him.

"I think the prince is all out of questions for this morning." She stood, indicating that Darcy was welcome to, also. "The princes and I will join the six of you for your afternoon session with Rubidius today. We'll see you then." She cleared her throat and Tellius sprang to his feet like his chair was on fire. He stared at Darcy's hand for a second, and then snatched it up in his. With a look of pure loathing on his face, he yanked it to his mouth and kissed it quickly before Darcy retracted it with horror.

She felt numb as Eleanor walked her to the door, and once out in the hallway, she stood still for a moment. She didn't mean to eavesdrop, but she distinctly heard Eleanor say to Tellius, "There now, not so bad as you imagined, was it?"

"Do I *have* to do this *every* morning?" he whined back. "I don't know what else to ask her!"

"I'm sure you'll think of more questions before tomorrow," Eleanor replied. "Why don't you apply yourself to the task right now?"

"I just want to play, like Cadmus. I never get to play."

"That's not true, highness," Eleanor answered calmly. "Why, you just played a game with him this morning."

Their voices grew too faint to hear, and Darcy jumped, realizing that she'd been caught listening in on a private conversation. She shot a guilty look at the two narks outside the door and took off down the hall.

Sam and Amelia had their heads together at the table when Darcy re-entered the great hall, and she knew instinctively that they were talking about her. She paused, unsure whether she should join them, but Sam looked up and saw her. Sam waved her over and scooted down so that Darcy could sit between her and Amelia.

"What did he want? Did he want to talk to you about getting married?" she asked breathlessly.

"No. He just wanted to ask me some questions." Darcy sounded nonchalant, but her hands were shaking. She hid them under the table.

"Questions like what?" Amelia asked.

"Stupid things . . . like what my favorite color is. I don't know what the point was."

"He probably just wants to get to know you a little bit," Amelia said, and Sam nodded.

"I don't think *he* wants anything to do with me," Darcy corrected her. "I got the idea that Eleanor made him do it."

"Eleanor's here?" Sam asked excitedly. "We haven't seen her for ages! I've been working on my Old Alitheian verbs, and I wanted to check them with her." She looked toward the tunnel as though expecting Eleanor to come walking through on cue.

Darcy followed her gaze. "I don't think we'll see her until session this afternoon. I think she's busy with the princes."

"Not with both of them," Amelia corrected her. "Cadmus is over there teaching Perry and Dean a new game." She pointed to the corner where the boys usually did their forms. The nark Tova was hovering over them, watching the young prince. Liontari and Alepo were also curled nearby. Every couple of minutes the boys would explode with laughter and the animals would raise their heads to gaze at them. They looked like they were having fun.

"So Rubidius is working with Lewis again this morning?"

"Yep." Sam's eyes stayed on the boys as she answered, "He's still having him write lines with that phoenix quill of his." She giggled and looked at Darcy and Amelia. "That sounds so bad—like he's in trouble, or something."

"Is he getting tired of it?" Darcy asked. "Writing every day, I mean."

"Are you kidding me? In case you didn't notice, Lewis always carries a backpack back home."

"Yeah, I've wondered what that was all about."

"Well, Lewis writes things . . . a lot of things. He says he wants to be an author someday."

"So, what does that have to do with his backpack?" Darcy asked.

Sam snorted softly. "He's *so* worried about somebody finding and reading his 'private' writings that he carries them around with him everywhere he goes."

"His backpack is full of journals?"

"Journals, notebooks, bits of napkin that he's scribbled on . . . you name it."

"How come you know about it if it's so private?"

Sam shrugged. "I'm his best friend. He's actually let me read a little of his stories. He's pretty good."

"He should be for how much energy he puts into it," Amelia said.

"I wouldn't be surprised to see him published someday," Sam added.

Session that afternoon was distinctly uncomfortable with Tellius and Cadmus there, but at least they were taking notes, too. Eleanor taught a history lesson about the centaur migration of 1065, and Darcy paid better attention than she had in a long time. She'd started in surprise when Eleanor said 'centaur,' but she tried to mask her awe. She didn't want to look stupid in front of the young princes, to whom the existence of centaurs was nothing new.

Eleanor made moving diagrams of the migration appear as stick figures in midair, adding to the interest of the lesson, and by the end of the afternoon, Darcy felt that she had taken a tolerably good stack of notes that even Rubidius couldn't complain about.

"Will you be back tomorrow?" Sam asked Eleanor as they packed up to leave. The shadows were long outside the windows, and a heavy snow was falling.

Eleanor laughed. "I'm not going anywhere in this weather, but yes, I was planning on teaching tomorrow, as well."

"Good, because I need to ask you about my verbs." Sam moved forward to continue talking with Eleanor, and Darcy surreptitiously watched the boys interact with the princes. Cadmus seemed to be formally introducing his older brother to the three teenagers, and they moved into an animated discussion of fighting and the forms. Darcy heard Perry asking questions about Baran, the weapons instructor, and Tellius and Cadmus laughed as they answered the questions with stories. Apparently Baran had a reputation.

She followed them out into the hall, leaving Amelia behind to wait for Sam, and shamelessly listened in on the boys' chatter. Why couldn't she talk that easily with people? Tellius looked more relaxed than she'd ever seen him as he laughed and talked along with his brother. Suddenly Cadmus looked over his shoulder and grinned wickedly at Darcy. Elbowing his brother in the ribs, he said, "Tellius, don't you want to walk with your future *wife*?"

Tellius became very still, and the rest of the boys turned around and sniggered, except for Lewis, who merely looked at her like she was something foul stuck to the bottom of his shoe. Darcy's ears flamed as the rest of her face blanched white.

"I don't know, Tel, she doesn't look very happy to see you," Cadmus continued. "Maybe you smell."

"Shut your mouth, Cadmus," Tellius said quietly. He was standing very still, but his ears were bright red, too.

"What? You don't like—"

But Cadmus didn't get to finish his sentence. Tellius launched at his younger brother and punched him in the face, knocking him flat on the ground and falling on top of him to continue the struggle. Cadmus howled in anger and pummeled back at his brother as they shouted unintelligible words at each other.

Darcy stepped back in horror as the three teenage boys reacted to the fight. Dean said, "Awesome!" and clapped his hands. Perry shot forward to try and disentangle Tellius from his younger brother, laughing as he did so, and Lewis watched the whole thing with a nervous, but mildly disgusted, look on his face.

The fight lasted only briefly, because the ever-present narks stepped in and pulled the boys apart. Perry had taken an elbow to the cheek for his trouble—he didn't look too upset about it—but Cadmus had had the worst of it. His nose was pouring blood and a fabulous black eye was blooming on the left side of his face. Tellius, obviously the more accomplished fighter of the two, stood cockily to the side once the narks removed him from his brother, sporting no more than a cracked upper lip.

"Whadya do that for?" Cadmus shouted at his brother, futilely struggling against Tova's firm grasp.

"You know why, you stupid garralump!" Tellius shouted back, but he didn't need to be restrained like his brother. He accepted a proffered rag from one of the other narks and put it to his lip.

Cadmus struggled a little more and then slouched, defeated. "Yeah, all right." He, too, took a rag and held it to his face. The narks seemed perfectly at ease, and Darcy wondered if fights between the two brothers were not uncommon.

Cadmus suddenly looked up and grinned at his brother. "That was a good one, Tel! You totally knocked me down before I even knew what was coming! I want Baran to teach me to fight like that someday. Then maybe I'll stand a chance."

Darcy was incredulous. If two girls had just fought like that, they wouldn't talk to each other for at least a month, and even then the relationship would probably be strained.

"Come on." Cadmus grabbed his brother's arm. "Let's go get some ice.

My eye's killing me." And with that, the company of boys and narks moved on. Only Lewis looked at Darcy, and he turned his back quickly when her gaze flitted to his.

She followed them down the hall and entered to the smells of cooking meat. She breathed deeply. They hadn't had a warm meal that wasn't soup or stew for dinner since they'd arrived. Apparently they ate better when royalty was around.

She sat at the table and put her head on her arms. She was tired, and her head hurt. She replayed the scene leading up to the fight in her head and wondered again what had provoked Tellius so violently.

She jumped as fur brushed her legs, and she looked down. Lykos stared back at her with his large, yellow eyes. *Hello!* She thought at him excitedly. She'd almost forgotten. She felt a very faint connection take hold between them, and Lykos answered her in measured tones.

Did you keep it between us? he asked her.

Yes. She frowned. *I didn't want to, really, but I gave you my word.*

Good, that's good. The wolf's voice was distinct in its inhumanness.

Where did you go last night when Tellius and Cadmus arrived?

He rested his head on her lap. *We probably shouldn't look like we're talking to each other. That boy is watching.*

Darcy looked up sharply and saw Lewis staring at her from across the table. She smiled wanly and laid her head on her arms like she was taking a nap. *Better*? she thought at him.

Yes, Lykos said. *I went to talk with my kind*, he answered her previous question.

About me?

Yes.

Darcy frowned to herself. *What happened to keeping it between us?*

My kind can be trusted. We've been waiting for someone like you for a long time. You're very special, Darcy.

Darcy felt a thrill of pleasure. At least someone treated her like she was important. *So, am I not allowed to tell any of my kind about this?*

Not yet. The great wolf shifted his head slightly. *There are many of your kind that can't be trusted, and some who would take advantage of you.*

Then who's going to train me? You?

Do you think you need training? Lykos's chest rumbled gently, and Darcy realized that he was chuckling. *What misguided thinking! Did you need training to discover your talent?*

No . . . I guess not. I did that on my own.

Just so, I will guide you as you develop it, but do not think of me as a teacher.

What do I think of you as, then?

A friend.

The weight on her leg abruptly lifted as Lykos trotted away from her without warning. Darcy looked up, surprised to see Sam and Amelia coming to the table. Sam scowled at Lykos's retreating form, but kept any comments to herself.

"What happened in the hall?" Amelia said. "Servants were cleaning up what looked like blood!"

"Oh, yeah . . . there was a fight." Darcy said, readjusting to vocal communication.

"A fight?" Sam's eyes grew large as she sat down next to Darcy. "Between who?"

"The princes. Tellius punched Cadmus, and they started fighting."

"Why?" Sam looked around the room. "Was anybody else involved?"

"I don't know," Darcy answered her first question first. "Perry tried to help, and I think he got knocked in the face, but that was it. It really didn't last very long."

"Perry got hit? Is he okay?" Sam asked anxiously. "Maybe I should go get him some ice." She started to rise, but Amelia pushed her back down.

"Too late," Amelia said, pointing. "He's already got some."

The two princes and Perry were emerging from the kitchen, laughing together, each holding a lumpy bag somewhere on his face. From their gestures, it looked like they were replaying the more exciting moments of the fight.

Asa Rhea was bringing out platters of succulent roasted meat with the help of a few servant girls, and Darcy's mouth watered in anticipation. The long table quickly filled as people from all over the warrens followed their noses to the best dinner in months. Even Rubidius joined them.

Perry sat across from Darcy, and when he lowered his ice bag, she could see a raised goose egg on his cheekbone that was slowly turning purple.

Sam gasped. "Perry! Are you okay?"

He grinned. "Nice, huh? But you should see Cadmus. Tellius totally messed him up."

"Fights between little boys should not be lauded," Rubidius said loudly, leaning forward to pin Perry with his gaze. "Tellius ought to learn to control his temper."

Perry kept a straight face until Rubidius looked away, but then he winked at the girls and bumped fists with Dean, who shared his enthusiasm. Perry leaned forward so that Rubidius couldn't hear him. "You should see how that little guy can fight! I mean, I think I could take him, but Dean would never stand a chance."

"Oy!" Dean smacked Perry on the back of his head.

Perry laughed and ducked but continued in his conspiratorial tone. "No, seriously though; Tellius is all right. He's been training for a lot longer than any of us. Baran told us he's not bad with a sword, either . . . for a ten-year-old," he added quickly.

"The food is served!" Asa Rhea declared to the room, and everyone began to pile cuts of meat onto their plates. There were roasted vegetables to complement the meal, and Darcy felt that she'd never been happier.

She loaded what smelled like pork onto her plate and was just reaching for the vegetables when loud shouting issued from far down the tunnel, and she, like everybody else on her side of the table, turned on the bench to look.

The shouting grew steadily louder and a large man clad in snow-covered furs burst into the great hall, followed closely by the redheaded Bayard. "Betrayed!" the man shouted, waving his arms. "This place is betrayed to the enemy! You must flee to Paradeisos, now!"

Chapter 29

The Flight

"My ladies, come *on*." Eleanor Stevenson breezed through their curtain and looked around at them impatiently, three heavy cloaks hung over her arm.

Darcy's shaking fingers scrambled over the tabletop, sweeping the few belongings she'd adopted as her own into a small satchel, which she then slung over her shoulder. She could hear shouting and people running past their room as Sam and Amelia finished gathering their own belongings.

Eleanor shoved a cloak at each of them. "Put them on," she said. "It's cold outside." She spun around, and the three girls followed her back out into the tunnel and then down into the great hall. The abandoned food mocked them from the table, and Asa Rhea was actually crying as she threw together her needed kitchen items.

Tellius and Cadmus were standing surrounded by their bodyguards on the far side of the table, and when Eleanor approached with the girls, they moved as a group to meet them.

"Quickly!" Darcy heard a shout. "They're not far away."

"Okay," Eleanor said in a rush. "When we get outside, we will split into two groups. Cadmus!" She snapped her finger under his nose; he'd been watching the chaos around them with wide eyes. "Are you listening to me?" He focused on her and nodded. "You and Tari Tova and Buto Hundi will go with Amelia. Take the easterly route. Tellius, Sam, Darcy, and you other two," she indicated the remaining two narks, "will go with me, west. Trust no one, and try not to be seen. The snow should help hide our tracks."

"Lady Eleanor." Yahto appeared at their side, his dark hair fluttering in his wake. "It's time. The way is clear, but we don't know for how long."

"Okay. Pateros guide our steps and hide us from evil eyes," she breathed. "Let's go."

She moved very swiftly for a woman of her age, and Darcy stepped quickly to keep up. Without warning, Sam, who was walking directly in front of her, stopped. Darcy ran smack into her back. "Oof! Sam! What are you doing? We have to go!"

Sam was staring hard at the man in furs who had alerted them of the danger. "I don't trust him," she said.

"What do you mean?" Darcy shoved her, exasperated and frightened. "We're falling behind."

"I don't know, I just . . . don't trust him," Sam said to her as she obediently jogged forward with Darcy. "Something about him gives me the creeps."

"What's . . . not . . . to trust?" Darcy panted. Their entire group was now moving at a full jog up the tunnel toward the stables. "He did . . . warn us . . . of the danger."

Sam didn't answer right away; she was clutching at a stitch in her side. "I guess . . . I'm just . . . scared," she finally managed.

They skidded around the corner into the stables and stopped. Darcy had been expecting to see the horses she'd grown to love, but instead her eyes met empty stalls. "Where are the horses?"

"Setting false trails," Yahto snapped at her, appearing at her side as only a nark could do. "Keep up!"

They moved to the end of the stables and to the wide door Darcy knew led outside but had never been through. They split into the two groups Eleanor had set up, and Yahto swung open the massive door. Cold air hit Darcy in the face like an anvil, and she gasped, trying to catch her breath. Snowflakes swirled in over the floor and a man just outside the door waved at them to move forward.

They stepped out into a very dense grove of cedar trees, and when the door swung closed behind them, Darcy noticed that it was camouflaged to look like part of the hillside. They moved as one until the grove thinned, and then Amelia was whisked away with Cadmus by their two narks, and Eleanor led Darcy's small group in the opposite direction.

Snow was falling heavily, making the world feel peaceful and quiet after the noise and chaos in the warrens, and Darcy couldn't help but thrill at being outside. She knew she should be as frightened as Sam was, but she just couldn't hang onto the feelings. Four months without fresh air! She inhaled deeply and watched her breath escape in a cloud of frost. But her euphoria was short-lived.

Sam squeaked as the two narks pushed them down behind a massive bush. One of the narks put his finger to his lips.

There were at least ten of them. They looked like men, but they moved slowly and deliberately, almost like prowling animals. Darcy had never seen a man move quite like that before. They were turning their heads from side to side, searching, and moving ever closer to the grove of trees that hid the secret entrance to the warrens. It looked as though their eyes contained no color—like the pupils had swallowed up the irises. Darcy gulped and tried to stay as still as possible.

Eleanor was muttering very softly under her breath, and their footprints to the bush faded instantly under an apparent layer of snow.

The prowling men disappeared into the cedar grove, and suddenly a loud and horrible sound filled the air. It was like a deep foghorn mixed with the snarl of a panther. It awoke terrible images in Darcy's mind and made her head feel as though two cymbals had just crashed in her ears. She cried out in fear, her outburst masked by the echoing bellow, and slapped her hands over her ears. They had found the entrance to the hideout.

"Let's go!" one of the narks shouted over the din.

Darcy struggled to rise in the foot-deep snow with Sam hanging onto her arm, but her effort was driven by adrenaline. What would happen if she were caught by one of those men? She shuddered to imagine, and with great effort threw herself after Eleanor and Tellius. The narks positioned themselves, one in front and one bringing up the rear, and they ran. Or, at least, they did the closest thing to running that they could in the snow. From snow-covered bush to massive boulder to grove of trees, they darted away from the hideout, putting as much space between them and the group of evil men as they could before they were once again forced to stop.

Darcy collapsed, dragging ice-cold air into her lungs in great gasps, and Sam was right beside her doing the same. Even Tellius was breathing hard, and Eleanor looked distinctly peaky. They'd been on the move for at least a half an hour and had finally taken shelter between two massive boulders that leaned together to form a sheltered area and a relatively dry patch of ground. It was dark out, but the landscape looked grey with all of the snow. It was falling lighter now, and they hadn't met up with any other enemy groups. The two narks watched diligently over their little hideout.

"I-I . . . always w-wondered . . . w-what it l-looked like h-here in . . . the wintertime," Sam gasped with effort.

"Here?" Darcy shivered. Now that they had stopped moving, the cold was beginning to close in on her. "You m-mean in . . . our w-world, right?"

Sam, apparently too winded to find any more words, merely nodded and waved her hand in a 'you know what I mean' sort of gesture.

Darcy leaned her head back against the rock and closed her eyes. Whatever those men were, they were evil, and she desperately hoped the boys had made it out before they found the warrens.

She felt a nudge on her shoulder and opened her eyes to find Eleanor Stevenson hovering over her. "Drink this," the woman said, holding out an uncorked canteen. "It's too strong for you, but it's all I have."

Darcy took it without argument and choked down a mouthful of very strong wine. She winced and handed the flask over to Sam, who coughed and choked on her own mouthful. She did start to feel her insides warm almost immediately, though, and she smiled gratefully at Eleanor.

"We can't rest here for long," Eleanor whispered to them. "We still have a long way to go, and we won't be safe until we reach Paradeisos." She put a hand to her forehead, and Darcy noticed that it shook. "We didn't expect this," she muttered, but then she looked up sharply. "What is it?" she spoke to the nark whose back was to them.

He was standing very rigidly. In a moment he was joined by his peer. They conferred silently together before turning to Eleanor. "We've been followed," one said.

"How many are there?" Eleanor whispered.

The narks closed their eyes and their ears twitched. "More than five," one said.

"Less than ten," the other completed.

Darcy peered between the narks' legs into the clearing. The boulders they were hiding between were two of many snow-blanketed mounds that rose like alien anomalies around an otherwise empty part of the forest. Trees closed in beyond the rocks, and Darcy imagined black eyes and pale faces hiding within their limbs and branches. She shuddered and sat back.

"Can we get away?" Eleanor asked the narks.

They shook their heads. "We shall have to fight. They are nearly upon us." They each drew swords and stepped away from the hiding place. "We will draw them out."

Tellius made a sudden movement. He sprang up and unsheathed his sword. He was halfway out of the hideout before Eleanor grabbed his arm and yanked him back. "Tellius, no!"

"I can fight!" he argued. "I want to fight."

"Now is not the time or the place," Eleanor hissed at him. "Let the narks handle it."

"But they killed my parents!" Tellius exclaimed. His hands were shaking madly, and there were tears in his eyes. "Let me go!"

"Oh, please, *please* be quiet," Sam whimpered. She was shaking like a leaf and sobbing. "I don't want them to hear us!" She buried her face on Darcy's shoulder.

Eleanor kept a firm hold on Tellius and forced him to look her in the eyes. "Sam's right, Tellius. Listen to me. These are not the same tsellodrin that killed your family. You must control your anger. Think of the girls; think of me. You mustn't betray our position to the enemy."

Tellius began to rock back and forth on his knees, and he dropped his sword arm with a gasp. He nodded his head as he rocked, and Eleanor pulled him in for a tight hug. "It's okay, highness," she crooned. "Pateros knows your pain."

Darcy's chest tightened as she watched the boy prince and his tutor. How would she feel if somebody killed her family? Would she want to avenge them? She turned her head to peer out of their hiding place and a sense of calm came over her. The narks stood back to back, armed and ready for battle. The snow had all but ceased falling and the dark limbs of the trees reached out closer about them.

Were they tree limbs? She squinted her eyes. Out of the blackness of the trees, a limb moved, followed by a human form. One tsellodrin moved into the clearing with deliberate steps; his form grew ever clearer and more defined the further he removed himself from the cover of the trees. He carried a broadsword at his side, dragging the tip of it in the snow with a drawn out scratching sound that resonated too loudly in the silent forest. He walked with his head thrust forward and lowered, like a tiger on the prowl, but his face contained no emotion. Blank, staring eyes and sagging mouth accentuated his haggard features.

As he came forward, more tsellodrin stepped out of the blackness, emerging from trees and bushes and from behind boulders. They moved and acted like the first one, without a hint of emotion as they circled the two narks and closed in on them.

Darcy's breath caught in her throat. She counted eight of them. The narks were outnumbered four to one. She clasped her hands together and wished desperately there were something she could do to help them.

"Turn away from this path," one of the narks called out. His voice, cool and musical and otherworldly, sounded confident despite the danger. "It's not too late for you. Turn back!"

The first hint of emotion appeared on the faces of the tsellodrin. Their eyelids widened and the black circles expanded to all but cover the whites of their eyes. A growl swept around the circle sounding almost like menacing laughter, and without warning, they attacked.

It wasn't at all like Darcy had imagined it would be. There were no Hollywood effects to distinguish the fighters from each other, and the tsellodrin attacked as a group, instead of one by one as they would have in the movies. At first it looked like the narks would be overwhelmed as they disappeared beneath a mass of tsellodrin bodies, but almost immediately three of the tsellodrin lurched and collapsed, and the narks whirled out of the fracas, their cloaks stained with a black, oily substance.

The narks were fast, impossibly fast, and agile with the special abilities of their race, but the tsellodrin did not fight like ordinary men. They were fluid, like dancers, and although they were slower than the narks, they moved and bent in ways that seemed to defy physics. The clang of swords hitting each other beat against her ears, and Darcy tried not to look at the injuries and fallen bodies, but they drew her eyes like magnets.

It happened so fast. Two more tsellodrin fell like rocks, black blood spurting across the white snow. As he met his fate, one of the tsellodrin, sandwiched between the backs of the two engaged narks, swiped his sword in a swift backhand across the back of the nark before him. Crimson blood bloomed across his back and he stumbled forward and fell on top of the tsellodrin he'd just slain.

Darcy's scream was cut short by Eleanor's hand as she whipped it around her face from behind, and the old woman hissed in her ear, "No! Not a sound!"

The tsellodrin didn't turn at her abbreviated scream, but the remaining nark gave a shout of grief and fell upon the remaining three with renewed vigor. He battled two at once, and the third circled around the back of him, poising for a killing strike.

Suddenly Eleanor shouted, "Tellius, no!"

She whipped around to see Tellius's small form rocketing from the other end of the hideout, having taken advantage of Eleanor's lapse in attention. She gasped as he ran toward the third tsellodrin; he looked tiny next to the other fighters. The tsellodrin turned, and when his eyes focused on the small boy with raised sword, he leapt upon him with a snarl, driving him to the ground. After a brief struggle, the tsellodrin lurched and both combatants lay still.

Eleanor screamed and scrambled forward, stumbling over her skirts and tripping over Sam's legs in her desperation. The remaining nark dispatched another tsellodrin, and the final tsellodrin took one look around him and fled into the trees. "He's seen the prince!" the nark shouted. "He must die!" With that, the nark sped off after the fleeing tsellodrin.

Eleanor pushed at the tsellodrin lying on top of Tellius. "I need help!" she shouted to Darcy and Sam. Darcy had never seen her lose control like this, and it frightened her.

Darcy untangled herself from Sam's frozen grasp and lurched forward. She dodged the fallen bodies, trying not to look at them, and reached Eleanor's side. Together they pushed the heavy tsellodrin off of the small prince and Eleanor let out a gasp of thankfulness.

Tellius was lying prostrate in the snow with his eyes squeezed shut, but he was breathing. His sword was clasped in both hands with the point facing upward and it dripped black blood. The tsellodrin had fallen on the blade, trapping Tellius beneath his dead weight.

Eleanor removed the blade from Tellius's grasp with shaking hands and pulled the boy into her arms. "Oh, thank you! Thank you, thank you, thank you!"

Tellius let himself be held, his arms limp and his shoulders rising and falling rapidly. He didn't open his eyes. Darcy looked around at the carnage and fought against the numbness that was overtaking her body, which had nothing to do with the cold.

The nark reappeared in the clearing and nodded at Eleanor. The deed was done; all of the tsellodrin had been killed. He moved to his fallen comrade and rolled him over gently, closing his eyes with two fingers and laying him delicately on the ground. With a hand over his brow, he bent his head for a minute, taking a moment of silent grief. Darcy watched all of this, distinctly uncomfortable, and Sam finally crept out of the hiding place.

When the nark was finished with his comrade, he went to Eleanor's side and gently removed Tellius from her grasp. Setting the boy on his feet, the nark handed him the sword and instructed him to clean it. As Tellius obeyed, the nark looked at Eleanor and said quietly, "His first. He'll be all right." He turned to the clearing. "Can you take care of this?"

Eleanor nodded and stood, wiping tears off her cheeks. With outstretched hands, she performed the same spell she'd used to erase their footprints earlier, but on a much larger scale. Even though it was no longer snowing, snow built up around each of the fallen bodies until they were no more than snowy lumps, not at all out of place in the boulder-strewn clearing.

"Thank you," the nark said. "Let's go."

Chapter 30

Paradeisos

The wolves moved like ghosts on either side of them. Their gray bodies flitted between the trees as their feet silently beat time. They were showing them the way.

Darcy was cold, freezing was more like it. And she was tired. The numbness that had crept over her in the clearing after the battle had not abated, physical cold added to her discomfort. They must be close to Paradeisos after all this time. It had been a long, dark hike through the forest, but Darcy had no idea how long it had been. It felt like hours.

According to Eleanor, the wolves were escorting them the rest of the way. She said it was a good sign, that it meant the other parties had made it safely to Paradeisos. They were the last. Darcy wondered if Lykos was among the wolves, but she was too tired to find out. She clung to the internal numbness. If it went away, she was afraid of what would replace it. She'd just seen people killing other people! Regardless of what the tsellodrin actually were, they looked human. And the poor nark who had died defending them—she'd seen it happen! Darcy swallowed convulsively and closed her mind to the images. She couldn't think of it; she had to stay numb.

She couldn't even bring herself to ask Sam how she was doing. The girl hadn't said a word since she'd emerged from the hiding place in the clearing. And Tellius—Darcy shot a sideways glance at him—was trudging through the snow like a person sleepwalking.

The wolves circled around them and faced an arch that emerged out of the darkness. Visible in the dark only because of the snow that covered it, it stretched twenty feet above their heads—an entrance through a broken-down wall on either side. The stones of the arch and wall were large and square cut and reminded Darcy of medieval ruins.

They passed through the arch with the wolves leading, and Darcy looked around to see other dilapidated stone structures littered throughout a large clearing, with the odd tree growing here and there. Enormous boulders, each one the size of the rock at Gnome's Haven or bigger, were scattered about. The snow beneath their feet was smooth and untouched. There was nobody in sight.

"Is this it?" she whispered. It couldn't be. It didn't look like anybody had been there in years.

Eleanor's face was gray and she looked ten years older than when they'd left the warrens at Sanditha. "These are the ruins of the castle of Paradeisos."

"But, where is everybody?" Darcy shivered.

"Hidden," Eleanor said simply. "Cloaked, remember?"

"Rubidius said that cloaking spells are complicated and that stepping out of a cloaked building destroys the spell. How does it work here?"

Eleanor actually smiled. "Because it is people and objects that are cloaked here, not the place itself, although the spell only works within the old walls of Paradeisos."

"So, w-what are we w-waiting for?" Sam's voice caught Darcy off guard.

"We're waiting for them to finish cloaking us," Eleanor replied. "Didn't you notice that the wolves are gone?"

Darcy started and turned a full circle. Eleanor was right. But when did it happen? She remembered following them in under the arch, but were they still there on the other side of the arch? She couldn't remember.

She must have been sleepy, because her vision was starting to blur. She blinked hard several times, but it didn't clear. Like a watercolor painting, the landscape was blurring about her, and different shapes and colors were taking form. She could also hear faint noises, like a television set turned on quietly in the background, growing ever louder. Something collided with her shoulder, and she spun around, but she could only see a large blob moving in the opposite direction. She turned to Eleanor, whom she could still see quite clearly, and the woman smiled serenely at her.

"We're almost there," Eleanor said encouragingly. Tellius stood dully at her side, staring at his feet.

Darcy blinked a few more times, and every time she did, the scene around her focused and grew sharper. She could now distinctly hear voices, and she thought that a few of the swimming blobs in front of her had faces she might recognize. With a final blink, the world around her finally settled and Darcy found herself in the middle of a bustling camp.

Amelia was hugging Sam, who was sobbing freely on her shoulder, and Yahto Veli stepped forward to greet the nark that had gone with them through the forest. Perry and Dean and Lewis came forward smiling to greet her, but Darcy couldn't bring herself to smile back. They didn't know what had happened in the clearing; she didn't want them to know. She didn't want their expressions to turn to ones of horror, and she couldn't handle the pity that she knew would be thrown her way. So, instead, she merely nodded her head at them and said, "Hey."

"Oh, man, wasn't that off the hook?" Perry said cheerfully. "Totally crazy! It was pretty nuts at first, but once we were clear of the tunnels, everything was fine. Which way did you guys go?"

"Um . . . west, I think," Darcy replied. She didn't want to talk about it.

"Didn't it feel weird to get cloaked?" Dean said. "Kinda made me dizzy."

"Yeah, so . . . what is all this? It's all cloaked, right?" She looked around at the colorful tents, roaring fires and moving people. There were a lot more people here than she'd ever seen at Sanditha, and the snow was trampled in all directions.

"Yeah," Perry answered. "It's all part of the hideout here. Torrin said that this cloaking spell only works here within the walls—something about the magical nature of the old castle, or whatnot. It's unique to this place, which makes it perfect to hide members of the rebellion."

"I don't care how it works," Lewis muttered. "At least we get to spend time outside here."

"True that!" Dean chimed in.

"But where do we sleep?" Darcy asked with a shiver. The prospect of sleeping in tents in the winter was not appealing. "I don't want to be outside *all* of the time."

"Let me show you," Eleanor said softly behind her. "I've sent Tellius off with his brother, and it's time for you all to get some rest. It's been a long night." She looked meaningfully at Darcy and Sam and then took them by the shoulders. "You boys should know where to go, correct? Did Torrin show you?"

"Yeah," Perry said. He and the other two said goodnight and Eleanor guided the three girls over to one of the large rocks.

It was strange-looking, because someone had set up a miniature pavilion next to the rock, connected to it like a porch, but when they ducked beneath the pavilion awning, they were faced only with the pock-marked and mossy side of the boulder. "Are you all here?" Eleanor looked over her shoulder. "Good. Watch closely." She placed her hand on the side of the boulder and waited. After just a few seconds, her hand melted into the rock and Eleanor pushed forward until her whole body disappeared into the boulder like it was made of Jell-O.

Darcy gasped. "What the—"

"It's really not that bad," Amelia said, stepping forward. "I did it earlier. You can't breathe for a moment, but it's really nice once you're inside." She imitated Eleanor by placing her hand on the rock, and in a moment she, too, pushed through and left them standing alone.

Sam still gaped, but Darcy said, "After you." So she went up to the rock.

Without a word she placed her hand on it. After a second, she exclaimed, "Oh! It's warm!" and then she pushed and was gone.

Darcy relished a moment alone, taking a few deep breaths before she followed her friends. The boulder was certainly large enough to contain a secret room, she supposed, but this was by far the strangest thing she'd done since arriving here. She went up to the rock and felt it warm under her hand, as Sam had said, and when the surface became permeable, she only had to push a little. Like a vacuum, it sucked her through to the space inside.

The room was toasty warm, the floor soft and covered in thick rugs, and a lantern swung from a hook above their heads. Like their room at Sanditha, three beds stood at even intervals around the walls, and the rest of the very small space was taken up by a round table and three chairs. That was where the similarities ended, though. The beds were four-posters with cedar-trunk poles rising up to the ceiling at each corner and draped in fabric that could be pulled down to enclose each one. Reds, oranges, and yellows dominated the color scheme of the bed dressings and rugs, and extra dresses in the same colors hung on rungs driven into the rock walls. A few books were stacked on the table, and Darcy noticed her favorite nursery rhyme book among them. Unexpected tears sprang to her eyes at the thoughtfulness of whoever had grabbed it, and she ducked aside to one of the beds to hide them.

"That's my bed," Amelia said. "Yours is over there. They've each got nightgowns on them for us."

"Thanks," Darcy said, trying not to sniffle. She went to the bed on the opposite side of the curved room and found a nightgown folded up on the pillow. When she unfolded it, it was indeed just her size. She silently removed her pack from her shoulders and untied the cloak strings at her throat. She was bone-achingly tired.

"All right," Eleanor Stevenson said, looking around. She sounded a little hoarse and Darcy noticed that her hands were still shaking. "Get dressed for bed and then drink these." On the table were three steaming mugs and Darcy recognized the scent of the broth she'd had the first night in Alitheia.

Her nightgown was a little scratchy, but the broth was good, and the sheets on her bed were fresh and warm. She sank her head into the pillow and looked at Eleanor with glazed eyes. The broth was taking effect, she knew, but she'd hardly needed it.

When they were settled, Eleanor turned down their lantern. "I'll be in the boulder across from you with the green pavilion out front. When you awaken, come and find me." And with that, she stepped to the rock wall and exited.

The three girls did not talk. Darcy figured that Sam had told Amelia what had happened in the woods, and she appreciated that Amelia did not ask them about it. As her eyes drifted closed, the last image in her mind was of red blood staining crisp, white snow.

Darcy could hear the ripping of fabric. She could smell the coppery scent of blood and the sweat of the tsellodrin. The thumping, the passing of blade through flesh and bone, the cracking sound of bones breaking and the utterance a man made just before he died. The stench of death. The nark's back, sliced open and spilling beautiful crimson, its droplets like tiny rubies on a white canvas. The shock and the grief of the surviving nark.

Dark, slack-faced images came at her. They raised their arms to strike at her with black eyes staring. But Tellius was there, just a little boy, driving his sword into them one after another . . . black oily blood spurted from their wounds, leaking toward her over the snowy ground, getting onto her clothes, her hands . . .

Darcy shuddered awake, drenched in sweat and shaking like mad. She swallowed. Her mouth and throat felt as dry as a bone, and she was suddenly aware that she was going to be sick.

She tried to throw off the covers, but they were twisted all around her legs. She kicked at them until they were lumped against the posts at the foot of her bed and she rolled to the floor, landing hard on her hands and knees. She couldn't stop shaking, and she knew that it was only a moment more that she could hold it in. Knocking over a chair as she passed, she jammed her palm against the cool stone. *Come on, come on!* She thought frantically. The bile was rising in her throat. She pushed hard and stumbled through into the pavilion. *Not here!* She took five more steps and burst through the tent flap, finally losing all the contents of her stomach onto the pressed snow at her feet.

She heaved and heaved, but she was mostly dry. They'd not had dinner the night before, she remembered, but she couldn't stop retching. If she could only get those images out of her head, she felt certain that she could stop, but she couldn't. Tears dripped down her cheeks and she collapsed to her knees. Blood and violence and death and sickness . . . these were not things that she'd counted on when she came to Alitheia. *I want to go home!* She thought desperately, and cried all the harder. But the harder she cried, the more she gained control of the retching, and soon she was only sobbing and shivering with her knees in the snow.

Snow crunched by her head and she heard a deep, exasperated sigh. She looked up, knowing that she must look wretched, and found Yahto staring down his nose at her. It must be near daybreak because his hair was chocolate brown and his eyes were lighter, but he was not Veli yet, and so he scowled at her. "Sick, are we?" His eyes flickered to her vomit and back to her.

She was shivering too violently to answer him.

"Well, you're not the only one," he groused. Without warning he reached down, took her shoulders, and set her on her feet. "Back to bed." He turned her around. "The last thing we need is for you to *really* get sick. I *trust* you can make it okay?" he asked coldly.

She bobbed her head; anything to get away from him. She was starting to feel a little better, and as she calmed, her sleepiness returned. Of course she couldn't go home. She couldn't go anywhere without Pateros's permission, whoever he was. She had to stay here, and she might as well get some sleep.

With leaden steps she re-entered the pavilion and a minute later was back in bed. The other two girls snored in their beds; she hadn't woken them. With some trepidation over what her dreams might hold, Darcy closed her eyes.

CHAPTER 31

LYKOS

Eleanor Stevenson was sick. Not sick like Darcy had been in the early morning with dream-induced vomiting, but really, actually sick. When the girls had dragged themselves out of their beds around midmorning and gone looking for her, they'd been turned away at the green pavilion by a stern-looking nurse who informed them that Lady Eleanor was not well enough for visitors.

"Go to the brown tent for breakfast, if that's what you're a-wanting," the nurse told them, "and leave Lady Eleanor to her peace."

"Is she going to be okay?" Sam asked anxiously.

"Only time will tell," the nurse replied.

"But, what's the matter with her?"

"She's an ailment in her lungs," was all the nurse would provide. "She's not a young woman, you know, and should not have been running around in the snow when she was already ill with a respiratory infection. Now off to breakfast with you!"

They had no choice but to obey the nurse. "I didn't know that she had a cold, did you guys?" Sam asked as they picked their way through the ruins to the brown tent. It was less colorful than the other tents in Paradeisos, but it was by far the largest and was set over the intact stone walls of one of the ancient buildings in the ruins.

"No," Darcy answered.

"She seemed okay yesterday," Amelia added. "But I get the idea that Eleanor's not the sort of person to complain if she's not feeling well."

"That's true," Sam said.

They ducked inside the brown tent, and as the tent flap closed behind them, they felt the warmth of a fire on their faces. Asa Rhea was inside with two other cooks, one of them a very round man with a handlebar mustache. Wonderful smells were emanating from three large pots set over three roaring fires.

The fires also served to keep the room warm, which was difficult because of gaping holes in the rock walls where stones used to be and the gusts of cold air that rushed through the room every time somebody opened the tent flap. Six wooden tables with benches were in the front part of the room and the three boys sat at them with Tellius and Cadmus sandwiched between them.

"Eleanor's sick," Sam said simply as they sat opposite the boys.

"We know," said Perry, nodding at the princes.

Cadmus looked cheerful enough, but Tellius sat with his head on one hand, playing with his breakfast. His brown waves hung low over his eyes, obscuring them from Darcy's view. She wished that she was bold enough to ask him if he was okay, but she wasn't. Instead she turned to Cadmus. "Does she get sick often?"

The younger boy shrugged his shoulders. "I dunno. Not often, I guess. I hope it means that we get to stay longer, though. Cousin Tullin was going to pick us up this week, but I don't want to go back. It's more fun here!"

"Where do you normally stay?" Darcy knew that she probably shouldn't ask, but her curiosity got the better of her.

Cadmus opened his mouth to answer, but Tellius suddenly looked up and glared at her. "That's none of your business!" He turned to his younger brother. "You know we're not supposed to say!"

"Yeah, but, Tel—"

"Do you want the same thing to happen to us and to Tullin as happened to Mother and Father?"

"No, but—"

Tellius slammed his hand on the table and shoved off the bench.

"Tel! Where are you going?" Cadmus stood, too.

"To find Rubidius," Tellius shouted back. "To tell him that we need to leave."

"Tellius, no! Come on, I don't want to leave yet. I wasn't going to tell them anything." Cadmus scrambled after his brother, and their argument faded as they left the tent.

Silence was heavy at the table after they left until Perry snorted softly and stabbed a sausage link with his fork. "Way to go, Darcy." He shoved the link in his mouth.

Darcy opened her mouth to protest, but Sam jumped in for her. "She didn't know that would happen!"

"Oh, come on." Perry rolled his eyes and waved his fork in the air. "What was she thinking, asking them where they stay? She knows as well as any of us that it's supposed to be a secret."

"Yeah, but we're all curious!" Sam shot back. "She didn't mean anything by it."

"Now they're probably going to have to leave," Dean said, siding with Perry.

"*So?* They weren't going to stay forever in the first place!"

"Sam," Darcy said quietly.

"And besides," Sam continued, "Tellius didn't have to get all mad at her."

"*Sam.*" Darcy put a hand on her arm. "It's okay," she whispered, even as she bristled inwardly at Perry and Dean.

"Cadmus told us that Tellius killed one of those tsellodrin last night," Perry changed the subject. He leaned close to them. "Is that true? Did you guys see it?" He sounded excited.

Sam's face lost all its color and Darcy abruptly stood. "I have to go," she said as her hands started to shake. She didn't look back as she stumbled out of the tent, the scent of breakfast suddenly nauseating to her. Once out in the cool morning air, she breathed deeply with her eyes closed.

She felt a bump against her thigh and opened her eyes. Lykos stared up at her, and she sunk down next to him, impulsively wrapping her arms around his furry neck. *Hello!* The link connected smoothly.

You are not hungry for breakfast? he rumbled back.

No, she answered.

Come with me, he said, working his neck free of her grasp and trotting off through the ruins.

She clambered awkwardly to her feet, encumbered by her skirts and cloak, and followed him as quickly as she could. She caught up with his bushy tail as he rounded a boulder in a deserted area of camp and entered the doorway of a structure that looked as though it used to be a part of the castle wall. The structure was small and dark, but mostly standing, and it still had a thatched roof intact. She ducked in after him and looked around as her eyes adjusted.

A hole in one wall bespoke where a fireplace used to be, and a couple of nooks and crannies held odds and ends that Darcy didn't recognize. There was an overturned bucket placed against one wall, and Lykos sat alert in the corner.

Where are we? Darcy asked him, lowering herself to sit on the bucket.

An old servants' quarters, he answered her. *I thought it would be a good place for us to talk. It's private, you know.*

She supposed he was right, but she shivered slightly, wishing that they could build a fire. *What do you want to talk to me about?*

Your talent, of course. Aren't you curious about it?

Darcy felt a slight thrill and the stress of the morning melted away. *Yes! You were going to help guide me, right?*

Right, and I think I've already come to understand more about it. He lowered his body so that he was lying with his head still upright and alert. *Think a private thought to yourself,* he commanded her.

Okay. She closed her eyes and concentrated. *I'm glad that I have Lykos as a friend*, she thought, and then she opened her eyes. *Well?* she asked him.

Did you do it? he asked.

Yes.

But the link was still open between us?

She wrinkled her brow. *Yes, I think it was.*

Then it is as I supposed.

What?

I can only hear that which you say directly to me. Your private thoughts are your own.

That's good, I suppose. Darcy thought to herself. *So . . . what exactly* is *the link between us? Do you know?* she asked the wolf.

I don't know what it is. It is unlike any magical talent that has ever occurred in Alitheia. Never before has any human been able to understand an animal's speech. It is remarkable. Lykos tipped his head thoughtfully to the side. *Rubidius has been a fool to ignore you*, he growled.

I suppose that we could let him in on it, Darcy thought, somewhat reluctantly. She rather liked having a powerful secret.

Lykos's ears flicked slightly. *I don't think that now is the time. Why not surprise him in a few months when you have achieved full mastery?*

Good idea. Darcy grinned at him. *So, what do we do next?*

We practice. Do you feel tired when you use it?

A little, Darcy answered, *but it's not nearly as bad as when Rubidius tested me for normal magic. Then I was really tired.*

I can help you with that, as well.

You can?

Of course. You didn't think humans were the sole recipients of magic, did you?

Darcy wrinkled her brow, trying to remember Eleanor's history lessons. She thought she remembered the old woman saying exactly that. *I thought . . .* she began, but Lykos interrupted her.

A common human lie, he laughed a little harshly. *The humans in Alitheia like to feel special, so they tell themselves that Pateros gave magic only to them. What an absurd notion! Of course the high animals have magic, too. Do you need a demonstration?*

I guess it would be nice, Darcy thought back apologetically.

With a wolfish grin, Lykos extended his head forward and blew on a spot in the middle of the floor. Blue flames sprang to life, despite the lack of wood or kindling.

Darcy clapped her hands and reached out to feel their warmth. It was a weak warmth, not nearly as comforting as a regular fire, but it was real. *I guess Eleanor was wrong*, Darcy thought. *Or she lied to us*. The thought disturbed her, especially with the old woman lying ill in her quarters. Darcy looked at Lykos, who seemed rather pleased with himself. *Please teach me what you know,* she said.

Yet again, my dear girl, he corrected her, *you do not need to be taught, but led. I can guide you on the path of discovery, but no more than that. Can you meet me here every morning after you have breakfasted?*

I think so; at least, I can try. What will you do if I can't get away?

I will wait. If you cannot make it one day, I will be here the next. And, I must insist that you continue to keep this between you and me. Your friends will not understand. Especially the blond girl; she is jealous of you.

Sam? Jealous of me? Darcy almost laughed, but then she caught herself. Maybe it was true. She *had* always followed her around like a lost puppy dog. Maybe there was more to Sam's behavior than met the eye. *Okay*, she agreed, and then she asked, *Lykos?*

Yes?

Is it just between you and me? This connection, I mean. You said to keep it between us, so I didn't try to speak with any other animals.

I think it is unique to us, he answered her. *But perhaps you can speak to all wolves? If I were Pateros, that is what I would have done for you.*

Why's that?

Because wolves are noble. We act and think in a pack, we support each other, and we are intelligent. You will find no other animal as devoted to you as I am.

She immediately thought of Hippondus, but she shrugged his image away. She didn't want this to get any more complicated that it already was . . . and she didn't want Lykos to be angry with her for doubting him.

She heard someone calling her name and looked at Lykos, feeling slightly panicky. *Why should I feel panicky, though?* she chided herself. *I'm not doing anything wrong.*

You should go, Lykos told her, standing up. With a poof of his breath he extinguished his magic fire and paced to the door. *Your friends are looking for you, and you don't want to alarm them. Remember, tomorrow morning, all right?*

Okay. See you tomorrow morning. She squeezed past him and jogged away from the ancient little dwelling.

CHAPTER 32

SURROUNDED

"Where have you been?" Amelia sounded irritated as Darcy jogged up to her. "We've been looking for you everywhere. Sam's on the other side of camp."

"I've been with . . . a friend," Darcy said haltingly. She wasn't sure if Lykos would want her to name him.

"A friend?" Amelia looked at her with a raised eyebrow but didn't push the issue. Together they walked back toward the red pavilion that marked their quarters. "Look," Amelia said after a moment. "Sam told me what happened to you guys on the way here, and I just wanted to say that I think Perry was a really big jerk to bring it up like that at breakfast."

"Oh, I—I wasn't mad at him. I mean, how could he know? He was just curious. I just . . . didn't feel like talking about it."

Amelia stopped walking and crossed her arms over her chest. "You know, it's one thing to have a crush on Perry. I mean, let's face it, I've been there, too. But, come on, Darcy, he's really not all that great. It's okay to say that he was a jerk, 'cause sometimes he is!"

Darcy felt a stab of annoyance and walked away. Who was she to pass judgment on Perry? It wasn't like she'd never had her moments of inconsiderateness since Darcy had met her. "We should probably find Sam. I don't want her to feel left out," she shot over her shoulder.

"Oh, *now* you're worried about Sam's feelings? Did you think about them when you were hiding all morning with your 'friend'?"

Darcy's ears flamed red and she stopped walking. She turned around to look at Amelia. "I care about Sam's feelings!"

"Only when it's convenient for you," Amelia retorted. She walked closer to Darcy and stuck her finger in her face. "Listen, I've been friends with Sam for a lot longer than you have, and I don't like the way you treat her. One second you're her best friend, and the next you're sneaking around trying to get away from her. What's the matter with you? Can't you see that she's the only person who really sticks up for you around here? If it were up to me, we never would have followed you into Alitheia, and none of this would be happening."

Amelia's words stabbed like knives in her heart and her stomach dropped. "I thought that you were okay with being here. That you were okay with *me*!"

Amelia shrugged one shoulder haughtily. "I go back and forth, on both counts." Amelia pushed past her. "I think Sam's over here. I'll let you explain to her where you have been."

They rounded a massive boulder, Darcy's blood pounding so loudly in her ears that she wasn't paying attention to where she was going. With a start she bumped into Amelia's back and was just opening her mouth to say something, when Amelia waved her back. Taken aback, she stepped backward twice until she and Amelia were both just hidden behind the curvature of the rock.

A large group of rebel leaders were talking just around the boulder at a large fire pit, and they sounded upset.

"Betrayed!" Torrin said loudly. "Flushed out like rats. If I could just get my hands on him, I'd make him tell me how long ago he turned."

"Get your hands on whom?" Voitto Vesa said impatiently. It sounded like she had just arrived.

"Freolgred," Yahto Veli answered quietly. "He betrayed the location of the warrens to the tsellodrin."

"Freolgred? But why?" Vesa cried. "He was one of our most loyal scouts!"

"Not as loyal as we thought," Torrin growled. "Does Ulfred know?"

"A message was sent to him this morning. He and his family should be safely away by now." Veli sounded uncharacteristically sad. "The days keep getting darker."

"If Freolgred betrayed us, then why did he warn us?" Vesa asked, sounding skeptical.

"The plan was to flush us out, make us come to them. Unfortunately for them, Freolgred warned us too soon, before their ambush was fully in place, and we were able to escape . . . most of us," Torrin answered her.

"At least they did not capture the princes," an unfamiliar voice said.

"No, but thanks to Freolgred, they now know that they are here . . . with us."

There was a general sharp intake of breath.

"Then we must flee again!" a man cried.

"But where can we go?" a woman chimed in.

"It's already too late," Torrin said over the din. "They are already here."

"What do you mean?" Vesa gasped. "Is the camp surrounded?"

"Yes, I'm afraid it is."

"We're trapped!" the woman called out.

"Pateros save us," someone else muttered.

"What will we do?" Vesa sounded dazed.

"We will outlast them," Veli called out. "We have water and we have supplies. They cannot see us, nor can they pass through the arch or beyond the old walls. Here we will wait for deliverance and continue to plan our offensive against the Shadow. It is all that we can do."

"I say we go out and meet them." Darcy recognized Baran's voice in the crowd. "Our warriors can take them. Why wait for them to grow stronger?" His proposal was met with a small number of cheers and the ringing of swords leaving their sheaths.

"Now is not the time," Torrin answered him. "What purpose would it serve? We cannot abandon this stronghold, and Tselloch will only send more. Perhaps it was Pateros's will for us to be forced into this time of preparation."

"What do you mean? Do you claim that Pateros *wanted* us to be betrayed?" an angry voice shouted.

"Don't be ridiculous," another added.

"To wait also works psychologically to our advantage," Veli declared over the din, ignoring the protesting voices. "If they never see us, they may lose faith in our even being here."

"That's not the way the tsellodrin operate," Baran said. "They don't think like normal men. They obey orders and that's all, to the death, if necessary. They do not reason on their own. If Tselloch tells them that we are here, they will wait out there for us to emerge until their legs drop off from hypothermia."

"Let their legs fall off," someone else said. "That's less for us to deal with."

"We don't know for certain how much of their own personality they retain. We've never had the chance to study them," Torrin said.

"What does Rubidius say?" another person shouted. "Rubidius will decide for us."

"What do I say?" Darcy and Amelia jumped as Rubidius's clipped voice sounded right behind them. He placed both his hands on their shoulders and walked out to face the crowd with them. He lowered curly brows on all of the people anxiously awaiting his verdict. "I say that we wait. Torrin and Veli speak wisely."

A few people looked disappointed, but most of them nodded their heads in agreement and turned to their neighbors to discuss the matter further.

"I also say," Rubidius added quietly to just the girls, "that it is time for lunch and session." He motioned across the circle and Sam, Perry, Dean, and Lewis emerged guiltily from behind an old well and part of a broken down wagon. They crossed the clearing, weaving in between the assembled people and joined them by the boulder.

"Rubidius," Sam said as soon as she was alongside him. "The man who betrayed us at Sanditha, Freolgred," she said, stumbling a little over the unfamiliar name. "Was he the one wearing all the furs?"

"Yes." Rubidius looked down his nose at her. "Why?"

"Oh . . . nothing. I just had a funny feeling about him that night, that's all."

"Did you now?" Rubidius looked very interested and then clapped his hands together. "Well, you were right. He was a rogue; a scoundrel. But never mind that now. We need to get onto lunch and session."

"How can we have session like normal with all those tsellodrin things out there?" Perry said incredulously. "Isn't Baran right? Shouldn't we be out there fighting them?"

"The best course of action is never to jump in unprepared," Rubidius said. "Although we have many capable fighters, we are in no position to fight an unknown number of tsellodrin. Given a little time, however, we will find ourselves better prepared. I think it wise," he turned to look at Dean, "for the spy and me to take some time together this week. Your talent will prove useful in very short order, I think. Come along, now. We shall dine in my cottage today."

"Your cottage is here?" Darcy asked him incredulously. "How did you have time to move your front door with all that went on last night?"

"I'm always prepared," Rubidius replied. "And it really is a very simple spell, as I've told you before. I have all your things, as well—your notes and quills and whatnot—although you really should take those things back to your quarters on a more regular basis. I should like to think that you are studying your notes in your down time."

Darcy wasn't the only one who looked guilty at this comment, and nobody said anything as they approached a bare rock near the west end of the camp. It was straight and tall and didn't look big enough to contain a secret room of any kind, let alone Rubidius's entire cottage, but Darcy knew that the magic didn't work that way.

"Pay close attention to where we are so that you can find it on your own later. I didn't allow them to put up a silly pavilion outside my front door. Like *I* want people bugging me all day! Harrumph. Better to reveal my home to only a select few. It is better this way."

"Oh my, I know where we are!" Sam suddenly declared. "I didn't recognize it right away because of the snow and the castle ruins, but this is Paradise Cove!"

"What?" Amelia squinted her eyes and looked around. "Are you sure?"

"Wait, yeah, Sam's right. This is the marker rock that the camp has that sign stuck to about having reached the trail end, and the lagoon is just over there." Perry pointed past Rubidius's rock.

"We hike out here every year." Sam turned to Darcy excitedly. "It's one of the most beautiful spots at Cedar Cove. There're all these rocks and boulders, just like here, and this beautiful lagoon area. I wonder if the old walls of Paradeisos encompass part of the lagoon."

"They do," Rubidius answered, somewhat impatiently, "but now is not the time to go look at it. If you will." He gestured toward the rock.

Sam, Darcy, Amelia, Perry, Dean, and Lewis one by one put their hands on the rock and passed through the stone into Rubidius's cottage, so much more out of place in Paradeisos than it had been in the warrens. As Darcy settled in to take notes, she let her mind wander to the next morning and her appointment with Lykos. What would he think of Amelia's attitude? What would be his opinion of the tsellodrin that surrounded their camp? She shuddered to think of those black eyes and vacant faces watching them over the wall. *No*, she reminded herself. *They can't see us.*

Chapter 33
Elemental Magic

"Okay, Dean, we get it. You're amazing! Now will you just come out?" Amelia put her hands on her hips and turned in a circle. It was just after lunch and they were making their way toward Rubidius's cottage for afternoon session. They'd been at Paradeisos for a month and in that time Dean had worked with Rubidius almost every day to develop his talent. And develop it he had.

Somewhat similar to Alepo, who was never far from Dean's heels these days, the boy was able to change color. Not seasonally like Alepo, who had become a beautiful white snow fox when winter had descended, but at will to blend into his surroundings. He flitted from rock to tree to snow-covered bush with ease, almost silently—another element of his talent)—blending into the colors and textures of each item he was next to. But then, just as easily, he could return to his normal appearance. He took great pleasure in sneaking up on the girls and jumping out at them at all times of the day. They wondered how his talent could line up so precisely with the natural tendencies he exhibited in their own world.

"Boo!" he shouted, stepping out from the rock in front of them and laughing hysterically when Darcy, Amelia, and Sam jumped.

"Dean, you jerk." Amelia sniffed.

"Don't you ever get tired of doing that?" Darcy added, her breath crystallizing in the air in front of her.

"Nope," he said with a grin.

"Yeah, I know that, but I mean, doesn't it make you physically tired? I mean, I'm always getting—" Darcy stopped abruptly, realizing that she'd been about to reveal that she knew, and was practicing almost daily, her talent. "What I meant to say is, doing magic at the beginning of our time here, when Rubidius tested me, was really tiring. Isn't it like that for you?" She avoided Amelia's gaze as she scrutinized Darcy with beady eyes. Her relationship with Amelia had not improved in the past month, and they coexisted tensely when they had to be together.

"Well, sure it *gets* tiring," Dean admitted. "But it's not nearly as bad as it was at the beginning. Rubidius said that the more I practice, the less tiring it will be."

"By 'practice' I don't think he meant using it to show off," Sam said loftily.

"Aw, but it's so much fun!"

"Why don't you go walk with Perry and Lewis," Amelia told him, waving her hand. "I don't want to be around you anymore."

Dean stuck his tongue out and disappeared, his presence only visible by the faintest of outlines against the snowy backdrop. They saw his footprints jog forward in the snow and then he tapped each of the other two boys on the back of the head.

"Hey!" Perry shouted, swatting in Dean's direction. "Knock it off."

Sam sighed. "It's actually kind of funny when it's not happening to you," she said, and then she looked at Darcy. "Don't worry, Darcy, I'm sure that Rubidius will work with you soon. He can't ignore you forever."

"What?" Darcy's mind was back with Lykos that morning when they'd once again practiced mindspeaking from a distance. In the last month they'd found that she could mindspeak with him up to the same distance that she could orally speak to a normal person, and increasing the distance meant that she had to shout in her mind to be heard by him, and vice versa. After a certain point, the connection naturally severed. They'd found that increasing the distance made Darcy have to work considerably harder, and it made her incredibly tired. Lykos was convinced, however, that the more she did it, the stronger she would become.

"I'm sure he'll help you figure out your talent soon," Sam prompted her again.

"Oh . . . yeah, probably." Darcy nodded and tried to look put out, but she couldn't help feeling a little smug. Wouldn't they all be so surprised when they found out what she could already do!

"Don't forget, we don't know what my talent is yet, either, and Rubidius only knows a little about Lewis's."

Darcy knew that Sam was trying to comfort her, assuming Darcy must be feeling pain, and she appreciated the sentiment, even if it was unneeded. For as far as she was concerned, Rubidius could work with the rest of them for their entire time in Alitheia. She was doing just fine without him.

"Hey, by the way." Sam stopped and turned to her right outside Rubidius's rock. "Did you ever figure out what your mirror was all about? That came out of my bag?"

"Oh!" Darcy had forgotten all about it. She supposed that it was tucked somewhere in the satchel she'd brought from Sanditha. "I forgot about that. Remind me and I'll take a look at it when we get back to our room tonight, okay?" She actually was curious, she realized. It was such a strange object to have appeared in Sam's satchel, especially since no other item had appeared in it before or since.

The boys were already inside and the girls quickly joined them; happy to be out of the bitter cold. December in Alitheia was, predictably, just as frigid as December in the upper peninsula of Michigan. They'd long ago been given new hooded winter cloaks of fur, furry mittens, and thick, fur-lined leather boots. As they stepped into the cottage and stripped off their outer garments, Darcy realized that there was an extra person in the room.

"Eleanor!" she exclaimed happily, somewhat begrudging the easy way that Sam and Amelia hugged the older woman in greeting. She'd never been able to hug people so easily; she always felt uncomfortable.

"You're all better!" Sam said, letting go of the woman's middle and looking up into her smiling face.

"Well, better enough, at least," Eleanor croaked. "It was a long battle, but my nurse has finally allowed me to leave my quarters."

"They never let us in to see you," Amelia said, pouting slightly. "We tried almost every day . . . at least, Sam and I did." She shot a malevolent glance at Darcy, but Eleanor didn't notice.

I didn't know that they tried to see her almost every day. They never told me! Darcy crossed her arms angrily, but the little voice in the back of her mind niggled at her. *Yes, well, you were always off with Lykos or Hippondus, so how would they have found you to tell you?* She shook off the reminder. She'd tried not to neglect Hippondus even in the midst of her sessions with Lykos, even though the great wolf told her that the horse would be fine without her. She still felt a curious bond with him, and if she went too long without seeing him, she felt depressed and empty inside. She always managed at least two visits a week.

"I should think not," Eleanor said in response to Amelia's complaint. "I was very ill; I had no desire for any of you to catch it."

"What did you have?" Lewis asked from across the room by the fire. He was holding his hands out toward the flames.

Eleanor looked thoughtful for a moment. "Well, they have a different name for it here, but I believe it was pneumonia. I certainly *felt* like I had pneumonia!"

"Will you be teaching us today?" Sam asked eagerly.

Eleanor laughed lightly, coughing a little at the end. "No, no! I don't have anything prepared, I'm afraid. I'm just here to stretch my legs and get out of my quarters. I'm sure Nurse Dembe will be after me in short order. I thought I would hide out with you for a time and enjoy my freedom." Eleanor settled easily into Rubidius's armchair and folded her arms over her lap. "The princes will want to see me, but I couldn't find them on my way here. Who's looking after them?" She looked questioningly at Rubidius.

Even though Eleanor spoke lightly, Darcy could tell that she was very anxious about Tellius and his rambunctious younger brother. She'd seen on their flight here how deeply she cared for the boys and couldn't imagine how she must have felt this last month, cooped up and sick, unable to take care of them herself.

Rubidius seemed to understand her concern and laid an uncharacteristically kind hand on the old woman's shoulder. "Torrin and Tari Tova have been overseeing their majesties, my lady. They have done well in your absence, but I know that they look forward to seeing you."

"Have they been coming to your afternoon sessions?" Eleanor asked, relaxing a little at his words.

"From time to time," Rubidius answered. "I invite them to come whenever I think we will be discussing something that will benefit them. They've already had most of this training, after all." He looked sternly at the six of them lounging around the room. "You six, on the other hand, are in desperate need of a good education," he barked. "I don't know what they teach you in the schools in your world, but it certainly isn't how to *pay attention*." He emphasized the last two words and stretched out his hand to catch a paper wad that Dean and Perry had been tossing back and forth. In Rubidius's hand the paper wad became a chunk of coal, which he tossed into his fireplace. "Sit!" he commanded them. "Today we will begin discussing the elements—earth, fire, water, and air—and their importance to Alitheian magical theory."

"But we can't *do* magic," Perry whined, taking his usual seat between Dean and Lewis. "Only Darcy can, and she doesn't even know how yet."

I know more than you think, Darcy thought smugly as Rubidius barked, "Doesn't matter! It will not hurt you to understand the theory. And what will you do, pray, when magic is used against you? Tell your assailant it's unfair for him to use magic and kindly ask him to attack you physically?"

Perry squirmed a little and looked at Dean out of the corner of his eye.

"No!" Rubidius banged his fist on the table, making them all jump. "You will stand no chance against magical assailants if you don't at least understand what it is that they are doing to you."

Darcy listened to Rubidius with interest. Lykos hadn't mentioned anything to her about magical theory, let alone elemental magical theory. She wondered if he knew about it. She would have to ask him in the morning, if she could get away. It was becoming more and more difficult to shake the other five in the mornings. Amelia was constantly suspicious of her, and Sam always wanted to come with her. No matter how much Darcy insisted that she was meeting with a friend who was very shy, Sam still wanted to come along. She would have to talk to Lykos about that, as well. She unrolled a fresh sheet of parchment and dipped her quill in the inkpot, ready to take notes.

"Almost all forms of magic in Alitheia deal with a manipulation of one of the four elements," Rubidius began. "Magicians that can manipulate two or more elements sometimes go onto become master magicians."

"Like you!" Sam said excitedly.

"Exactly, but it is not always so. For example, Lady Eleanor performs earth and water magic, but she is not a master magician." They peered interestedly at Eleanor as Rubidius continued. "Now, the most commonly manipulated element is, of course, earth, because it represents all physical objects. It is most uncommon for anybody to be born in Alitheia who does not have the ability to perform earth magic, and almost every time a person is born with the ability to manipulate two of the elements, earth is one of them."

"How many elements can you manipulate?" Perry interrupted.

"Three." Rubidius scowled at Perry. "I have no talent with air. Now don't interrupt!"

"He didn't yell at Sam when she interrupted," Perry muttered under his breath to Dean. Darcy smirked a little and ducked her head. She was actually finding the lesson quite interesting. She wondered what type of magic she possessed. *I must possess earth*, she thought logically. For some time now Lykos had helped her move small items around their little hideout. That sort of magic, however, always left her much more drained than using her talent did, so she didn't like to practice it.

Rubidius took the rest of the afternoon to discuss the nature of the earth element and informed them that the next day they would go into how the manipulation of the earth element could be used against them in combat and how to recognize its use. Rubidius promised he would do what he could to prepare them to non-magically oppose an earthly magical threat. "And then we'll move onto the other elements," he concluded for the day. "I expect this discussion to take us through the winter. When it warms up, I would like to take you all outside for some practical survival exercises and identification of magical plants and fungi."

"Yippee," Dean said under his breath to Perry and Lewis. Perry laughed, but Lewis only looked annoyed.

The sun was already down as they exited Rubidius's tent and picked their way, as they'd become used to, using the light of torch lanterns that had been set up next to every residential rock. The boys went off to their quarters and Darcy, Sam, and Amelia turned the other direction to head to theirs. As they passed an area close to the old, dilapidated wall of the city, Sam suddenly clutched at Darcy's arm and squeaked.

"What is it?" Darcy frowned at her.

"Oh! Why do they have to do that?" Amelia asked next to her. She shivered and moved closer to Sam's other side.

Darcy looked up and felt her heart skip a beat. Standing just on the other side of the wall were three tsellodrin, identifiable by their vacant stares and sagging mouths. She gulped and tried to tear her eyes away from them, but it was difficult. "Remember," she hissed in a wavering voice to Sam and Amelia. "They can't see us and they can't hear us."

"And they can't cross the wall," Amelia added quietly.

Darcy knew that Amelia, like her, spoke what they all knew out of an effort to stay calm. For a month, ever since they'd first surrounded the camp, a handful of tsellodrin prowled close around the wall every night, staring vacantly in at the camp they couldn't see, but knew was there. They acted as a nightly reminder that the rebels were not free to leave the camp. The first night they'd seen them, Sam had screamed until she was blue in the face and then run back to Rubidius's cottage and wouldn't re-emerge until he agreed to walk her back to their quarters.

"But why do they have to *do* this? They're so creepy!" Sam sniffed; she sounded close to tears.

"They're just trying to scare us," Amelia said fiercely.

It's working, Darcy thought, but instead she said, "Come on. It's pointless to watch them. They don't even know we're here!" With some effort she turned her back on them and pulled Sam and Amelia after her. She could feel Sam shaking, and when they reached their rock, she pushed Sam toward it first. "You go in first," she encouraged her. "We'll be right behind you."

Darcy remembered her little mirror the moment she entered their cozy quarters and thought it would be a good way to distract Sam, who was sitting on her bed staring into space. "We have a few minutes before dinner," Darcy said to her. "Why don't we check out that mirror?"

"Okay," Sam said, a little dully, but she adjusted herself so that she was watching Darcy.

Darcy fumbled around in her satchel until she found her grandmother's compact on the very bottom under a pair of forgotten undergarments. With shaking hands, she pulled it out and examined it in the lantern light. It was definitely the one she'd inherited from her grandmother; it was exactly the right size and had all the right markings.

Her thumb found the latch and she clicked it open, peering at the inside before she looked in the mirror. When she caught her reflection, she started and blinked her eyes.

"What is it? What do you see?" Sam said, perking up.

"Ahhh . . ." Darcy fished around for something to say. She didn't really know how to describe it—or she didn't want to. She looked again in the mirror, this time wincing at the image. She looked *old* and *ugly!* Really ugly. In fact, she looked like the wicked witch from the *Wizard of Oz*, but with her own features. This couldn't be what she *actually* looked like at the moment. She went quickly to the mirror that was tacked to their wall and compared the images. In the wall mirror she looked like herself—a little tired perhaps, but nothing out of the ordinary. But in the compact mirror . . .

She snapped it closed and handed it to Sam. "I don't really get it. You tell me what you see in it."

Sam clicked it open and peered inside. "Oh! I look great! Wow, is that me? I look totally fit! And my skin." She touched her cheek gently. "It's amazing. Amelia, look in it!"

She tossed it to Amelia who caught it and looked apprehensively between the two of them. Raising it to her face she wrinkled her nose a little and quickly lowered it. She shot a glance at Darcy, who knew almost immediately that she hadn't seen the same glowing image as Sam had.

"What did you see?" Sam asked her eagerly.

"Nothing," Amelia said. "It looked just like me, like normal." She shoved the compact back at Darcy like it was going to burn her.

"Well, of course. You're already beautiful," Sam said flatteringly. "I'm sure it was the same for Darcy."

Darcy wasn't about to correct her.

"Well, I have no idea what it means. Maybe you just needed to comb your hair or something when it came to my bag." Sam giggled and bounced up from her bed. "I'm hungry. Are you guys ready?"

"Sure, just let me put this away." Darcy buried the compact back in her satchel. As far as she was concerned, it could stay hidden.

They carefully kept their eyes away from the walls as they trekked to the food tent, and Darcy reminded herself to ask Lykos about elemental magic when she saw him. From time to time he still sat with her at night, but it was different now that they were no longer in the warrens. The food tent was not the warmest place to hang out for any extended amount of time, and he never came back to her quarters with her. What if he said that Rubidius was lying about the elements, too? Whom should she believe? He'd once or twice contradicted the teachings of Rubidius or Eleanor since he'd proven them wrong about high animals not possessing magic, and Darcy was always uneasy whenever he did so. Maybe there wasn't *one* truth when it came to magical matters. Perhaps both Lykos and Rubidius were right.

She shook off her thoughts as they entered the tent to find Tellius and Cadmus happily sitting next to Eleanor, who had been allowed to join them in the food tent for supper. Cadmus was leaning against Eleanor's side and Darcy could tell by the relaxed set of Tellius's shoulders that he was truly happy to see her.

"Darcy! I'm glad you're here," Eleanor said, looking up when the girls entered the tent. "After you get your food, come and sit by us, please."

"Okay," Darcy said, wondering why she was being singled out from the other two. With a shrug at Sam and Amelia, she trotted up to the food line and reluctantly received her bowl of stew and piece of bread. *How many times can they serve us stew?* she thought, but she took it back to the table and sat down.

"Tellius and I would like for you to join us in the morning in my quarters," Eleanor began without preamble.

Darcy's spoon froze on the way to her mouth and she shot a glance at Tellius. His shoulders had gone rigid and he looked like he wished Eleanor were still sick. "Um, all right," she said.

"You remember which one it is, right? The green pavilion," Eleanor reminded her.

"Yes, ma'am," Darcy said quietly. *More dumb questions*, she thought grimly, and worst of all, she wouldn't be able to meet with Lykos.

She shoved stew in her mouth and looked around the tent. There. She saw his great grey form curled up in the corner with one of his fellow wolves. *Lykos!* She called out to him.

His head didn't rise to acknowledge her, but she felt the connection take hold anyway. *Yes?* he answered her. *You called?* He sounded amused, almost mocking.

She frowned, but continued, *I won't be able to meet with you tomorrow. I have to meet with Tellius and Eleanor in the morning.*

How very dull for you. He commiserated in the same, slightly mocking tone, but then he grew more serious. *I'll wait for you. If you cannot come tomorrow, meet me on the next day.*

What if he tells me to come back every day this week?

Lykos sighed in her head. *I will wait*, he said simply.

Chapter 34

An Offensive Plan

It was over a week before Darcy was able to meet with Lykos again. Every morning was the same thing: a summons to Eleanor's tent to spend the morning with her and Tellius as the boy prince asked her a series of inane questions. Sometimes they argued, but as long as they kept it relatively calm, Eleanor did not interfere. She seemed to think it was important for them to interact, even if it involved conflict.

At all other times of the day, Tellius ignored her and Darcy was only too happy to let him do so. She remembered what Rubidius said about Tellius continuing to age when she returned home, but she just couldn't imagine someday marrying the spoiled and stiff little boy.

It was Resting Day and Tellius was playing a game with the other teenagers. Darcy feigned disinterest and took advantage of the opportunity to sneak away. It was only shortly after the breakfast hour, and she hoped Lykos hadn't given up on her.

When she reached their little shack, it was to find Lykos patiently waiting, but he wasn't alone. By his side was a handsome charcoal-grey wolf with a white snout. The newcomer was somewhat smaller than Lykos, and she could tell by his demeanor that he deferred great respect upon her friend. She smiled uneasily at the newcomer and sat down on her overturned bucket.

Hello, she opened the link. *Who's this?*

One of my subjects, Lupidor, Lykos responded. *He's been keeping me company this week while you have been away.*

There was a slightly accusatory tone in Lykos's voice, and Darcy chafed inwardly. *I didn't want to be away, but I had no choice!*

Didn't you, now? Lykos raised a shaggy eyebrow at her.

He's the king . . . well, that is, he will be the king. I'm not allowed to turn down his summonses.

Be that as it may, Lykos said, *we've lost valuable time, and we don't know how often he will force you to grace him with your presence.*

He put a strained emphasis on the word 'force' and Darcy scowled at him. Why was he being so mean to her? *Valuable time for what?* she snapped. *Do we have a deadline to meet, or something?*

I just mean, Lykos said in more measured tones, *that it is not good to go so long between practice sessions.* His eyes went from her to the other wolf and she thought that they exchanged a look. She didn't like feeling like they were talking about her. She looked again at the charcoal-grey wolf and wondered if he would be with them the whole morning. Unlike Lykos's, his eyes were blue and looked like polished marbles in a bed of fur.

Is Lupidor going to stay with us all morning? she asked.

If he bothers you, I'll send him away, Lykos answered matter-of-factly.

No. There was something cool and comforting about those blue eyes. *It's okay, he can stay.*

Darcy shivered and wrapped her cloak tightly around her. *Can you make your fire? It's freezing in here.*

Certainly. With a poof the blue flames crackled to life in the middle of the floor and Darcy scooted her bucket closer to them. As she looked at them, she was reminded that she had some questions for Lykos about the elements.

Rubidius has been teaching us elemental magical theory, she said. *Do you know anything about it? You've never mentioned the elements to me before.*

Lykos laughed, the sound more like a growl in her head, and answered her, *Elemental magical theory? That is very outdated. We have a much more forward understanding of magical theory now.*

Oh, Darcy frowned, *then why do you suppose that he's teaching it to us?*

Because he is an old man stuck in old ways, Lykos said. *Do you want to know the truth, Darcy?*

Yes.

He lowered his head conspiratorially. *The elements exist, of course, but all that nonsense about being able to control only certain elements is outdated. Any magical person or animal can control any of the elements, and anyone is capable of achieving master magician status.*

But . . . how come everybody isn't a master magician if that's the case?

Because it requires an open mind. If you'd been taught your whole life that you could only manipulate the earth element, would you ever try to do anything else?

I guess not. It made sense, what Lykos was saying, but it also made her uncomfortable. She didn't want to believe that Rubidius was wrong; she *liked* studying the elements. Why wasn't Lykos a master magician, if what he said was true? She was too afraid to ask, so they moved into their practice exercises.

She was able to meet with Lykos on and off for the rest of the winter. Sometimes Lupidor was there, quietly watching. It was cold in Paradeisos and at times Darcy almost wished for the warm underground warrens at Sanditha, but she knew that that hideout was spoiled for good. She'd grown used to the tsellodrin outside their walls at night, and occasionally even made faces and taunted them when she was feeling particularly brave. Yahto Veli caught her doing this one time, though, and chastised her. He said that it was wrong to mock them, even if they were her enemy. Lykos said that doing it would increase her bravery.

Lykos had some other very interesting ideas, and she wondered if he was serious about them. He seemed to think that Darcy was going to be the deliverer of Alitheia all on her own. Like Joan of Arc, she would ride into battle with her sword blazing, cutting down her foes and demanding the surrender of the Shadow, Tselloch. She laughed every time he hinted at it and waved him off, but it was nice to know that somebody had faith in her. Nobody else seemed to take her seriously.

The leaders of the rebellion at Paradeisos—Torrin, Yahto Veli, Voitto Vesa, Baran, Rubidius and others—were busy with plans all winter long. They took great hope in Dean's chameleon-like abilities and had even included him in a few of their top-secret councils. Darcy didn't know what they were planning, but she was sure it didn't involve her. She knew they were confused about the role of the Six, that much she'd overheard one night. Rubidius still insisted they needed more training and that, though they might help in the storming of the castle, their ultimate role would center on the permanent removal of Tselloch and all his tsellochim.

She thought they might even have an offensive plan put together, but the problem remained that they were besieged by tsellodrin, and once they left the ruins of Paradeisos, they likely wouldn't be able to get back. And so they waited.

March was upon them and Darcy wondered where the time had gone. It seemed like just yesterday that she had led the other five teenagers through the gateway at Gnome's Haven. In a way, she missed the funny little gnomes, even if they were annoying, and she definitely missed the fairies and nymphs. The world around them was still exaggerated in its beauty; the rocks looked sharper, the snow whiter, and the pine needles more emerald green than they ever would be in her world, but the effect was dimmed by the long winter and the many months already spent there.

Sam had given up trying to follow her to her covert morning meetings with Lykos, but her worried eyes followed Darcy every time she left the others. Darcy had finally had to reveal to Sam, and Amelia only because she walked in on them when they were talking, that it was Lykos she was meeting with. She could still hear Sam's words ringing in her ears from the encounter.

"But I don't trust him, Darcy! What could he possibly want to talk to you about all the time? Why won't he let anybody else come to your meetings?"

"He's my friend, Sam. Does he need a reason to want to be around me? Plus, he's a part of the rebellion; there's nothing to worry about."

But her easy smile hadn't alleviated Sam's worries. She wondered if Sam and Amelia had told anybody else about her meetings. She didn't know why, but she rather thought that Rubidius would be angry. *Not like he has any right to be*, she thought huffily. *If he'd train me himself, I wouldn't have to meet with Lykos all the time!*

Between mornings spent with either Lykos or Tellius and afternoons in session, the only real time that she had with the other teenagers for relaxation and fun was in the evenings, and Darcy felt herself further and further removed from them. She didn't know if it was because of the limited time, or because of her magical growth with Lykos, but she commonly felt like it was her against them. She knew that they talked among themselves about the progress they were making in their talents with Rubidius, but aside from the dropped comment here and there, Darcy was excluded from these conversations. She didn't think it fair, considering that Sam's talent hadn't even been revealed yet, but they still included her! Darcy figured her old suspicions were true: she was different from other people, and they didn't understand her.

But Lykos did. He listened quietly when she belly-ached about the others and he assured her that he understood exactly what she was going through. He'd even planned a birthday surprise for her today. The others hadn't even remembered. When Perry had turned fourteen just two weeks earlier, they'd thrown him a huge surprise party, complete with a special meal cooked for him by Asa Rhea. Breakfast had come and gone this morning without so much as a nod in Darcy's direction; not even Sam remembered.

She was on her way to meet Lykos that very moment to find out what her birthday surprise was. She was excited; she'd always loved her birthday and she was looking forward to some celebration, even if the others hadn't remembered. *Lykos?* she called out as she drew near to their little shack.

Inside, he answered her. He sounded a little sly.

She ducked inside to find him waiting for her, lying down with his great shaggy head on his crossed paws. *Happy Birthday*, he said, raising his head.

Lying in the space between his chest and his paws was a circlet of silver with small black stones wrought into it at even intervals. It looked like a crown and it winked and glimmered in the pale blue light of his flames. *Oh! It's beautiful! Is that for me?*

Of course it's for you. Try it on. He took it in his mouth and held it out to her.

With shaking hands, she took it and lowered her fur hood so that she could place it on her head. It was surprisingly heavy and felt cold on her temples where it sat snug around the crown of her head. *Thank you,* she said, stroking it with her fingers. *It's so pretty, but I don't think I'll be able to wear it around the others; it might raise too many questions,* she added.

It's not meant to be worn around the others, Lykos said to her. *It is a very special piece of ornamentation. Would you like to know what it does?*

Okay. Darcy sat on her bucket and looked at him.

It will enhance your natural magical abilities.

Really? How?

He laughed. *One question at a time. Yes, it really will. How? Well, let's just say that I imbued it with special powers. It took me all winter to create, but it is finally finished.*

You created this for me? Out of what? Silver? What are the stones?

I didn't need materials to craft the crown; I just created it, on my own.

Darcy frowned. According to the elemental magical theory that Rubidius was teaching them, everything had to come from something. You could not simply cause materials to exist without them being drawn from something that already existed. According to Rubidius, the power to create from nothing belonged only to Pateros.

As for the stones, Lykos continued, *they are very special and rare. I searched long and hard to find the six that I needed. The stones, not the crown, contain the power you can draw on to enhance your magic. The metal of the crown binds the stones together harmoniously.*

What do you mean by 'enhance'?

Why don't you try something? Something that would have tired you out before.

Um . . . okay. Darcy searched the room until her eyes fell on a broken pot in the corner. It was large enough that moving it would give her a sizeable headache on a normal day. Stretching out her hands, she latched onto the pot with her mind and willed it to move across the room to her. With a jolt, the old pot flew off the floor and into her waiting arms. She held it out, surprised.

How do you feel? Lykos's silky voice entered her thoughts.

I feel great. I don't feel tired at all! She turned the pot over and over in her hands. *This is really cool, Lykos! What else can I do with the crown on?*

Many things that you have never done before, but most importantly, you will lead the wolf army to retake Ormiskos and defeat the Shadow.

Darcy laughed out loud and held the pot out to Lykos. "Moving pots across the room is one thing," she spoke in the silence, "but commanding armies is another. You *can't* be serious."

Oh, but I am.

"But, Lykos," she spoke in exasperation. *I don't know the first thing about leading armies in war. Why would your subjects want, or even allow, me to lead them?*

Because we believe you are the one we have been waiting for all these years. The other humans are incompetent; they move from hideout to hideout, always scared, always looking over their shoulders. But you, Darcy Pennington, you are brave, you are talented, and you are ready for this task. Haven't you imagined what it would be like?

Well . . . Darcy had to admit, she'd had a few Joan of Arc-like daydreams over the last couple months.

Imagine how grateful they all would be. While they are holed up here, hiding from the tsellodrin, you will be saving them. How indebted they will be to you! And how sorry that they did not take you more seriously. Perhaps . . . he trailed off a little and squinted his eyes.

What?

Perhaps they will even make you their queen.

Darcy sighed and rolled her eyes. *They're already going to do that, remember?*

What I mean is, Lykos continued, *perhaps they will crown you queen without making you marry the spoiled boy prince, Tellius.*

Darcy felt her stomach lurch. What Lykos was saying was dangerous, and incredible! Oh, how she would love to be released from the marriage expectation! But . . . she shook her head. *It's too crazy, Lykos. I don't believe that any of that could actually happen.*

Oh, but the wheels are already in motion.

What do you mean? She felt startled.

I've spoken with my people, those outside the walls.

How?

In the same manner that you and I speak, of course. This ability is nothing new among the high animals; it is only unique now because you, a human, can speak with me, a wolf. They are ready, Darcy, ready to follow you.

But . . . Darcy grappled for some bit of logic that might stop this crazy train. *But we can't leave Paradeisos. We'll be seen!*

We will? Lykos raised a shaggy eyebrow at her. *You are forgetting your crown. Try to make yourself blend into your surroundings, like the spy, Dean, does.*

Rubidius said those talents are unique to each of us; they're not regular natural magical abilities, Darcy countered.

Just try, Lykos insisted.

With a small degree of trepidation, Darcy closed her eyes. She didn't even know what to do to become chameleon-like, like Dean, so she settled on thinking of him and imagining that she *was* him, blending into the stone wall behind her.

Ah. Perfect, Lykos crowed in her mind.

She opened her eyes and looked down. Indeed, she was mottled and gray like the stones behind her. She gasped and lost her hold on what she was doing, popping back to normal like a snapped rubber band. "I don't believe it!"

Why not? It was in you all the time; the crown's power just helped you on your way. Rubidius has been holding you back!

This is . . . totally nuts, Lykos!

He looked puzzled at her choice of vernacular. *I assume that you mean to say that it is crazy. I assure you, it is not. To do this thing is your destiny, Darcy. Can you be ready to go to war when I give you word that the time is right?*

I— Darcy spread her hands. *Lykos! I don't think I can do this!*

You can, and you will, he said. *Alitheia is depending on you.*

Chapter 35

Another Birthday Surprise

'*Alitheia is depending on you,*' Darcy grumped to herself. *But no pressure, right?* She tromped through the mud toward the food tent, her stomach grumbling almost as much as her mind. Her beautiful crown was hidden deep inside an inner pocket of her cloak, which hung off her shoulders as the sun rose higher in the sky and the day warmed. Pretty soon she would put away her fur cloak entirely.

She'd left Lykos marginally satisfied, for the time being, promising that she would think about what he wanted her to do, even though she didn't really believe it was possible. What was the likelihood of his plans coming to pass before the leaders of the rebellion were ready to carry out *their* offensive plan? She shivered remembering the horrible fight in the clearing the night they'd come here, and she hoped against hope that she would not have to enter battle ever again. Then again—she stuck her hand in her pocket and fingered cold metal and smooth stones—if this crown was really as powerful as Lykos claimed it was, perhaps she could lead the wolves without ever seeing any bloodshed? Maybe she could cast a spell so powerful that Tselloch himself would cower before her? She smirked and took her hand out of her pocket.

She ducked into the brown tent and stopped abruptly. On the table was a three-tiered cake and Sam, Perry, Lewis, and a reluctant Amelia were gathered around it, talking. Sam looked up and noticed her.

"Oh! You took us by surprise! It was supposed to be the other way around. Come on you guys, let's sing!"

Sam and Perry, who didn't seem to mind that sort of thing, were the only ones to sing "Happy Birthday". Amelia didn't even try, and Lewis only moved his mouth, no sound coming out.

"Happy birthday, Darcy!" Sam said when the song ended, practically glowing.

They did remember, Darcy thought, surprised.

"It *is* today, right? March 2nd, yeah?" Sam's face fell a little and she looked from side to side, as though seeking help from the other teenagers.

Darcy realized she hadn't said anything, probably hadn't even smiled, and she quickly stepped forward. "Yeah, sorry, you just took me by surprise." She grinned at Sam and looked at her cake. "Wow, this looks great. Did Asa Rhea make it?"

"Yep! But it's only a white cake," she added apologetically. "Asa Rhea said that supplies for things like this are running low."

"That's okay, I like white cake. We should probably eat dinner first, though, huh?"

"Yes, let's. I'm starving," Amelia huffed with the air of somebody who'd been made to wait. She breezed past Darcy without so much as a glance and made for the food line.

"Where's Dean?" Darcy asked as she and Sam went to stand behind Amelia in line.

"He's not feeling well," Sam said with a frown. "I think maybe they've been working him too hard."

"What's he sick with?"

"I don't know if I'd call it a sickness, really. He was fine this morning at breakfast, and then right in the middle of sword practice with Perry, he doubled over like he'd been hit in the stomach."

"Stomachache?"

"No . . . he said he felt like something took hold of his insides and pulled. And then when he stood up straight again, he was all sweaty and out of breath, like he'd been using his talent for too long."

"That's really weird."

"Yeah. He's in bed recovering. I think Eleanor's with him. Oh! I almost forgot . . . something appeared in my bag today and I think it's for you." Sam fished around in her pocket and pulled out a small, ancient-looking, iron key. It was about the size of her house key back home.

Darcy took it from Sam. "Um . . . thanks?"

Sam giggled. "Yeah, I know, great birthday present, huh?"

Darcy turned it over in her palm. She'd never seen it before and didn't have a clue what it could belong to. "What makes you think it's for me?"

"Because it came into my bag when I was thinking about your birthday this morning; just as I was wishing I had a present to give you, there it was! Thanks," Sam said to Asa Rhea, taking her plate of food. "I don't know what it's for, but I thought you should have it."

She waited for Darcy to take her plate of food and then whispered to her, "Did you know that they've been talking about sending him outside the walls? They think he'll be able to fool the tsellodrin with that talent of his."

"Sorry, who?" Darcy's mind was still on the key.

"Dean."

"Oh, right. Really?"

"Yeah, but Rubidius says they should wait until all of our talents are revealed. And then that made them argue about you, naturally."

"Why? Because Rubidius won't work with me?" Darcy dropped the key into the pocket of her cloak and heard it ping as it hit her crown.

Sam shrugged. "I think so. It is weird, isn't it?" She sat down by the cake and picked up her fork as Darcy went to sit across from her. "Is there anything that Rubidius told you that you had to do before he would train you? Anything that he's waiting for?"

Darcy frowned. It had been a while since she'd thought about that long-ago conversation with the old alchemist. What *had* he told her to do? She thought it might have had something to do with encouraging the other five teenagers, but she couldn't remember. "I don't know," she said to Sam. "What is this?" she pointed with her fork.

"Rabbit meat and potatoes," Sam said, taking a bite. "It's not bad. It's a nice change after all the fish."

"Mmm!" Darcy agreed with her mouth full. Access to the lagoon within the old city walls meant a lot of their meals at Paradeisos had consisted of small, salty tasting fish. She swallowed hard and watched Sam eat for a moment. For the first time she noticed that Sam was thinner; it wasn't a huge change, but it was something. She wondered how long the change had been noticeable and mentally kicked herself for neglecting her friend. "Thanks a lot for the cake, Sam," she said. "I really do appreciate it. I . . . I thought you guys had forgotten about me."

Sam shrugged as if to say "It was nothing" and smiled at Perry and Lewis as they took seats next to them. "Anything new going on with your talent, Lewis? Rubidius seemed pretty intent on working with you this morning."

Lewis glanced at Darcy and shook his head.

Catching the gesture, Darcy slowly put down her fork. "What?" she asked, feeling her stomach drop. The others never seemed to want to discuss their talents around her. It was time for them to level with her. "What is it? You don't want to talk around me?" She leveled a hard gaze on him.

"It's nothing," Sam said quickly, trying to draw her attention. "He's just being stupid."

Perry ate with his head down, pretending not to listen.

"No, really . . . what is it?" Darcy put her fork on her plate and crossed her arms over her chest. "You guys never let me know what's going on with your training."

"Well, it's not like you care," Amelia said from the other side of Perry.

"Yes, I do!"

"Okay . . . okay . . ." Sam interceded, trying to head off disaster. "Darcy,

I'm really sorry. It's all my fault, but I never meant for it to be taken this far."

"*What's* your fault? Can't you guys just tell me what's going on?"

"Well, I—that is—Amelia, told the others, the boys, about how you meet with that wolf all the time—"

"Lykos."

"Right, him . . . anyway, I accidently mentioned how I don't really trust him, and Am—that is, one of the *others* made up this elaborate story about how he's a spy for Tselloch and all the wolves are his minions—"

Darcy dropped her arms in disbelief. "*What?*"

"I know, I know, it was totally ridiculous, and we didn't really believe it. I mean, it was just a stupid story we made up. But then the more we talked about it, the more we, at least, *some* of us," she glared at the others, "actually started to believe it. They all decided that we shouldn't tell you anything critical about our talents in case you passed the information onto *him.* I'm really sorry, Darcy, but I didn't know what to do about it!"

It all makes sense now. "Is that why Dean stopped jumping out at me?" Darcy asked in a dull voice. "He doesn't want to practice his talent in front of me?"

"Um, yeah," Sam answered, her voice very small.

"I see." The blood pounding through Darcy's veins was making her head hurt. She should have known that Amelia would figure out some way to alienate her from the rest of them. And to think that they all went along with it! Even Sam was guilty of participating. She pushed her plate of food away and scooted back to get up off the bench.

"Darcy," Sam began, but Amelia interrupted her.

"Oh, don't be a baby, Darcy. Can't you take a joke?"

Darcy looked at her slowly, incredulity in her eyes. "A *joke*? You've accused me of passing information to the enemy, and you've accused my best friend of being a spy!"

Amelia had the decency to look slightly ashamed, but she merely looked down.

"Darcy, please!" Sam looked close to tears.

"Forget it, Sam," Amelia said, "she's just going to go sulk somewhere."

Darcy couldn't comfort Sam. She couldn't argue with Amelia anymore. She couldn't stand to be around any of them any longer. She gathered her cloak around her and breezed out of the tent. She almost wanted to put her new crown on and go back in there and show them what she could do, but she knew that Lykos would be angry if she did that.

She kicked viciously at a sludge pile and dodged around a group of soldiers standing and laughing in a group. What was the matter with everybody, anyway? While the enemy surrounded them outside the walls, the soldiers inside them did nothing and their leaders just talked endlessly. Her own "friends" made up ridiculous stories behind her back and Rubidius and Eleanor taught them inane lessons about magic—that Rubidius wouldn't even train her in—history and languages. What use was Old Alitheian going to be against an army of tsellodrin? And Tellius! She didn't even want to think about him. If she had to spend one more boring morning with him and his stupid questions, arguments, and uncomfortable silences, she was going to scream!

Whatever Lykos wanted her to do, she would do it. She would *show* them how loyal she was to the rebel cause. They all would be jealous of her when they found out what she could do, what she *had* done. She had to find Lykos; she was ready to leave.

CHAPTER 36

LEAVING PARADEISOS

Darcy didn't know why, but she'd chosen a bright red dress to wear for the occasion. It had been such a nice surprise to find clothing other than the plain, brown woolen dress that had been her only garment at Sanditha when they first arrived in Paradeisos, but she hadn't worn the other garments very often. When it came down to it, she felt that although they were also made out of wool, they were far too fancy to mess up in the snow and mud. But tonight she would wear it. She guessed that she wanted to feel regal and confident; red was a good color for that.

She lay in bed feigning sleep and counting the minutes. She'd had to go to session that afternoon; Lykos had told her that it would raise suspicion for her to miss it, but she'd not said a word to any of the others, not even to Dean, who walked in halfway through the afternoon session and didn't have any idea what had happened at lunch. She'd even eaten dinner with them, but she still hadn't talked. She wouldn't have bothered with food, but she knew that she had a long night before her, and she needed her strength. After dinner she'd pretended to be sick and went straight back to their quarters, changed her clothes, made sure her crown was still in her cloak pocket, and gotten into bed.

Now it was just a matter of time. When she'd gone to Lykos during lunch, he'd told her to meet him by their shack once everybody was asleep. At the time she'd been worried that she would fall asleep while she waited for the others to drift off, but she knew now that she would not. She felt like she'd taken caffeine pills and she chafed under the need to lie still and wait.

She heard the faint sucking sound that announced the entrance of somebody else to their room, and she squeezed her eyes shut, willing her breathing to slow. She'd not pulled the hangings down on her bed; she wanted them to see her in it.

She heard the whisper of clothing and a second sucking sound before Sam's worried voice penetrated the silence.

"Is she asleep?" Sam whispered.

"Looks that way," Amelia said. She didn't sound concerned. "I told you she would be."

"Amelia, I think she's really mad."

Darcy couldn't see either of them, but she imagined the older girl swatting the air dismissively. "Darcy's always mad about something."

"No . . . I mean I think she's *really* mad. I've never seen her like this before."

Amelia didn't answer, and Darcy heard her rummaging around by her bed. "Look," Amelia finally hissed, "if you're that worried about it, why don't you just tell Rubidius?"

"Because I promised I wouldn't!" Sam hissed back; she sounded scandalized.

"Yeah, but . . . if you honestly believe that she's in danger, why wouldn't you break that promise?"

"I . . . I guess you're right." Sam sighed. "Let's do it in the morning, though. I don't want to bother him tonight."

"Okay."

They quietly rustled around as they readied themselves for bed, and after what felt like an hour of waiting, one of them finally turned down the lantern and Darcy heard them settle into their beds.

"G'night, Amelia," Sam whispered sleepily.

"Good night, Sam."

Okay. Darcy quietly let out a pent up breath and opened her eyes. She was facing the wall, so she wasn't concerned about them seeing her awake with the lights off. *Sam's so ridiculous,* she thought peevishly as she listened to the other girls' breathing. *What does she have against Lykos? Is she jealous that I spend so much time with him?* She snorted softly and inwardly shook her head.

Okay . . . Amelia's out. Amelia was one of those people who had the amazing ability to fall asleep almost as soon as her head hit the pillow. Her breathing always deepened and slowed and she sometimes made little sighing sounds in her sleep. Sam, on the other hand, always tossed and turned for at least twenty minutes before dropping off, and Darcy could hear her now, adjusting and readjusting in her bed. *Come on, Sam, it's easy. Just close your eyes and lie still.* Even when Sam fell asleep, she would often twitch convulsively and mumble incoherent sentences. It was difficult to know when she was really out.

It took an eternity, but Darcy finally felt that it was safe for her to sneak out. She climbed carefully from her bed, thankful for the straw mattress and stone floor that didn't creak. She swiftly let down the hangings around her bed; she wanted them to think in the morning that she had awoken in the night and pulled them down. She hoped that it would buy her and the wolves a little more time. Swinging her fur cloak about her shoulders, she tiptoed to the exit wall and placed her hand on the stone. As it warmed, she took one last look back at the girls' sleeping forms, and then she stepped through to the outside.

She took a moment inside their entrance pavilion to calm herself and go over her selected path again. It was late, but there were always people wandering around the encampment. The outskirts of camp by the walls were always more deserted, though, and she'd chosen to sneak to the wall and make her way along it until she came to the shack. She knew that she would probably have to pass very close to some of the watching tsellodrin, but at least they couldn't see her.

She dug the crown out of her pocket and set it snuggly on her head; then she tucked her long braid inside the cloak and pulled the hood up over it all. Closing her eyes, she pulled on the power in the crown and willed herself to become like a chameleon. *It worked!* she thought excitedly before she even opened her eyes. *I can feel it! Okay . . . it's time.*

She opened her eyes and took two steps, then a third and she was out in the open. She looked right and left. A cluster of three soldiers stood talking by a bonfire twenty paces to her right, but the way to her left was clear. *That's the way I need to go.* She turned left and continued on, feeling horribly exposed but knowing that unless they really focused on her faint outline, they couldn't see her. She breathed as quietly as she could and mentally cheered that the ground had frozen again. After a few days of thaw, much of the snow had disappeared, but with the refreezing, her feet would leave no prints in the frozen mud.

Dodging around two more boulders, she suddenly came up short as two young men, the camp nurse, and Yahto Veli rushed past her.

"What's the matter with him?" she heard Yahto snap briskly at the two men.

"We don't know, sir!" one of them panted. "We just found him doubled up outside his rock and he's shakin' like the dickens!"

"Same as this morning," Nurse Dembe muttered.

And then they were too far away for Darcy to hear anymore. She hesitated, concerned, torn between continuing straight to the wall and following them. Just before they disappeared behind a bend of bushes, she took off after them. *I can still get to the wall from over here,* she rationalized.

When she caught up to them, Nurse Dembe was helping a very green-looking Dean to his feet outside the blue pavilion that marked the boys' rock. Darcy gasped and put her hand over her mouth. His limbs were shaking and his lips trembling as sweat matted his hair to his forehead. Alepo, who usually slept under the boys' pavilion, was yipping nervously at

Dean's side and nosing his legs.

Suddenly Alepo stopped jumping and looked in Darcy's direction, his nose in the air. A deep growl started in his throat. With a lurch, Darcy realized that he could smell her. *But why would he growl at me? He's never growled at me before.* With cautious steps, she backed away.

Loyalty to Dean kept the fox at the boy's side, but his amber eyes and rumbling growl followed her until she slipped behind another rock and was hidden from sight. She let out a deep breath and closed her eyes for a moment. *Okay, no more detours,* she promised herself. She put Dean out of her mind.

With darting steps, she dodged around boulders, ramshackle ruins, trees, and bonfires until she reached the line of the old wall. Thankful for the progress she'd already made, she trotted along the wall at a brisk pace until the ruins thinned and she came into a region she thought must have been an inner courtyard at some time. The shack was visible now in the misty gloom and she breathed a sigh of relief.

Lykos? I'm coming!

We're ready for you, he replied. He sounded excited. *Were you followed?*

No. I'm wearing the crown.

Excellent.

A moment later she ducked into the shack to find it packed with shaggy bodies. In addition to Lykos and Lupidor, there were four other wolves that Darcy had seen from time to time around Paradeisos. She released the spell that cloaked her and grinned at Lykos. She was terrified of what Lykos was asking her to do, but for some reason her fright was coming out in energetic, excited waves.

We must move quickly, Lykos said to her when she appeared before him. *My people already know the plan. You are to cloak us here, and then we will pass through the gap in the wall that is fifty paces east of our current location. Once through, do not speak aloud. Make no noise whatsoever as we pass through the ranks of tsellodrin. My people outside the walls tell me that they are many. Five miles from here we will rendezvous with them and rest before we continue on to Ormiskos.*

Darcy tried to get everything he'd just told her to stay in her brain. *Okay . . . but what then? How are we supposed to storm the castle?* She felt almost silly asking the question, like she was an actor in a movie or on stage.

Leave that to me, Lykos told her. *We will have time yet to go over those details.*

Lykos, Darcy hesitated, her fear becoming icy cold for the first time that night, *are you sure you don't want to bring anybody else with us? Like some soldiers, or . . . or Yahto?*

Lykos growled in his throat. *Are you questioning the capability of my people?*

No! I just . . .

He gentled and interrupted her. *It would be best, Darcy, for us to do this alone. The others here will not understand the power you possess until you demonstrate it to them with the re-conquest of Ormiskos. And you are also sparing them.*

Sparing them?

From bloodshed and possible death. Did you not consider how you will be protecting them through your actions tonight?

Oh . . . um, no . . . I guess I didn't think about it that way. Darcy felt her cheeks warm and she smiled nervously. Everything was going to be okay.

Are you ready? Lykos asked her.

Yes. Raising shaking hands, she placed the spell over herself, Lykos, Lupidor, and the other four wolves until they all resembled chunks of the wall and the pressed dirt of the ground.

Without another word, Lykos dodged past her and out the door and Darcy felt the other wolves press around her legs as they juried for position to pass through the open entrance. *Lykos?* Darcy called out in her mind, slightly panicky as she felt herself being left behind.

Follow the link, he answered her, and she remembered this was one of the exercises they'd practiced over the long winter months. She could actually pinpoint the wolf's location by following the thread of the magic that linked them.

When she came up alongside him, she was finally able to make out his very faint outline. *Lay your hand on my head,* he instructed her. *If you lose me, just follow the link again to find me. Don't worry,* he chuckled roughly in his throat, *I'm not leaving you behind.*

They passed like ghosts to the section of wall that Lykos had spoken of. Many parts of the old walls of Paradeisos were no higher than Darcy's armpits, and in several places the wall had crumbled entirely. It didn't matter to the enchantment that kept the camp safe, though, because it worked according to the original location of the walls, not the walls themselves. Standing just outside the gap in the wall was a leering tsellodrin. Darcy came up short. Now that it came to it, was she brave enough?

Pay him no mind, Lykos instructed her. *Remember, he cannot see you.*

Okay.

Now! With me! Lykos lurched forward and she went with him, clinging to the fur between his ears.

CHAPTER 37

A DIFFERENT SORT OF RENDEZVOUS

It was really very simple. In a few steps they were through the gap and past the servant of the Shadow. A few more paces took them under heavy tree cover, and Darcy breathed easier.

That wasn't so bad, she thought, but a moment too soon. She realized that between every tree trunk in her line of sight, tsellodrin stood silently waiting. Their blank, black eyes betrayed no emotion as they stared toward Paradeisos. There were hundreds of them—no, thousands of them! Every direction she looked, they were there.

She gasped and clapped a hand over her mouth to muffle the sound. *This way,* Lykos's voice sounded in her brain. Numb, she followed his lead in front of the line of tsellodrin. At some point, she knew, they would have to find a break through them. *Don't look at them, don't look at them,* she chanted in her mind, but it was difficult not to. Their sullen faces and bristling weapons drew her eyes like magnets, and she was suddenly back at the battle on her way to Paradeisos. *I never even found out what the nark's name was who died that night,* she thought. What was the matter with her? Was she really so selfish? *Not now*, she ordered herself. It was not the time for introspection, and Lykos was nudging her closer to the tsellodrin.

There was a stream, still frozen, that cut through the enemy line. No tsellodrin stood on the ice, and Darcy realized that this was the only path they could take. *I'll try not to slip,* she promised Lykos.

That would be good, he answered wryly. *Don't let go of my fur; I can help you balance.*

They stepped cautiously onto the ice. Darcy held her breath and continued forward. A few cracks snapped under her feet and the tsellodrin they were passing looked their way curiously.

Just keep going, Lykos growled tensely in her head.

Keep going she did, legs shaking and feet slipping sideways from time to time, and none of the tsellodrin ever challenged them. Their ranks were thick, however, and Darcy felt sick thinking about her friends stuck in the center of their midst. Did they even know how many tsellodrin were out here? *It won't matter soon,* she reminded herself. *Once we defeat Tselloch, they will be free to leave Paradeisos!* The thought spurred her onward.

Fifteen minutes later they finally passed the last of the tsellodrin and stepped from the stream to the bank. Darcy was weary with exertion and nerves and would have asked to rest for a while, but Lykos urged them onward. *Five more miles,* he told her, *and then you can rest.*

She sighed. *Okay.*

The next five miles were quicker, but no easier. Sure, they didn't have leering tsellodrin on every side, but they still had to exercise caution as they passed through forest and dense undergrowth that snagged Darcy's cloak and skirt. There were black spots in the forest, too; spots that, even at night, looked like all life had abandoned them completely. From time to time they even passed great swaths of blackness, like some sort of creature had come through and sucked the life out of everything in its path.

She wasn't that far off the mark. When she finally asked Lykos about them, he told her that they were the marks of the tsellochim.

What do the tsellochim look like?

Like shadow, he answered, exasperatedly. *Why do you think we call him the Shadow?*

Oh. Darcy fell silent. She'd only been able to carry on the conversation at all because of the crown, which lent her magical strength. On any other day, she would never have been able to carry on the clipped pace and mindspeak at the same time.

Finally, after many scrapes, bruises, and banged shins, Lykos called a halt to their group and sent up a bone-chilling howl. His call was answered by a wolf very close by and Darcy saw the forest around them swell with furry bodies.

Release the spell, Darcy, Lykos instructed her. She did so, marveling again at how she felt no fatigue from having kept it up for so long.

The wolves looked at her with curious interest; grey, white, black, charcoal, brown, and golden coats shimmering between the rocks and trees. Lykos breathed and his blue flames encircled her.

What are you doing? Darcy asked in alarm.

Letting them get a good look at you, he replied, amusement in his voice.

The wolves made many interesting, and sometimes frightening, sounds as they milled around her. She couldn't count their number, but it was great. For the first time she found herself believing that they would be able to retake Ormiskos. They examined her for several minutes, and Darcy didn't know if Lykos was talking to them during that time, but finally, beginning with the wolves closest to her, every animal bent their front legs into an unmistakable bow.

What are they doing?

Paying you homage. It is now time for you to address them.

Address them? I don't know what to say! Darcy sputtered mentally at Lykos.

I will give you the words. Speak them aloud.

She wrung her hands nervously, but nodded her head. "Noble people of the fur," she spoke the words as Lykos said them in her mind, "I bring you greetings."

As one, the wolves sent up a collective howl in response to her greeting and she had to wait until they quieted down to continue. "Today we begin a new era; one in which the wolves will be glorified!"

More howls and joyful yips, growls, and barks.

"I am pleased to be the bearer of these good things for you. If you follow me to Ormiskos, all your hopes and dreams will come true." She glanced at Lykos incredulously. This was like a bad politician's speech, but the wolves seemed to like it. Many of them were now standing on their feet and wagging their tails. "By this time tomorrow," she continued at Lykos's prompting, "you will be elevated to the status of princes!"

The din that followed this announcement was so loud that Darcy actually put her hands over her ears.

Okay, Lykos whispered in her brain, *that's enough for now.* With a puff of air, he extinguished the flames surrounding her and faced the wolves himself. Darcy assumed that he spoke to them because they became very silent and attentive to him for several minutes. Then they broke off into groups and a large chunk of them disappeared into the woods. *I've given them your preliminary instructions,* he said, turning to face her.

My preliminary instructions? she repeated weakly.

Of course, he said slyly. *I told you that you wouldn't have to worry about anything. I'll command the troops and you'll take all the glory.*

Okay . . . I guess so.

But now, we rest, he said. *The forward guard must perform their duties, and then they will send a messenger back to let us know when it is time.*

What will I need to do?

Only what I tell you. Just remember to obey me completely and without question, and you will be fine.

Okay.

Sleep now, if you can. You won't have a chance to later.

Darcy sank wearily to the ground. She wished she'd thought to bring some food with her, but she guessed she was probably too worked up to eat anyhow. She curled up next to Lykos and closed her eyes. She would sleep . . . if she could.

Darcy lurched awake when a wet nose bumped her on the chin. "What's going on? Sam?" she mumbled, confused.

Lykos bumped her again, and she realized that in her sleep she had let the connection between them break. *Sorry, Lykos,* she reconnected with him, *I'm awake now.* She sat up and rubbed her eyes. She felt foggy and disoriented, like she'd been wrenched from a very deep sleep.

It's time to go, Lykos told her. *Hurry!*

Okay, okay. How long was I out for?

Four hours. It's near dawn; time for our attack.

Darcy suddenly felt very wide awake. Dawn. They were going to attack at dawn. "Lykos—" she wavered.

It's too late for second-guessing; your path is set, he growled in her mind.

She felt ill. She pulled herself to her feet and brushed off her skirt with shaking hands. She was a fourteen-year-old girl! What did they need her for? Lykos was the one instructing them! She peered down at him in the predawn gloom and noticed his yellow eyes watching her. Her questions died in her throat. She had no choice now but to go forward.

CHAPTER 38
THE VISION

They'd been camped close to what Lykos called the 'Old Highway.' Darcy couldn't see any signs of the road itself under thick, oily-looking vines, growth, and piles of muddy snow and slush, but Lykos assured her that it was there. The Old Highway led to the gates of Ormiskos, and the way was lined with wolves. In the distance Darcy could see turreted towers of gray blocks scraping the sky—four of them, with a larger fifth tower on the side of the fortress furthest from the road. No banners flew from them, and more of the thick vines clung to their sides.

Darcy felt like she was being led through a gauntlet. On both sides of the road the wolves lolled with their tongues hanging out, watching her and Lykos tread their way slowly toward the palace gates. She didn't know why they looked so relaxed. She didn't know why there was, as of yet, no sign of tsellodrin or tsellochim, or guards of any sort, for that matter. *This is wrong,* she thought to herself. *Lykos . . . shouldn't we be hiding or something? Tselloch is going to see us coming!*

Don't worry, he assured her again, *it's all taken care of. My troops have done their part.*

So . . . just like that? We can just walk right up to the castle?

Lykos didn't respond.

Fear twisted in Darcy's belly. She told herself she should stop walking, that she should plant her feet and refuse to go any farther until Lykos explained exactly what was going on, but she was compelled to move forward. One foot in front of the other, on and on . . .

The sun was about to peek over the horizon, but Darcy didn't feel any comfort from the thought. With a jolt Darcy recognized the terrain. Even though it was clogged with menacing shapes and plants that did not exist in Michigan, Darcy realized that she was walking up the highway along the coast, and that any second now they would reach the castle gates, which had to be the east entrance to Glorietta Bay.

They drew up parallel to the towers and Lykos swung a hard right. Darcy obediently followed him. She didn't understand what the matter with her was. Why couldn't she control her own body? With a jolt she stopped next to Lykos and the wolves all down the road sent up a chilly howl as one.

Directly before her were the gates of Ormiskos. They were massive, at least twenty feet high. But she hadn't seen them from a distance because they were masked on either side by towering cedar trees. The gates were hinged on either side to two massive cedar trunks so that they looked more a part of the forest than anything else. Wrought of planked wood and black iron, strange insignia and words had been burned into them, giving them the appearance of finely engraved furniture. The same thick, oily vegetation that cloaked the Old Highway clung to either side of the cedar trees to which the gates were hinged, concealing the massive brick wall through which the gate gave passage.

Darcy absorbed all these things in a moment, though, because the wolves began howling almost as soon as she'd stopped. Lykos didn't howl, but stood stiffly at her side, with his bottlebrush tail cocked out behind him. *Why are they doing that?* Darcy cried to him, putting her hands over her ears. *What's going on?*

Lykos didn't answer. His eyes were riveted on the gate and Darcy heard a groan of hinges. Terrified, she wondered what had gone wrong. Was this part of the plan? Was the castle already taken? Why wouldn't Lykos talk to her?

The gates opened very slowly, and between them Darcy could see only blackness. But it wasn't an empty blackness; it moved and roiled and breathed . . . like it was alive. *Run, run, run, run.* Beat instinctively through Darcy's brain with every pulse of her heart, but her feet were riveted to the ground.

The gates were open. The blackness inside came out to meet her. Four shadow creatures—*tsellochim!* Darcy thought frantically—formless . . . but with form. They were like beings of black fog that scattered and coalesced in an undulating pattern. When they came together they resembled giant, four-legged spiders with knobby legs extending far above their globular, suspended bodies.

With moaning and whispering, they surrounded Darcy and nudged her forward through the gate. Shaking like a leaf, she was powerless to resist them. She tried to call out to Lykos, but the connection was gone, severed. She moved forward like a sleepwalker, her feet dragging on the ground as she resisted with all her strength. She couldn't even see Lykos anymore; all she could see was blackness.

With a groan and a thud, the gates closed behind her. Darcy was alone in Ormiskos with the tsellochim. Lykos had betrayed her.

No! It can't be . . . Darcy thought numbly. *How could he do this to me? Why?* She was stumbling forward with no view of where she planted her feet. The tsellochim surrounded her with their fog, their indecipherable voices muttering, their passage making no sound. She could hear the wolves howling again outside the walls; they sounded joyful, ecstatic. Was this the job Lykos had intended for them to do? Deliver her to Tselloch? Were they to be rewarded for their actions? *Of course they are! Don't be so stupid.*

She felt the tsellochim lift her feet one at a time. They were climbing a staircase cut out of stone. She heard water passing beneath her as her feet hit wooden planking. *But . . . why me?* she moaned inwardly. *Why would Tselloch want me?*

Because, the logical part of her brain answered—the part that all along had warned her against her friendship with Lykos. *Because you are to be the future queen of this land. Because the rebellion would pay any ransom to get you back. Because the prophecy states that only the Six, working together, can fully expel Tselloch from this land.*

Darcy swallowed hard and the tears finally came. How could she have been so stupid? Why didn't she recognize early on that Lykos was deceiving her? Sam knew that he couldn't be trusted. *Oh, Sam! I'm sorry!* She wailed out loud, covering her mouth with her hands to cut off the sound. What was going to happen to her now? What would they do with her?

Her feet suddenly stopped moving and she lurched to stay upright. One by one the four tsellochim coalesced into their spider-like forms and withdrew from her, leaving her standing alone in a large, cold, high-ceilinged chamber.

She blinked through her tears at the heavy black drapes that covered the walls and the winking and sparkling chandeliers and candelabras that lit the space, giving her the stifling feeling that she was stuck inside a large, padded jewelry box. There were no chairs or furniture of any kind in the room aside from a menacing black throne that sat in a half-moon shaped alcove on the far wall. The throne was empty.

Darcy shivered and wrapped her arms around her chest. She'd never felt such despair and loneliness in all her life. The four tsellochim lurked along the walls, hissing to each other from time to time. Darcy wanted to turn around to see what was behind her, but she still couldn't move her feet.

She felt his approach before she heard it. Soft, padding feet stepped with measured treads behind her, growing ever nearer. She tried hard not to squeak with fear, imagining another shadow-beast like the tsellochim, but bigger, sneaking up on her from behind. She tried to slow her breathing, but she was shaking too hard.

She felt a hand brush her shoulder, cool like ice to the touch, but human. She frowned as the man rounded her side and stood before her. If this was Tselloch, he was not at all what she'd expected. He was, indeed, a man . . . but Darcy could tell that it was not his natural form. He looked perfect—too perfect to be human. His skin was like ink, the embodiment of the oil that bled from his dead tsellodrin. Darcy had to hold herself back from reaching out and grazing her hand along his high cheekbone, overcome with a need to know whether touching him would leave liquid on her skin. His jet black eyes bore into her, his smooth black hair falling about his shoulders. He stood nearly seven feet tall, his nose, chin, full lips, and powerful build looking chiseled from onyx. He was dressed in simple, but rich, black robes and he carried no items at all. Darcy may have thought he was a tsellodrin were it not for the charisma in his bearing and the interest betrayed in his eyes. No tsellodrin showed that much emotion.

"You expected me to be a monster, didn't you? That's what they told you, I am sure."

His voice was deep and melodious. Against her will, Darcy felt her shoulders relax. She shrugged at his words.

"Of course you did. They all do." He turned his back on her and walked slowly toward his throne. Against her will, Darcy followed him until he was seated, and she stood just a few feet in front of him.

He sat and observed her, lounging at ease while she stood stiffly watching him. She felt less fear now that she stood before him and found him to be not as terrible as she'd imagined.

"So young," he murmured, his voice compassionate. "And they expect so much from you."

Darcy didn't answer. She didn't want to agree with him.

"*I* would never ask so much of you," he continued.

"What do you mean?" Darcy finally ground out.

He laughed, throwing his head back. "Do you mean that they have brainwashed you into thinking it is a small thing? What they are requiring of you?"

"I don't know what you are talking about."

"To think that they have told you that you must marry that prince—a child!—in order to come into your rightful inheritance."

Darcy's mind spun. "My . . . my what?"

His face grew very grave. "Did you not know that this kingdom belongs to you?"

"What?"

He stood and went to her shoulder. With a touch of his hand she regained movement of her body, but she didn't run. "There are older writings than the prophecy they parade around like truth," he said very deeply. "There are prophecies that speak of you, Darcy Pennington. You were made to rule this land. I. . ." he chuckled softly, "I have only kept it safe for you."

Darcy shook her head. She didn't understand what he was saying, but it must be a lie. "No." She took a step backward. "No . . . they told me about you. You haven't been keeping it safe for me; you've taken it for yourself!"

Tselloch folded his hands in front of him and shook his head sadly. "Oh, the lies they tell. They probably also told you that my servants and I destroy the beauty of this land. That we cover it up?"

Darcy shrugged. She couldn't deny it.

"I've only covered what I've needed to in order to survive. Do you think I enjoy living like this?" He gestured to the draped walls. "No! It is to keep me safe from prying eyes." His gaze became more intense. "But if you step into your birthright here today, I can give you a glimpse of what Alitheia will once again become." He clapped his hands loudly and then threw them wide. With the gesture, the drapes covering the walls flew back to reveal walls of windows open to the brilliant morning sunshine. Inside the chamber, the only pieces to remain the same were the chandeliers and candelabras; everything else became different, brighter colors, and the hall filled with couches and tables and Tselloch himself stood before her in bright robes of yellow and white. Darcy's cloak slid off her shoulders and her red and gold dress gleamed while her arms and neck were suddenly bedecked in fabulous jewels.

Darcy gasped and fingered the jewelry at her wrist. She walked hesitantly to one of the floor-to-ceiling windows, which opened at her touch out to a veranda. Tselloch followed her as she walked outside and leaned on the railing, breathing deeply.

"It's beautiful, isn't it?" he asked from behind her. "It is Alitheia as it was meant to be."

Darcy didn't answer, but her heart swelled to see the sparkling green on the cedar limbs and the impossibly bright-colored wildflowers that poked up through the slush. She absorbed the effects of the morning silently for a moment, but then she frowned. She looked at the view outside. The sea sparkled nearby and the trees and flowers looked just as magical as she remembered from her first day in Alitheia, but where were the creatures that *made* them magical? She saw no fairies, no gnomes, and no nymphs of any kind. In fact . . . her frown deepened. The woods were silent. She knelt down to look more closely at a wildflower poking through onto the veranda. When she touched it with her finger, it crumbled like dust.

Darcy stood up quickly and glanced up at Tselloch to see if he had noticed. He was watching her, of course, but his eyes betrayed no anger at her actions. With as much courage as she could muster, she turned her back on the glorious outdoor morning, and marched back into the hall. She heard Tselloch follow her in and the soft click of the window closing. When it was closed, the curtains suddenly fell back down and the room returned to its black interior.

"It was only a vision of the future that I showed you," Tselloch murmured, walking past her to sit on his throne. "That is why the flower could not withstand your touch."

"Where were the magical creatures?" Darcy challenged him. "Where were the fairies and all the others?"

His eyes flickered and Darcy worried that she had made him angry, but he calmly replied. "They will return when you are queen."

"Rubidius told me that the rocks and plants only look so spectacular because of the fairies and magical creatures that indwell them and make them so. How could you show me a world without the magic, but with the effects of the magic? It doesn't make any sense!"

"It was only a vision," Tselloch said again, and this time there was a cold undertone to his words.

They glared wordlessly at each other. "So . . .," Darcy finally ventured, "according to you, all I need to do to return Alitheia to its former splendor is accept my rightful inheritance."

"Yes. All of Alitheia would thank you." He was suddenly smooth and charming again.

"So, how exactly would I *do* that?" Darcy asked.

"All you have to do is reach out," he extended his hand to her, "and touch my hand."

"That's it?" Darcy sputtered, taken aback. Her guard dropped a little as she stared at his hand.

"A lot simpler than marrying some prince, wouldn't you agree?" He smiled beguilingly at her.

"Yes," she murmured. Her heart was pounding, but she felt drawn to him. She took a step forward. She mentally screamed at herself, but her hand was rising. She suddenly remembered learning about the tsellodrin; how they willingly gave themselves over to eternal slavery to Tselloch. She remembered their blank faces and black eyes. She remembered learning that there might be no way to change a tsellodrin back.

As images from her experiences with the tsellodrin flashed through her mind, Darcy balled her hand into a fist and dropped it to her side. "No," she said firmly.

Tselloch raised an eyebrow at her. "No?"

Darcy shook her head. "I don't want it."

He lowered his hand slowly and his eyes blazed. "Are you certain?"

Darcy quavered under his furious gaze but nodded her head again. "Yes," she whispered.

With a snap he stood up, and his presence seemed to fill the room. His robes billowed around him like they were alive and he raised his arms ominously. "Perhaps you need some time to consider your options," he said. His voice didn't sound at all pleasant anymore. He dissolved into a coagulated shadowy mass before her eyes and retreated up the wall even as his tsellochim came forward to take her. The last image she saw of Tselloch before they shuffled her from the room was of a massive spidery shape hanging above the throne.

Chapter 39
The Dungeon

She was cold and frightened, and sleep offered her no relief. When she was asleep she drifted between disturbing dreams, images, and black voids of unconsciousness.

She didn't know how long she'd been in the dungeon, but it must have been a great deal of time, because she could feel that she had changed. Her ribs stuck out from her chest and her cheeks were sunken in. She could count every bone in her hands and she knew that if she was left there much longer, she would die. They fed her, it was true, but it was a meager meal at best, and it was brought by a sallow-faced tsellodrin only once a day.

She hadn't seen the tsellochim since her first day in Ormiskos, but a black panther paced outside her bars for several hours every day. She could tell that it was a panther only because her eyes had grown so accustomed to the dark, and she heard its deep, growling purr as it walked to and fro. There was a voice in her head some days, and she suspected that it belonged to the panther, but that *should* be impossible. Lykos had told her she could only communicate with him. Even if he'd lied about that, she *did* know that she had to initiate the contact; it didn't work the other way around. Yet the inhuman voice spoke to her, whispering comforts and promises and rewards if she would only reach out and touch the panther's nose. She ignored him . . . most days.

Some days she talked back, but at those moments she wondered if she was in her right mind. When it came to a logical thought pattern, she only knew for certain that she had screwed up, badly, and she would likely pay for it with her life. But beyond that, she was deeply sorry for having let her friends down. She now knew that they cared about her, and not just Sam. It wouldn't bother them so much that she spent all her time with Lykos if they didn't care about her.

Today she lolled in the back of her cell, pushing her skull against the cold, dripping stones behind her. The crown that Lykos had given her was still on her head, and she realized quickly after his betrayal that the magic it contained was not anything that she actually controlled. She couldn't remove it, either, even though she tried to almost every day. It cut deeply into her head, and it was always cold, no matter how long it connected with her body heat. She sighed and shifted her weight. They'd never given her a change of clothing, and her beautiful red dress was soiled beyond recognition. Her nails were long and broken and her teeth felt rough and grimy. She vaguely remembered watching movies in her old life with people locked in prisons and recalled how they would do pushups and other exercises to keep up their morale, but she just didn't have the energy. She was listless, empty of all hope. Did the rebellion even know what had happened to her? Would they come and find her?

She grew tired of asking herself those questions.

Are you ready to be finished with your time here? The panther's voice entered her mind.

She ignored him.

It's very simple, Darcy, you know what to do.

She suddenly flared up, squinting at the prowling animal outside her cage. *Right . . . just touch your nose and become a tsellodrin. No thank you.*

The panther laughed softly. *Is that what you think will happen? Who told you that?*

Nobody told me that . . . but I'm not stupid; I know what will happen.

I can make all the pain go away, Darcy. How can that be a bad thing?

Yeah, right, you make all the pain go away because I'll be a zombie when you're through.

You won't be like the others. You're special.

Darcy leaned her head back again and closed her eyes. He'd tried this tactic with her before. *Special?*

Yes. I do not need to tell you again that your rightful place is on the throne.

With you ruling over me, right? Darcy thought back.

Not over you . . . with you. Coequal. Partners, Darcy. Wouldn't that be nice?

Darcy curled up into a ball and turned her back on him. She wished he would go away.

After several moments of silence, his voice entered her head again. This time he sounded sad, sorry for her. *They're not coming for you, you know.*

Darcy felt her chin start to tremble and she bit her lip furiously.

They don't care about you, he continued. *They were afraid of your power. Rubidius wouldn't train you because they feared you would discover all that you could really do. They are relieved to be rid of you.*

That's not true! Darcy shouted at him.

It's not? Did he ever give you a satisfactory reason why he would not train you?

He—I—I don't remember.

He wanted to keep you docile until the others were trained enough to control you. And then they were going to use you and marry you off to the spoiled boy prince. It will destroy your magic, you know.

What will?

Marrying Tellius. Oh, you'll keep the run of the mill abilities, but your special talents will disappear.

Why?

It's how marriage in Alitheia works . . . it's how Pateros designed it. Didn't Rubidius ever tell you? He sounded slightly amused.

No.

When two people become one, their magical abilities fuse, and the stronger is subordinated to the weaker; in your case, you are the stronger, and Tellius is the weaker.

Darcy frowned and sat up. Rubidius had never mentioned anything about that before. *Why would Pateros do that?*

Because he wants to keep you weak; it is how he regulates the growth of magic in humans. The panther abruptly turned tail and made for the stairs. *Your meals will come every other day, now. Perhaps it will help you realize how good your life could be, if you will let it.*

Darcy didn't even have the strength to protest. His words circled in her head, over and over. Was he telling the truth about Rubidius and why he didn't train her? Would she really be stuck here until she died? It had already been so long! She gulped a sob and put her head in her hands. Perhaps she should just take the panther's—Tselloch's—way out. Wouldn't it be better to be a tsellodrin for the rest of her life than to be stuck in the dungeon, slowly starving to death?

Just give them a little more time, the logical part of her brain insisted. But that voice was becoming weaker.

Days . . . weeks, it felt like. One meal every other day had caused Darcy to fall into a state of half consciousness for most of her waking hours. The panther continued to come and go every day and whispered words of hope to her. She was so sluggish she could hardly move, and she worried that it was too late to take his way out, even if she wanted to.

One night she jolted awake from a deep, dreamless sleep to find the panther inside the cage with her, his head very close. Outside her bars in the dim hall lurked four tsellochim in their spidery forms and she recoiled with revulsion. Why had Tselloch entered her cell? He'd never done that before.

Now, Darcy Pennington, he said to her. *It is now or never.*

Something about his demeanor was more tense than usual, and Darcy sat up with a great effort, more aware and alert than she had been for a long time. The contrast between his raw beauty and the horror of the shadow creatures watching them caused her mind to spin and she shook her head.

Now is the time to make your decision. Touch me! he growled. *I will never offer again. If you do not do it now, you will die.*

Darcy stared at him with large, frightened eyes. She was so weary and so tired of waiting to be rescued. She knew she was close to death. Tselloch was not lying this time. "I—" she rasped. Her voice sounded strange from disuse. "I'm afraid." Her eyes flickered to the tsellochim.

You don't need to be, he answered back, drawing her attention back to himself. *It will be painless.*

Is this really the only way? Darcy thought frantically to herself, but she seemed incapable of rational thought. She reached her hand up tentatively and the panther lowered his wide head to her. She snatched her hand back quickly. "Wait, I'm not ready!"

He growled low in his throat and turned his back on her. As he turned to leave, the four tsellochim advanced, coming through the bars as though they didn't exist. Their aura was malicious and Darcy knew that he had brought them to kill her. She didn't want to die. "Wait!" she cried hoarsely.

He spun back around, and Darcy, for the first time, clearly saw Tselloch in the eyes of the panther. She scrambled weakly on hands and knees over to him. "I'll do it," she breathed. "I want to live."

His growl turned to a purr and he once again lowered his head.

As Darcy reached toward him, she heard the sound of crashing and shouting. Human voices. They were coming for her! With a gasp, she snatched her hand back a second time, but it was too late. Her fingertips were damp; she'd just brushed the tip of the panther's nose before she'd taken her hand away. She was going to become one of them.

"No. No, no, no," she gasped over and over. She held her hand out in front of her like it was contaminated. It felt strangely cold and dead to the touch. "I take it back!" she cried. "I didn't mean it!"

The panther didn't answer. In fact, he was no longer there. She looked around frantically, blinking back the darkness that was creeping into her vision. What had she done? People were here, real live people. They were here to rescue her, but they were too late; she'd ruined everything.

She continued to blink furiously. Her vision was going blurry, and it wasn't because she was crying. Whatever she'd done when she'd touched the panther's nose, she'd changed something within herself . . . or let something in. She breathed in shallow gulps, trying to stay conscious.

"Help!" she rasped uselessly. Her voice was barely louder than a whisper now. "Somebody help me; I'm down here!"

The dungeon door scraped at the top of the stairs. She clung desperately to awareness, but her heart plummeted when she saw the creature coming toward her.

He was obviously in a hurry. As he hobbled toward her, he breathed with a deep rattle on every other step. He muttered darkly under his breath and fumbled with a ring of keys at his waist. He was not a tsellodrin; Darcy could see that much through her fading vision. He was human, but hunched over and deformed. He was one of those who swore allegiance to Tselloch without becoming a tsellodrin. Why was he here? Was he going to take her away?

His key clicked in the lock and he swung open the door of her cage just as Darcy lost her battle to stay conscious. Her vision of his leering face blurred to the side as she slumped over and knew no more.

CHAPTER 40
THE SEA

Darcy swayed on a sea of unconsciousness. Back and forth, up and down . . . she felt her world moving without regard to the normal laws of physics. She had no conscious thoughts aside from an awareness that she'd screwed up again. Suddenly, in the midst of her darkness, she heard music. At first it sounded harsh and unnatural, like it didn't belong, but as it grew louder, it became more pleasant, and Darcy began to be aware of her surroundings.

The melody rose in a gentle rhythm. Darcy had never heard music like it before, and she couldn't identify the instrument, but it was like an organic voice. Her psyche began to center itself, and she thought her world would cease its unnatural rocking sensation, but it did not. Instead, the rocking became more punctuated, and Darcy could hear the distinct sound of oars hitting water.

As her consciousness returned, the music slowly faded, leaving her feeling alone, but bolstered with hope, and alive. What was happening to her? She wasn't in the dungeon any longer. In fact . . . she could hear sounds distant, yet close: yelling and screams of pain and the clashing of metal against metal. A battle was being fought. At the castle. It sounded so far away even as it was strangely magnified. She must be in a boat on the sea. *They're taking me away!* she thought with a jolt.

She lay still, thinking of what to do, and soon she could discern the rattling breathing of the man who had taken her away from the dungeon. With every dip of the oars, he rumbled deep in his chest. She didn't know how far from shore he'd already taken her; she couldn't see a thing.

She reached a finger out tentatively and it brushed against fur. She recoiled immediately with disgust. Was she being held by some monstrous creature? She held her breath for a moment and then let it out slowly. No. That couldn't be. She felt no warmth in the fur; it was nothing more than a cloak. In fact . . . she brushed it again, her hands moving together because they were shackled. It felt familiar, like the one that she'd worn all winter long in Paradeisos. Could it be that they had wrapped her in her very own cloak? She held her breath again in expectation. If that was the case, then she must find her inner pocket.

The key that Sam had given her was still in the inner pocket. She'd often looked at it in her cell, and of course she'd tried it on her cell door, but to no avail. But what if it was meant for something else? Or some other time?

Darcy fumbled for the pocket, listening very attentively to the rower. He didn't break his rhythm. He must have his back to her. With a swell of jubilation, Darcy found her pocket. She dug into it and felt the cool metal key with trembling fingers. *Please, oh please,* she pled inwardly. *There has to be a hole for a key on these shackles.* She turned the key so it was facing her wrists and poked. Nothing. She moved it slightly and poked again. Still nothing.

She took a moment to close her eyes and breathe deeply before trying it again, aware that every stroke of the rower took her farther from shore. She moved the key the other direction and twisted it. This time when she poked, it hit a hole and, with some more fumbling, slid into it. Darcy held her breath. With her heart pounding, she turned the key and felt the shackles click and fall off of her left wrist. With a twist the other direction, her right wrist was free.

She muffled her gasp of joy and rotated her wrists beneath the cloak. *Okay, so what next?* After hearing the music that woke her from her sleep, she felt like she was thinking more clearly than she ever had before. The weight on her head reminded her that she still wore Lykos's crown. Her arms brushed against the fur of her cloak, she very carefully reached up to her head and pushed on the cold metal. It slid off like it had never been stuck and she eased it down to her chest, her heart singing in elation. She was finally free of it!

Okay, she thought, trying to make herself focus on the next thing. *It's time to take a look outside.*

Darcy prodded with her fingers into the fur of the cloak, searching for a slit or opening. Whoever he was, the man had just wrapped her in it willy-nilly like she was a dead body or a sausage. With deft movements she finally found an edge, but it was almost underneath her. Easing herself to the side very slowly, she grasped the edge and lifted it up.

Warm wind buffeted her face as she breathed freely. Peeking over to the side, she saw that the rower did indeed sit with his bent back to her, and she lay on the floor of a small, wooden coracle. Looking the other direction, she saw the winking lights of Ormiskos castle about five hundred yards away and noticed with a surge of joy that the curtains in the throne room were thrown open. Surely that meant that her friends were prevailing. Dark shadows battled beings who wielded flaring lights on the battlements. A wide wharf extended out into the bay where the camping sites at Cedar Cove sat, and Darcy knew that if she had the strength, she could swim to them.

She eased herself free of the cloak, trying not to imagine how difficult it would be to swim in a skirt and in her present state of weakness. *I can't think about that. I just have to try!* Soon she lay in the boat on top of the heap that was her fur cloak. Her movements had been completely muffled by the sound of the oars in the water and the man's labored breathing and muttering.

Darcy sat up with infinite care and rested her hands on the side of the swaying vessel. *Okay . . . one, two, three!* With a heave and a wild kick, she threw herself over the edge. The salty, cold water slapped against her face and she went under for a brief moment, her feet entangled in her skirt as she struggled to right herself in the water. She was not a strong swimmer, but she kicked furiously and finally broke the surface again, sputtering and splashing.

She heard the man in the coracle give a shout and a snarl. She struck out for the wharf, which was closer than the beach next to the castle. She already felt winded, like she could hardly move, and the cold fingers of the depths threatened to pull her down. She swam without a particular stroke in mind, flailing her arms and legs in an effort to keep moving forward.

A splash from the boat warned her of pursuit. The man had entered the water to bring her back. He was close behind her.

As his cold hands grabbed her hair, she let out a piercing scream, cut off quickly as he forced her under the water. She turned, unsure from where her strength was coming, and kicked out against him, but he wouldn't let go. Resurfacing, she screamed again as he began to drag her slowly back to the boat. She reached up with both hands and dug her nails into his arm, but he was undaunted and dunked her again.

Looking up from under the surface of the water, Darcy saw a strange, reddish light arcing through the air toward her and her captor. As though in slow motion, it grew closer and closer to them, flickering slightly. It was a flaming dart! It sailed toward them and Darcy felt the man holding her thud and shudder as it met its mark. For a terrifying moment he dragged her down to the depths with him as his dead weight sank, but then his hand relaxed and she bobbed upward alone.

Darcy's head broke the surface and she gasped and coughed. Somebody had helped her. Or had they? Perhaps the arrow had been meant for her? And how could anybody see two small people in the vast bay with enough precision to shoot an arrow at them? Darcy sobbed and shook as she painfully pulled herself toward the wharf. All she knew was that her strength was almost gone, and she was still far from the shore.

Moving her limbs felt like trying to lift skinny saplings with bricks tied to them. Every time a swell hit her in the face, she passed through it, unsure if she would come out the other side. It was still too far. The lights on the shore hadn't even grown closer in her estimation, and she could see no form coming out to rescue her. Whoever had shot the flaming dart was long gone.

With a shudder Darcy gave a final stroke and her strength went out. She may have escaped Tselloch, but he had won anyway in the end. She would die, and the prophecy would not be fulfilled. For the second time that night, Darcy lost consciousness.

Chapter 41

Recovery

Darcy awoke to the feel of grainy sand beneath her and anxious voices in her ear. She blinked her eyes open, once, twice, three times . . . but she couldn't keep them open. The periphery of her vision was completely red and searing bright. What was that? Light? Sunrise? It had been so long since she'd last seen a sunrise.

"Is she okay?"

"She's waking up."

"We have to get her up to the castle."

"What happened to her?"

"Did anybody see that bear?"

Darcy felt strong hands pass beneath her back and legs and suddenly she was swung up in the air.

"Veli, please inform those at the palace that we found her."

That voice. It sounded so familiar, but it felt like ages since Darcy had last heard it. Torrin? She frowned and scrunched her eyes closed again. When she reopened them, it was to find Sam's face bobbing next to hers as the man carried her.

"Darcy?" Sam said. "Can you hear me?"

Darcy parted her lips to speak, but no sound came out. She nodded instead and squeezed her eyes closed again.

"We've been looking for you everywhere!" Sam said in a rush. "Then I noticed this great big bear sitting down here on the beach. He wasn't here anymore when we got down here, but you were! Just lying on the beach like you were taking a nap!"

"Sam," the man spoke again. It was definitely Torrin, Darcy decided. "Don't overload her. She's been through a lot."

"Sorry," Sam said, and then there was no sound other than the crunch of Torrin's boots on the ground and the soft trotting noise that Sam made.

Soon Darcy heard the sound of many people bustling about. They passed through an entrance into the castle and the air became closer, but not oppressive as it had been under Tselloch. Tselloch! What had happened to him? Darcy's brain hurt just trying to think about it, so she refocused on the sounds around her.

She didn't know where Torrin was taking her. She'd never been anywhere in the castle other than the throne room and the dungeon. It felt like they were climbing stairs now. People passing them going down made exclamations of surprise, but Darcy didn't try to look at any of them. She could hear Sam panting behind Torrin; it sounded like she was falling a little behind.

Off the stairs and onto a solid landing, two more quick turns took them to a door, which Torrin pushed open with his foot. He must have paused in the doorway, though, because she heard him say, "Sam, wait out here. This is no place for a young lady." He then turned and Darcy heard the door close softly behind them.

"She's expecting you." Darcy heard Veli's voice again. "Over there, she had a bed prepared away from the others."

The others? For a moment Darcy felt a stab of fear. Were the rest of her friends injured, too? *No, Sam would have said something*. Of course, there was a battle last night; there would be injured soldiers. And as Darcy focused, she could smell the coppery scent of blood and hear murmurings and groans.

"You found her!" That was Nurse Dembe. "Put her here. I've put up a screen for her. Where was she?"

Darcy felt her head hit a soft bed, followed by the rest of her body as Torrin gently laid her down.

"She was on the beach," Veli answered.

"The beach? Great Gloria, how did she get down there?"

"We don't know."

"Pateros was with her," Torrin said very quietly.

"Oh! I see!" Nurse Dembe sounded very excited. "Well, I think it's safe to say that she will make a full recovery. But, my, my, she looks starved. Did they not feed her these two months?"

Two months! Darcy's eyes flew open, and she immediately squinted against the early morning light pouring in through an open window. After so long in the dark, it would take her a long time to adjust.

"Lady Darcy?" Nurse Dembe took her hand and touched her cheek. "Can you hear me?"

Darcy nodded.

"You're in the sick ward. You will be here for some time until we can get you nursed back to health. Do you think that you can take some drink?"

Darcy nodded again. She simply felt too tired to talk.

Nurse Dembe helped her to sit up, and Veli supported her back while she choked down a mug of broth. She was able to keep her eyes open while she drank, and she looked around at the three familiar faces. She wanted to say thank you and she longed to know everything that had happened since she'd left them. She wanted to say she was sorry, but the words wouldn't come. Instead her eyes burned, and she closed them again as they urged her to sleep.

"You should have *seen* him; he was amazing," Sam gushed over a month later from her perch on the foot of Darcy's bed. Nurse Dembe had insisted that Darcy's friends wait until most of the soldiers had left the ward before they come in and visit her, and Darcy herself had taken a long time to recover. Darcy kept her right hand, the hand she'd touched the panther with, subconsciously curled in a ball beneath her covers. It still felt colder than the rest of her body, but she was too ashamed to tell anybody about it, so she kept it to herself.

"I don't know about *amazing*," Perry muttered, but he grinned widely at Darcy anyway. He'd certainly changed since she'd last seen him. He was a little bit broader in the shoulders and had a more compassionate look about him, even as he lounged casually against the stone wall by the window.

"Yeah?" Darcy said. "Your talent really paid off, huh?"

"More than we ever could have imagined," Sam continued. "We weren't supposed to be watching the actual fighting, Amelia and I, but we climbed up to the top of the wall where we could see some of the battle in the courtyard. Man, Perry was awesome. He kept busting out these moves that none of us had ever seen before, and every time he swung his sword, a tsellodrin fell."

"That wasn't the coolest part, though," Amelia said. "Even Rubidius didn't know that he'd be able to kill the tsellochim."

"That was a surprise to me, too," Perry said. "I wasn't thinking about where I was swinging my sword. A shadow came at me, and I swung at it. When it fell, everybody was like, 'Whoa!' and so I tried to target them from then on."

"Sounds like it was really exciting," Darcy said, smiling.

"The whole thing was exciting," Sam said. "I wish you could have been there, but in a way, it's thanks to you that it all went over so smoothly."

"What do you mean?"

"Well, when you showed up missing the day after your birthday, we were all really upset."

"Yeah . . . I know . . . I'm sorry."

"It's okay." Sam waved her off. "Let me tell my story. Amelia and I went straight to Rubidius and told him everything about you and Lykos and how you'd been acting really strange. And we also told him how rotten we'd been to you. Well, naturally, he was concerned."

"Yeah, you should have seen him," Lewis said, nodding vigorously. "He went storming around camp, shooting fireworks from his beard—"

"What?" Darcy laughed.

"Okay, well, not exactly fireworks, but his beard was definitely on fire."

"Lewis, you're no good at telling the story," Sam butted in. "You can write them, but you should stick to that. The *important* part is that we didn't have to wait very long to find out what had happened to you, and it explained Dean's illness, too."

"Wait, what?" Darcy frowned at her. "What did Dean's sickness have to do with anything?"

"It had to do with a lot, actually. This great big wolf came breezing into camp around midday with a hundred tsellodrin on his tail, but naturally they couldn't cross the wall with him. Once he was cloaked, he scratched some pictures on the ground, one of which was a crown with six rocks in it. Rubidius was really interested in the crown."

"Yeah, it was bad; I figured that out too late, of course." Darcy frowned. "What did the wolf look like?"

"He was a charcoal grey, and he had really blue eyes. I remember that because Amelia pointed them out."

"Lupidor!" Darcy exclaimed.

"Rubidius said he thought he knew what the crown was; well, actually what the rocks in the crown were. He said they were shadow stones, which aren't really stones at all. They are coalesced, broken-off bits of tsellochim. People in contact with them can steal magic from others, but they can also be controlled by any element of the Shadow."

"Okay . . . I had figured out the controlling part, but what was that about stealing magic?"

Sam looked apologetic. "Um, are we right in assuming Lykos told you to cloak yourself like Dean is able to?"

Darcy nodded, and then gasped. "That's how we got away! I cloaked myself like Dean and even threw the cloaking to cover Lykos and the other wolves." She turned chagrined eyes on Dean. "I'm so sorry! Is that why you were so sick?"

He shrugged and tilted the corner of his mouth up in a half-smile. "It's no big deal, Darcy."

"Actually, it was a big deal," Amelia said quietly. "He almost died."

"I'm *so* sorry!" Darcy repeated. "I didn't know what I was doing."

"Really, Darcy; it's okay," Dean said.

"But it was really a good thing in the end," Sam insisted, "because it was the piece that Rubidius needed in order to put everything together. So, naturally, the plans to escape Paradeisos and attack Ormiskos escalated. The adults figured that Tselloch wouldn't kill you. They figured that he would first try to get you to join him and then try to break you if he failed in that. Meanwhile, the five of us were feeling really left out of the mix, and we wanted to do something useful."

"You'd already been useful, I was the useless one who ran away," Darcy said.

"Whatever. We met together and discussed our talents. That's when we figured mine out."

"You did?" Darcy sat up a little straighter. "What is it?"

"Trust," Amelia said. "Whoever Sam trusts is trustworthy, whomever she doesn't, isn't. We ran a few tests, naturally, just to make sure."

"What sort of tests?"

Sam giggled. "Dean would go off and do his invisible thing, and he would tell the other boys where he would be hiding to jump out at me. Then I would take a walk with the boys and one would try to lead me toward him, while the other one would try to lead me away from him. I could always tell who was trying to lead me toward him."

"Right, so that was valuable right away." Amelia continued, "But we wanted to do something else, too. We felt kind of responsible, you know."

"Why?" Darcy asked in exasperation.

"Because we hadn't been very nice to you. Well, everybody except Sam, that is. And when it comes down to it, you are our friend."

"*So*, we decided to take a look at Lewis's writings," Sam said, eager to finish her story. "And we found an awful lot of stories and poems about hiking to Paradeisos—that is, to Paradise Cove back home, which is the same place geographically as Paradeisos. And suddenly Amelia got this look on her face like 'duh!' and grabbed her lyre. Then she told us all to follow her to a spot where there was a break in the wall.

"See, none of us had ever really thought about the hiking trail existing in Alitheia, and Amelia had the idea that it might have been overrun by the enemy, but maybe it could be revealed."

"It would explain why Lewis had so much written about the trail," Amelia said. "I just figured it was worth a try."

"It was impressive," Perry said. "We got to the place where the trail should come in, back home, you know, and Amelia started playing her lyre while Lewis read aloud from his writings."

"We felt kind of silly," Sam said, "but it paid off. There were all these oily-like vines in that area of the woods that didn't belong, and the more Amelia played and Lewis read, the more they receded."

"And pretty soon we could see clearly that the trail was there," Lewis added.

"Better yet, the tsellodrin couldn't see it," Amelia said. "It was cloaked like the ruins."

"That's cool!" Darcy said. "So you guys figured this out right away after I left?"

"Oh! No." Sam laughed. "Sorry, we kind of condensed the story. That was what, like two weeks before the attack?"

"Yeah, something like that," Amelia said.

"We wanted to take off right away to rescue you, but there were still battle preparations to be made."

"And they were studying that old map that Amelia had found at Sanditha in the great hall," Perry reminded them. "We ended up using some of the tunnels on the map. I'm not sure we would have been able to breach the castle without it."

"But what we want to know is, what happened to you. How did you end up on the beach?" Sam asked her.

Darcy quickly recounted her time in the dungeon, but she left out everything having to do with Tselloch as the panther. She didn't want them to know how close she'd come to becoming a tsellodrin . . . at least not yet. Sam was thrilled to hear about the key from her wallet, and they all were interested to know who had shot the flaming arrow that killed the man in the water with her. For that matter, Darcy wanted to know how she got to shore safely, but nobody had an answer to those questions.

"It's time to go." Nurse Dembe finally bustled into her partitioned area and shooed the other five teenagers away. "Lady Darcy still needs more rest. You can come back tomorrow after Tellius visits with her."

Darcy almost choked at those words. "Tellius is coming here?"

"Naturally. He was here almost every day when you were sleeping."

Darcy's face registered her horror, but Sam grinned at her. "It's actually kind of cute, Darcy. He's been really concerned about you."

Darcy closed her eyes and lay down. "I'll see you guys tomorrow."

Sam and Amelia laughed as they left the room.

Chapter 42
Going Home

"Perhaps I owe you an apology." Rubidius stood contritely at the foot of her bed and Darcy spun around in surprise. She was just finishing up packing her stuff into her small satchel and was looking forward to surprising Sam and the others with her release from the sick ward. She hadn't seen Rubidius since she'd left Paradeisos three and a half months ago, but he looked aged since then.

"You what?" she sputtered.

Rubidius moved into her space and sat on the edge of one of the many chairs that had been moved in since Darcy had recovered enough to have visitors. "I should apologize," Rubidius repeated, "for driving you away. Perhaps I was too hard on you. You are, after all, barely older than a child."

"Well, okay," Darcy said, embarrassed. "But I don't think you need to apologize. I think *I* should. You were right; I wasn't ready to be trained. I used a magical instrument that almost killed Dean because I was too stupid to think about what I was doing."

Rubidius held a hand up to stop her. "But I could have given you more attention, and for that, I am sorry. And," he looked up and smiled, "you discovered your talent without me!"

"Is that really my talent?" Darcy sat down as well. She'd been afraid to try to talk to any animals because of her experience with Lykos.

"Indeed it is, and it truly is remarkable."

"And I can talk to all animals? Not just Lykos?"

"It would be absurd to assume that you could talk to only one. We will have to explore the extent of your talent. But not now." Rubidius stood and folded his hands in front of him. "Now is the time for rest and relaxation. I expect that you all will be going home very soon."

"But . . . Tselloch isn't defeated yet!"

"No, far from it, I am afraid."

"Then how can we leave?"

"Tselloch has been driven back," Rubidius explained. "He will not be found until he wants to be found, and we have much to do here at the palace to prepare."

"I don't understand how you drove him back, and how you fought the tsellochim."

"It takes very strong magicians to do it. I will teach you all more about it at a later time. Young Perry was a great help. Tselloch feared himself mortal for the first time and fled as soon as he heard of the great warrior who could slay his tsellochim." Rubidius chuckled softly. "Alitheia will be a different place the next time you are here."

Darcy slung her satchel over her shoulder and made a face. "We really have to wait a whole year to come back? I feel like I threw away so much of the time I was given here this year."

"I do not know exactly when Pateros will call you back, but it is logical to assume it will be when you six are next at the summer camp." Rubidius turned to leave, holding the partition open for Darcy to pass through with him.

"Sir, I . . . I was wondering about Pateros—"

"Many do."

"That is . . . I know I haven't met him, but I'm pretty sure I've been around him at least twice!"

"Is that so?" Rubidius said politely, but he didn't seem surprised.

"Back home, before I came here, there was a moment in the woods when I felt really scared and I saw this shadowy thing. I don't know how a tsellochim got to our world, but I know that's what it was! I felt like it was going to attack me, and then out of the woods came this great big bear—way too big to be a normal bear. At the time I thought that it was coming after me, but thinking back . . . " Darcy frowned thoughtfully. "I think it was protecting me." She laughed nervously. "Is that totally crazy?"

"No," Rubidius answered thoughtfully, holding the door to the sick ward open for her. "Eleanor Stevenson met Pateros in his bear form in your world, as well. As for the tsellochim . . . I do not know their rules of passage to your world, but I would imagine it to be very rare." He smiled as they descended the stairs together. "When was the second time you saw Pateros?"

"Well, I didn't see him, but I think that Sam saw him, sitting by me on the beach when they found me. Does that make any sense?"

Rubidius laughed. "Of course! It makes perfect sense. He was the one to pull you from the water and, I expect, the one who shot the flaming dart at your captor."

"Oh! Really?"

Rubidius winked at her. "What a foolish question! Who else could it have been?" He stopped and faced her. "I look forward to talking with you more, Darcy Pennington. You have grown a great deal." With that he left her and meandered off down the hall, whistling softly to himself.

Darcy watched him go and then continued down the stairs. It seemed strange that Pateros should have shown himself to her when so few others had ever seen him. What made her so special?

She had a vague idea where the girls' room was from Sam's descriptions of the palace, and she was determined to find it on her own without any help. Everywhere she looked, workers were busy scrubbing floors, walls, and ceilings, airing out tapestries, and moving plants and furniture into long-abandoned rooms. She smiled. It would take them a while to put the castle back in the shape it was before Tselloch took over, but they had a good start.

She bumped into somebody as she rounded the landing on the first floor and excused herself quickly.

"Oh, hi."

Tellius wrinkled his nose at her. "Hi."

They stood awkwardly, staring at each other.

"So . . . you've fully recovered?" Tellius finally asked, breaking the silence.

"Yes. Nurse Dembe told me I could leave this morning."

"That's good."

"Mm-hm." Darcy rolled her eyes inwardly as Tellius obviously sought a means of escape. "Do you know where Sam and the others are?" Darcy finally asked.

"I believe they are in the dining hall having lunch," Tellius replied.

"Thanks." Darcy nodded and dodged around him.

"Darcy?" Tellius called after her.

She turned. "Yes?"

"I'm glad you're feeling better."

Darcy smiled. "Thanks."

"Cause you really looked awful for a while there," he finished. With a short wave, he turned and jogged up the stairs with Darcy scowling at his back.

In the end, Darcy had to admit defeat and find Sam and the others before finding their room. There were just too many twists and turns in the castle of Ormiskos for her to keep track of on her own without ever having seen them before.

Her friends were thrilled to see her up and about, and even Amelia gave her a warm hug of welcome. In fact, the whole palace decided to celebrate her return to full health, and they had a great pig roast in the castle courtyard that night with lots of dancing and music and fireworks. The fairies were out in full force, and Darcy thought she'd never experienced a more lovely and fun-filled evening in her entire life. The six of them wore their special jerkins once again, with the emblems of their animals on their chests.

Amelia gave a special performance on her lyre, and although people held their breath and looked around expectantly for something to be revealed, it was purely for entertainment. The music of the piece, however, sounded strangely familiar to Darcy, and she listened intently, trying to figure out where she knew the tune from.

When Amelia came and sat down after her performance, her cheeks aglow in the firelight, Sam leaned over to her and said, “That sounded a lot like that pretty song you played during the battle.”

“What?” Darcy leaned around Amelia. “She played a song when everybody was fighting?”

Amelia shrugged and plucked her strings absentmindedly. “It was really unexpected, but of course I had my lyre on me, anyway. When we were sitting on the wall watching the fighting, the urge suddenly came over me to play something, and it was a song I’d never heard before. Sam was nervous that it would attract attention, but all I knew was that I *had* to play it.”

“And it sounded like the one you just played?”

“Sort of. I was just now trying to remember the song from the battle, but I don’t think I did it justice. That song I played . . .” Amelia’s eyes took on a far-off look, “it was unlike anything I’d ever heard before.”

Darcy sat back, astonished.

“What’s the matter, Darcy? You’ve gone all pale,” Sam said, leaning around to look at her.

“It’s just,” Darcy looked at Amelia, “I recognized that tune, and I couldn’t put it together until now, but . . .” she trailed off and shook her head.

“What?” Sam said eagerly.

“That was the song that woke me up in the boat; after the man had taken me from the dungeon. That song is the reason I’m sitting here with you.”

“Oh! Wow,” Sam said, awed. “I guess that’s why you had to play it, Amelia.”

“Yeah,” Amelia said, looking at Darcy with wide eyes. “I guess so.”

Darcy and Amelia shared a long look, and Darcy felt the tenuous and frayed link between them solidify into an unshakeable bond.

The approach of Perry’s gigantic lion, Liontari, announced the imminent arrival of the three boys, who plopped down next to the girls with smoke-stained faces, laughing and coughing.

“Man. That game was totally nuts,” Perry laughed. “We should try that back home.”

“Something tells me that my parents won’t approve of ‘smokeball,’ ” Lewis said morosely, but he grinned anyway.

“This is great, isn’t it? No lessons, no training, no enemy to worry about . . . just fun for the rest of the summer,” Dean said, leaning forward to rub Alepo between the ears.

Amelia wrinkled her nose. “I don’t know about the rest of the summer; I’d guess that we’re going to be heading home pretty soon. Actually . . .” she trailed off and began counting on her fingers. “Yeah. Next week Sunday is exactly one year since we left home.”

“So,” Perry said, “it doesn’t mean we will be going home then.”

“How *are* we getting home?” asked Sam. “I mean, we have to get back to the other side and all the way out to Whitetail Point to get back to the gateway. How will we know when to go?”

“I’m not going to worry about it,” said Perry. He leaned back against Liontari’s broad side and closed his eyes. “We’ll get back when we’re supposed to.”

Darcy inwardly agreed with Perry, but she also agreed with Amelia. They were likely to head home in a week on Sunday, a year after they’d left home. But she wasn’t ready to go home yet! For all her months in Alitheia, the good times, like now, far overshadowed the miserable ones. She still couldn’t shake the feeling that she belonged here in Alitheia and that she would never feel at home in her own world again.

She watched five flower fairies dancing in a circle around the bonfire, and she looked over to see Eleanor Stevenson sitting with the two princes nestled up against her sides. Torrin and Yahto Veli were deep in conversation at a table laden with food and Voitto Vesa played an unfamiliar game with a handful of nymphs. Crowds upon crowds of cheerful faces and friendly animals crammed into the space of the courtyard, and it was only beyond the castle walls that the dark forest loomed.

Darcy shivered. She knew there was still a great evil out there lurking. She also knew that the Shadow knew how close she’d come to succumbing to him . . . knew that she *had* succumbed to him just before the end. She clenched her right fist and felt the coolness of her fingers in comparison to her other hand. She must never tell anyone what she had done. “It doesn’t matter now,” she whispered to herself.

“What did you say?” Sam said.

“Nothing.” Darcy smiled. “I’m just enjoying the party.”

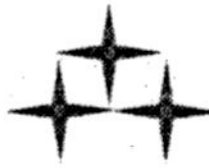

It was Sunday, one year after they had first arrived in Alitheia. Darcy stretched in her bed and swung her feet over the edge, her toes brushing the cool flagstones. She appreciated how cool the stones in the castle stayed even as the temperatures climbed in the summer. She made quick work of shrugging out of her nightshirt and into a pretty blue dress with short sleeves that tied with bows around her upper arms. She tried to ignore her sense of premonition as she readied to go downstairs.

She left Amelia and Sam still sleeping and went down to the kitchens, preferring to eat with the servants rather than with the nobles in the dining hall. As she ducked into the pantry quarters, she heard a familiar voice.

"I thought that you all would enjoy a sailing voyage today."

She spun around and smiled at Yahto Veli. "Very much! I love sailboats. When will we be going?"

"As soon as your friends are up and breakfasted, you can come and find me. I will be on the terrace." The nark bowed and walked away.

Darcy opted to snatch a biscuit to go, despite Asa Rhea's loud insistence that she sit down and take a full, warm meal, and jogged back up the winding staircase to the second floor and down the hall to their room. Banging open the door, she called, "Get up!" She ran to the window and pulled the heavy woolen draperies apart, allowing bright morning sunshine to pour in.

Sam grumbled in her sleep and rolled over, but Amelia peeked her eyes open and pushed her hair out of her face. "What is it?" she mumbled sleepily.

"Come on, Sam. Get up!" Darcy went to Sam's bed and pulled the covers back.

"Darcy," Sam sat up and grimaced at her.

"Veli's going to take us sailing!" Darcy announced excitedly. "But we can't go until everybody is up."

"Sailing!" Sam's eyes lit up, and she kicked her covers the rest of the way off. "That sounds like so much fun."

It took several minutes, but before long, the three girls were dressed and ready to go. They banged on the boys' door on the way down to the kitchen, but there was no answer. In the kitchen they found the three boys munching away on one of Asa Rhea's famous warm breakfasts, and they couldn't be persuaded to move until they had eaten their fill.

Finally, at long last, the six of them traipsed out to the terrace to find Yahto Veli talking with Eleanor.

"Eleanor!" Sam exclaimed, giving the old woman a hug. "Are you coming with us?"

"No, no." Eleanor smiled at them, her hazel eyes kind. "I'm just seeing you off. I hope that you enjoy your day trip. It's been some time since I've been on a sailing vessel." Her gaze looked a little wistful.

"Well, then, why don't you come with us?"

"No, not today, my darlings. This voyage is meant for you. I'll say farewell." She touched Sam on the head fondly and then re-entered the palace through one of the giant floor-to-ceiling windows.

"Are you ready?" Veli asked them, but his gaze was fixed on something far off.

They affirmed they were ready to leave, but it was with great reluctance that Darcy turned her back on Ormiskos castle and followed the others down to the wharf and a waiting sailboat with red sails.

Darcy swallowed hard and was so distracted for the first part of their voyage that Sam finally asked her what was wrong.

"Huh? Oh . . . nothing," Darcy answered, but her gaze met Amelia's and she knew they were thinking the same thing.

There was a small crew on the boat—it couldn't be larger than a twenty-footer—and they deftly managed the sails and rudder so that the six of them and Veli could relax and enjoy the breeze on their faces and the beautiful view of Glorietta Bay.

"What's that?" Perry suddenly said loudly over the snapping of the sails. He pointed overhead and the others looked up.

"It's an eagle," Veli answered calmly.

"An eagle?" Sam wrinkled her nose. "I've never seen eagles at Cedar Cove before!"

"Yeah, but you've also never seen lions or badgers or any other number of animals in our world that we've seen here in Alitheia," Perry pointed out reasonably.

"It looks like it's leading us," Amelia said softly, watching the great golden wing strokes of the eagle above them.

Amelia was right. As the eagle veered to the right, the man steering the vessel followed it. And they carried on that way for the better part of an hour, not in a straight line, but crisscrossing the bay until they had rounded Whitetail point and the eagle dove for the rocks at the edge of the forest.

"Look!" Dean pointed. Instead of an eagle on the shore, there now stood a great brown bear, enormous and imposing.

Darcy stood up and looked at Yahto Veli, who merely smiled back at her. He tapped the captain on the shoulder and indicated that they should drop anchor. The bear stood on the shore, watching them and waiting. Without a word, Veli dropped a small coracle over the side of the boat and helped each of them down into it. They all complied without asking any questions, each knowing now what the day voyage was about.

Finally, once they were all settled, Veli said, "Follow him; he will not lead you wrong."

"Aren't you coming with us?" Sam asked, her lip quavering slightly.

Veli laughed lightly. "No. You'll be fine. It's not far from here. I look forward to your return." With that he handed Perry and Dean the oars and pushed the coracle toward the shore.

It wasn't a great distance to the rocks on the beach, but the great bear waiting for them made the trip seem very long. When they finally scraped the bottom of the boat on the rocks and splashed their way through the shallows to dry ground, the bear turned his tail and disappeared into the trees.

"Quick!" Darcy said, following the great beast. "We don't want to lose him."

They plunged into the woods, hearing the mad giggles of gnomes. "We must be close to Gnome's Haven," Sam panted just before they broke out of the trees into that very clearing. The gnomes were scampering all over the rock and pointing into the trees on the far side where a stag stood watching them.

"What's going on?" Lewis puzzled. "What happened to the bear?"

"It's him!" Darcy said excitedly. "The stag is the bear, who was also the eagle."

"How do you know that?" Perry huffed.

"I just do; come on!" Darcy followed the stag, knowing exactly where it was leading them. She wasn't at all surprised to find the stag waiting for them beside the two trees between which the gateway stretched.

The stag inclined his head toward the gateway, shimmering with energy, and twitched his ears toward them.

"It's time, you guys," Darcy breathed. "Time to go back." Her excitement at following the stag faded away. She swallowed hard and turned around to look at the other five teenagers. "Are you ready?"

Amelia squared her shoulders and stepped forward. "I'll go first." She took two steps forward, looked at the stag, and then plunged through the gateway and disappeared.

One by one, the others passed through until it was just Darcy and the stag standing alone in the forest. Darcy walked right up to the gateway and then turned back to look at the stag. She hesitated for a few moments, unanswered questions circulating in her head. So much she wanted to ask, and yet now was not the right time. She clasped her fists, feeling the coldness in her fingertips and gave a short nod. With that, she passed through the gateway.

Epilogue

Cedar Cove Again

"Ugh," Sam said, looking around, "we're young again."

Amelia laughed and looked down at herself. "Yeah. I hadn't realized how much I'd changed."

"It feels weird," Darcy admitted.

"Think about us!" Perry said, looking between Dean and himself. "We were in the best shape of our lives! I don't even think I could do a full morning's forms in this body."

"Oh, so it's worse for you than for us?" Sam said sarcastically. "What about me? I'd lost weight. Now I'm back to being just as chubby as before."

They started to make their way back to the path.

Somehow they were all in the clothes they'd worn when they'd left home, and Lewis even had his backpack on. It made them feel almost like they'd never left at all.

"Look at the colors," Sam said sadly as they began their hike back toward camp. "Kind of depressing, huh?"

It was true; there were not the same brilliant greens and sharply colored flowers here as in Alitheia. In fact, everything looked rather muted.

"I never thought I'd see the day when I'd actually wish that Cedar Cove was *more* beautiful," Sam added.

"Yeah, but there aren't any fairies here," Amelia reminded her.

They hiked in silence, all processing their return in their own way before Perry asked, "So, what now?"

"What do you mean?" Sam asked.

"What now? When do we go back?"

"I'd guess next year," Amelia said, "wouldn't you say, Darcy?"

"Yeah."

Lewis sighed. "So we have to live this whole year over again? I already turned fourteen!"

"Well, you get to do it again. We all do!" Sam said brightly. "Just think about it this way, we have even more to look forward to next year."

"I miss Alepo," Dean said.

"Yeah, Pinello, too," Sam added.

"We'll see them again," Amelia said bracingly.

"What time is it?" Perry asked Lewis.

"Same time as when we left," Lewis answered, checking his watch. "We just missed the four o'clock ferry."

They hurried across the rocky isthmus and into the woods on the main body of land. As they came upon the camp buildings, they looked around sadly, reminded of the marvelous stone structures in Alitheia.

"What is the part of camp over there, again?" Sam asked, looking around.

"Kenidros," Amelia answered, "the twin castle to Ormiskos."

"Maybe we'll get to see it when we go back next time. I'd sure like to!"

They stopped short. Marching toward them on the path was Colin Mackaby, his pale blue eye gleaming in his pallid face. He stopped and faced them, scowling maliciously. "You're back," he said quietly.

Darcy shot a furtive glance at the others, who looked as baffled as she felt.

"What do you mean?" Amelia shot back at him, her hands on her hips.

Colin threw back his head and laughed harshly. "You know what I mean. Think you're special, don't you? Well, I know the truth."

"I don't think you know anything at all, and you should mind your own business," Amelia snapped at him. She marched past him and the others followed in her wake.

"Creep," Perry muttered under his breath, purposefully knocking into Colin with his shoulder.

Darcy watched uneasily, and when she passed Colin, their eyes met and locked. "I know what you did," he mouthed at her. "You won't ever forget."

Darcy dropped her eyes and hurried to catch up with Sam. She didn't know how or why, but Colin Mackaby knew something. *Just brush it off*, she told herself as they rounded a corner and came into the main area of camp. *It's not important what he thinks.*

They waited listlessly for the next ferry and finally boarded and began the ride back to the Glorietta Bay side of camp. Darcy was eager to see her parents, and even Roger, and convince them that they had to come back next year. She knew that they wouldn't understand her change of heart. How could they? She'd tried her hardest not to come here this year. But hopefully, with Sam's help, she could convince them of her sincerity. She had to; she had no other choice.

Choice. She smiled and closed her eyes as the breeze played over her face, imagining what Rubidius would say if he could hear her thoughts now.

"Pateros always gives us a choice."

The Gateway Chronicles
Book 2

The Oracle

Chapter 1
Darcy's Dream

Darcy started awake. Her heart pounded in her ears and a fly beat idly against the windowpane next to her bed with an annoying *buzz* thunk, *buzz* thunk, *buzz* thunk. She rolled over and looked at her clock. *Seven thirty! Too early for summer break.* She rubbed her face with both hands and tried to pinpoint what had woken her. She'd been having a bad dream, she knew that, but she didn't have any idea what it had been about now that she was awake.

With a sigh Darcy sat up and stretched. Other than the sound of the fly beating against the window, the house was eerily silent. She frowned. Usually her mom was up by now making breakfast for Roger, who rose with the sun. Darcy stood and opened her window to let the fly out and then padded across her carpet to crack open her door.

Nothing. Not a sound in the entire house. Her parents' door was still shut across the hall, as was Roger's just right of hers. She shrugged. *They must be sleeping in. Guess I'll get a head start on them.*

Darcy walked to the bathroom and shut the door gently. She went straight to the shower and turned on the faucet to get the water nice and hot before she got in. Going back to the sink, she brushed her teeth distractedly, unable to shake the feeling that something was amiss in her house. As steam began to fill the bathroom, she spit and took a drink to rinse out her mouth before glancing up in the mirror.

She froze.

No! She looked closer. It couldn't be. It must be the fog on the mirror obscuring her vision. She raised a shaking arm to wipe off the glass and brushed her hair out of her face with her right hand, the dead hand, as she often called it in secret.

She peered closer and felt herself go pale. It was undeniable. Her eyes were black, as if her pupils had enlarged to swallow up her usually grey irises.

She lurched against the sink as panic overtook her. Grabbing at the counter, she knocked the soap dispenser onto the floor. Shards of white ceramic flew everywhere and she stumbled backward in horror, stepping down hard on a jagged piece, but the pain didn't register. Instead she stared numbly at her foot as her blood spread across the tiles in an ever-widening circle. But it wasn't red; it, too, was black.

Black and oily, it spurted and spurted in nauseating waves. Darcy could feel herself hyperventilating. Her nightmare had come true. She was one of them, a *tsellodrin*.

The ever-present coldness in her right fingertips began to spread, up her arm and into her chest. In a few moments it would cover her entire body. She screamed.

CPSIA information can be obtained
at www.ICGtesting.com
Printed in the USA
LVOW10s2255280317
528833LV00009B/135/P

9 781612 133003